Super

英文 領隊導遊

PAPAGO

考證照PASS、帶團GO!

滴兒馬、方定國 ◎著

提升領隊導遊專業英語力，
帶旅客體驗旅遊的樂趣！

台北101有什麼No.1的事蹟？
中正紀念堂階梯數目有特殊涵意？？
全台23大景點，
用英語帶外國人在台灣趴趴走！！

迷路了怎麼問路？突然生病或護照掉了怎麼處理？？
8大主題旅遊英語快速通關，帶團或自助都方便！！

哪些是年年都出來的考題？哪些單字用法一定要會？？
題庫總練習，亦加強旅遊英語能力，共**480題**全速前進！！

兼具**考照功能性**與**帶團實用性**！！輕鬆準備！！ 輕鬆讀！！

適用於：旅遊業從業人員、準備領隊導遊證照者、觀光旅遊科系學生

作者序

　　本書分為三個章節。第一個章節以中英文對照的方式介紹了台灣各大景點，第二個章節列出了許多出國旅遊實用的短句與對話，而第三個章節則是囊括了這幾年外語導遊領隊考試的題目與解析。

　　希望能夠幫助要考外語領隊導遊的朋友們，順利地通過考試，並在工作中可以自然地使用。也希望讓其他的朋友們，能夠把台灣的景點用英語介紹給我們的外國友人，並在自己出國旅遊的時候通行無阻。畢竟，我們在某些時刻，都可能導遊，也都可能是領隊。

　　而本書最特別之處就是，雖然這看似是一本英語學習書，但裡面包含了台灣各地的介紹，除了歷史與地理，還描述了這些地方什麼特別、哪裡好玩。與坊間現有的其他外語領隊導遊考用書比起來，更多了實用性與趣味性。

　　台灣真的是一個很美的地方。在這本書的寫作過程中，我常常覺得非常感動。我們所在的這片土地，是一個如此充滿記憶與美麗的福爾摩沙，有著說不完道不盡的風景與故事，值得我們好好地告訴這個世界。

歡迎交流與指教：http://facebook.com/jamie.cyc

hola@dearmaa.com

　　2013年來台觀光的旅客高達800萬人次，這也讓外語與華語導遊的需求日益攀高。自從導遊與領隊考試在民國92年成為國家考試後，每年都有為數可觀的應考人數，而在外語導遊口試的部分語言也隨著旅客多元的背景而增加到13種語言之多。有此可見，觀光產業目前為台灣最有市場開發性的產業之一。

　　此書希望能幫助您在準備考試時亦可強化自身英語導遊的功力，讓您游刃有餘地介紹台灣的美麗風光，讓英語不是文化交流的阻礙，反而是最好的助力。此書的內容設計，從實際介紹景點的對話，學習導覽與觀光常用的單字句子，藉此提升專業英文能力且提高考試的分數。

　　也望可以幫助想將台灣好山好水及溫暖人情味介紹給來自世界各地旅客的讀者，讓英語能力提升，順利通過導遊與領隊的證照考試。

倍斯特編輯部

目 錄

PART 1 帶旅客趴趴走遊台灣

Unit 1	故宮	012
Unit 2	台北 101	016
Unit 3	中正紀念堂	020
Unit 4	國父紀念館	024
Unit 5	大稻埕	028
Unit 6	華西街與龍山寺	032
Unit 7	北投	036
Unit 8	淡水	040
Unit 9	基隆	044

Unit 10	九份	048
Unit 11	烏來	052
Unit 12	大甲	056
Unit 13	阿里山	060
Unit 14	集集	064
Unit 15	日月潭	068
Unit 16	台南	072
Unit 17	高雄	076
Unit 18	墾丁	080

Unit 19	花蓮	084
Unit 20	台東	088
Unit 21	宜蘭	092
Unit 22	澎湖	096
Unit 23	馬祖	100

2 PART
旅遊英語快速通關

Unit 1	機場會用到的英語	106
Unit 2	飛機上會用到的英語	112
Unit 3	入境會用到的英語	118
Unit 4	觀光會用到的英語	124
Unit 5	住宿會用到的英語	130
Unit 6	餐廳會用到的英語	136
Unit 7	逛街購物會用到的英語	142
Unit 8	其他時候會用到的英語	148

PART 3 近年試題練習

Unit 1	101 外語領隊英語考試 — 試題	156
	101 外語領隊英語考試 — 解析	166
Unit 2	102 外語領隊英語考試 — 試題	176
	102 外語領隊英語考試 — 解析	186
Unit 3	103 外語領隊英語考試 — 試題	196
	103 外語領隊英語考試 — 解析	206
Unit 4	101 外語導遊英語考試 — 試題	218
	101 外語導遊英語考試 — 解析	228
Unit 5	102 外語導遊英語考試 — 試題	238
	102 外語導遊英語考試 — 解析	248
Unit 6	103 外語導遊英語考試 — 試題	258
	103 外語導遊英語考試 — 解析	270
附錄	考前單字	282

◎應考資格：

一、高中畢業，領有畢業證書。

二、初等考試或相當等級特種考試及格，並曾任有關職務滿四年，有證明文件。

三、高等或普通檢定考試及格。

◎外語導遊人員類科考試第一試筆試應試科目，分為下列四科：

（本考試外語導遊人員類科分二試舉行，第一試筆試錄取者，始得應第二試口試。第一試錄取資格不予保留。）

一、導遊實務（一）（包括導覽解說、旅遊安全與緊急事件處理、觀光心理與行為、航空票務、急救常識、國際禮儀）。

二、導遊實務（二）（包括觀光行政與法規、臺灣地區與大陸地區人民關係條例、兩岸現況認識）。

三、觀光資源概要（包括臺灣歷史、臺灣地理、觀光資源維護）。

四、外國語（分英語、日語、法語、德語等十三種，由應考人任選一種應試）。

◎外語導遊及格方式：

考試總成績滿六十分及格。外語導遊人員類科第一試以筆試成績滿六十分為錄取標準，其筆試成績之計算，以各科目成績平均計算之。第二試口試成績，以口試委員評分總和之平均成績計算之。筆試成績占總成績百分之七十五，第二試口試成績占百分之二十五，合併計算為考試總成績。

◎外語領隊人員類科考試應試科目，分為下列四科：

一、領隊實務（一）（包括領隊技巧、航空票務、急救常識、旅遊安全與緊急事件處理、國際禮儀）。

二、領隊實務（二）（包括觀光法規、入出境相關法規、外匯常識、民法債編旅遊專節與國外定型化旅遊契約、臺灣地區與大陸地區人民關係條例、兩岸現況認識）。

三、觀光資源概要（包括世界歷史、世界地理、觀光資源維護）。

四、外國語（分英語、日語、法語、德語、西班牙語等五種，由應考人任選一種應試）。

◎外語領隊及格方式：

以應試科目總成績滿六十分及格。前項應試科目總成績之計算，以各科目成績平均計算之。本考試應試科目有一科成績為零分，或外國語科目成績未滿五十分，均不予及格。缺考之科目，以零分計算。

◎外語口試規則：

外國語言，指英語、法語、德語、日語、西班牙語、阿拉伯語、韓語、俄語、義大利語、土耳其語、馬來語、泰語、葡萄牙語、越南語、印尼語及其他指定之語言。外語口試分為下列三種，得視考試性質選定其中一種或併採二種舉行：

一、外語個別口試：指個別應考人就指定之外國語言回答外語口試委員之問題，藉以評量其外語表達能力、語音與語調、才識見解氣度。

二、外語集體口試：指二位以上之應考人依序分別以指定之外國語言回答外語口試委員之問題，必要時外語口試委員並得指定其他應考人提出評論，並由該應考人予以答復，藉以評量其外語表達能力、語音與語調、才識見解氣度及應變能力。

三、外語團體討論：指五位以上之應考人輪流擔任主持人，藉以評量其主持會議能力、外語表達能力、決斷力，及共同參與討論時之影響力、外語表達能力及積極性。

外語口試得依考試等級、類科、應考人數、時間分配，分組舉行。

PART 1
帶旅客趴趴走遊台灣

GO!

 景點介紹

　　故宮博物院位於台北市的外雙溪，是全台灣最大的博物館，也是全世界最大的中華藝術品集散地。館內珍藏了六十多萬件從新石器時代至今的各類文物，包含了繪畫、書法、銅器、玉器等。最著名的文物有翠玉白菜、肉形石、毛公鼎等。院內文物以時間軸概念陳設約數千件展品，其中，器物類展件相隔半年至兩年輪換一次，書畫和圖書文獻類展件則每 3 個月定期更換。近年來故宮推動「時尚故宮」與多個創新計劃，致力於藏品數位化與故宮創新化。

 帶外國朋友認識台灣

Frank and Jamie are discussing the treasures in the National Palace Museum.
Frank 與 Jamie 正在討論故宮博物院的寶物們。

Jamie　Look at that piece! It is so much like the braised pork chunk that we had for lunch!
看看那個作品！看起來好像我們中午吃的滷肉塊！

Frank　You are right. We call the pork "Tungpo Meat". It is the Meat-shaped Stone from the Qing Dynasty.
對啊。我們叫那種豬肉東坡肉。這是從清朝時代的肉塊石。

Jamie　It is just amazing. I wonder how the craftsman can make it so lifelike.
太厲害了。我好奇那個工藝師怎麼能把它做的這麼像。

Frank　It is made from jasper. The craftsman made use of this naturally occurring stone and turn the layers and impurities into this masterpiece. He carved it precisely and stained the skin, and it became the way it is now. You can see the layers of skin, fat, and lean meat.

這是由帶狀紅褐色碧玉做成的。工藝師利用這個自然形成的石頭，把它的分層跟雜質變成了這個傑作。他精確地雕刻並染色之後，就變成了它現在的樣子。你可以看到皮、肥肉、還有瘦肉的層次。

Jamie How about this cabbage artwork beside the Meat-shaped Stone?

肉形石旁邊的那個白菜作品呢？

Frank It is called Jadeite Cabbage with Insects. The figure was carved from a single piece of half-white, half-green jadeite. The maker used the color variations of the jadeite to create this artwork. The shape is just like the real cabbage, and the translucency of the jadeite makes it look so real.

這個叫做翠玉白菜。它的形狀是由一半白色一半綠色的硬玉雕刻成的。創作的人運用這個硬玉顏色的變化來創出這個作品。它的形狀就像是真的白菜一樣，而且這個硬玉的半透明性讓它看起來好真實。

Jamie There are two insects camouflaged in the leaves! It is a great work. Who made this?

有兩隻昆蟲藏在葉子裡面！這個作品太棒了。是誰做的呢？

Frank Yes. It is a great artwork. The sculptor of the Jadeite Cabbage is unknown. The only thing we know is that it was originally placed in the Forbidden City's Yung-ho Palace, which was the residence of the Guangxu Emperor's Consort Chin. Let's move on to the next one!

是啊。這是一個很棒的藝術作品。這個翠玉白菜的雕刻師已經不可考了。我們唯一知道的是這個作品一開始是放在紫禁城的永和宮，就是光緒皇帝的瑾妃寢宮。我們去看看下一個作品吧！

Words

braise [brez] v. 以文火燉煮	masterpiece [ˋmæstɚ͵pis] n. 傑作；名作
dynasty [ˋdaɪnəstɪ] n. 王朝；朝代	carve [kɑrv] v. 刻；雕刻
lifelike [ˋlaɪf͵laɪk] adj. 栩栩如生的	camouflage [ˋkæmə͵flɑʒ] v. 偽裝；掩飾
occur [əˋkɝ] v. 出現；存在	palace [ˋpælɪs] n. 皇宮；宮殿

輕鬆學導遊英語短句　　念過一次請你打「√」

It is said that the history of the museum can be traced back to the Song Dynasty, in which the emperor opened a gallery to preserve rare books and artworks.

據說博物館的歷史可以追溯到宋代，那時候的皇帝建了一個藝廊來收藏稀有書與藝術作品。

The National Palace Museum has a collection of more than 600,000 pieces, which makes it one of the largest museums in the world.

故宮博物院收藏了超過六十萬件的作品，讓它成為了全世界最大的博物館之一。

Due to the insufficient space to display more than 600,000 artworks, only a few thousand pieces of the museum's collection can be viewed at a given time.

因為空間不夠擺上超過六十萬件的藝術品，同一個時間只能看到博物館收藏的幾千件。

The antiques are priceless.

這個古物是無價的。

Most calligraphers in early China are from a privileged class, because the kind of art needs endless hours of time for individuals to practice and acquire the skills.

早期中國大部份的書法家都是出生於權貴人家的，因為這是一種需要花掉很多時間來練習然後取得技藝的一種藝術。

You cannot bring a bottle of water into the museum.

你不能把瓶裝水帶進博物館裡面。

You will have to go through the security check before getting into the museum.

在進入博物館以前，你必須要做安全檢查。

The National Palace Museum did a good job in digitizing the artworks in the collection.

故宮博物院在把收藏的藝術品數位化的部分做得很好。

Please tell us the history of the National Palace Museum.
請告訴我們故宮博物院的歷史。

It was established on October 10, 1925 after the last emperor, Puyi, left the Forbidden City in Beijing. The articles in the museum consisted of the valuables of the former Imperial family. In 1931, the Japanese attacked the north of China and threatened Beijing, and Chiang Kai-shek asked the museum to evacuate the most valuable items out of the city. The valuable artifacts were brought to Nanjing and other places. The most valuable pieces were shipped from Nanjing to Taiwan during the Chinese Civil war in 1948 and 1949. They were landed in Keelung and stored in Taichung. In 1965, the museum was finally reopened again in Waishuangxi.

它是在 1925 年的 10 月 10 號建立的，在最後一個皇帝溥儀離開北京的紫禁城之後。博物館裡面的這些文物是由之前的皇室的寶物組成的。在 1931 年，日本人襲擊中國北方，並威脅到了北京，蔣介石先生要求博物館把最珍貴的東西撤出北京，這些珍貴的文物到了南京與其他的地方。國共會戰在 1948 年與 1949 年的時候，最珍貴的物件從南京被運到了台灣，它們在基隆登陸，並且存放在台中。在 1965 年的時候，博物館終於在外雙溪重新開放。

What is a ding?
鼎是什麼呢？

Dings were made mostly by bronze, and some are made by ceramics. Originally, a Ding was a vessel used for cooking, storage, and ritual offerings to the gods or to ancestors. Later, when a Ding was associated to the person who has the privilege of performing related rituals, it became a symbol of authority.

鼎大多是由青銅製成的，有些是由陶做的。在一開始的時候，鼎是用來烹飪、儲物、還有對神明或祖先進行儀式的容器。後來，當鼎與權力進行相關儀式的人產生連結之後，它成為了權威的象徵。

02 Unit 台北 101

 景點介紹

　　台北 101 是大台北地區的地標性建築，建於 2004 年，高度 508 公尺，世界第三高的大樓。結合了傳統精神與尖端科技，台北 101 外觀除了傳達許多東方哲學之外，作為環地震帶最高的建築，它的設計採用了特殊工程技術，並設置世界最大的阻尼器，對抗地震與颱風。台北 101 也是世界上最大最高的綠建築，乘坐世界數一數二快的電梯上觀景台，可以鳥瞰整個大台北的面貌。夜間的外牆會打上燈光或傳達節慶訊息，這裡還是全世界跨年夜最大的倒數計時鐘，並在新年有絢爛的煙火表演。

 帶外國朋友認識台灣

Jamie and Frank are climbing the Xiangshan Hiking Trail.
Jamie 與 Frank 在爬象山登山步道。

Jamie
Wow! What is the skyscraper up there?
哇！那是什麼摩天大樓啊？

Frank
It is TAIPEI 101, which was once the tallest building in the world.
那是台北 101，曾經是全世界最高的建築物。

Jamie
It is stunning! The architecture looks oriental.
好壯觀！這個建築看起來有東方風情。

Frank
It is. The shape looks like pagoda, and you see Ruyi, the Chinese talisman and symbol of good fortune. There are a lot of oriental elements in the building.
是的。它的形狀看起來像是寶塔，而且你看到如意，如意是中華文化裡的護身符，也是好運的代表。這個建築還有很多東方的元素。

Jamie

Is it safe? There seems to be many earthquakes and typhoons in Taiwan.

它安全嗎？台灣似乎有不少地震跟颱風。

Frank

Yes. The architects build the skyscraper like bamboo, not only because of its cultural symbol but also because of its structural benefits, which makes the gravity point stay in the center. The skyscraper also has the world's largest and heaviest visible damper that helps stabilize the building. The building is resilient and able to meet the nature's conditions.

安全的。建築師把摩天大樓蓋的像是竹子一樣，不止是因為竹子的文化象徵，而且也是因為它在構造上能夠讓重心維持在中間。這個摩天大樓還有全世界最大最重的可以看見的阻尼器，幫助這個建築維持穩定。這個建築是有彈性的，能夠承受天然環境的狀況。

Jamie

I cannot believe that such a tall building exists in this seismically active zone. It's awesome.

我不敢相信這樣高的建築會出現在地震活躍的區域。太厲害了。

 Frank

Yes. It is a man-made marvel. Let's go there and take one of the fastest elevators in the world to get to the observatory, so we can take a look at the city.

對。這是一個建築奇觀。我們去那邊，然後坐坐全世界數一數二快的電梯到景觀台看看這個城市吧。

📝 Words

skyscraper [ˋskaɪˌskrepɚ] n. 摩天樓

stunning [ˋstʌnɪŋ] adj. 極漂亮的

oriental [ˌorɪˋɛntl] adj. 東方的

pagoda [pəˋgodə] n. （東方寺院的）塔；（公園等的）涼亭

talisman [ˋtælɪsmən] n. 護身符；法寶

damper [ˋdæmpɚ] n. 阻尼器

resilient [rɪˋzɪlɪənt] adj. 彈回的；有彈力的

seismic [ˋsaɪzmɪk] adj. 地震的

marvel [ˋmɑrvl] n. 令人驚奇的事物（或人物）

observatory [əbˋzɝvəˌtorɪ] n. 觀景台

TAIPEI 101 is the landmark of Taipei.

台北 101 是台北的地標。

It consists of a mall, observatory, and office center.

這裡是由購物中心、觀景台、還有辦公大樓所組成的。

If you want to go to the observatory, please go to the 5th floor and buy the ticket in the booth.

如果你想要到觀景台，請到五樓的售票處去買票。

It takes only 37 seconds to get to the indoor observatory, which is on the 89th floor.

只要 37 秒的時間，就可以到 89 樓的室內觀景台。

You can see the world's largest damper weighing 660 metric tons in the observatory.

你可以在觀景台看到 660 公噸的世界最大的阻尼器。

You can find a lot of gifts for friends in TAIPEI 101 souvenir shops.

你可以在台北 101 的紀念品店找到很多的紀念品給朋友。

Have you seen the fireworks display in TAIPEI 101 in the New Year?

你有看過台北 101 在新年放的煙火嗎？

The construction of TAIPEI 101 was started in 1999 and was completed in 2004.

台北 101 從 1999 年開始動工，2004 年完工。

Let me take you to the best spot to take a photo of TAIPEI 101.

讓我帶你去拍台北 101 最好的地方。

We will assemble here at 3 p.m.

我們三點在這裡集合。

 口說題問答時間

What are the things to do around TAIPEI 101?
台北 101 的附近有什麼事情可以做呢？

The Taipei World Trade Center is located near TAIPEI 101. There are a variety of shows and exhibitions all year. In the pedestrian areas, you will see many interesting street performances. In addition, the largest Eslite Bookstore is in the area.

台北世界貿易中心就在台北 101 的周圍，一年當中有各式各樣的展覽。在行人步行區，你會看到很多有趣的街頭表演。此外，最大誠品書店也在這個區域。

Is there any cultural activity around TAIPEI 101?
台北 101 附近有什麼文化活動可以做嗎？

Although TAIPEI 101 is located in the Xinyi district, one of the busiest business areas in Taipei, there are many cultural activities that are offered around it. Only a few steps from TAIPEI 101, you will see Four Four South Village, a restored military dependents' housing complex. Sometimes, there is an outdoor market that sells organic food and creative crafts.

雖然台北 101 位於全臺北最繁忙的商業區之一的信義區，這周圍還是有不少文化與休閒的活動。只有距離台北 101 幾步的距離，你會看到四四南村，一個被保存的眷村。有時候這裡有露天市場賣有機的食品和創意手工品。

Is there any place around TAIPEI 101 where residents in Taipei like to go on weekends?
101 附近有哪裡是台北居民週末常去的地方呢？

The residents in Taipei like to go to the Xiangshan hiking trail or other trails in Sishou Hills in order to look down on the city from the mountains and enjoy nature. The night view from the mountains is just breathtaking.

台北居民喜歡到象山登山步道或者四獸山其他的步道，可以從山上眺望城市，並享受大自然。從山上看到的夜景非常的漂亮。

03 Unit

中正紀念堂

景點介紹

中正紀念堂建於 1976 年，為了紀念蔣中正總統所建立，顏色採用的是中華民國國旗中的青天白日的顏色，中正紀念堂除了蔣公銅像之外，設有展覽室，陳列蔣總統生前的文物。紀念堂內也有三軍儀隊每個小時的交接儀式，也可提供旅客參觀。中正紀念堂前的廣場與牌坊，象徵了台灣許多的民主運動與政治轉變，中正紀念堂所在的中正紀念公園內，並有國家音樂廳與國家戲劇院，舉辦各種活動與展覽。

帶外國朋友認識台灣

Frank and Jamie are talking on the phone.
Frank 跟 Jamie 在電話中聊天。

Jamie What a lovely day! Let's go somewhere for a walk.
今天天氣真好！我們去哪裡走走吧。

Frank Where should we go?
我們應該去哪裡呢？

Jamie How about going to National Chiang Kai-shek Memorial Hall?
中正紀念堂怎麼樣？

Frank I have never been there. What can we do there?
我從來沒有去過那裡，我們去那裡可以做什麼呢？

Jamie Really? It is one of the famous spots in Taipei. Both tourists and residents like to go there. As the name implies, it is in memory of Mr. Chiang Kai-shek, the former president of the Republic of China, who led people to retreat from Mainland China to Taiwan in 1949. He passed away in 1975, and the government built the monument in 1976. In addition to his statue, there is a library and museum that documents the history of his life.

真的嗎？那是台北最知名的地方之一了，遊客跟這裡的居民都很喜歡去那裡。顧名思義，那是為了紀念 1949 年帶領人們從中國撤退到台灣的蔣介石先生。他在 1975 年過世，政府在 1976 年建了這個紀念館。除了他的雕像之外，裡面還有圖書館與博物館記錄那段歷史與他的生平。

Frank
Sounds interesting! Let's go there. What else can we do in the area?

聽起來很有趣！我們就去那裡吧。那邊還有什麼可以做的嗎？

Jamie
In the National Chiang Kai-shek Memorial cultural center, there are the National Theater and National Concert Hall near the memorial hall. We can go to an exhibition there or go to the National Central Library across the street. How about we meet in the National Chiang Kai-shek Hall Station Exit 5 one hour later?

在中正文化中心那邊，除了紀念堂，還有國家戲劇院跟國家音樂廳。我們可以去看個展覽，或者去對面的國家圖書館。我們一個小時以後就在捷運中正紀念堂站五號出口見面怎麼樣？

Frank
That's nice. See you then.

很好！到時候見。

 Words

lovely [ˋlʌvlɪ] adj. 【口】令人愉快的；美好的	statue [ˋstætʃʊ] n. 雕像
spot [spɑt] n. 場所；地點	museum [mjuˋzɪəm] n. 博物館
imply [ɪmˋplaɪ] v. 暗指；意味	document [ˋdɑkjəˏmɛnt] v. 用文件證明
retreat [rɪˋtrit] v. 撤退	exhibition [ˏɛksəˋbɪʃən] n. 展覽
monument [ˋmɑnjəmənt] n. 紀念碑	

National Chiang Kai-shek Memoral Hall is one of the most famous tourist attractions in Taiwan.

中正紀念堂是台灣最有名的遊客景點之一。

You may put your luggage in the information desk, when visiting the hall, and take it back before you leave.

你可以在參觀紀念堂的時候把行李放在服務台，然後在離開的時候再把行李拿回來。

Free tour service is available at 10 a.m., 2 p.m., and 4 p.m.

免費的導覽服務在早上十點、下午兩點、還有下午四點。

You can take the information brochure in the souvenir shop, and it is free of charge.

你可以在紀念品店拿參觀手冊，這是免費的。

The ceremony of changing the guard takes place every hour in the hall.

衛兵交接儀式每個小時在紀念堂舉行。

Do you want me to take a picture for you in front of the archway?

你要我幫你在牌樓前面拍張照嗎？

There are baby carriages and wheelchairs available for use.

這裡有嬰兒車與輪椅提供使用。

The National Chiang Kai-shek memorial hall is beautiful in the daytime, and it is even prettier at night with the lights on.

國立中正紀念堂在白天很好看，在晚上有燈光的時候更是漂亮。

If you like cultural activities, you can buy a ticket and watch a show in the National Theater or Concert Hall. The facilities there are state-of-the-art.

如果你喜歡文化活動，可以買張票在國家戲劇院或者國家音樂廳觀賞個表演。那裡的設備是一流的。

There are two ponds there and you will see the beautiful landscape of a Chinese garden.

那裡有兩個池塘，你會看到美麗的中國庭院造景。

口說題問答時間

Could you introduce the design concept of the National Chiang Kai-shek Memorial Hall?
你可以介紹一下中正紀念堂的設計概念嗎？

The designer of The Grand Hotel, Yang Cho-cheng, designed the National Chiang Kai-shek Memorial Hall. The colors of the building echo the colors of the national flag. It is said that Mr. Yang's design of the roof is fashioned in the form of the Temple of Heaven in Beijing, China. The octagonal roof design creates many "ren", (Man) symbolizing the idea of "unification of Man and Heaven". The total 89 stairs in the front of the hall represent the age of Mr. Chiang Kai-shek when he died.

圓山大飯店的設計師楊卓成設計了中正紀念堂。這個建築物的顏色呼應了國旗的顏色。據說楊先生設計的屋頂仿效了中國北京天壇的設計，八角形的屋頂設計創造出很多個人字，象徵了「天人合一」的概念。紀念堂前的階梯總共 89 階，代表了蔣中正先生過世的年紀。

What are the places that the locals go to in the surrounding area of the National Chiang Kai-shek Memorial Hall?
當地的人在中正紀念堂附近都去什麼地方？

In the surrounding area, the locals like to go to the Nanmen Market, which is known for its wide range of regional specialty goods, as well as dishes originated from the various provinces of Mainland China. There are also a lot of great traditional Taiwanese food in this area, for example, braised pork rice and pork thick soup.

在附近，當地人喜歡去南門市場，南門市場著名的是販賣多種中國各省的地方特產還有餐點。那裡還有很多好好吃的台灣食物，像是滷肉飯跟肉羹。

04 Unit 國父紀念館

景點介紹

　　國父紀念館是為了紀念國父孫中山的百年誕辰而建立，於 1965 年由蔣中正先生舉行奠基典禮，1972 年落成啟用，並由蔣中正先生寫下「國父紀念館」五個大字做成黑底金字的橫匾，懸掛於館之正門上方。國父紀念堂的裡面有孫中山先生的銅像，銅像基座刻有孫中山先生以毛筆親自書寫的《禮記·禮運》首段部分內容，此外，紀念館裡面展有許多中山先生與現代史相關的文物與書籍。除了主館之外，館外還有碑林、廣場、中式庭園，讓此處成為了一個結合戶外運動、休閒、藝文與知性活動的綜合公園。

帶外國朋友認識台灣

Roger and Jenny are taking a stroll in Chungshan Park of Sun Yat-sen Memorial Hall.
Roger 跟 Jenny 正在國父紀念館的中山公園裡面散步。

Roger　Look at the willow trees! They are so pretty. Can you take a photo of me and the trees?
看看那些柳樹，真漂亮。你可以幫我跟這些樹照張相片嗎？

Jenny　Sure. My phone camera has the wide-angle mode, and I will also put the reflection of TAIPEI 101 from the pond in the shot.
當然，我的手機相機有廣角模式，我會把湖上面的台北 101 倒影也拍進去。

Roger　Thanks a lot! I really love this garden. The flowers are so lush, the trees are so verdant, and the air is so fresh.
太感激了！我真的很喜歡這個庭園。花好茂盛，樹好翠綠，而且空氣真好。

Jenny
I am glad that you like it. The moisture in the air makes it humid today. I want to rest in the library.

我很高興你喜歡這裡。空氣裡的濕度讓今天感覺很潮濕，我想要去圖書館裡面休息一下。

Roger
What library?

什麼圖書館？

Jenny
There is a library inside of the main building of Sun Yat-sen Memorial Hall. The library includes 400 seats and 140,000 books! I am sure that we can find seats and books that we like. Most importantly, the library definitely has air conditioning.

在國父紀念館的主樓裡面有一個圖書館。圖書館裡面有四百個座位還有十四萬本書！我確定我們可以找到位置還有喜歡的書的。更重要的是，圖書館裡面一定有冷氣。

Roger
Wait. My friend told me that he went to a dinner meeting in Sun Yat-sen Memorial Hall before, and he said that the meeting was literally in the hall. This just came to my mind.

等等。我的朋友以前告訴我他去國父紀念館參加一個晚餐會面，而且他說真的就是在紀念館裡面。我剛剛才想到。

Jenny
Really? Let's go to check it out! Maybe afternoon tea is served in the restaurant.

真的嗎？我們去看看吧。說不定餐廳裡面還有下午茶呢。

Words

reflection [rɪ`flɛkʃən] n. 映象；倒影	moisture [`mɔɪstʃɚ] n. 濕氣；潮氣
pond [pɑnd] 池塘	humid [`hjumɪd] adj. 潮濕的
lush [lʌʃ] adj. 蒼翠繁茂的；多汁的	definite [`dɛfənɪt] adj. 一定的，肯定的
verdant [`vɝdnt] adj.（指植物、田野）青翠的	literally [`lɪtərəlɪ] adv. 實在地；不加誇張地

If you like to see the changing of guards and the marching performance, you can come back here at 1 p.m. It will last for 10 minutes.
如果你喜歡看衛兵交接與行進表演，你可以在一點的時候回來這裡。表演會持續十分鐘。

The plaque on the top of the main entrance was written by Chiang Kai-shek.
正門上面的匾額是蔣中正先生題字的。

If you have time, you should go to the galleries and exhibition rooms. They showcase a lot of great works.
如果你有時間的話，你應該去那些藝廊跟展覽間看看。裡面有很多很棒的作品。

The records of Dr. Sun Yat-sen's life and the revolution that he led are displayed in the hall.
孫中山先生的一生與他所領導的革命的記錄，陳列在紀念館裡面。

You will see the reflection of TAIPEI 101 on the Emerald Pond.
你會在翠湖上面看到台北 101 的倒影。

Local people like to go to the Sun Yat-sen Memorial Hall to fly kites, walk dogs, play Taichi, jog, or just take a stroll. It is a relaxing place.
當地人很喜歡到國父紀念館來放風箏、遛狗、打太極、慢跑、或者就是散散步。這是一個很令人放鬆的地方。

If you are lucky, you will get to see the water show in the fountain plaza. At night, the show will be presented with lights, and it is just amazing.
如果你夠幸運的話，你會看到在噴泉廣場的水舞，在晚上的時候，還會有燈光一起表演，真的非常棒。

The Sun Yat-sen Memorial Hall serves as a relaxing civic space within the hustle and bustle of the Xinyi District.
國父紀念館在信義區的熙來攘往中，是一個很輕鬆的市民空間。

Later, I will take you to Songshan Cultural and Creative Park. It is a creative center built after Huashan Creative Park.
等一下，我會帶你去松山文創園區，這是一個在華山文創園區之後建立的創意中心。

口說題問答時間

Who is Dr. Sun Yat-sen?
孫中山先生是誰呢？

Dr. Sun Yat-sen was a Chinese revolutionary. He overthrew the Qing Dynasty and terminated 2,000 years of imperial rule in China. He was the founder of the Republic of China, the first democratic republic in Asia, and he was called 'the father of the nation'. You can see his portrait on the 100 NTD bill.

孫中山先生是一個中華革命家，他推翻了清朝，結束了中國 2000 年的帝國統治。他是亞洲的第一個民主共和國中華民國的創始者，被稱為國父。在新台幣 100 元的紙鈔上面可以看到他的肖像。

Please introduce the history of Sun Yat-Sen Memorial Hall.
請介紹一下國父紀念館的歷史。

Sun Yat-sen Memorial Hall was built in order to commemorate Dr. Sun Yat-sen. The hall was first built in 1965, during which President Chiang Kai-shek officiated the groundbreaking ceremony, and it was competed in 1972. It has been the place to hold many important events in Taiwan,for example Gold Horse Film Festivals and Awards.

國父紀念館是紀念孫中山先生所建立的。這個紀念館在 1965 年開始建立，是由蔣中正總統主持動工儀式的，並在 1972 年完成。這個地方已經成為台灣舉辦許多重要事件的地方。例如，金馬獎。

Please describe the facilities in Sun Yat-sen Memorial Hall?
請描述國父紀念館的設施？

The main building in the park is Sun Yat-sen Memorial Hall. Within the main building, there is an auditorium, library, gift shop, galleries, exhibition rooms, and several rooms for civic activities.

在園區裡面主要的建築物就是國父紀念館。在主樓裡面，有大會堂、圖書館、禮品店、藝廊與展覽室、還有一些市民活動的空間。

Unit 04 國父紀念館

Part 1 遊台灣

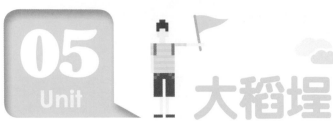

05 Unit 大稻埕

 景點介紹

　　大稻埕位於台北的西南部分,曾經是台灣非常繁華的一個地方,在經濟上與文化上都有著非常重要的地位。大稻埕為台灣舊時的地名,在 18 世紀初期,因為這個地方原為一大片曬穀廣場而得此名。在 19 世紀中期淡水開港通商之後,大稻埕成為北台灣許多其他產品的交易中心,帶來了大稻埕的繁榮與生氣。在大稻埕商圈中,迪化街是最熱鬧的一條街,也是臺北市現存最完整也最具歷史意義的老街。

 帶外國朋友認識台灣

Judy and Michael are walking on Dihua Street.
Judy 與 Michael 正在迪化街走路。

Michael Dihua Street is the most well-preserved old street in Taipei.
迪化街是台北保存最好的一條老街。

Judy The stores seem to be small.
那些商店看起來好像很小。

Michael They look small in the front, but they are very deep inside. The purpose of their sizes was to accommodate more stores on the street. People used to manufacture and store the products in their stores. Some of the people even live in the stores.
它們前面很小,但是裡面很深,目的是為了在這條街容納更多的店面。以前他們會在店裡面製造跟存放貨品,有的人甚至住在裡面。

Judy Wow! It sounds amazing. Was it a busy street in the past?
哇!聽起來很酷。這在過去是一條熱鬧的街道嗎?

Michael

Yes. It was very busy in the past. All kinds of local products are sold on the street. It is not only a retail market, but also a wholesale market for products.

對啊。這裡以前非常熱鬧。這個街道有賣各種當地的產品，這裡不只是零售，還是批發市場。

Judy

Interesting. The buildings are beautiful. What styles are they in?

有意思。這些建築很漂亮，是什麼樣的風格呢？

Michael

Because of the profound history of the street, you will find Fujian, Western, Baroque, and other styles of architecture on the street. The styles speak of the history and mixture of cultures here.

因為這條街道的豐富歷史，你會在這條街道上看到福建、西式、巴洛克式、還有其他樣式的建築。這裡的建築代表了這裡的歷史還有文化的融合。

Judy

Indeed. I have fallen in love with this place. It is so rich in culture. Let's go buy some dried fruits, and the vendors might tell us more stories about the street!

的確。我已經愛上這個地方了，它的文化很豐富。我們去買一些果乾吧，說不定小販會告訴我們這條街道更多的故事！

Words

preserve [prɪ`zɝv] v. 保護；維護	wholesale [`hol͵sel] adj. 批發的
seem [sim] v. 看來好像；似乎	profound [prə`faʊnd] adj. 深刻的；深度的
busy [`bɪzɪ] adj. 熱鬧；忙碌	mixture [`mɪkstʃɚ] n. 混合
retail [`ritel] adj. 零售的	vendor [`vɛndɚ] n. 小販；叫賣者

You can experience the tea ceremony in a tea shop here.

你可以在這裡賣茶的店裡面體驗一下泡茶的儀式。

The Queen was amazed by the oolong tea refined in Dadaocheng, and she named it the Oriental Beauty.

英國女皇為這個大稻埕來的烏龍茶感到驚豔，所以她叫這種茶東方美人。

You can buy dried fruits, nuts, candies, and herbal medicines on Dihua Street.

你可以在迪化街買果乾、核果、糖果、還有草藥。

In Yongle Market, you will find all kinds of fabrics.

在永樂市場，你會找到各式各樣的布料。

A lot of textile companies in Taiwan were started on Dihua Street.

在台灣有很多紡織的公司都發跡於迪化街。

During the Lunar New Year, Dihua Street is always packed with people who are trying the food samples and buying items for the New Year celebrations.

在農曆新年的時候，迪化街總是擠滿了人在試吃跟買東西，為了新年的慶祝做準備。

The atmosphere here is very festive during Lunar New Year.

在農曆新年的時候，這裡的氣氛非常的熱鬧歡樂。

Young people go to the Xiahai City God Temple to pray for a good spouse or long-lasting relationship.

年輕人到霞海城隍廟去，祈求一個好的配偶或者長久的關係。

There are more than 5,000 puppet artworks in the Lin Liu-hsin Puppet Theater Museum.

在林柳新偶戲博物館裡面有超過五千個玩偶作品。

Puppet-carving workshops, puppet-master demonstration shows, and puppetry skills teaching sessions are offered in the Lin Liu-hsin Puppet Theater Museum.

在林柳新偶戲博物館裡面，有刻製玩偶的工作坊、展示偶戲的表演、還有偶戲教學的課程。

口說題問答時間

Please describe the history of Dadaocheng.
請描述大稻埕的歷史。

Dadaocheng started to develop in the mid-1800s, when some immigrants from Fujian moved from Wanhua to the area. In 1860, Dadaocheng Wharf began to serve as a pier to the Tamsui Port, and the area started booming. In 1885, the first railway of Taiwan and a station at Dadaocheng were planned. Many foreign companies set their offices there, and the area was also become the distribution and trading center for products, such as Chinese medicine, fabrics, camphor, and tea. Although, it is no longer the most prosperous area in Taipei, it certainly keeps the cultural heritage.

大稻埕從 19 世紀中期，一些從福建來的移民從萬華搬到這個區域的時候開始發展。在 1860 年，大稻埕碼頭開始作為淡水港的一個碼頭，這個地方也開始繁榮發展。在 1885 年，台灣的第一條鐵路計劃開始規劃，並以大稻埕作為其中的一站，許多的外國公司在這裡設立辦公室，而這裡成為了像是中藥、織物、樟腦、還有茶等貨物的交易與集散中心。雖然這裡不再是台北最繁榮的地方，但還是保有了這樣的文化資產。

Please introduce the Xiahai City God Temple.
請介紹一下霞海城隍廟

The Xiahai City God Temple is located on Dihua Street, and it was built in 1865. The City God originally protected the wall and moat of the city. Later, it became a deity responsible for protecting the people and the affairs of the particular city.

霞海城隍廟位在迪化街，建立於 1865 年。城隍原本是保護一個城市的城牆與護城河的，後來，它變成了負責保護這個城市的人們與事務的神明。

Unit 05 大稻埕

Part 1 遊台灣

06 Unit

華西街與龍山寺

景點介紹

　　龍山寺與華西街位於台北市的萬華區。萬華舊稱艋舺，是台北最早開發的一區，在 18 世紀初期，漢人渡海來台，便以此地作為交易市集，這裡便開始日益繁華，並於 1738 年建立了龍山寺，從此龍山寺漸漸成為台北的一座非常重要的廟宇。龍山寺總面積約 1,800 坪，坐北朝南，為三進四合院之中國宮殿式建築物，神祇有百餘尊，主要分為前殿、大殿、與後殿，一共七個香爐，香火非常鼎盛。位於龍山寺附近的華西街，也因為過去萬華的繁榮與龍山寺的人潮，讓華西街成為了全台灣第一座的觀光夜市。

帶外國朋友認識台灣

This is a conversation between Stella on Huaxi Street.
這是一段 Stella 與 Ono 在華西街的對話。

Stella　We are now in the oldest area of Taipei. The Huaxi Night Market, one of the quirkiest night markets in Taiwan, is located here.
這裡就是台北最古老的一區，台北最奇特夜市之一的「華西街夜市」就在這裡。

Ono　Great! Is there anything that we should not miss?
太好了！我們有什麼不能錯過的嗎？

Stella　You may treat yourself to some snake meat.
你可以吃吃看蛇肉。

Ono　Snake meat? Sounds terrible!
蛇肉？聽起來很可怕！

Stella
This is the most distinguished and featured food of Huaxi Street. This is why the street is also called Snake Alley. It is said that snake meat can relieve inflammation, make your skin smoother, etc. Besides snake meat, the vendors also make snake liquor and snake powder.

這是華西街最特別的食物，這也是為什麼這條街叫做蛇街。據說蛇可以降火氣，讓人皮膚變好，還有很多其他的好處喔！除了蛇肉，小販也做蛇酒、蛇粉等。

Ono
I should at least try it once. Do all Taiwanese eat snake meat?

我應該至少要嘗試一次看看。所有的台灣人都吃蛇肉嗎？

Stella
Not really. Because this area used to be the most prosperous place in Taipei, you would see a lot of old-time delicacies from the mountain and sea. We may also go to Guangzhou Street. You will see food that the Taiwanese eat on a daily basis.

沒有啦！因為過去這一整個區域是商業很繁華的地方，華西街這裡賣的都是過去的山珍海味。我們也可以去廣州街，那邊就有很多台灣在地人平常在吃的東西。

Ono
Sounds good. Let's go!

聽起來不賴，走吧！

Words

terrible [`tɛrəb!] adj. 可怕的；嚇人的	inflammation [ˌɪnfləˋmeʃən] n. 炎症；發炎
distinguishing [dɪˋstɪŋgwɪʃɪŋ] adj. 有區別的	liquor [`lɪkɚ] n. 酒；含酒精飲料
feature [`fitʃɚ] n. 特徵；特色	powder [`paʊdɚ] n. 粉；粉末
relieve [rɪˋliv] v. 緩和；減輕	delicacy [`dɛləkəsɪ] n. 美味；佳餚

輕鬆學導遊英語短句 念過一次請你打「√」

There are a lot of worshippers in the Longshan Temple.
在龍山寺有很多拜拜的人。

The temple was built in 1738 by settlers from Fujian, China.
這個寺廟在 1738 年由福建移民所建立的。

The temple has been rebuilt and renovated several times.
這個寺廟已經被重建與整修過幾次了。

The main God worshipped in the Longshan Temple is the Goddess of Mercy.
龍山寺主要供奉的是觀世音菩薩。

You can take the subway to the Longshan Temple Station to get to the Huaxi Night Market.
你可以坐到捷運龍山寺站到華西街夜市。

There are a lot of religious supply shops on Xiyuan Road, a road that borders the Longshan Temple. If you are interested in religious craftworks, you might find enjoyable to go there.
西園路有很多的宗教用品商店，如果你對於宗教的工藝品有興趣，你可能會喜歡去那裡。

There is a traditional Chinese style archway with Chinese lanterns in front of the Huaxi Night Market.
在華西街夜市的前面有一個中國傳統風格的牌樓與中式燈籠。

Later, we can go to Ximending to experience the contemporary culture in Taipei.
等一下，我們可以到西門町去體驗一下台北的當代文化。

There is a pedestrian area in Ximending.
西門町有行人徒步區。

The Red House is Taipei's first modern market and movie theater.
紅樓是台北的第一個現代的市場與電影院。

Please describe the features of Longshan Temple.
請描述龍山寺特色。

The Longshan Temple mixes the features of Buddhism, Taoism, and Mazu, one of the folk deities. The temple was decorated with lots of fine stone, wood carvings, and bronze works. Notably, it has the only dragon columns with bronze in Taiwan.

龍山寺結合了佛教、道教、民間信仰與媽祖。這裡有很多的精美的石塊、木雕、與銅質藝術品。值得注意的是，這裡有全台僅見的銅鑄龍柱。

Please describe the importance of the Longshan Temple for people in Taipei.
請描述龍山寺在台北人心中的重要性。

The Longshan Temple was built in 1738 and is listed as the second level historical monument in Taiwan. During wartime, people used the Longshan Temple as an asylum. At one point, they left it because of the countless mosquitos, and very soon, an air attack destroyed the asylum. People thought this was a miracle, and they considered it to an act of the Gods to protect them from disasters. The Longshan Temple has been believed to be a very efficacious temple since then.

龍山寺建於 1738 年，在台灣列為二級古蹟。在戰爭的時候，人們把龍山寺當作避難所。有一次，他們因為太多蚊子而離開避難所，不久之後空襲來臨毀掉了寺廟的避難所，大家把這個當成了神蹟，他們認為是神幫助他們遠離了災難。從此之後，龍山寺就被當成了一座非常靈驗的寺廟。

What do you suggest me to eat in Huaxi Night Market?
你建議我在華西街夜市吃什麼呢？

The Huaxi Night Market is well-known for its snake cuisine. Besides eating snakes, you can try squid thick soup, braised pork rice and Chinese herb tea.

華西街夜市以蛇的料理聞名。有很多種的蛇料理。除了吃蛇之外，你可以試試魷魚羹、滷肉飯與青草茶。

07 Unit

北投

 景點介紹

　　北投區位於台北的最北邊，在大屯火山境內，因此火山和地熱溫泉特別發達，是非常著名的溫泉聖地，也是台灣第一家溫泉旅館設立的地方。北投此名源自於以前巴賽族認為地熱谷是女巫施法才會冒煙，巴賽語裡的女巫念起來是 PATAW，與北投的台語發音很像，所以命名為「北投」。北投區有許多著名的景點，其中，稱為台北後花園的陽明山國家公園也部分位於北投區。陽明山國家公園是台灣離都會區最近的一座國家公園，火山活動的特殊景觀與亞熱帶與溫帶氣候的豐富動植物生態，讓陽明山成為北部的一大觀光景點。

帶外國朋友認識台灣

Frank and Jamie just arrived at the terminal station for Bus Route 260.
Frank 與 Jamie 剛剛抵達 260 公車的終點站。

Jamie
We finally arrived in Yangmingshan.
我們終於到陽明山了

Frank
Yes. What's next?
對啊，下一步呢？

Jamie
We will have to decide what part of the mountain that we want to visit this time. Yangmingshan is large, and it comprises several mountains. There are many attractions in Yangmingshan. Last time, I went to Zhuzihu and had so much fun picking calla lilies.
我們要決定這次我們要去山的哪個部分。陽明山很大，是由幾個山組成的，在陽明山有很多的景點。上次，我去了竹子湖，採海芋超好玩的。

Frank: Why is it called Zhuzihu? In Chinese, it means 'the bamboo lake'. However, I don't think there are any lakes in Zhuzihu now.

為什麼要叫竹子湖啊？在中文的意思是竹子湖吧，但是，我想現在竹子湖那邊應該沒有湖吧。

Jamie: Zhuzihu used to be a barrier lake, formed by volcanic eruptions a long time ago. The water receded, and it became a fertile land. In the past, it was a bamboo plantation, and it is the reason why this place is called Bamboo Lake. Now, Zhuzihu has become a place to plant vegetables and flowers.

竹子湖在很久以前曾經是一個因為火山爆發所產生的堰塞湖。水退掉之後，就變成了一塊肥沃的土地。過去，那裡是種竹子的地方，所以這是為什麼這個地方叫做竹子湖。現在，竹子湖變成了種植蔬菜與花卉的地方。

Frank: Thank you for telling me that story. How about now? Is there any specific spot that you want to go to this time?

謝謝你告訴我這個故事。現在呢？這次你想要去什麼地方呢？

Jamie: I prefer to go to Qixingshan this time. We can follow the trail and get to the top of Taipei, and we will see the panoramic view of the city.

我這次想去七星山。我們可以爬步道到台北的最上端，可以看到這個城市的全景。

Frank: The weather is nice, and the sky is clear today. It must be great. Let's go.

今天天氣很好，天空也很晴朗。一定會很棒的，我們走吧。

Unit 07 北投

Part 1 遊台灣

📖 Words

comprise [kəmˋpraɪz] v. 包含	fertile [ˋfɝtl̩] adj. （土地）肥沃的；富饒的
pick [pɪk] v. 採；摘	specific [spɪˋsɪfɪk] adj. 特殊的；特定的
eruption [ɪˋrʌpʃən] n. （火山）爆發；（熔岩的）噴出	trail [trel] n. 小道
recede [rɪˋsid] v. 退；後退	panoramic [͵pænəˋræmɪk] adj. 全景的

Yangmingshan National Park is very close to the metropolitan area of Taipei, and it is called Taipei's backyard garden by the local residents.

陽明山國家公園非常靠近台北都會區，被當地的人稱作台北的後花園

In Yangming Park, there is a flower clock, composed of a variety of colorful, seasonal flowers.

在陽明公園，有一個由許多種類的彩色季節花朵組成的花鐘。

The spring water in Lengshuikeng is not cold. It is just below the temperature of other hot springs in the area.

在冷水坑的溫泉水不是冷的，它只是比這個地區其他的溫泉溫度還要低。

You should go take a look at Milk Pond. The white-colored water in the pond was formed by the sulfur deposits from the bottom of the pond.

你應該去看看牛奶池。在池子裡面白色的水是由硫磺沉澱在池子的底部所形成的。

If you want to see post-volcanic geological landscapes, you can go to Xiaoyoukeng. You will definitely see and smell the sulfurous fumes. Sometimes, you can even see the fumaroles.

如果你想看看後火山的地理景觀，你可以到小油坑。你一定會看到並聞到硫磺的氣味的。
有時候你甚至可以看到火山噴氣孔。

Qingtiangang is a terrace formed by lava, and it is now a beautiful meadow.

擎天崗是一個由火山熔岩產生的平台，現在是一片美麗的草地。

The Grass Mountain Chateau was the residence of the late President Chiang Kai-shek, and it has now become an art exhibition space, as well as a restaurant.

草山行館曾經是已故總統蔣中正先生的住所，現在已經變成一個藝術展覽空間與餐廳。

口說題問答時間

Please describe the history of hot springs in Beitou.
請介紹北投的溫泉歷史

Beitou started to be viewed as a hot spring resort in 1896, when a Japanese businessman opened Taiwan's first hot spring hotel in Beitou. Hot spring water in Beitou has been considered as having great therapeutic effects and as being good for health. The hot spring hotels reached their peak during World War II and the Vietnam War because of the business brought in by the soldiers. After the end of the war, the business went down greatly. After the MRT stopped in Beitou and peopled viewed the hot springs soaking as a leisure and healthy activity, the hot spring hotels in Beitou revived and became popular.

北投在 1896 年，從一個日本商人在北投開了第一家溫泉旅館的時候，開始被當作一個溫泉度假村。北投的溫泉水被認為有很好的療癒效果，對健康很好。當地的溫泉旅館在第二次世界大戰跟越戰的時候，因為士兵們帶來的生意而到達了全盛時期，在戰爭結束之後，生意大不如前，直到捷運在北投開站，以及大家開始把泡溫泉當作一個休閒與健康的活動，北投的溫泉旅館又恢復生氣，並且變得熱門。

What is special about the Public Library Beitou Branch?
台北市立圖書館北投分館有什麼特別之處？

The Public Library Beitou Branch is a work of green architecture. It was built mainly by wood, and everything in the library is recyclable. The plants on the rooftop make the temperature of the building stay cool, and the rainwater that drops on the building can be gathered and used. There are many other eco-friendly and well-designed highlights of this building, and the building itself is an aesthetic masterpiece.

它是一個綠建築的作品。圖書館主要是由木頭蓋成的，而且所有的東西都是可以回收利用的。在屋頂的植物讓這個建築的溫度保持涼爽，而且落在建築物上的雨水是可以被收集與利用的。這棟建築還有很多的環保與精心設計的特點，而建築物本身就是一個美學的傑作。

景點介紹

　　淡水位於臺北盆地淡水河系出口，由於地理位置的關係，曾經是一個重要的港口。歷經了西班牙人與荷蘭人入侵、清代政府、還有日據時代的歷史，走在淡水街道上，可以看到一座座的洋式、日式、閩式的老房子。其中，中正路、真理街、重建街、三民街、清水街一帶，最能展現老街古風及各時期建築特色。另外，出海口的漁人碼頭、渡輪可到達的對岸八里，都是在淡水不可錯過的景點。追尋古蹟、看夕陽、觀山、坐船、吃美食，讓淡水成為台北周圍一個充滿魅力的地方。

帶外國朋友認識台灣

Roger and Jenny are walking on an old street of Tamsui.
Roger 跟 Jenny 正走在淡水的一條老街。

Jenny
The weather is very nice today. I can clearly see the mountain on the other side of the river. What is the mountain?
今天天氣真好，我可以清楚的看到在河另一邊的山，那是什麼山啊？

Roger
It is Guanyin Mountain. There are six hiking trails, and you can get to the top of the mountain by walking on the trails.
那是觀音山，有六條登山步道，你可以由這些步道到達山頂。

Jenny
Guanyin Mountain? I have heard of it. Is it a volcano?
觀音山？我聽過，它是一個火山嗎？

Roger
Yes. It is a dormant volcano. The rocks on Guanyin Mountain were very famous for construction purposes, because they are very solid and come from molten lava.

是的，它是一個休眠的火山。觀音山上的石頭曾經在建築的用途上很有名，因為這些石頭很堅固，是由熔岩變成的。

Jenny
Why is it called Guanyin Mountain? Does the word Guanyin mean Goddess of Mercy in Chinese?

為什麼要叫觀音山呢？觀音在中文的意思不就是那個慈悲女神嗎？

Roger
You are right. It is said that the there are four Goddess of Mercy (Guanyin) temples on this mountain, and this is why it was named Guanyin Mountain. Two of the temples have been there for more than 200 years. Some people say that the ridge of Guanyin Mountain, when viewed from Tamsui, is like the face of the Goddess of Mercy. See? What do you think?

答對了。據説這座山裡面有四座觀音廟，所以就變成了觀音山。其中有兩座廟已經有超過兩百年的歷史。有的人説觀音山從淡水這邊看過去的山脊線，很像觀音的臉，有看到嗎？你覺得呢？

Jenny
Wow! Yes! I see it. It is so cool. Shall we go there next time?

哇！真的！我看到了，好酷喔。我們下次要去嗎？

Roger
It is only one hour past noon. We can take the ferry to Bali and hike to the top of the mountain. The night view from the top is awesome. You can see Guandu Bridge, The Grand Hotel, and even TAIPEI101. I am ready!

現在才中午過後一點。我們可以搭渡輪去八里，然後爬到山上，山頂的夜景超棒的，你可以看到關渡大橋，圓山飯店，甚至是台北 101。我準備好了！

Words

volcano [vɑl`keno] n. 火山	temple [`tɛmp!] n.（佛教的）寺院
molten [`moltən] adj. 熔化的；熔解的	ridge [rɪdʒ] n. 屋脊；山脊
lava [`lɑvə] n. 熔岩	ferry [`fɛrɪ] n. 渡輪
mercy [`mɝsɪ] n. 慈悲；憐憫	awesome [`ɔsəm] adj.【俚】極好的

You can take the ferry to Bali or Fisherman's Wharf.

你可以坐渡輪到八里或者漁人碼頭。

You can pay by cash or by EasyCard.

你可以用現金或者悠遊卡付錢。

You can also take a cruise. It will take you to the mouth of the river, and dinner is served on the cruise.

你也可以坐遊艇。他們帶你到河口，然後在遊艇裡面吃晚餐。

Along the river, you will see the Tamsui River Mangrove Nature Reserve, which is not far away.

沿著河，你將會看到不遠處的淡水紅樹林自然保留區。

There are a lot of snacks served on the old streets in Tamsui. You should try the fish ball soup, the fried fish cracker, and Agei.

淡水的老街有很多小吃。你應該試試魚丸湯、魚酥、還有阿給。

Agei is a fried tofu pocket, stuffed with mung bean noodles, and sealed with fish paste, and it is best served with sweet and spicy sauce.

阿給是炸豆腐包裡面放了冬粉，然後用魚漿封起來做成的。最好跟甜辣醬一起食用。

The store sells antique toys and old-fashioned candies.

這個商店販售以前的玩具還有古味的糖果。

The Fisherman's Wharf has some eateries and coffee shops.

漁人碼頭有一些小餐廳跟咖啡店。

It is very comfortable in Tamsui. Even just watching the river flow and feeling the breeze are enjoyable.

在淡水很舒服，即使就是看看河水的流動、感受微風，都是愉快的。

There are tons of historical sites in Tamsui. Don't miss them!

在淡水有很多的歷史遺跡，不要錯過了！

Please briefly describe the developmental history of Tamsui.
請簡單描述淡水的發展歷史。

In the 17th century, the Spanish occupied Tamsui and used it as an important port for business, before the Dutch came and expelled them. After the Dutch, the Chinese Ming and Qing Dynasty administrations took over Tamsui.

在十七世紀的時候，西班牙人佔領了淡水，並且把它作為一個重要的商業港口。接著荷蘭人來了，並且驅趕了他們。在荷蘭人之後，中國明朝與清朝接著統治了淡水。

Please tell us the story of Fort San Domingo.
請告訴我們聖安東尼堡（紅毛城）的故事。

Fort San Domingo is also called 'Hong Mao Cheng', which means 'the fort of the red-haired barbarians' in Chinese. It is said that this is what the local people called the Dutch during that time. Fort San Domingo was originally built by the Spanish and was razed, before it was rebuilt by the Dutch. The building was renovated many times, and it has become one of the most important colonial architectures in Taiwan.

聖安東尼堡又叫做紅毛城，在中文的意思就是紅頭髮的野蠻人的堡壘。據說這是當地人在當時稱呼荷蘭人的方式。聖安東尼堡一開始是西班牙人蓋的，接著被破壞了，然後荷蘭人重建了它。這個建築物被整修了很多次，而現在已經成為台灣最重要的殖民建築之一。

What are the other buildings that are worth seeing in Tamsui?
淡水還有哪些值得看的建築呢？

Tamsui is a place with rich historical heritage. You can go to places like Oxford College, Hobe Fort, Temple of Blessings, Tamsui Church, Tomb of Rev. G. L. Mackay, etc.

淡水是一個充滿歷史古蹟的地方。你可以去的地方像是理學堂大書院、滬尾炮台、福佑宮、淡水禮拜堂、馬偕墓等等。

基隆

景點介紹

　　基隆是台灣最北端的城市，古稱「雞籠」，由於是深水谷灣的天然港灣地形，雞籠成為了北台灣的航運樞紐，優良港灣加上豐富的礦產，讓基隆的商業與貿易的發展一度達到巔峰，在日據時代更成為了台灣的第四大城。由於基隆地勢多屬於丘陵，聚落多是沿河或者港口而建，成為了一個美麗、充滿文化與自然風光的基隆北海岸。

帶外國朋友認識台灣

Judy and Michael are discussing their schedule in a hostel in Keelung.
Judy 跟 Michael 正在基隆的一個民宿討論他們的行程。

Judy　Good morning! What do you plan to do today?
早安！你今天打算要做什麼？

Michael　I am thinking of renting a car and driving to the north coast today. Do you want to join?
我在想今天要租一台車，然後開到北海岸。你要加入嗎？

Judy　Sure! Do you know where the car rental place is?
當然！你知道哪裡租車嗎？

Michael　I saw one near the Keelung Train Station. Let's go check it out.
我看到有一家靠近基隆火車站的，我們去看看。

Judy　Okay! Let me buy some breakfast on the way to the train station. I am craving fried dough sticks and soymilk. How about you?
好！我要在路上買早餐。我現在很想要吃油條跟豆漿。你呢？

Michael I just had some sandwiches and milk tea from the breakfast shop across the street. For today's schedule, I am thinking of visiting Heping Island in the morning. I really want to see the oddly weathered rock formations on the northeast coast. We can come back to the Port of Keelung and eat lunch in a seafood restaurant. In the afternoon, we can go to the Yeliu Scenic Area. There are also a lot of extraordinary sandstones, shaped by the weather and erosion.

我剛剛在對面的早餐店吃過三明治跟奶茶了。時間安排上，我在想早上要去和平島看看。我真的很想要看看那些在東北海岸奇特風化石頭的形成。我們可以回到基隆港，在一個海鮮餐廳吃午餐。下午的時候，我們可以到野柳風景區，那裡也有很多經過風化與侵蝕形成特別形狀的砂岩。

Judy Will we come back to the city and have dinner in the Keelung night market?

我們會回到市區來在基隆夜市吃晚餐嗎？

Michael Haha! I know it is a must-do. Let's go now and indulge in the yummy local snacks of our choice tonight!

哈哈！我知道這是必須的。我們現在出發，然後今晚享受一下我們選擇的當地美味小吃吧！

🖊 Words

crave [krev] v. 渴望獲得

oddly [`ɑdlɪ] adv. 古怪地

weathered [`wɛðəd] adj. 風化的

formation [fɔr`meʃən] n. 構成，組成

extraordinary [ɪk`strɔrdn͵ɛrɪ] adj. 非凡的

sandstone [`sænd͵ston] n. 砂岩

erosion [ɪ`roʒən] n. 侵蝕；腐蝕

indulge [ɪn`dʌldʒ] v. 滿足（欲望等）

If you have any problems, please go to the tourist information center located in the train station.

如果你有任何的問題，請到火車站裡面的旅遊服務中心。

There is a lot of fresh seafood in the Port of Keelung.

基隆港有很多新鮮的海鮮。

Many natural wonders in Taiwan are located on the north coast.

台灣很多自然奇觀都在北海岸。

Most of the rocks have fanciful names. For example, this rock is called 'Queen's Head Rock'.

大部份的石頭都有富想像力的名字。舉例來說，這叫做女王頭。

Keelung is the northernmost city of Taiwan.

基隆是台灣最北邊的城市。

It is also Taiwan's second-largest port.

它也是台灣第二大的港口。

Keelung city is surrounded by hills and mountains.

基隆市被丘陵與山圍繞。

There are numerous bridges and tunnels in Keelung.

基隆有很多的橋樑與隧道。

Keelung's most famous landmark is the white statue of the Goddess of Mercy.

基隆最有名的地標就是觀音的白色雕像。

The Keelung Temple Mouth Night Market is one of the biggest night markets in Taiwan.

基隆廟口夜市是台灣最大的夜市之一。

Where are the attractions in the northwest of Keelung?
基隆東北邊有什麼景點呢？

Keelung connects the North Coast and Northeast Coast. You can easily get to places from Keelung. For example, you can go to Jinshan, and Jinbaoli Street is one of the few places in Taiwan to see architecture from the Qing Dynasty. In the Ju Ming Museum, you can see the works of Ju Ming, one of Taiwan's famous sculptors. In the Yeliu Scenic Area and Yeliu Geopark, you will see a lot of stunning sandstones. They make the scenery magnificent.

基隆連接了台灣的北海岸跟東北海岸。你可以從基隆輕鬆地到很多地方。舉例來說，你可以去金山，那裡的金包里老街是台灣少數可以看到清代建築的地方。在朱銘美術館，你可以看到台灣有名的雕刻家之一，朱銘的作品。在野柳風景區還有野柳地質公園，你將會看到很多美麗的砂岩，形成了壯觀的景色。

What are the attractions in the southeast of Keelung?
基隆東南邊有什麼景點呢？

You can go to Ruifang. It is the first stop of the Pingxi Branch Railway, which was originally built in order to carry coals from the mountains to Keelung. It has now become the train that is mostly used for tourism purposes. By the Pingxi Branch Railway, you can go to the Shifen Waterfall, Coal Memorial Museum, Jingtong Old Street, and many other natural and cultural attractions. Among all of the attractions, you must not miss Pingxi Old Street and the sky lanterns.

你可以去瑞芳，這是平溪支線鐵路的第一站，平溪支線鐵路一開始是為了從山上運送煤礦到基隆而建立的，而它現在成為主要為了旅遊目的而在的火車。經由平溪支線鐵路，你可以到十分瀑布，煤礦博物館，菁桐老街，還有很多其他的自然以及文化的景點。在這之中，你千萬不要錯過了平溪老街，還有天燈。

九份位在新北市瑞芳區，在 1893 年在九份地區發現金礦之後，出現淘金的人潮，也帶給九份將近 100 年的繁榮時光。九份臨山靠海，與基隆山遙遙相望；整個小鎮座落於山坡地上，也因此形成了獨特的山坡和階梯式建築景觀，因電影《悲情城市》在九份取景，而成為熱門的觀光景點。近年也因日本動畫片《神隱少女》在九份取景也吸引眾多日籍觀光客慕名而來。老街有許多很有魔幻情調的茶樓。可以在觀景茶樓喝一杯茶享受依山面海的美景與古樸的氛圍。

 帶外國朋友認識台灣

Jenny is standing in front of the information board in a bus station while Michael is approaching her.
珍妮正站在一個公車站的看版前面，當麥可正往她靠近的時候。

Michael Hi. Do you need help?
嗨！你需要幫忙嗎？

Jenny Hi! Yes. I am looking for the bus route to Jiufen.
嗨！對的，我正在找去九份的公車。

Michael We are at Taipei Main Station and there is no bus that goes to Jiufen.
我們在台北車站，這裡沒有公車到九份。

Jenny Oh, no! Could you tell me how to get there?
哦！不！你可以告訴我怎麼去那裡嗎？

Michael Sure. There are several ways to get to Jiufen. First, you can take the train to Ruifang and then take a bus or taxi to Jiufen. Second, you can take the subway to the Zhongxiao Fuxing Station and then take bus 1062 directly to Jiufen, and I think it is easier and faster. Third, you can just take a taxi from here to Jiufen. It takes approximately NTD 1,000 to get there.

當然。去九份有幾種方法。第一，你可以搭火車到瑞芳，然後再搭公車或者計程車到九份。第二，你可以坐捷運到忠孝復興站，然後再搭 1062 號巴士直接到九份，我想這會比較簡單也比較快。第三，你可以從這裡搭計程車到九份，大約台幣一千塊。

Jenny Can the taxi driver charge by meter? Is there any surcharge? Where can I find the taxi stand? Or can I hail a taxi on the street?

計程車司機可以用計費表來收費嗎？有什麼附加費用嗎？我在哪裡可以找到計程車招呼站呢？或者我可以直接在路上招車嗎？

Michael Of course you can, and there should not be any surcharge. There is a taxi stand outside of the Taipei Main Station. However, I think it is better not to take the taxi because the traffic is very heavy right now. It is easier to take the mass transportation service. What do you think?

當然可以，而且應該不會有附加費用的。台北車站外面有一個計程車招呼站，但是，我覺得還是不要搭計程車的好，因為現在這個時間的交通很壅塞。搭乘大眾交通工具會比較方便一點，你覺得呢？

Jenny Good suggestion. I would rather go to Zhongxiao Fuxing to take the bus. Thank you very much.

很好的建議，我寧可到忠孝復興那邊去搭巴士。非常謝謝你。

📝 Words

board [bord] *n.* 牌子；布告牌；黑板	surcharge [`sɝ͵tʃɑrdʒ] *n.* 額外費
approach [ə`protʃ] *v.* 接近，靠近	stand [stænd] *n.* 停車處；候車站
route [rut] *n.* 路；路線	hail [hel] *v.* 招呼
meter [`mitɚ] *n.* 計量器；儀表	heavy [`hɛvɪ] *adj.* 繁忙的；大量的

Jiufen is a beautiful mountain town.

九份是一個美麗的山城。

Many people like to stay overnight in Jiufen.

很多人喜歡在九份過夜。

There are many bed and breakfast inns that you can choose.

有很多的民宿小旅館可以讓你選擇。

If you want to stay for the night in Jiufen, you better book a room or bed beforehand, in case they are all fully booked.

如果你想要在九份待一個晚上的話，你最好提前訂房間或者床位，以免他們都客滿了。

Some teahouses stay open for the whole night.

有些茶館是開一整晚的。

You gotta try the taro rice ball sweet soup, taro rice cake, and herbal rice cake.

你一定要試試芋圓湯、芋粿、還有草仔粿。

The town is even prettier at night. The tranquil beauty of the town is very comforting.

這個城鎮在晚上更漂亮，它平靜的美讓人覺得很舒服。

Some people avoid coming to Jiufen on the weekends, as it is always packed with crowds.

有些人會避免在週末來到九份，因為這裡那裡總是擠滿了人群。

You can feel the rise and fall of the town that once relied heavily on mineral mining.

你可以感覺到這個曾經仰賴採礦的城鎮的起與落。

Some scenes in the movie *Spirited Away* look like the sceneries in Jiufen.

在《神隱少女》電影裡的有些場景看起來像是九份的景色。

口說題問答時間

What is the origin of Jiufen's name?
九份這個名字的來源是什麼？

The name Jiufen means 'nine portions' in Chinese. It is said that there were only nine households in Jiufen in the past, and the residents would buy or order everything in nine portions from the market outside of the village. Later, Jiufen became the name of the village.

九份這個名字在中文的意思代表了九份東西。據說以前那裡只有九戶人家，他們在村子外面的市集採買或者訂購任何東西都會要九份，後來九份就變成了這個村莊的名字。

Please summarize the development and history of Jiufen.
請簡述九份的發展與歷史。

Jiufen was a small village before its gold was discovered in 1893. The gold-mining activities made Jiufen become a prosperous town during the Japanese Colonial Era. The gold-mining activities lasted for almost 100 years before the town was mostly forgotten. The town was brought back to people's memories by the movie *A City of Sadness,* which is a film set in Jiufen. The nostalgic scenery of Jiufen revives people's memories of the old times, and it has become a popular tourist attraction.

九份在 1893 發現金礦以前是一個小村莊，開採金礦讓九份在日據時代成為了一個蓬勃發展的城鎮，幾乎持續了一百年的風光時光，直到這個城鎮幾乎被忘記之前。它再被大家想起的時候，是《悲情城市》這部電影，九份懷舊的景色，喚醒了人們對於舊時的回憶，也讓它變成了一個熱門旅遊景點。

烏來區位於新北市的南邊,是台灣分布最北的原住民山區。居民以泰雅族為主,「烏來」這個名稱來自於泰雅族語裡面的 Ulay,就是冒煙的熱水的意思,指的就是烏來的溫泉。烏來除了溫泉之外,還有台車、纜車、櫻花、瀑布、老街、原住民文化,以及雲仙樂園。春天這裡可以看到許多品種的櫻花,夏天這裡的溪流與瀑布成為消暑的好去處,還有秋天的楓葉與冬天的溫泉,烏來是個四季都適合旅遊的好地方。

 帶外國朋友認識台灣

Stella and Ono are getting off the bus outside of the Wulai Parking Structure.
Stella 與 Ono 正從烏來立體停車場的外面下公車。

Stella Hurray! We are finally here! I can smell the fresh air from the mountains.
喔耶!我們終於到了!我可以聞到山裡來的新鮮空氣了。

Ono Yes. I am so excited! Let's go to our hotel and check in first.
對啊!我好興奮!我們先到我們的飯店辦理入住手續吧。

Stella Okay. I called the hotel this morning, and they told me how to get to the hotel. The receptionist said that we can walk through the old street, and then we can walk through the bridge, after we see the river. After crossing the river, we should turn left and should be able to see the hotel on the left side of the street.
好的。今天早上我打電話到飯店,他們已經告訴我怎麼到飯店了。飯店的接待員說,我們可以穿過老街,然後我們看到河之後穿過那座橋,在過了河之後,我們要左轉,然後應該就會看到他們的飯店在馬路的左手邊。

Super 英文領隊導遊

Ono

Thank you, darling. Let's go. I can't wait to soak in the hot springs and come back to the old street in order to treat myself to some yummy food.

謝謝你，親愛的。我們走吧。我等不及要泡在溫泉裡面，然後回到老街上享受一些好吃的食物了。

Stella

The receptionist also suggested that we check out the Wulai Atayal Museum. He also recommended that we stroll in the Neidong National Forest Recreation Area.

那個接待人員還建議我們去看看烏來泰雅民族博物館，他還建議我們去內洞國家森林遊樂區散散步。

Ono

Maybe we can leave Neidong for tomorrow. Oh! Look at the Taiwanese sausages that the vendors are grilling. I am drooling.

或許我們可以把內洞留到明天。喔！你看看小販正在烤的台灣香腸，我都流口水了。

Stella

Me, too. Did you see the grilled rice cake that we just passed by? It is just tempting.

我也是。你有看到我們剛剛經過的那個烤麻糬嗎？那真是太吸引人了。

Ono

Yes, I saw it. Let's move faster to our hotel and start with the hot springs. I am already in love with this place!

嗯，我看到了。我們快點去到我們的飯店，然後從溫泉開始吧。我已經愛上這個地方了！

📝 Words

receptionist [rɪˋsɛpʃənɪst] *n.* 接待員	yummy [ˋjʌmɪ] *adj.* 好吃的；美味的
cross [krɔs] *v.* 越過；渡過	stroll [strol] *v.* 散步；溜達
soak [sok] *v.* 浸泡	grill [grɪl] *v.* （用烤架）烤（魚、肉等）
treat [trit] *v.* 請客；款待	drool [drul] *v.* 流口水

Wulai is a famous hot spring resort.

烏來是一個著名的溫泉度假勝地。

You can savor the aboriginal cuisine on the street.

你可以在街上品嚐原住民的美食。

If you want to go to the Yun Hsien Resort, you can take the cable car from Wulai Waterfall to get there.

如果你想要去雲仙樂園，你可以從烏來瀑布坐纜車到那裡。

Hot spring soaking is good for your health.

泡溫泉對身體好。

Swimwear is required in some hot spring pools, and it is prohibited in other ones.

在有些溫泉池穿泳衣是必須的，而有些是禁止的。

You can enjoy some snacks or meals after soaking in the hot spring.

你可以在泡完溫泉之後享用點心或者餐點。

Please take a shower before and after soaking in the hot spring.

請在泡溫泉的前後都沖個澡。

I suggest that you take a stroll along the river.

我建議你沿著河邊散散步。

Many tourists are fascinated by the Wulai Waterfall.

很多的遊客被烏來瀑布給吸引住了。

Ethnic dances will be performed in the museum.

博物館將會有民族舞蹈演出的。

口說題問答時間

In Wulai, what is the function of the mini train?
在烏來，台車的功能是什麼呢？

The mini train in Wulai was originally built for the purpose of transporting timber, and it is now used to haul tourists from the riverside to the gorge. The length of the rail is 1.6 kilometers, and you will see the beautiful mountain views along the way. If you go to Wulai, you must take the mini train and enjoy the nature.

烏來的台車本來是為了運送木頭所建造的，現在的用途是運送旅客從河邊到峽谷。鐵路的長度是 1.6 公里，你將會在沿途看到美麗的山景。如果你來到烏來，你一定要坐這個台車，享受大自然。

What can I do in Wulai?
我在烏來可以做什麼呢？

There are a lot of things to do in Wulai. You can choose a place to soak in the hot springs. You can experience Atayal aboriginal culture and taste the indigenous cuisine. You may also go to the Neidong National Forest Recreation Area, where you can see exquisite waterfalls and hike on the trails.

在烏來有很多事情可以做，你可以選一個地方來泡溫泉，你可以體驗泰雅族原住民文化，並且品嚐原住民美食。你也可以到內洞國家森林遊樂區，看看漂亮的瀑布，爬爬步道。

Who is Atayal?
誰是泰雅族？

Atayal, also known as Tayal, is one tribe of Taiwanese aborigines. The word Atayal means 'the brave man'. It is one of the three largest aboriginal groups in Taiwan, and it is believed they have existed in Taiwan since 5,000 years ago.

泰雅族（Atayal），也叫做 Tayal，是台灣原住民的一個族。泰雅族的字面意思就是勇敢的人的意思。這是台灣原住民的三大族之一，而且據說五千年前就已經台灣存在了。

Part 1 遊台灣　Unit 11 烏來

 景點介紹

　　大甲鎮瀾宮，俗稱大甲媽祖廟，位於台中市的大甲，主奉天上聖母媽祖，據說是清雍正 8 年（西元 1730 年）自湄洲天后祖廟恭請媽祖神像來臺，香火鼎盛，為台灣媽祖信仰的知名廟宇之一。大甲鎮瀾宮媽祖最有名的就是大甲媽祖南下遶境進香活動，每年的春天舉行九天八夜的活動，沿途經過 20 多個鄉鎮市區，80 餘座廟宇，跋涉 300 多公里路，依照傳統舉行十大典禮，每個典禮都有既定的時間跟地點，是台灣民間宗教界每年的一大盛事。

 帶外國朋友認識台灣

Roger and Jenny are discussing their trip to Dajia.
Roger 跟 Jenny 正在討論去大甲的旅行。

Roger　When is the pilgrimage to the Dajia Zhenlan Temple this year?
大甲鎮瀾宮今年的遶境進香是什麼時候呢？

Jenny　I am not sure. I know it has to be before March 23th of the Lunar year.
我不確定，我知道一定是在農曆年的 3 月 23 日以前。

Roger　Why? What does it refer to?
為什麼？典故是什麼呢？

Jenny　The date refers to the birth of Mazu, the patron saint of fishermen.
這個日子代表的是漁夫的守護神媽祖的生日。

Roger Do you want to participate in the pilgrimage?

你想要參加繞境進香嗎？

Jenny Definitely not! There will be thousands of pilgrims packed on the street. I bet you wouldn't want to be there during that time.

當然不要！到時候街上會有成千上萬的進香者擠在街頭，我打賭你一定也不會想要在那裡的。

Roger I agree with you. This means that we will go there after the pilgrimage.

你說的有道理。意思就是我們要在繞境進香之後去囉？

Jenny Yes. Let's do it after the pilgrimage. We can drive along the coastal expressway to get there and enjoy the town without the crowd.

是的，我們在那之後去吧，我們可以開車沿著沿海快速道路到那裡，享受那個沒有擁擠人群的城鎮。

 Words

lunar [`lunɚ] *adj.* 陰曆的	coastal [`kost!] *adj.* 海岸的；近（或沿）海岸的
refer [rɪ`fɝ] *v.* 涉及；有關	expressway [ɪk`sprɛsˏwe] *n.* 高速公路，快速
patron saint *ph.* 保護聖徒；守護神	道路
fisherman [`fɪʃɚmən] *n.* 漁人；漁夫	crowd [kraʊd] *n.* 人群
packed [pækt] *adj.* 塞得滿滿的；擁擠的	

輕鬆學導遊英語短句　念過一次請你打「√」

Mazu is widely worshiped in Taiwan and in the southeastern coastal areas of China.

媽祖在台灣還有中國東南沿岸廣為信奉。

Mazu is the Goddess of the sea.

媽祖是海上女神。

The Zhenlan Temple is one of the three biggest Mazu temples in Taiwan. The other two are the Chaotian Temple in Beigang and the Guandu Temple in Beitu.

鎮瀾宮是台灣前三大的媽祖廟，另外兩個是北港的朝天宮跟北投的關渡宮。

The temple with the statue of Mazu has been there for more than 500 years or more.

這個有媽祖雕像的寺廟已經在那裡超過五百年了。

Please be respectful when entering the temple.

當進入廟裡的時候，請保持莊重。

You don't need to take off your shoes in the temple.

進入寺廟的時候不需要脫鞋。

Every year, the pilgrimage is seen as one of the biggest festivals in Taiwan.

每年的繞境被視為台灣最大的節慶之一。

The temple has been renovated many times.

這個寺廟已經被整修很多次了。

Don't forget to check your personal belongings when leaving the temple.

離開寺廟的時候，請不要忘記檢查一下你的個人隨身物品。

Please stay humble at any religious site.

在任何的宗教場所，請保持謙遜。

Who is Mazu?
媽祖是誰呢？

According to legend, Mazu was a girl named Muoniang Lin. She was born during the Song Dynasty. One day, the severe typhoon took the lives of her family members, and she was very sad. From this time on, she always brought a lamp to the port and led the boats back to the port. After she died, the fishermen in the village claimed that they often saw a woman holding a red light lamp in bad weather. It is believed that it is Mazu, making her presence felt and helping people come back home safely. People started to build temples to commemorate her and worship her.

根據傳說，媽祖是一個叫做林默娘的女孩。她出生在宋代。有一天，嚴重的颱風奪走了她的家人的性命，她非常的難過。從那個時候開始，她總是帶著一盞燈到港口，引領漁船回到港口。在她死了以後，村子裡面的漁夫們說，他們常常看到一個女人在天氣不好的時候，提著一個紅色的燈。大家相信那是她顯靈了，幫助人們安全地回到家裡，大家便開始建立寺廟來紀念與敬拜她。

Please tell us about the celebration of the pilgrimage to the Dajia Zhenlan Temple.
請跟我們說說大甲鎮瀾宮的繞境進香慶典。

Every year, the administration of the Dajia Zhenlan Temple tosses red divination blocks in order to request Mazu's instructions on the time that the pilgrimage must be held. The pilgrimage will last for nine days and walk through about 300 kilometers. The special worship ceremonies would be held in specific places at specific times.

每年大甲鎮瀾宮的管理當局會擲紅色的筊來尋求媽祖的指示，問繞境進香的時間。繞境進香會持續九天，走過三百多公里，特別的敬拜儀式會在特定的時間在特定的地方舉行。

Unit 13 阿里山

景點介紹

阿里山國家風景區位於台灣嘉義縣東部，阿里山實際上並不是一座山的名稱，只是特定範圍的統稱，正確說法應是「阿里山區」，地理上屬於阿里山山脈主山脈的一部份，東鄰玉山山脈，北接雪山山脈。阿里山區的林相豐富，從亞熱帶的闊葉林到寒帶的針葉林都有，多樣的林相也造就了多種動物棲息的生態，阿里山著名的五奇之景是小火車、雲海、日出、晚霞、森林，另外原住民鄒族的文化、高山茶、農作物、處處可見的美麗山谷、瀑布、與其他天然景觀，都是阿里山美麗的代表。

帶外國朋友認識台灣

Jamie and Frank are in the front of the Chiayi Railway Station.
Jamie 與 Frank 正在嘉義火車站的前面。

Frank
We can take the Alishan Forest Railway from Beimen Station. Let me see. It departs at 9 a.m. in the morning or 1:30 p.m. in the afternoon. We passed the departure time and will have to take the train tomorrow morning.
我們可以從北門車站坐阿里山森林鐵路。讓我來看看，火車早上九點還有下午一點半開，我們已經錯過時間，必須要坐明天早上的火車了。

Jamie
This means we have only one day in Alishan.
意思是我們只有一天在阿里山了。

Frank
Or we can rent a car and drive there.
不然我們可以租台車開過去。

Jamie What do you think? I have heard that the sceneries that Alishan Forest Railway passes on the way are very beautiful.

你覺得怎麼樣？我聽說阿里山森林鐵路沿途經過的風景非常的漂亮。

Frank However, if we take the train, there are places that we cannot go. It's easier if we drive.

不過，如果我們坐火車的話，有些地方我們就到不了了。我們開車比較方便。

Jamie Where do you want to go?

你想去哪裡呢？

Frank I want to go to oolong tea plantations, Zhaoping Park, Celebration Mountain, and Danayi Valley. I have heard that Danayi Valley is exquisite, but it is hard to get there by public transportation.

我想去阿里山烏龍茶茶園、沼平公園、祝山、還有達娜伊谷。我聽說達娜伊谷超漂亮的，但是大眾交通工具很難到那裡。

Jamie OK. Let's go to the tourist information center and ask them where we can rent a car.

好吧。我們去旅遊服務中心，問看看他們哪裡可以租到車吧。

 Words

forest [`fɔrɪst] n. 森林

railway [`rel͵we] n. 鐵路；鐵道

rent [rɛnt] v. 租用；租入

scenery [`sinərɪ] n. 風景；景色

plantation [plæn`teʃən] n. 農園；大農場

valley [`vælɪ] n. 山谷；溪谷

exquisite [`ɛkskwɪzɪt] adj. 精美的；精緻的

transportation [͵trænspɚ`teʃən] n. 運輸；運輸工具

We will take the train to get to the mountain.

我們會搭火車到山上。

When you get off of the train at Fenqihu Station, you can buy a lunchbox there and enjoy the traditional taste of the food in Taiwan.

當你在奮起湖站下火車的時候，你可以在那邊買個便當，享受一下台灣食物的傳統風味。

You can get on and off a train at any station.

你可以在任何一站上下車。

Alishan is one of the most well-known tourist attractions in Taiwan.

阿里山是台灣最著名的觀光景點之一。

The chance of seeing a sea of clouds is higher in the fall and winter.

在秋天與冬天看到雲海的機會比較高。

The main aboriginal tribe in Alishan is Tsou.

阿里山最主要的原住民族群是鄒族。

You can see the ways that oolong tea was grown and processed in oolong tea plantations in Alishan.

你可以在阿里山的烏龍茶茶園看到烏龍茶種植還有處理的方法。

Oolong tea that was grown in Alishan tastes sweet and smooth. It is a popular souvenir.

在阿里山種植的烏龍茶喝起來甜甜的，很順口，是一個非常熱門的紀念品。

Alishan is famous for its production of high mountain tea and wasabi.

阿里山以種植高山茶與芥末聞名。

Giant trees are the symbols of Alishan.

神木是阿里山的象徵。

Please introduce the Alishan Forest Railway.
請介紹阿里山森林鐵路。

The Alishan Forest Railway was built in the early 1900s. The original purpose was to build a railway to transport timber, and this narrow-gauge mountain railway has become a marvel of engineering. The system is mostly operated by diesel locomotives, and there are occasional public runs that use the old steam-powered Shay locomotives. There are four lines running in the railway, and it has become a famous tourist railway.

阿里山森林鐵路是在二十世紀初建立的，一開始的目的是為了建立一條運送木材的鐵路，而這個窄軌山中鐵路也成為了工程上的一大巨作。整個系統主要是以柴油火車頭來運作，有的時候會用舊式的 Shay 式蒸汽火車頭來行駛，讓民眾搭乘。阿里山火車現在行駛的線路有四條，已經轉變成為一個知名的觀光鐵路了。

Please tell us the story of the giant trees.
請告訴我們神木的故事。

The giant trees in Alishan are red cypress. The oldest giant tree discovered in Alishan is aged at more than 3,000 years, and it was seen as a sacred tree by the Tsou. Unfortunately, the tree was destroyed by rain and thunderbolts in 1997. There are still a few trees in Alishan that are aged at more than 2,000 years. If you travel to Alishan, you must take a walk on the giant tree trails. You will be amazed by the beauty and sacredness of the nature.

阿里山的神木是紅檜。在阿里山被發現的最老的一棵神木有 3000 年以上的樹齡，被鄒族的人視為聖樹。不幸的是，它在 1997 年被雨水與雷擊給毀壞了。在阿里山現在還有一些樹的樹齡高達了 2000 年以上，如果你到阿里山旅行，一定要到神木群棧道走一走。你會為大自然的美麗與神聖感到驚奇。

14 Unit

集集

 景點介紹

　　集集位於南投縣的西部，依山傍水，以鐵道觀光小鎮聞名，是台鐵支線集集線的其中一站。集集線原為運輸發電機組而建立的，後來也成為當地農產品的運輸工具。集集線的多個車站在九二一大地震的時候遭受嚴重的毀損，修復之後成為觀光的熱門景點，沿線搭乘火車或者騎腳踏車遊覽，別有一番風味。附近景點有集集大山、集集攔河堰、綠色隧道、明新書院、水里蛇窯等，緊臨的還有溪頭、杉林溪，玉山國家公園、信義梅園、東埔溫泉等。

 帶外國朋友認識台灣

Judy and Michael are debating about where to go in Nantou.
Judy 與 Michael 正在猶豫要去南投的什麼地方。

Michael
Where are we going today?
我們今天要去哪裡呢？

Judy
I heard from my friend that Jiji is a lovely small town. Do you want to go there?
我從我朋友那邊聽說，集集是一個美麗的小鎮。你想要去那裡嗎？

Michael
I don't know what is in there. What can we do in the town?
我不知道那裡有什麼。我們在那裡可以做什麼呢？

Judy
We can take a train from Ershui to Jiji. The Jiji station was built during the Japanese Colonial Era. It was destroyed in the 921 Earthquake and was rebuilt later. We can go there to take a look.
我們可以搭火車從二水到集集。集集火車站是在日據時代建立的，它在 921 地震的時候被毀掉，後來又被重建。我們可以去看看。

Michael

What else can we do there?

我們在那邊還可以做什麼呢？

Judy

Many people go there for cycling. We can rent a tandem and ride around the town. A beautiful road called Green Tunnel is in the town. The length of the tunnel is roughly 4.5 kilometers. There are about 500 camphor trees on both sides of the road, and this is why it is called Green Tunnel. There are a few coffee carts along the way. We can ride our bikes for a bit and find a coffee cart to get a cup of coffee.

很多人去那裡騎腳踏車。我們可以租一台協力車，然後騎車遊這個城鎮。在這個城鎮有一條美麗的路叫做綠色隧道，全長 4.5 公里，路的兩側約有五百棵樟樹，而這就是為什麼它被稱為綠色隧道。沿途有一些行動咖啡車，我們可以騎一下車，然後找一個咖啡車喝杯咖啡。

Michael

Sounds good. Let's do it.

聽起來不錯，就這樣吧。

📝 **Words**

debate [dɪ`bet] v. 辯論；討論	tandem [`tændəm] n. 協力車
earthquake [`ɝθ͵kwek] n. 地震	ride [raɪd] v. 騎車；乘車
rebuilt [ri`bɪld] v. 重建	tunnel [`tʌn!] n. 隧道；地道
cycling [`saɪk!ɪŋ] n. 騎腳踏車兜風	roughly [`rʌflɪ] adv. 大約；大體上

輕鬆學導遊英語短句 念過一次請你打「√」

Cycling has become a very popular activity in Taiwan.

騎腳踏車在台灣成為了一個非常熱門的活動。

Do you want to rent a normal bicycle or tandem?

你要租一般的腳踏車還是協力車呢？

Jiji was named one of the Top 10 Small Tourist Towns by the Tourism Bureau of Taiwan.

集集被台灣觀光局列為了十大旅遊小鎮。

Jiji was the epicenter of the 921 Earthquake.

集集是九二一地震的震央。

We will take a short break at Jiji. You have one hour to take a walk in this picturesque small town.

我們會在集集停留一下。你有一個小時的時間可以在這個風景如畫的小鎮走一走。

It is very comfortable to cycle under the shade of the trees with a gentle breeze.

在樹蔭下伴著微風騎腳踏車是很舒服的。

The banana is an important local product in Jiji.

香蕉是集集當地重要的產物。

In addition to the banana, other agricultural products, including lychees, grapes, pitahayas, guavas, and sunflowers are grown in the area.

除了香蕉之外， 這個區域還有種植其他的農產品，包括荔枝、葡萄、火龍果、芭樂、與太陽花。

Jiji used to be the agricultural products' distribution center of the region in the past.

集集在過去曾經是這個地區的農產品集散地。

If you have any questions, please call me by using your cell phone.

如果你有任何的問題，請用你的手機打給我。

Please give me some information about the Jiji Railway Line.
請給我一些集集鐵路線的介紹。

Jiji Line is a narrow-gauge railway that spans the countryside between Changhua and Nantou counties. It was originally built in order to facilitate the construction of Mingtan Dam's hydroelectric power plants The railway was later used to transport timber and agricultural products. Nowadays, it has become a popular tourist railway.

集集線是一條窄軌的鐵路，跨越了彰化縣與南投縣的鄉間。它一開始建立是為了方便明潭水庫水力發電廠的建造，後來被用來運輸木材與農產品。現在，它已經成為了一條熱門的觀光鐵路。

What can I do in Jiji?
我在集集可以做什麼呢？

You will get to see the rustic charms of Jiji. You can cycle and hike there. Besides, there are a lot of attractions around Jiji. You can go to the Green Tunnel, Ming Hsin Academy, Jiji Military History Park, Endemic Species Research Institute, Wuchang Temple, Jiji Dam, and so on.

你會在集集看到鄉間的魅力。你可以在那邊騎腳踏車與登山。此外，在集集周圍有很多景點，你可以到綠色隧道、明新書院、集集軍史公園、特有生物研究保育中心、武昌廟、集集攔河堰等等的。

What are the other attractions in the Jiji Line?
在集集線還有哪些景點呢？

In Checheng, the last stop of the Jiji Line, the train station was rebuilt from a wooden structure, after it was damaged in the 921 Earthquake. The view of the rural architecture style, with a backdrop of green mountains, is very captivating.

車埕，在集集線的最後一站，這個火車站在921地震毀壞之後，以木頭結構來重建。這個鄉村風格的建築，搭配上綠色的山作為背景的景色，看起來非常地美麗。

15 Unit

日月潭

景點介紹

日月潭位於南投縣的魚池鄉，這個美麗的高山湖泊是台灣最大的天然湖泊。日月潭此名源於潭面南邊的形狀像是月鉤，北邊的形狀像是日輪，所以拉魯島為界，分成了日潭與月潭，合稱為日月潭。位在中高度海拔，群山圍繞，造就日月潭宛如圖畫山水，氤氳水氣及層次分明的景色變化。環潭公路長約 33 公里，沿途部分設有自行車道，沿途景色優美，早晨到黃昏，都有不同的風光。除了美麗的自然風光以外，日月潭具有豐富的原住民文化，是台灣原住民邵族的居住地。

帶外國朋友認識台灣

Jamie and Roger are talking about Lalu Island.
Jamie 與 Roger 正說到拉魯島。

Roger Look at the island on the lake. It was called Guanghua Island in the past.
看看湖上面的哪個島。這個島以前叫做光華島。

Jamie Yes. It is called Lalu Island now.
對，它現在叫做拉魯島。

Roger Why is it called Lalu? Is it a term in an aboriginal language?
為什麼叫做拉魯？這是原住民語言裡面的一個詞嗎？

Jamie Correct. Most of the Thao reside around Sun Moon Lake. It is said that the Thao were originally from the South, and their ancestors found a white deer and chased it to Lalu Island. The white deer became a tree on the island. The island was a lot bigger at that time, and they decided to live there and worship the tree. This is the story of Lalu Island, and this is a sacred island of great importance to the Thao.

是啊。大部份的邵族人住在日月潭周圍。據說邵族人原本來自於南方，他們的祖先發現了一隻白鹿，並追逐它到了拉魯島，在島上白鹿變成了一棵樹。這個島在那個時候比現在大的多，他們決定住在島上，並且敬拜那棵樹。這就是拉魯島的故事，而且這是對邵族非常重要的一個聖島。

Roger
Why are there floating fields around the island?

為什麼在島的周圍有一些浮塊呢？

Jamie
Some aboriginal herbs are planted in the floating fields. They are ecologically and culturally important to the Thao and Sun Moon Lake.

在浮島上種的是一些原住民植物。這些植物對於邵族以及日月潭在生態上與文化上是重要的。

Roger
Will we get to walk on the island?

我們可以上島上去走走嗎？

Jamie
I don't think so. We can take a boat there and take a look. I think the boat will stop there for a while, and we can get a closer look of the island.

我想不行。我們可以坐船去那邊看看，我想船會在那邊停一陣子，然後我們可以更靠近地看一看。

Words

term [tɝm] n. 詞；名稱

aboriginal [ˌæbəˋrɪdʒən!] adj. 原始的

originally [əˋrɪdʒən!ɪ] adv. 起初；原來

ancestor [ˋænsɛstɚ] n. 祖先

worship [ˋwɝʃɪp] v. 信奉；敬拜

sacred [ˋsekrɪd] adj. 神的；神聖的

floating [ˋflotɪŋ] adj. 漂浮的

ecologically [ikəˋladʒɪk!ɪ] adv. 生態意義上

Sun Moon Lake is the largest lake in Taiwan.
日月潭是台灣最大的湖。

Sun Moon Lake is located in Nantou, a county with abundant natural resources and beautiful sceneries.
日月潭位於南投，南投是一個有著豐富自然資源與美麗景色的縣。

Tourists come to Sun Moon Lake for the nearby high mountains and lake, indigenous culture, and nature and ecology.
旅客們來到日月潭來看高山與湖泊、原住民文化、還有自然生態。

The Sun Moon Lake International Swimming Carnival is the world's largest mass participation in open-water swim.
日月潭萬人泳渡活動是全世界最大的公開水域的集體游泳活動。

The Sun Moon Lake Swimming Carnival is a 3,000-meter cross-lake race that usually takes place around the time of the Mid-Autumn Festival.
日月潭萬人泳渡活動是一個三公里的橫渡比賽，通常都是在中秋節附近的時間舉辦。

If you want to see a Daoist shrine, you can go to Wenwu Temple. In the temple, Confucius, Guangong, and Yuefei are worshipped.
如果你想要看道教的聖殿，你可以到文武廟。在這個廟裡面敬拜的是孔子、關公、還有岳飛。

The Xuanzang Temple was built with the Tang Dynasty's architectural style, and it is meant to commemorate Xuanzang, the monk who made a pilgrimage to India, brought back sutras, and translated them into Chinese.
玄奘寺是依照唐代的建築風格建成，為了紀念玄奘。玄奘是一個去印度朝聖的和尚，帶回了佛經，並翻譯成了中文。

Some relics of Xuanzang are stored in the Xuanzang Temple.
玄奘的遺骸被放在玄奘寺裡面。

You must take a ride on a bicycle on the bike path along the lake. The best time to do this would be after sunrise or before sunset.
你一定要沿著湖的自行車道騎腳踏車，最好的時間就是日出之後或者日落之前。

Please give a brief history of Sun Moon Lake.
請簡述日月潭的歷史。

The entire area around Sun Moon Lake, including today's Yuchi, Toushe, and Puli, was once known as Shuishalian. The originally residents were the Thao, and they made a living by hunting. Immigrants from Mainland China joined the land during the Qing Dynasty, and they began to cultivate the land. In 1919, the Taiwan Power Company started to build a dam on Sun Moon Lake for hydro-electric generation. When the Nationalist Government came to Taiwan, Sun Moon Lake became the favorite vacation spot for the late President Chiang Kai-shek, and he invited a lot of international guests to Sun Moon Lake. It gradually became a popular destination for domestic and international tourists.

整個日月潭周圍的區域，包括現在的魚池、頭社、還有埔里，都曾經叫做水沙連。這裡最一開始的居民是邵族人，他們以打獵維生。從中國大陸來的移民在清朝的時候來到這個土地，並且開始開墾這裡。在 1919 年，台灣電力公司開始在日月潭興建一個水力發電的水庫。當國民政府來台的時候，日月潭成為了已故總統蔣介石先生最喜歡的度假勝地，他也邀請了很多的國際貴賓來到日月潭。這裡逐漸成為了一個國內與國際旅客喜愛的地方。

What are the other attractions near Sun Moon Lake?
日月潭附近還有什麼其他的景點呢？

Black tea grown around Sun Moon Lake is very famous, and you can choose to visit a tea plantation and drink some tea that has the best quality. Besides, the Puli Winery is a place that is worth visiting. The winery is known for making good Shaohsing Wine, a kind of wine made from rice.

在日月潭附近種植的紅茶非常的有名，你可以選一家茶園來參觀，並且喝點品質最好的茶。此外，埔里酒廠是一個值得參觀的地方，它以製作優良用米做成的紹興酒聞名。

16 Unit 台南

 景點介紹

　　台南市位於台灣西南沿海地帶，舊稱府城。台南有二百年的時間曾為臺灣首都，是臺灣政治、經濟、文化的中心。台南歷經了荷蘭殖民時期、明鄭時期、清領時期、日據時期到現在，造就了台南豐富的文化遺產與古蹟，如延平郡王祠、安平古堡、赤崁樓、億載金城、台南孔廟等。台南在自然風光也是不容錯過的，如台江國家公園、西拉雅國家風景區等。除此之外，台南的小吃保留了台灣小吃傳統的味道，也是到台南旅遊一定要好好品嚐的。

 帶外國朋友認識台灣

Jenny and Roger are strolling on the campus of Cheng Kung University.
Jenny 與 Roger 正在成功大學散步。

Jenny　It's always relaxing to stroll in the banyan garden.
在榕園散散步真輕鬆。

Roger　Yes, I feel the same way. So what do you plan to do today?
對啊，我也覺得。所以你今天打算做什麼呢？

Jenny　I don't know. How about you?
我不知道。你呢？

Roger　Oh, okay. I surfed the Internet before we came to Tainan. We can revisit Qigu, Anping, and we can go to Sicao, which has been a very popular spot in recent years.
喔，好吧！在我們來台南以前，上網瀏覽了一下。我們可以再去看看七股還有安平，然後我們可以去四草，它最近這幾年很熱門啊。

Jenny

Sounds good. What can we do in Qigu?

聽起來不錯啊！我們在七股可以做什麼呢？

Roger

We can go to the Qigu Salt Fields. They were once the largest solar salt fields in Taiwan. Although they are no longer used to produce salt, they have been turned into a recreation area. There is a museum where you can learn the history of the salt industry in Taiwan, see the antique machinery, and even stand on the peak of the salt mountain. It should be a very interesting experience. In addition, we can go to see Qigu Lagoon and the oyster farms.

我們可以去七股鹽田，它曾經是台灣最大的日曬鹽場。雖然那裡現在不再產鹽，現在轉變成了一個休閒區域。那裡有一個博物館，你可以學到台灣在鹽業的歷史，看看古老的機器，還可以站在鹽山的頂端，是一個非常有意思的體驗。除此之外，我們可以去看看七股瀉湖還有蚵田。

Jenny

What about Sicao?

那四草呢？

Roger

Sicao Wetlands is a protected ecological area, and there is a mangrove forest within it. We can take a boat in the famous Sicao Green Tunnel, which takes about 30 minutes. After that, we can go to the Black-faced Spoonbill Bird Ecology Exhibition Hall and see if we will be lucky enough to see them!

四草溼地是一個生態保育區，裡面有一座紅樹林。我們可以到四草有名的綠色隧道坐船，大約 30 分鐘的時間。接著，我們可以到黑面琵鷺生態展示館去，看看我們夠不夠幸運可以看到它們！

Words

revisit [ri`vɪzɪt] v. 再訪；重遊

field [fild] n. （廣闊的一大片）地

solar [`solə] adj. 太陽的；利用太陽光的

recreation [ˌrɛkrɪ`eʃən] n. 休閒

antique [æn`tik] adj. 古董的

lagoon [lə`gun] n. 瀉湖

wetland [`wɛtˌlənd] n. 濕地；沼地

mangrove [`mæŋgrov] n. 紅樹林

The National Museum of Taiwanese Literature is the only museum that dedicated to Taiwanese literature. The museum building was built by the Japanese, and it served as city hall before it was turned into a museum.

台灣文學館是唯一一個致力於台灣文學的博物館。博物館的建築是在日本人建立的，這裡在變成博物館之前，是市政府的所在。

The Eternal Golden Castle was a fortress built in 1874 in Anping, Tainan, in order to defend the invasion of the Japanese.

億載金城是在 1874 年在台南安平所建立的一個碉堡，為了抵擋日本人的入侵。

The Koxinga Shrine was built in memory of Zheng Chenggong, the hero that saved Taiwan from the hands of the Dutch.

延平郡王祠是為了紀念鄭成功所建立的，他是把台灣從荷蘭人手中搶回來的英雄。

Tainan's Confucius Temple is the first temple dedicated to Confucius.

台南的孔廟是第一個供奉孔子的廟宇。

Chikan Tower was built on an old Dutch fort during the Qing Dynasty. It was the administrative center in Taiwan during the time.

赤崁樓是在清朝的時候，建立在以前荷蘭人的碉堡上的。這在當時是台灣的行政中心。

If you like traditional Taiwanese food, you should not miss Yongle Market. You will love the simple, yet satisfying, taste of the local food.

如果你喜歡傳統的台灣食物，你應該不要錯過永樂市場，你會喜歡當地食物簡單、但是令人感到滿足的滋味的。

Great Queen of Heaven Temple in Tainan is one of the oldest Mazu temples in Taiwan, and the face of Mazu is stained by smoke, and as a result, it is now black.

大天后宮是台灣最老的媽祖廟之一，廟裡面的媽祖的臉被煙熏的，現在已經變成黑色了。

Shennong Street was one of the best preserved streets in Tainan. The street is vintage, but this used to be a busy business area in the past.

神農街是台南保存最好的街道之一。這條街道看起來古色古香的，但是它以前可曾經是一個忙碌的商業區。

Please briefly describe the National Cheng Kung University.
請簡述國立成功大學。

National Cheng Kung University is one of the most prestigious universities in Taiwan, and it has cultivated many successful alumni. Some historical monuments were reserved in the university, such as the original dormitory of the 2nd infantry division of the Japanese Army. There is also a banyan garden with a century-old banyan tree.

國立成功大學是全台灣最好的大學之一，它培育了許多成功的校友。大學裡面保存了一些歷史遺跡，像是原日軍步兵第二聯隊營舍。還有一個榕園，裡面有一個百年歷史的榕樹。

What are the attractions in Anping?
安平的景點有哪些？

It is amazing, and you simply cannot miss it was formerly called Fort Zeelandia and was built by the Dutch in 1624 and used it as their administrative center in Taiwan. Zheng Chenggong took it over after the Dutch surrendered. Additionally, Old Tait & Co. Merchant House is a colonial-style building with arcades that were built after the Second Opium War.

這裡很棒，你千萬別錯過了。安平古堡過去叫做熱蘭遮城，是荷蘭人在 1624 年所建立的，作為它們在台灣的行政中心。鄭成功在荷蘭人投降之後接管了這個地方。此外，英商德記洋行是一個有著拱廊的殖民風格的建築，在第二次鴉片戰爭之後建立的。

What can I do in Guanzi Hill?
我在關子嶺可以做什麼呢？

The hot springs in Guanzi Hill have a special kind of muddy springs emerging from the rocks. It is perfect for relieving the weariness and is a great source for skincare. In Guanzi Hill, you can try some rice in bamboo tubes and other mountain products after you are finished with your hot springs soak. You will love this satisfying experience.

關子嶺的溫泉是一種特別的從岩石中湧出的泥狀溫泉。它對於消除疲勞非常有效，而且是很好的護膚用品。在關子嶺，你可以在泡完溫泉之後，嚐點竹筒飯還有其他的山產。你會愛上這種令人滿足的體驗的。

高雄

 景點介紹

　　高雄是台灣的第二大城市，舊名為打狗，傳說是因為早期在高雄沿海這一帶的平埔族叫做 Takau，後來漢人移民把它譯成了打狗。而在日據時代，由於日語的高雄(Takao)與打狗(Takau)的讀音相似，於是把這個地方的名稱改為了高雄。高雄全境屬於熱帶，由於受到海洋氣候的調節，全年陽光普照，四季都適合觀光。除了有許多的歷史古蹟與自然美景以外，海港文化與多族群的融合，也都深深的影響了高雄，使高雄成為了一個觀光旅遊的好去處。

💬 帶外國朋友認識台灣

Roger and Jenny are discussing where to go in Kaohsiung.
Roger 與 Jenny 正在討論在高雄要去哪裡。

Jenny
Have you been to Meinong?
你去過美濃嗎？

Roger
No. I have not been there.
沒有，我沒有去過那裡。

Jenny
I want to go there to buy a paper umbrella to Lidia as a wedding gift.
我想要去那裡買一把紙傘送給 Lidia 當作結婚禮物。

Roger
Why do you want to buy an umbrella as a wedding gift?
為什麼你想要買紙傘當做結婚禮物呢？

Jenny
It was a local Hakka tradition. In the past, people would give two paper umbrellas to a bride as a wedding gift. The umbrellas were seen as auspicious. It is not common now, but I really like the beautiful hand-

made paper umbrellas. The craftsmen made an umbrella with a bamboo frame and paper. The paper is painted using calligraphy brushes and waterproofed with oil. It is decorative and practical.

這是當地客家的傳統。在過去，人們會給新娘兩把紙傘作為結婚的禮物。這些傘被認為是吉祥的代表。雖然現在這個習俗已經不常見，但是我真的很喜歡這些美麗的手工紙傘。工藝師用竹架與紙來做成雨傘。傘紙用毛筆來作畫，並且上油來覆蓋防水，既有裝飾效果，又很實用。

Roger

Okay. If we go to Meinong, I want to go to Meinong Hakka Culture Museum. The Hakka culture is introduced in the museum. In addition, Meinong was once an important region for tobacco production. After joining the WTO, the tobacco production business could not compete internationally, and it went down. The history is presented in the museum, and you can see the rise and fall of the town.

好的。如果我們去美濃，我想要去看看美濃客家文物館，在文物館裡面有介紹客家的文化。此外，美濃曾經是一個菸草的重要產地，在加入 WTO 之後，沒有辦法在全球競爭，於是這門生意就沒落了。這段歷史被呈現在文物館裡面，你也會看到這個城鎮的起落。

Jenny

Who exactly are the Hakkas?

客家人到底是誰呢？

Roger

They are a linguistic and cultural minority among the Han Chinese. They represent 15 percent of the population in Taiwan. Let's go to Meinong to learn more about paper umbrella and the Hakka culture!

他們是漢人裡面的一個語言與文化的少數族群。他們在台灣人口中代表了百分之 15 的人口。我們去美濃了解更多紙傘與客家文化吧！

Words

auspicious [ɔ`spɪʃəs] adj. 吉兆的；吉利的	practical [`præktɪk!] adj. 實用的
calligraphy [kə`lɪgrəfɪ] n. 書法	tobacco [tə`bæko] n. 菸草；菸草製品
waterproof [`wɔtɚ‚pruf] v. 使不透水；使防水	decline [dɪ`klaɪn] v. 衰退；衰落
decorative [`dɛkərətɪv] adj. 裝飾性的；裝潢用的	linguistic [lɪŋ`gwɪstɪk] adj. 語言的

The Port of Kaohsiung is the largest harbor in Taiwan as well as one of the largest container ports in the world.

高雄港是台灣最大的港口，也是全世界最大的貨櫃碼頭之一。

I suggest that you take a stroll along the Lover River and feel the breeze. It is especially comforting at night, and you can even choose a cafe on the riverbank to listen to live music or just enjoy the beautiful skyline of the city at night.

我建議你沿著愛河散散步，感受一下微風。在晚上更是特別地舒服，你甚至可以在河邊找一個咖啡店，聽聽現場演奏，或者就享受一下這個城市夜晚美麗的天際線。

The Pier-2 Art Center showcases contemporary art. The numerous abandoned warehouses on the Pier-2 Port of Kaohsiung formerly stored fishmeal and granulated sugar, and they have been transformed into a venue for exhibitions, festivals, and performances.

駁二藝術特區展示了當代藝術。在高雄港二號碼頭，很多個過去存放魚粉跟砂糖的廢棄倉庫變成了展覽、藝術節、還有表演的場地。

You can see large-scale installation and creative graffiti artwork at the Pier-2 Art Center.

在駁二藝術特區，你可以看到大型的裝置藝術作品還有創意塗鴉作品。

If you like seafood, you can go to the Kezailiao Fish Market. You can buy fresh fish and have the restaurants cook them for you. It is a fun and authentic experience.

如果你喜歡海鮮，你可以到蚵仔寮魚市去。你可以買新鮮的魚，然後請餐廳幫你把它們煮熟。這是一個有趣、在地的體驗。

Crystal Clear Lake is the largest lake in the Kaohsiung area, and it is a very important source of drinking water.

澄清湖是高雄地區最大的湖泊，也是高雄飲用水的重要來源。

In Xizi Bay, if you feel hot or tired, you can find a café and have a huge, shell-shaped bowl of shaved ice. It will cool you down and take your weariness away.

在西子灣，如果你覺得很熱或者很累，你可以找一家店，點一碗裝用大貝殼形狀的碗裝的刨冰來吃。這一定會讓你冷卻下來，並且趕走你的疲勞。

 口說題問答時間

Please describe Cijin.
請描述一下旗津。

Cijin is an island 11 kilometers long and only 200 meters wide. It is accessible by ferry, and it takes 4 minutes to get to the island from the mainland. It was the first Chinese settlement in the Kaohsiung area. There are temples, a lighthouse, pier, and parks. You can go to those attractions, or simply enjoy great seafood, watch the boats near the shore, and feel the sea breeze. Don't miss the three-wheeled carts that await you by the ferry. They are rarely seen elsewhere, and they will take you anywhere you want on the island.

旗津是一個長 11 公里，寬僅兩百公尺的島嶼。可以坐渡輪到達，從本島過去只需要 4 分鐘的時間。這裡是高雄地區第一個華人聚居的地方。這裡有廟宇、燈塔、碼頭、還有公園。你可以到這些景點看看，也可以就享受一下這裡超棒的海鮮、看看岸邊附近的船、然後吹吹風。不要錯過了在渡輪旁等著你的三輪車，它們在其他地方很少見的，而且它們會帶你到這個島上任何你想去的地方。

Please describe the attractions in Xizi Bay.
請描述西子灣的景點。

Xizi Bay is a black-sand beach, and it is also the location of National Sun Yat-sen University. The Former British Consulate at Takao is on the hill in the harbor entrance, and it is the oldest complete example of the colonial architecture in Taiwan. You can see the beautiful sunset on the beach of Xizi Bay or at the Former British Consulate at Takao.

西子灣是一個黑色沙粒的沙灘，這裡也是國立中山大學的所在。打狗英國領事館就在港口入口的山坡上，這是台灣保存殖民時代最老的完整建築。你可以在西子灣的沙灘上或者打狗英國領事館，看到美麗的日落。

79

18 Unit 墾丁

 景點介紹

　　墾丁是台灣的第一座國家公園，位於恆春半島，三面環海，東鄰太平洋、西鄰台灣海峽、南瀕巴士海峽，是一座涵蓋陸域與海域的國家公園，同時，也是台灣唯一一座熱帶氣候的國家公園，終年氣候宜人，由於地形與氣候的因素，造就了墾丁的地形景觀變化多、動植物種類豐富的得天獨厚環境，是觀察大自然的一個絕佳地點。墾丁的熱門景點眾多，是台灣南部最熱門的旅遊景點之一。

 帶外國朋友認識台灣

Frank and Jamie are driving from Kaohsiung to Kenting.
Frank 與 Jamie 正從高雄開車到墾丁。

 I am so excited about our trip to Kenting.
我們要去墾丁玩了，我好興奮。

 Me, too. We will be arriving at Hengchun very soon. Do you want to rest?
我也是。我們快到恆春了，你想要休息一下嗎？

 I am not tired. What is special in Hengchun?
我不累。恆春有什麼特別的嗎？

 We can take a look at Hengchun Old Town. It was built in 1875, and it is the only castle town in Taiwan where all four original gates are intact. Around the east gate, you will see a notable geological phenomenon. The fire literally comes from the earth.

我們可以去看看恆春古城。它建立於 1875 年，是台灣唯一一座完整保留四個門的城池。在東門的附近，你會看到一個特別的地理現象。地上真的生出火來。

Jamie

How can this happen?

這怎麼可能？

Frank

There is gas within the earth to feed the flame, and the fire burns eternally. We are now in Hengchun old town. Let's go to see the four gates and the geological phenomenon. Afterwards, we can grab some lunch and head to Kenting.

地底下有天然氣供應給火，所以火一直都在燒著。我們現在到了恆春古城了，我們去看看那四個門還有那個地理現象吧。然後，我們可以帶點午餐，然後往墾丁去。

Jamie

Awesome. We will start to see the beautiful coastline while driving on Provincial Highway 26, after passing the old town, right?

太棒了。在過了古城之後，我們開在 26 號省道就可以開始看到美麗的海岸線了，對吧？

Frank

You are right. Let's go!

沒錯，我們走吧！

 Words

castle [`kæs!] *n.* 城堡

intact [ɪn`tækt] *adj.* 完整無缺的；原封不動的

notable [`notəb!] *adj.* 值得注意的；顯著的

geological [dʒɪə`lɑdʒɪkl] *adj.* 地質的

phenomenon [fə`namə‚nan] *n.* 現象

earth [ɝθ] *n.* 陸地；地上；土；泥

eternally [ɪ`tɝnəlɪ] *adv.* 永恆地；常常

coastline [`kost‚laɪn] *n.* 海岸線

輕鬆學導遊英語短句 念過一次請你打「√」

Kenting is located in the Hengchun Peninsula.

墾丁位於恆春半島。

Guanshan is a great place to watch the sunset.

關山是觀賞日落的絕佳地點。

It is perfect for swimming from April to October.

從四月到十月很適合游泳。

You need to hire a instructor if you want to ride a water motorcycle.

如果你想要玩水上摩托車的話，你需要請一個教練。

Longluan Lake is the best place to watch tropical and migratory water birds.

龍鑾潭是觀賞熱帶與遷徙水鳥最好的地方。

Kenting is the perfect choice for a beach vacation.

墾丁是海灘度假地的最好選擇。

The movie *Cape No. 7* was filmed in Kenting.

電影《海角七號》是在墾丁拍攝的。

The National Museum of Marine Biology and Aquarium is a place worth visiting.

國立海生館是一個值得去的地方。

Kenting National Park was established in 1984, and it was the first national park in Taiwan.

墾丁國家公園建立於 1984 年，是台灣的第一座國家公園。

The sharp peak that you can see from many places in Kenting is Mount Dajian.

你從墾丁很多地方看到的那個尖端就是大尖山。

口說題問答時間

What are the popular attractions in Kenting?
墾丁有哪些熱門景點呢？

If you are a nature lover, you should go to the Nanrenshan Ecological Reserve Area, Longkeng Ecological Protection Area, Longluan Lake, Sheding Nature Park, and National Museum of Marine Biology & Aquarium. If you like beautiful sceneries and geological landscapes, you might like Maobitou Park, Baisha Bay, Longpan Park, Kenting National Forest Recreation Area, Guanshan, and Fongchueisha.

如果你是大自然愛好者，你應該要到南仁山生態保護區、龍坑生態保護區、龍鑾潭、社頂自然公園、還有國立海洋生物博物館。如果你喜歡漂亮的景色與地理景觀，你可能會喜歡貓鼻頭公園、白沙灣、龍磐公園、墾丁國家森林遊樂區、關山、還有風吹沙。

When is the best time to travel to Kenting?
什麼時候是去墾丁最好的時候呢？

It depends. Most people like to go there in the summer to enjoy the glorious sunshine. Some people like to go there during other seasons to enjoy the less-crowded town. You can go there during any season.

不一定，大部份的人喜歡在夏天去那邊享受熱情的陽光，有的人喜歡在其他的季節去，享受比較不那麼擁擠的墾丁。你可以在任何一個季節到那裡去。

Is there any festival in Kenting?
在墾丁有什麼節慶活動嗎？

Yes. The Spring Scream music festival started in the early 1990s and is the biggest festival in Kenting. It is held annually in April, and bands and artists from all over the world have performed almost nonstop there. If you like indie music, you might not want to miss the festival.

有的，從 1990 年代初期就開始舉辦的春天吶喊音樂節，是墾丁最大的節慶活動。春吶每年四月在鵝鑾鼻燈塔那邊舉辦，從世界各地來的樂團與藝人在那邊幾乎不間斷地表演。如果你喜歡獨立音樂，你應該不會想要錯過這個活動。

景點介紹

　　位於台灣東部，花蓮縣是台灣面積最大的一個縣。花蓮的西邊是中央山脈，西邊是太平洋，平原僅占全縣面積的十分之一，人口主要聚集在花東縱谷與海岸山脈東側的沿海地帶。花蓮是全台灣原住民人口最多的地方，占花蓮縣人口的四分之一，其中，以阿美族的分佈最廣。花蓮有山有海，氣候宜人，有許多知名的景點，包括太魯閣國家公園、花東縱谷國家風景區、東部海岸國家風景區、七星潭風景區等。

帶外國朋友認識台灣

Frank and Jamie are planning their trip to Taroko Gorge.
Frank 與 Jamie 正在計劃他們去太魯閣的旅行。

Frank

Have you been to Taroko National Park?

你有去過太魯閣國家公園嗎？

Jamie

I went there when I was young. I went to Yanzikou and the Tunnel of Nine Turns. The scenery was marvelous. How about you?

我在小的時候去過。我去了燕子口，還有九曲洞。景色超級棒的，你呢？

Frank

I have been there, too. The farthest point I visited in Taroko is Tianxiang. I thought it was everything Taroko offers, but recently I found the park is much more than the attractions we usually hear about.

我也去過，太魯閣我到過最遠的地方是天祥。我以為那就是太魯閣的全部了，最近我才發現太魯閣不只有我們常聽到的那些景點。

Jamie

You sound so excited. What impresses you?

你聽起來好興奮喔！什麼讓你這麼印象深刻？

Frank First, I learned about how the place was formed. The rocks seen in Taroko now were sediment on the bottom of the ocean 200 million years ago. Tectonic compression between the Eurasian Plate and the Philippine Sea Plate created pressure and made the limestone metamorphose into marble, and uplifting forces from the plate collision pushed the rocks above the surface of the ocean to where we see it today.

首先，我發現了它是怎麼形成的。我們現在在太魯閣看到的石塊來自於兩億年前海底的沈積物。菲律賓海板塊與大陸板塊的地殼擠壓創造了壓力，讓這些石灰岩變成了大理石。板塊碰撞產生的上升作用力把石塊推到了海平面以上，也就是我們現在看到的這些石塊。

Jamie That is remarkable. I know the Taroko gorge itself was carved into the marble by the erosive power of the Liwu River, but I did not know much about its formation until you told me just now.

真是了不起。我知道太魯閣峽谷本身是由立霧溪侵蝕這些大理石而產生的，但是在你現在告訴我以前，我不知道它是怎麼形成的。

Frank Yes. This time I want to go deeper, to other places in the park. I want to go to the Baiyang Falls and Wenshan Hot Springs, where we can enjoy a natural hot spring at its source.

對啊，這次我想要去走更裡面去其他地方。我想要去白楊瀑布，還有文山溫泉，在那裡我們可以在源頭享受天然的溫泉。

Jamie I am getting into the mood to visit. Let's plan for it now.

我開始想要去看看了，我們現在開始計劃吧！

📖 Words

sediment [`sɛdəmənt] n. 沉澱物；沉積物

tectonic [tɛk`tɑnɪk] adj. 地殼構造上的；構造的

compression [kəm`prɛʃən] n. 壓縮；壓擠

plate [plet] n. （地質學中的大陸）板塊

metamorphose [mɛtə`mɔrˌfoz] v. 變形；變質

collision [kə`lɪʒən] n. 碰撞；相撞

remarkable [rɪ`mɑrkəbl] adj. 值得注意的；非凡的

rewarding [rɪ`wɔrdɪŋ] adj. 有益的；值得的

When we pass the Su-Hua Highway, you will see spectacular views of the Pacific Ocean and Qingshui Cliff.

當我們經過蘇花公路的時候，你將會看到太平洋與清水斷崖壯麗的景色。

After an approximately ten-minute drive from downtown Hualian, we will arrive at Qixingtan Beach, a beautiful shingle beach.

從花蓮市區開車十分鐘的距離，我們就會到七星潭，一個美麗的礫灘。

Hualien is on the Pacific side of the Central Mountain Range. The East Rift Valley also runs through Hualien. 90 percent of its land is mountainous, and the landscapes, which feature mountains, valleys, rivers, and the ocean, are magnificent.

花蓮在中央山脈的太平洋這端。花東縱谷也經過花蓮。這裡有百分之九十的山，結合了山、河谷、河流、還有海洋的景色非常的美麗。

Most of the beaches in Hualien are shingle or coral, and Jiqi is one of the few sandy beaches in Hualien. In winter, the beach's sands are black, and they turn golden in the summer.

在花蓮大部份的海灘都是礫石或者礁石的，磯崎是在花蓮的少數幾個沙灘之一。在冬天的時候，海灘的沙是黑色的，在夏天的時候就變成了一個金色沙灘。

Liyu Lake is a barrier lake, and it is the largest lake in eastern Taiwan. Only twenty minutes from downtown Hualien, you can sail a small boat in the lake or ride a bicycle around it.

鯉魚潭是一個堰塞湖，也是東台灣最大的一個湖泊。距離花蓮市區 20 分鐘的時間，你可以在鯉魚潭以輕舟閒遊，或者沿著潭邊騎單車。

The Amis, the largest aboriginal group in Taiwan, are scattered throughout Hualien. If you are interested in learning more about their culture, you should arrange a tour to visit one of their tribes.

阿美族是全台灣最大的原住民族群，他們的部落散佈在花蓮。如果你想要了解更多他們的文化，你應該安排去遊覽一下他們的其中一個部落。

What is river tracing?
什麼是溯溪？

River tracing is a kind of outdoor adventure activity similar to canyoning, and it is very popular in Taiwan. River tracers start at the end of a river and go to its beginning, and they will need to swim through fast currents, climb from rock to rock, and jump from the rocks to the water. River tracing requires skills such as swimming, rock climbing, and the understanding of the geographical features of rivers and valleys.

這是一種戶外的冒險活動，類似於峽谷探險，這個活動在台灣非常的盛行。溯溪的人從河的下半段往源頭去，他們要游過激流，在岩石間爬行，還有從岩石跳到水裡。這種活動需要一些技巧，像是游泳、攀岩、還有對於河流於峽谷地理特性的了解。

What are popular activities in Hualien?
花蓮有哪些熱門的活動呢？

River tracing is very popular is Hualien. In addition, rafting is a popular activity in Hualien. Xiuguluan River is the only river that cut through the Coastal Mountain Range, and it is one of the best rivers for rafting.

溯溪在花蓮非常的盛行。還有，泛舟也是花蓮一個非常很受青睞的活動，秀姑巒溪是唯一一條橫跨海岸山脈的河流，也是泛舟最適合的河流之一。

What can I do in downtown Hualien?
在花蓮的市區可以做些什麼呢？

In addition to favorite attractions around downtown Hualien, like the Pine Garden and Qixingtan Beach, there are a lot of fun things to do downtown. You can ride a bike on Hualien City Coastal Bikeway and enjoy the great ocean view. At night, you can also go to Ziqiang Night Market to enjoy the great food.

除了在花蓮市區附近最受歡迎的一些景點，像是松園別館跟七星潭之外，市區還有很多好玩的事情可以做。你可以在花蓮雙潭自行車道上騎腳踏車，然後享受一下美麗的海景。在晚上，你還可以去自強夜市享受絕佳的美食。

20 Unit 台東

 景點介紹

　　台東縣是台灣最美的地方之一，位於台灣的東南方，大致可分為中央山脈、花東縱谷平原、卑南溪三角洲、海岸山脈及泰源盆地等地理區，以及蘭嶼、綠島兩個島嶼。這裡是台灣較晚開發的地方，也是原住民人口比例最高的地方。自然資源相當豐富，天然景觀、物產、以及人文的多樣性，讓台東成為一個旅遊的好去處。看山、泡湯、看海、欣賞海岸的特殊地形、體驗豐富的原住民文化與各種民俗慶典，台東是個一年四季都適合來旅行的地方。

 帶外國朋友認識台灣

Lidia and Jamie are debating about visiting Orchid Island or Green Island.
Lidia 與 Jamie 正在想要去蘭嶼還是綠島。

Lidia　I want to go to Green Island's Zhaori Hot Spring, a special oceanic hot spring. It is one of the most rare hot springs in the world.
我想去朝日溫泉，它是特別的海底溫泉。這是全世界一種特別的溫泉。

Jamie　Now I remember it. I have heard that it is quite pleasurable to soak in the hot spring, listen to the sound of the surf, and observe the coral reefs. It's even greater to soak in the hot spring during the sunrise, sunset, or at night. It's superb.
現在我想起來了。我聽說超級享受的，可以泡在裡面，然後聽聽波浪的聲音，觀察身旁的珊瑚礁。在日出、日落、或者晚上泡的話更棒。超讚的。

Lidia　How about you? Do you want to go to Orchid Island?
你呢？你想去蘭嶼嗎？

Jamie Yes! Most of the inhabitants on Orchid Island are Dao, the only oceanic aboriginal tribe in Taiwan. I want to join the Flying Fish Festival this year. Every spring, Dao holds the Flying Fish Festival. For them, it means more than constructing a canoe itself, and it represents the courage and pride of a family. In this season, you can literally see the fishes leaping into the canoes. In addition to the Flying Fish Festival, a lot of traditional Dao culture can be seen on Orchid Island. For example, now, you can still see some traditional Dao houses built partly below the ground.

對！蘭嶼大部份的人都是達悟族，他們是台灣唯一的海洋原住民族。我想去參加今年的飛魚節，在每年春天，達悟族人會舉辦飛魚節。對於他們來說，這其中的意義不只於造船本身，而是代表了一個家庭的勇氣與驕傲。在這個季節，你真的會看到魚兒們跳進船裡面。除了飛魚節以外，在蘭嶼可以看到很多傳統達悟族文化。舉例來說，你到現在還可以看到一些傳統的達悟族房屋是部分改在地底下的。

Lidia I read in an article that there are many taboos on Orchid Island, and tourists need to follow the rules. The island is believed to be one of the most pristine places in Taiwan.

我讀到一個文章說，在蘭嶼有很多的禁忌，旅客需要去遵守這些規則。據說那裡是台灣最原始的地方之一。

Jamie Don't worry. We will be respectful and follow the rules. Both islands are accessible by flight and boat. Let's go.

別擔心，我們會保持敬意，遵守他們的規則的。兩個島都可以坐飛機或者坐船到到達。我們走吧！

 Words

rare [rɛr] adj. 稀有的；罕見的	leap [lip] v. 跳；跳躍
pleasurable [`plɛʒərəb!] adj. 使人快樂的	taboo [tə`bu] n. 禁忌；忌諱
superb [sʊ`pɝb] adj. 極好的	pristine [`prɪstin] adj. 原始的
canoe [kə`nu] n. 獨木舟	accessible [æk`sɛsəb!] adj.可（或易）接近的

Taitung is the county with the longest coastline in Taiwan.

台東是台灣海岸線最長的縣。

Aboriginals represent one-third of the population in Taitung.

原住民占了三分之一台東的人口。

Taiwan's earliest prehistoric relics were found in the Baxian Caves.

台灣最早的史前遺跡出現在八仙洞。

The Baxian Caves, formed by sea erosion, were originally in the sea, and they are now on the cliff because of the rise of the Earth's crust on the east coast of Taiwan.

由海洋沖蝕而成的八仙洞本來是在海裡的，它們現在在峭壁上，是因為台灣東海岸的地殼上升的緣故。

Sanxiantai is composed of offshore islands and coral reefs, and there is a dragon-like bridge that connects the mainland and the terrace.

三仙台是由離岸小島跟珊瑚礁所組成的，有一座像是龍的橋樑鏈接本島陸地跟三仙台。

It takes about two hours to walk around the round island trail in Sanxiantai, and there are a lot of exotic plants and geological sceneries formed by corals.

三仙台的環島步道大概需要走兩個小時的時間，沿途會有很多奇特的植物與珊瑚形成的地理景觀。

Jinzun has one of the most beautiful bays and beaches in Taiwan. Sitting in the gazebo to see the sparkling ocean and feel the breeze is quite pleasant.

金樽有著台灣最美的海灣與沙灘之一，坐在瞭望台上面看看閃閃發光的海洋、感受一下微風，是很美妙的。

Some people like to stay in Zhiben for one night. After spending time in the Zhiben National Forest Recreation Area and going forest bathing, it is quite a pleasure to soak yourself in the hot springs and then just rest at the hotel.

在知本森林遊樂區一段時間享受森林浴之後，把自己泡在溫泉裡，然後就待在飯店裡面休息，是一大享受。

Please give a brief history of the settlement in Taitung.
請簡介人們定居台東的歷史。

Thirty percent of the inhabitants in Taitung are indigenous people. The other inhabitants are the descendants of people who immigrated to Taitung in the past 150 years. Some immigrants were from Fujian and other places in China; some were veterans; and some were Hakka people. Nowadays, Taitung has become the multiethnic society.

在台東有百分之三十的人是原住民。其他的人都是在這 150 年間移民台東的人的後代。有的移民者是從福建與中國其他地方來的，有的是榮民，有的是客家人。現在，這裡已經變成了一個多元族群的社會。

Please describe the attractions in Taitung City.
請描述台東市的景點。

Taitung Forest Park is a 280-hectare beautiful and serene park with three lakes, and it is very agreeable to walk, jog, or bike in the park. If you are interested in archaeology, you must go to the National Museum of Prehistory and Beinan Cultural Park, where the Beinan site is preserved. Also, the prehistoric and present-day aboriginal cultures are displayed there.

台東森林公園是一個 280 公頃的美麗寧靜的公園，裡面有三個湖泊，在裡面走路、慢跑、或者騎腳踏車都很舒服。如果你對於考古有興趣，你一定要去史前博物館跟卑南文化公園，在那裡卑南遺址被保存著。還有史前與現代的原住民文化也在博物館裡面呈現。

Please describe the attractions of East Rift Valley in Taitung.
請描述在台東的花東縱谷景點。

Guanshan and Chishang are the farming villages. There are many agricultural products in these areas, and the loop bikeways will take you to see many farms and related facilities. In Luye, there are tons of tea plantations, and they offer nice views of the valley. Luye Plateau is an ideal place for paragliding, and hot-air balloons events are also held every year there.

關山與池上是農村。在這個區域有很多的農產品，環狀的腳踏車道會帶你見識到很多的農田與相關的設備。在鹿野，有很多的茶園，它們提供了看到縱谷的絕佳視野。鹿野高台是一個玩飛行傘完美的地點，每年的熱氣球活動也在這裡舉辦。

Unit ❹ 台東

Part **1** 遊台灣

21 Unit 宜蘭

 景點介紹

宜蘭是台灣東部最早開發的地方。舊稱「噶瑪蘭」，在噶瑪蘭原住民的語言裡面，這是平地人的意思。宜蘭位於台灣的東部，三面環山，東臨太平洋，而平地的主體是由蘭陽溪所沖積形成的蘭陽平原。宜蘭是一個自然與文化資源都很豐饒的地方，從山中天然美景、溫泉、冷泉、龜山島賞鯨、與烏石港衝浪，到各種博物館、體驗行程、與種各種美食，宜蘭的觀光景點類型非常的多元。尤其在雪山隧道開通之後，更促進了宜蘭的觀光與休閒產業的繁榮。

 帶外國朋友認識台灣

Jamie and Frank are visiting the Lanyang Museum.
Jamie 跟 Frank 正在參觀蘭陽博物館。

Jamie

This museum is just marvelous.
這個博物館真是太棒了。

Frank

Yes. In the Langyang Museum, the stories of Yilan's pioneers, aboriginals, and present-day inhabitants, as well as stories about its geology and biology, are told. It is a must-go museum if you want to learn more about Yilan. Besides, the Langyang Museum itself is a great architectural work.
對啊。宜蘭的開拓者、原住民、現在的居民，還有它的地理與生物的故事都在蘭陽博物館裡面被訴說著。如果你想要對宜蘭了解更深的話，這是一個必去的博物館。此外，蘭陽博物館本身就是一個很棒的建築作品。

Jamie

Look at that! What is grappling with the ghosts?
你看那個！搶孤是什麼？

Frank

I just read the introduction board. It is a competition held during Ghost Month. On the last day of Ghost Month, there is a competition for grappling with the ghosts by pole-climbing to celebrate the end of the month.

我剛剛才讀了那個介紹看版，這是一個在鬼月舉行的競賽。在鬼月的最後一天，舉辦搶孤爬竿比賽來慶祝這一個月的結束。

Jamie

How exactly does it competition be held?

這個競賽到底是怎麼辦的呢？

Frank

It is a competition for participants to seize the sacrificial goods. The food is put in the tower, and the tower is divided into three sections. Some pillars are covered by oil. Participants team up with other people and climb the pillars. They throw the food to the people on the ground. The competitors continue to race, and the one who gets the flag at the top wins the competition. It is believed to bring luck to the winner.

這是一個給參加者搶奪祭拜物品的比賽。食物會被放在搶孤的塔上面，而塔會被分成三個部分。有些支柱上會塗上油，參加者跟其他人組成團隊，爬這些支架。他們會把食物丟給在地上的人，然後繼續競賽，拿到最上面的棋子的人獲得了勝利。據說棋子會帶給勝利者好運。

Jamie

It is very interesting.

真的非常有趣。

---

marvelous [`mɑrvələs] adj. 令人驚歎的

pioneer [ˌpaɪə`nɪr] n. 開拓者；拓荒者

inhabitant [ɪn`hæbətənt] n. （某地區的）居民

grapple [`græp!] v. 抓住；扭打

seize [siz] v. 抓住；奪取

sacrificial [ˌsækrə`fɪʃəl] adj. 獻祭的

divide [də`vaɪd] v. 分；劃分

Yilan Plain is very fertile, and it is abundant with agricultural products.

宜蘭平原非常的肥沃，有著豐富的農產品。

The four treasures of Yilan are sweet gelatinized red-bean cake, smoked and corned duck meat, candied jujubes and plums, and salty liver. All of them are made from the local products of Yilan.

宜蘭四寶是羊羹、鴨賞、蜜金棗跟梅子、還有膽肝，都是用宜蘭當地的產物做成的。

The Taiwanese Folk Opera, Gezaixi, is a form of the traditional drama in Taiwan, and it originated in Yilan.

台灣民俗戲曲歌仔戲是台灣的一種傳統戲劇表演，起源於宜蘭。

Wushi Harbor is the paradise for surfing lovers.

烏石漁港是衝浪愛好者的天堂。

In Toucheng, you may not want to miss trying the taro ice. It is traditional Taiwanese ice cream, and it used to be sold by street carts.

在頭城，你應該試試芋頭冰。這是台灣傳統的冰淇淋，過去都是在街上的小車賣的。

The vegetables grown in Jiaoxi are of the best quality because the farmers grow them with spring water. They taste sweeter and fresher.

在礁溪種的蔬菜是品質最好的，因為農夫用溫泉水來種植。這些蔬菜嚐起來更甜更新鮮。

You can try green onion pancakes in Yilan. Most of them are made from the green onions in Sanxing, a town that is famous for its green onions.

你可以試試宜蘭的蔥油餅。這裡的蔥油餅大部份用的都是三星來的蔥，三星是一個以蔥聞名的鄉鎮。

Smoked and corned duck meat is made by duck cured in salty water and smoked over sugar cane. It is the most popular local specialty food in Yilan.

鴨賞是用鹽水醃過的鴨肉然後以甘蔗煙燻做成的。它是宜蘭受歡迎的特產。

If you have more time in Yilan, we can go to Taiping Mountain. Cuifeng Lake, the largest alpine lake in Taiwan, is in the area.

如果你有更多的時間在宜蘭的話，我們可以去太平山。台灣最大的高山湖，翠峰湖，就在那個區域。

Please describe the National Center for Traditional Arts.
請描述一下國立傳統藝術中心。

It is located by the bank of the Dongshan River in Yilan. If you are interested in traditional art and culture, this is a place you need to visit. The buildings and streets were built to present Taiwan in the old days. You can see organized displays and performances of traditional culture and art in the center.

它位在宜蘭冬山河岸邊。如果你對於傳統藝術與文化有興趣的話，那就是你應該要來看看的地方。那裡的建築與街道建造呈現了舊時的台灣。在這個地方，你可以看到傳統文化與藝術被有系統地陳列與表演。

What is special in Suao?
蘇澳有什麼特別的？

Suao is located in the south of Yilan. There are two things that make Suao special. Firstly, the springs are the cold springs that have a temperature of 22 degrees Celsius. The water from the cold springs is drinkable. It is the only calcium hydroxy carbonic spring in Taiwan. In fact, this rare type of cold springs is only found in a few places around the world. Second, Nanfang Ao, a fishing port south of Suao, is famous for its seafood.

蘇澳在宜蘭的南方。蘇澳有兩個特別的地方。第一，這裡的泉水是攝氏 22 度的冷泉，這裡的泉水可以飲用。它是台灣唯一的碳酸氫鈣泉。事實上，這種稀有的冷泉全世界只有少數幾個地方有。第二，南方澳是蘇澳南邊的一個漁港，以海鮮聞名。

Where is Guishan Island?
龜山島在哪裡？

Guishan Island is located 10 kilometers east of Toucheng. It is the only active volcano in Taiwan, and the geology and ecology on the island are very special. There were people living in the island, but it is now uninhabited. If you want to visit the island, you will need to apply for a permit beforehand.

龜山島位於頭城的東方十公里處。它是全台灣唯一的活火山，那裡的地址與生態都很特別。以前曾經有人住在島上，但是現在沒有人住了。如果你想要登島的話，你需要事先提出申請。

22 Unit 澎湖

景點介紹

　　澎湖群島位於台灣西邊 50 公里的海域，由 90 個大小島嶼所組成，是台灣的第一大離島群。澎湖的縣花為天人菊，天人菊不受風吹雨打的影響，象徵澎湖人面對惡劣環境生生不息的生命力，因此澎湖又稱為「菊島」。澎湖大多數的島嶼都是玄武岩組成，平坦面是熔岩流台地面，有許多特殊的自然景觀。除了許多自然美景之外，澎湖也是海上活動的絕佳地點，由於東北季風的加持，更是許多風帆船選手愛好的地方。此外，漁村景觀、釣魚、賞鳥、海鮮、花火節，都是澎湖讓人流連忘返的原因。

帶外國朋友認識台灣

Frank and Jamie are discussing their schedule at a bed and breakfast inn in Penghu.
Frank 跟 Jamie 正在澎湖一個民宿裡面討論他們的行程。

Frank

Where are we going today?
我們今天要去哪裡呢？

Jamie

My friend enthusiastically recommended that I visit Zhongshe Historical House in Wangan, Penghu. It is also named Huazhai, the Flower Houses.
我的朋友強力推薦我去看看在望安的中社古厝。那裡又叫做花宅。

Frank

What is special there?
那裡有什麼特別的呢？

Jamie

There are traditional Fujian three-section compound houses with courtyards that were built more than 300 years ago. The houses are believed to be the oldest ruins of the type in Taiwan. The ancient inhabit-ants used local materials to build the houses, and the walls were composed largely of coral reefs.

那裡有三百多年前的傳統閩南氏三合院。那些房子據說是台灣這類建築最老的遺跡。以前的居民用當地的材料建造了這些房子，而且牆壁很多都是用珊瑚礁堆成的。

Frank

It is amazing. I can't help imagining what kind of lives the maritime pioneers had when they lived there a long time ago. It must have been tough, but they were smart and enduring.

太厲害了。我忍不住想像這些勇敢的海上開拓者，很久以前在這裡過的是什麼樣的生活。一定很艱苦，不過他們非常聰明、有毅力。

Jamie

Exactly! We can go there first. Then, we can go to the Green Turtle Tourism and Conservation Center to gain more knowledge about its conservation. From the website, I learned that the record of green turtle conservation can be traced back to 130 years ago.

真的！我們可以先去那裡，接著，我們可以去綠蠵龜觀光保育中心，去得到更多保育的知識。我從網站上看到綠蠵龜的保育記錄可以追溯到 130 年前耶。

Frank

It is pretty cool.

好棒喔。

Jamie

Yes. Let's go to Wangan first. Then, we can go to the Twin Hearts Stone Weir in Cimei.

對啊。我們先去望安吧，然後我們可以到七美的雙心石滬去。

📝 **Words**

enthusiastically [ɪnˌθjuzɪˈæstɪkḷɪ] adv. 熱心地；滿腔熱情地

compound [kɑmˈpaʊnd] n. 有圍牆（或籬笆等的）住宅群，大院

courtyard [ˈkortˌjɑrd] n. 庭院；天井

ruin [ˈrʊɪn] n. 廢墟；遺跡

maritime [ˈmærəˌtaɪm] adj. 海的；航海的

tough [tʌf] adj. 棘手的；費勁的

enduring [ɪnˈdjʊrɪŋ] adj. 持久的；堅持下去的

conservation [ˌkɑnsəˈveʃən] n. （對自然資源的）保護；管理

The Penghu Islands are an archipelago in the Taiwan Strait.

澎湖群島是在台灣海峽上的列島。

Penghu consists of 90 islands and islets.

澎湖是由九十個島跟嶼所組成的。

Only about one quarter of the islands in Penghu are inhabited.

大約只有四分之一的島嶼是有住人的。

Jibei, Wangan, Cimei, and Magong are the four most popular islands for tourists in Penghu.

吉貝、望安、七美、馬公是澎湖最受旅客歡迎的島嶼。

The Sand Beach Beak is in the southwest of Jibei, and it is a white-sand beach mainly composed of corals and shell fragments. It is spectacular.

沙尾沙灘在吉貝的西南方，是一個白色的沙灘，主要由珊瑚與貝殼碎片所組成。非常的美麗壯觀。

Many inhabitants in Penghu make a living by fishing, so you can see the fishing culture of the village here.

很多澎湖的居民以捕魚為生，所以在這裡你可以看到漁村文化的存在。

Most people go to Penghu in the summer, but it gets windy from October to March.

大部份的人都是在夏天去澎湖，但從十月到三月那裡風非常大。

Penghu is one of the best places in the world for windsurfing.

澎湖是世界上玩風帆船最棒的地方之一。

Penghu Trans-Ocean Bridge connects the islands of Baisha and Xiyu, and this bridge was the first sea-crossing bridge in East Asia.

澎湖跨海大橋連接了白沙嶼跟西嶼，是東亞的第一座跨海大橋。

Walking on the bridge is enjoyable. You can watch the oceanic views, listen to the roaring tides, and feel the sea breezes.

走過這個橋是很享受的。你可以看看海洋的樣子、聽聽潮汐的聲音、並感受一下海洋的微風。

Please briefly describe the early settlements of Penghu.
請簡述澎湖早期定居的情況。

Penghu was visited by people approximately 5,000 years ago, but the people did not settle permanently. Penghu started to be inhabited in the 9th or 10th centuries by Han, which was approximately 400 years earlier than the time that they settled on the island of Taiwan.

澎湖在五千年前就有人來過，但是這些人並沒有定居在這裡。從第九或者第十世紀，開始有漢人居住在這裡，比他們到台灣本島定居還早了約四百年。

What are the activities to do in Penghu?
在澎湖可以做什麼呢？

You must be able to find an activity that you love doing in Penghu. The majority of islands in Penghu are made of basalt, and there are many places where you can see basalt columns and other basalt landscapes. Penghu is also a great place for bird watching. If you like cultural attractions, you must not miss the Erkan Historical House and Huazhai Historical House. If you are an outdoor enthusiast, you can go surfing, windsurfing, wakeboarding, kiteboarding, snorkeling, scuba diving, sea kayaking, and so on.

你一定能夠找到一個你在澎湖喜歡做的活動。澎湖大部份大島嶼都是由玄武岩組成的，這裡有很多的地方你可以看到玄武岩柱與其他的玄武岩景觀。這裡也是賞鳥絕佳的地方。如果你喜歡文化類型的景點，你一定不要錯過了二崁古厝落跟花宅古厝。如果你是戶外活動的愛好者，你可以去玩衝浪、風帆船、寬板划水、風箏衝浪、浮潛、潛水、海上獨木舟等等的。

What are the fishing-related activities that a tourist can experience in Penghu?
旅客可以體驗澎湖哪些捕魚相關的活動呢？

In addition to going fishing, you can experience other fishing-related activities. For example, you can feed cobia and lure squids, as well as collect seaweed and oysters.

除了釣魚以外，你可以體驗看看其他捕魚相關的活動。舉例來説，你可以餵海鱺、誘花枝、還有採海菜與蚵。

 景點介紹

　　馬祖列島位於台灣海峽，在台灣本島的西北方，由南竿、北竿、莒光及東引等數十座島嶼所組成。氣候屬亞熱帶海洋性氣候，四季分明，在地理上，由於部分島嶼與中國大陸距離不到十公里，這裡是非常重要的軍事重地，也形成了許多的戰地風光。馬祖的地形多山丘、谷地、與灣澳，成為了許多美麗的風光，當地的傳統聚落的建築不管是風格、建材、還是功能，都與台灣有很大的不同。此外，由於馬祖特殊的位置與氣候，這裡成為了賞鳥的絕佳去處。

 帶外國朋友認識台灣

Lidia and Jamie are discussing the architecture in Matsu.
Lidia 與 Jamie 正在討論馬祖的建築。

Jamie　I have heard a lot about the architecture in Matsu.
我聽說很多關於馬祖建築的事情。

Lidia　You mean the traditional Fujian style architecture?
你指的是傳統福建形式的建築嗎？

Jamie　Yes. The culture and architecture in east Fujian is presented in Matsu, and they are rarely seen in other places in the world, even in East Fujian itself.
對，在馬祖可以看到福建東部的文化與建築，這在世界上其他的地方已經很難見到了，甚至是在福建東部本身。

Lidia　Why?
為什麼呢？

Jamie Because of the destruction from Mao Zedong's rule, the traditional culture in East Fujian was not well-preserved in China. Most inhabitants in Matsu are the descendants of the immigrants from East Fujian, and this is the reason why the culture in East Fujian can be seen in Matsu.

因為毛澤東統治時代的破壞，在中國傳統的福建東部文化並沒有被好好保存。大部份馬祖的居民是來自福建東部的移民的後代，這是為什麼福建東部的文化在馬祖還看得到的原因。

Lidia What is special about the architecture in Matsu?

馬祖的建築有什麼特別的地方？

Jamie The granite blocks are largely used in the buildings in Matsu. Most of the traditional buildings are in square shapes and look like Chinese ink stamps. The roofs are not fixed; they are covered with large rocks for protection from the strong wind in winter and for easier maintenance. This results in better ventilation, and the buildings are called 'breathing houses'. In addition, if you pay attention to the temples in Matsu, you will see that many of them have exaggerated curving eaves that look like fire, and they would help in preventing the spread of fire.

在馬祖，花崗岩塊被大量地運用在建築物上面。大部份的傳統建築是正方形的，看起來像是印章。這些屋頂並不是封死的，屋頂上放了大量的石頭，用來防止冬天的大風，也讓維修更為方便。這樣的建築形成了更好的通風，被稱為了「會呼吸的房子」。除此之外，如果你注意到那裡的寺廟，你會發現它們很多都有誇張的彎曲屋簷，看起來像是火焰，用途是幫助防止火災的蔓延。

Lidia Sounds interesting. Let's plan a vacation to Matsu!

聽起來好有趣。我們來計劃一個到馬祖的假期吧！

 Words

present [priz'ɛnt] v. 呈現

destruction [dɪ'strʌkʃən] n. 破壞；毀滅

descendant [dɪ'sɛndənt] n. 子孫；後裔

immigrant ['ɪməgrənt] n. 移民

maintenance ['mentənəns] n. 維修；維持

ventilation [ˌvɛnt!'eʃən] n. 通風；流通空氣

exaggerated [ɪg'zædʒəˌretɪd] adj. 誇張的

spread [sprɛd] n. 蔓延；伸展

Matsu's islands are located on the offshore frontlines between Taiwan and China.

馬祖是位在台灣與中國之間離岸的前線。

Many people think the village of Qinbi reminds them of a European village by the Mediterranean.

很多人認為芹壁讓他們想到地中海沿岸的一個歐洲小鎮。

Qinbi in Beigan and Niujiao in Nangan are the two most popular stone house villages.

北竿的芹壁與南竿的牛角是兩個最受歡迎的石屋村落。

Matsu is named after the Goddess of the sea, Mazu, and it is believed that she was buried in Matsu's Nangan Tianhou Temple.

馬祖是因海上的女神媽祖而得此名，據說她葬在馬祖南竿天后宮裡面。

The world's tallest Mazu statue is located in Nangan, Matsu.

全世界最大的媽祖雕像就在馬祖的南竿。

Matsu consists mostly of granite islands. The dominant landscape is the hilly terrain.

馬祖是由花崗岩組成的島嶼。最主要的景觀就是丘陵的地形。

There are numerous boards with military slogans in Matsu. This creates a special atmosphere in Matsu.

在馬祖有很多有著軍事標語的看板，塑造了馬祖特殊的氣氛。

The density of the military tunnels in Matsu is the highest in the world.

馬祖的軍事隧道的密度是全世界最高的。

Please describe the history of Matsu.
請描述馬祖的歷史。

The earliest historical relics found in Matsu were from the Neolithic Era. Some people from Fujian started to immigrate to Matsu during the Yuan Dynasty. What is special is that in contrast to most islands in Taiwan, Matsu was not occupied by Japanese troops. After the Nationalist Chinese retreated to Taiwan in 1949, they retained Matsu and used it as an important military base.

在馬祖所發現的最早的歷史遺跡是來自於新石器時代。在元朝的時候，福建開始有一些人移民到馬祖。特別的是，馬祖與台灣大部份的島嶼不同，馬祖從來沒有被日本軍隊佔領過。

What are the main attractions in Nangan and Beigan?
南竿與北竿主要的景點有哪些呢？

In Beigan, the most popular attraction is Qinbi, which is believed to be one of the most beautiful villages in Matsu. Because most people left Qinbi for better lives, the village was able to keep its traditional appearance. In Nangan, you should not miss the Beihai Tunnel, a hidden port hewn from solid granite. It was a big achievement at that time, and it also reflected the military importance of Matsu.

在北竿，最熱門的景點是芹壁，這裡被認為是馬祖最漂亮的村落之一。因為大部份的人都離開這裡去尋求更好的生活了，這個村落的以保存了它傳統的樣子。在南竿，你應該不要錯過了北海隧道，這是一個由堅硬花崗石所挖成的隱秘的港口。這在當時是一個很大的成就，也反映了馬祖的軍事重要性。

What are the main attractions in Dongyin and Juguang?
莒光與東引主要的景點是什麼呢？

Dongying is the northernmost territory of Taiwan. You will see a lot of military outposts in this area. The Andong Tunnel, built during the Cold War, is an impressive one, with eight branches connecting to the seashores. In the tunnel, there are arsenal, military barracks, a meeting hall, and pigsty that are no longer used.

東引是台灣最北的領土。你會在這個區域看到很多的軍事哨站。在冷戰期間所建立的安東隧道是令人很印象深刻的一個隧道，有八個孔道通向海岸。在隧道裡面，有已經不復使用的軍火庫、軍營、會議室、還有豬舍。

PART ②

旅遊英語
快速通關

GO!

01 Unit

機場會用到的英語

訂票

I am looking for a round-trip ticket.

我正在找一張來回的機票。

Does the fare include tax?

整個機票價格含稅的嗎？

May I get an open return ticket?

我可以買一張回程不限時間的機票嗎？

What are your departure and arrival dates?

你出發以及回來的日期是什麼？

Do you have any preferences for the seats and meals?

你有偏好的座位跟餐點嗎？

辦理報到手續

Where is the group check-in counter?

團體的報到櫃檯在哪裡呢？

Is there any isle seat available?

有靠走道的座位可以選擇嗎？

Please give me the passports and itinerary.

請給我護照還有行程單。

Is there any special need or condition that we should know about?

有什麼我們需要知道的特殊需求與情況嗎？

We are a group of six people. Can we sit together?

我們是六個人的團體，可以坐在一起嗎？

Words

round-trip [`raʊnd͵trɪp] *adj.* 來回的

departure [dɪ`pɑrtʃə] *n.* 離開；出發

arrival [ə`raɪv!] *n.* 到達

counter [`kaʊntə] *n.* 櫃臺

itinerary [aɪ`tɪnə͵rɛrɪ] *n.* 旅程

condition [kən`dɪʃən] *n.* 條件

行李檢查

Please take off your jacket and shoes.

請脫下你的外套與鞋子。

You need to take out all your personal belongings and walk through the security gate.

你需要拿出你所有的隨身物品，然後走過這個安檢門。

Hold out your arms, please.

請伸開你的手臂。

Is there any liquid in your luggage?

你的行李裏面有液體嗎？

You cannot carry this on the plane. You can either check this in or throw it away.

你不可以帶這個上飛機，你可以選擇託運或者丟掉。

登機

The flight has been cancelled. Please go to the information desk for assistance.

這個班機已經取消了，請到服務台來，我們會協助你。

The boarding gate has been changed. Please proceed to Gate C5.

登機門已經換了，請到C5號門去。

Welcome aboard. May I see your boarding pass?

歡迎登機。我可以看你的登機證嗎？

Could you tell me where my seat is?

可以請你告訴我，我的座位在哪裡嗎？

You must put your luggage under the seat in front of you or in the overhead compartment.

你必須要把你的行李放在你前面的座位下面，或者放在上面的行李置放箱裡面。

Words

take off 脫去 (衣物)	proceed [prə`sid] v.（沿特定路線）行進
belongings [bə`lɔŋɪŋz] n. 財產；攜帶物品	boarding pass 登機證
hold out 向外伸	compartment [kəm`pɑrtmənt] n. 行李置放箱

 旅遊主題式對話

帶錯文件

L: Sir. This is not a valid passport.

領隊：先生，這不是有效的護照。

T: Oh! I am so sorry. I took the old one by mistake and left the new one at home. What should I do now?

旅客：啊！很抱歉，我搞錯拿成舊的了，然後把新的留在家裡了。現在我應該怎麼做？

L: What I can do now is to book the next flight for you. You need to go back home to get your new passport and come back here to catch the flight.

領隊：我現在可以做的就是幫你預定下一個航班。你要回家拿你的新護照，然後回到這裡來趕飛機。

T: OK. Please let me know how to catch up with you after arrival.

旅客：好的。請告訴我到目的地後要怎麼趕上你們。

(L: Tour Leader；T: Tourist)

辦理報到手續

L: Please be careful with the luggage. It is fragile.

領隊：請小心這個行李。這是易碎的。

A: Okay. I will put a fragile sticker on it. Please put the luggage on the scale, and I will help you check in the luggage.

航空公司接待人員：好的。我會放上一個表示易碎的貼紙。請把行李放在秤上，我會幫你辦理託運這個。

L: Thank you. Also, this is the membership card for this lady. Please help her add the mileage to her membership card.

領隊：謝謝。還有，這是這個女士的會員卡，請幫她把里程數累計到她的會員卡裡面。

A: Sure. Not a problem.

航空公司接待人員：好的，沒有問題。

(L: Tour Leader；A: Airline receptionist)

行李檢查

I: Please take out all your electronic devices and put them in the tray.

檢查人員：請拿出你所有的電子設備，把它們放在盤子裡。

T: How about my cell phone?

旅客：那我的手機呢？

I: Yes. Take it out, put it in the tray, and proceed to the gate.

檢查人員：也是的，要拿出來，放在盤子上，然後通過這個門。

(I: Inspector；T: Tourist)

Words

valid [`vælɪd] adj. 合法的；有效的	mileage [`maɪlɪdʒ] n. 總里程數
catch up with 趕上	device [dɪ`vaɪs] n. 設備；儀器
fragile [`frædʒəl] adj. 易碎的；易損壞的	tray [tre] n. 盤子；托盤

飛機誤點 🛄

P: When is the boarding time? Is it delayed?

乘客：登機時間是什麼時候呢？誤點了嗎？

G: I am sorry. It is delayed for one hour, and the boarding gate is D3 now.

地勤人員：我很抱歉，飛機誤點了一個小時，而且登機門現在改成D3了。

P: Is it in this terminal?

乘客：是在這個航廈嗎？

G: No, it is in another terminal. You can take the shuttle bus, and it takes only 5 minutes to get there.

地勤人員：不是，是在另一個航廈。你可以坐接駁巴士，只要五分鐘就到了。

(P: Passenger；G: Ground crew)

免稅商店 🛄

T: Could you tell me what the duty-free special deal here is?

領隊：你可以告訴我這裡的免稅特別優惠是什麼嗎？

S: Sure. If you buy three boxes of the chocolate, you will get one extra box for free. The expiration date is one year from now, so it is a pretty good deal.

銷售人員：當然。如果你買三盒巧克力，你會得到另外一盒免費的。有效期限是從現在開始一年之後，所以這還蠻划算的。

T: OK. Let me ask my group members and come back to tell you.

領隊：好的，我來問問我的團員，然後再回來告訴你。

S: No problem. Please come back to tell me the number of boxes, and I will wrap them for you.

銷售人員：沒有問題，請再回來告訴我要幾盒，然後我會幫你把盒子包裝好。

(L: Tour Leader；S: Sales)

登機

L: We have heard the final boarding call. We need to proceed to Gate 6 immediately.

領隊：我們聽到最後的登機廣播了，我們需要立刻到六號門登機。

T: I need to go to the restroom.

旅客：我需要用一下洗手間。

L: Please get on board first. You may use the lavatory on the plane.

領隊：請先登機，你可以使用飛機內的洗手間。

(L: Tour Leader；T: Tourist)

Words

terminal [`tɝmən!] *n.* 航空站；航廈

shuttle [`ʃʌt!] *n.* （車輛、飛機等在兩地間的）短程穿梭運行；短程穿梭運輸線

deal [dil] *n.* 交易

expiration [ˌɛkspə`reʃən] *n.* 終結；期滿

wrap [ræp] *v.* 包；裹

lavatory [`lævəˌtorɪ] *n.* 廁所；洗手間

02 Unit

飛機上會用到的英語

▶ 輕鬆學旅遊短句　念過一次請你打「√」

起飛前

This is Captain Tracy Wu speaking. On behalf of China Airlines, we would like to welcome you aboard.

這是機長吳崔西的講話，我們想要代表中華航空歡迎你登機。

For safety reasons, the use of all electronic devices is prohibited during take-off and landing.

為了安全起見，所有的電子儀器在起飛以及降落的時候都是禁止使用的。

Sir, please switch off your cell phone.

先生，請關掉你的手機。

Ma'am, please straighten the seat back and stow the table.

女士，請豎直椅背，並把餐桌收好。

If you need any assistance, please let us know.

如果你需要任何的協助，請告訴我。

機上服務

Could you give me a blanket and a pillow?

可以給我一條毛毯跟一個枕頭嗎？

Excuse me. I think my headset is broken. Could you give me a new one?

不好意思，我想我的耳機壞掉了。你可以給我一個新的嗎？

Are you ok? Your lips are pale. Do you need some water?

你還好嗎？你的嘴唇看起來很蒼白。你需要一些水嗎？

Please lower your voice, because other passengers are resting.

請降低你的音量，因為其他的乘客正在休息。

My group member is airsick. Do you have some medicine?

我的團員暈機了。你有藥嗎？

Words

takeoff [`tek͵ɔf] n. 起飛；起跳

landing [`lændɪŋ] n. 降落，著落；登陸

switch off 關上

stow [sto] v. 貯藏，收藏

blanket [`blæŋkɪt] n. 毛毯，毯子

headset [`hɛd͵sɛt] n. 戴在頭上的收話器；雙耳式耳機

供餐

We will serve dinner very soon.

我們很快就會供應晚餐。

Have you ordered the vegetarian meal?

你預定了素食的餐點嗎？

Do you mind to get me some snacks? I am hungry.

你介意給我一些點心嗎？我餓了。

We have pork with rice and beef with eggs, which would you like?

我們有豬肉配飯跟牛肉配蛋，你想要哪一種？

What kind of drinks do you have?

你們有什麼樣的飲料？

購買免稅品

Can I get a catalogue of the duty-free products?

我可以要一本免稅商品的型錄嗎？

When can I buy the duty-free items?

我什麼時候可以買免稅品呢？

What currencies do you accept?

你們接受哪種貨幣？

You can pay by credit card, US dollars, euros, or New Taiwan Dollars.
你可以用信用卡、美金、歐元、或者新台幣來支付。

Are there other colors or sizes that I can choose from?
有其他的顏色或者尺寸可以選擇嗎？

Words

serve [sɝv] v. 侍候（顧客等）；供應（飯菜）

vegetarian [ˌvɛdʒə`tɛrɪən] adj. 素菜的

snack [snæk] n. 點心

catalogue [`kætəlɔg] n. 目錄

item [`aɪtəm] n. 項目

currency [`kɝənsɪ] n. 貨幣

旅遊主題式對話

起飛前

F: Do you need any help?
空服員：你需要幫忙嗎？

P: Excuse me. I cannot find a space in the overhead compartment for my hand luggage.
乘客：不好意思，我在上面的行李箱找不到一個空間來放我的隨身包包。

F: Let me help you find a space for it. There you go!
空服員：讓我幫你找到一個地方吧。找到了！

P: Thank you very much!
乘客：非常謝謝你！

(F: Flight Attendant ；P: Passenger)

機上服務

P: Excuse me. I think my remote control is broken.

乘客：不好意思，我想我的遙控器壞掉了。

F: Let me see. Hmm, I think there is a problem with the screen. Do you mind changing to another seat?

空服員：讓我來看看。嗯，我想是這個螢幕的問題，你介意換掉另一個座位嗎？

P: No, not at all.

乘客：不會，我不介意。

F: Thank you for your understanding. Let me take you to your new seat.

空服員：謝謝你的理解。讓我帶你到新的座位吧。

(F: Flight Attendant；P: Passenger)

供餐

F: Can I get you anything to drink?

空服員：我可以給你來點什麼喝的嗎？

P: Please give me a cup of water. Also, do you have ginger ale?

乘客：請給我一杯水。另外，你們有薑汁汽水嗎？

F: Yes, we do. Let me get it for you.

空服員：有，我們有。讓我去幫你拿。

(F: Flight Attendant；P: Passenger)

Words

overhead [`ovɚ`hɛd] *adj.* 在頭頂上的	remote control 遙控；遙控器
luggage [`lʌgɪdʒ] *n.* 行李	not at all 一點都不
there you go 給你的；拿去吧	besides [bɪ`saɪdz] *adv.* 此外；而且

遇到亂流

L: We are now experiencing some turbulence. Please return to your seat and buckle your seatbelt.

領隊：我們正在經過不穩定的氣流，請回到你的座位上，並且繫上你的安全帶。

P: Is it dangerous? I am beginning to panic.

乘客：有危險嗎？我開始慌張了。

L: No, it is normal. For your own safety, please keep your seatbelt fastened until the seatbelt sign is turned off.

領隊：不會的，這是正常的。為了你的安全起見，請把你的安全帶繫好，直到安全帶指示燈熄滅為止。

P: Okay. I will go back to my seat and fasten my seatbelt immediately.

乘客：好的，我會立刻回到我的座位，並繫好安全帶的。

(L: Tour Leader；P: Passenger)

索取入境表格

P: Could you give me some disembarkation and custom declaration forms?

乘客：可以請你給我入境表格還有海關申報表格嗎？

F: Of course! Are you travelling alone?

空服員：當然！你是一個人旅行嗎？

P: No, I am with my group members. We have ten people.

乘客：不是，我跟我的家人一起，我們一共有十個人。

F: OK. Everyone should fill out a disembarkation card. Each family needs only one declaration form. Let me get them for you.

空服員：好的。每個人都要填一張入境表格，一個家庭只要填一張海關申報表格，讓我去幫你們拿。

(P: Passenger；F: Flight Attendant)

降落前

F: We are now descending and will be landing soon.

空服員：我們現在正在下降高度，很快就會降落了。

P: How is the weather?

乘客：天氣怎麼樣呢？

F: The weather is great. The temperature is 28 degrees Centigrade, so it should be very comfortable.

空服員：天氣非常好。溫度是攝氏28度，所以應該是非常舒服的。

(F: Flight Attendant；P: Passenger)

Words

turbulence [ˋtɝbjələns] n. （氣體等的）紊流，亂流

buckle [ˋbʌk!] v. 扣住；扣緊

disembarkation [ˌdɪsɛmbɑrˋkeʃən] n. 登陸；上岸

declaration [ˌdɛkləˋreʃən] n. （納稅品等的）申報

descending [dɪˋsɛndɪŋ] adj. 下降的；下行的；梯降的

centigrade [ˋsɛntəˌgred] n. 攝氏

03 Unit 入境會用到的英語

輕鬆學旅遊短句　　念過一次請你打「√」

入境檢查

These are the immigration counters for citizens. Please go to the counters for visitors.

這些是給本國籍人士的櫃台，請到訪客的櫃台去。

How long do you plan to be here?

你計劃在這裡待多久的時間？

Are you travelling alone?

你是一個人旅行嗎？

Where do you intend to stay?

你計劃住在哪裡？

Do you have any relatives here?

你有任何的親戚在這個嗎？

轉機

I am transferring in Hong Kong.

我正在香港轉機。

Where is the transit counter?

轉機櫃台在哪裡呢？

Could you tell me where the transit lounge is?

可以告訴我哪裡是轉機休息室嗎？

I am waiting for a connecting flight.

我正在等轉接的班機。

Please check the electronic information board to see if your flight is delayed.

請確認電子資訊看版，看看你的飛機有沒有延誤。

Words

citizen [`sɪtəzn] n. 公民	transfer [træns`fɝ] v. 轉車；轉乘
intend [ɪn`tɛnd] v. 想要；打算	transit [`trænsɪt] n. 通過，經過；過境；中轉
relatives [relə`tɪvz] n. 親戚	lounge [laʊndʒ] n. 候機室；休息室

領取行李

Where is the baggage claim area?

領取行李的地方在哪裡呢？

Which one is the carousel for flight A368?

請問A368班機的行李轉盤是哪一個呢？

Please check the baggage tag and make sure you take your own bag.

請確認一下行李條，確定你拿到自己的行李。

My luggage is missing. Where can I report it?

我的行李不見了，我可以在哪裡報失呢？

My suitcase is broken. Who should I talk to about this problem?

我的行李箱壞掉了，我應該把這個問題跟誰說？

兌換貨幣

Where can I exchange some money?

我在哪裡可以換錢？

What is the exchange rate between the Japanese Yuan and U.S. Dollars?

日圓跟美金的匯率是多少？

How much is the transaction fee?

手續費是多少呢？

I would like to change 2000 euros.

我想要換兩千歐元。

 Could I have some small change?

可以給我一些零錢嗎？

Words

claim [klem] *v.* 要求；認領；索取

carousel [‚kærʊˋzɛl] *n.* （機場的）旋轉式行李傳送帶

suitcase [ˋsutˌkes] *n.* 小型旅行箱；手提箱

exchange [ɪksˋtʃendʒ] *v.* 交換；調換；兌換

transaction [trænˋzækʃən] *n.* 交易

change [tʃendʒ] *n.* 零錢；找零

 旅遊主題式對話

海關詢問

C: What is the purpose of your trip?

海關人員：你這趟旅行的目的是什麼？

T: I am travelling with a tour group.

旅客：我是跟著旅行團來旅遊的。

C: Okay! Have a nice trip and enjoy your stay!

海關人員：好的！祝你旅行愉快，並玩的開心。

T: Thank you. I will!

旅客：謝謝你，我會的！

(C: Custom Officer; T: Tourist)

出關行李檢查

C: Please open your suitcase.

海關人員：請打開你的行李箱。

T: Okay, sir. I don't think there is anything I need to declare.

旅客：好的，先生。我想我沒有東西需要申報的。

C: I need to check if there are any prohibited items. If yes, I will have to confiscate them. Okay, you can leave now.

海關人員：我需要看看是不是有禁止攜帶的東西。如果有的話，我就需要沒收。好了，你可以離開了。

T: Thank you, sir.

旅客：謝謝你，先生。

(C: Custom Officer；T: Tourist)

領取行李

T: Excuse me. Where are the carts?

旅客: 不好意思，請問推車在哪裡呢？

G: They are over there. Did you see them?

地勤人員：在那裡啊，你看到了嗎？

T: Yes, I saw them. My bags are overweight, so it will be easier for me to use a cart. Thank you!

旅客: 嗯，我看到了。我的包包都太重了，如果用推車會比較方便。謝謝你！

(T: Tourist；G: Ground Staff)

📝 **Words**

purpose [`pɝ·pəs] n. 目的；意圖	confiscate [`kɑnfɪsˌket] v. 沒收；將……充公；
attend [ə`tɛnd] v. 出席；參加	cart [kɑrt] n. 小車；手推車
prohibit [prə`hɪbɪt] v. 禁止	overweight [`ovɚˌwet] adj. 超重的；過重的

行李遺失

T: I think my baggage is lost. The carousel stopped, but I did not see my baggage.

旅客: 我想我的行李不見了，行李轉盤已經停了，但是我沒有看到我的行李。

G: I am so sorry. Is this your final destination?

地勤人員：我感到很抱歉。這裡是你最終的目的地嗎？

T: No. I am transiting here, and my final destination is Boston.

旅客: 不是的，我在這裡轉機，然後最終目的地是波士頓。

G: Please fill out the form. As soon as we locate your baggage, we will arrange to deliver it to you. Also, we will compensate you for this mistake. Sorry for the inconvenience.

地勤人員：請填好這個表格。我們一旦找到了你的行李，我們會安排送到你那邊。還有，我們會針對這個錯誤賠償給你。不好意思造成你的不便。

(T: Tourist；G: Ground Staff)

機場交通

T: How do we get to the downtown?

旅客：我們要怎麼到市區呢？

L: Our bus will be outside waiting for us and take us downtown. I will tell you how to come back to the airport by public transportation, because you will stay here for one more day.

領隊：我們的巴士會在外面等著我們，然後帶我們去市區。我會再告訴你要怎麼乘坐大眾交通工具回到機場來，因為你會在這裡多停留一天。

T: How much is the fare by taxi?

旅客：坐計程車的話車資是多少呢？

L: It takes about 50 US dollars. If you have time, you can choose to get there by bus. It costs only 5 US dollars.

領隊：大概要五十美金。如果你有時間的話，你可以選擇坐公車，只需要五美金。

(T: Tourist；L: Tour Leader)

轉機誤點

G: This is an announcement from China Airlines. The flight is delayed because of the weather conditions in Hong Kong. We will arrange for our guests to take a rest in our transit hotel.

地勤人員：這是中華航空的廣播。我們的航班因為香港天氣的原因誤點了，我們會安排我們的貴賓到我們的過境旅館休息一下。

T: How do we get there?

旅客：我們怎麼去呢？

G: The shuttle bus will be here very soon.

地勤人員：接駁車很快就會到了。

(G: Ground Staff；T: Tourist)

Words

baggage [`bægɪdʒ] n. 行李	compensate [`kɑmpən͵set] v. 補償；賠償；酬報
fill out 填寫（表格、申請書等）	
arrange [ə`rendʒ] v. 安排；籌備	fare [`fɛr] n. 車資
deliver [dɪ`lɪvɚ] v. 投遞；傳送；運送	announcement [ə`naʊnsmənt] n. 宣告；宣布

Part 2 旅遊英語

Unit 03 入境會用到的英語

04 Unit

觀光會用到的英語

▶ 輕鬆學旅遊短句　　念過一次請你打「✓」

宗教景點

The mosque is magnificent. Many Muslims come to this town for this mosque.

這個清真寺很壯觀。許多的穆斯林為了這個清真寺來到這個城鎮。

It is one of the most popular pilgrimage destinations in Spain.

這是西班牙最受歡迎的朝聖景點之一。

The doors in the temple are decorated with fine carvings.

這個寺廟的門裝飾了精緻的雕刻。

When visiting a religious monument, please stay humble and respectful.

當拜訪宗教遺址的時候，請保持謙遜與莊重。

Please respect the code of conduct in any religious site.

請尊重任何宗教場所的規範。

博物館／美術館

This is one of the greatest contemporary art museums in Asia.

這是亞洲最棒的現代美術館之一。

What are the special exhibitions in this cultural center?

這個文化中心的特展是什麼呢？

In this neighborhood, you will see a lot of galleries.

在這附近，你會看到很多的畫廊。

Is there any admission fee?

這裡有入場費嗎？

Photography is not allowed in our museum.

我們的博物館禁止拍照。

Words

mosque [mɑsk] *n.* 清真寺；回教寺院	code of *conduct* 行為準則；規範
Muslim [`mʌzləm] *n.* 回教；伊斯蘭教徒	contemporary [kən`tɛmpə,rɛrɪ] *adj.* 當代的
pilgrimage [`pɪlgrəmɪdʒ] *n.* 朝聖；朝覲	gallery [`gælərɪ] *n.* 畫廊；美術館

自然風景

What is the most beautiful national park in your country?

你們國家最漂亮的國家公園是什麼？

The landscape of the national park is breathtaking.

這個國家公園的景色非常的迷人。

You don't need reservations to enter this national park, but you do have to make a reservation for its campgrounds.

你不需要預約進入這個國家公園，但是你需要預約露營的營地。

The fire can only be lit in designated areas in the national park.

在這個國家公園裡面，只有一些指定的地方才能夠點火。

The natural resources are abundant in this national park.

這個國家公園的天然資源很豐富。

娛樂

The street is filled with exotic restaurants and local shops. It is a famous tourist destination.

這條街道充滿了異國風味的餐廳與當地商店，是一個有名的旅遊景點。

Is there any amusement park for kids?

有給小朋友玩的遊樂園嗎？

Most people go to Macau for its casinos.

大部份的人去澳門是為了那裡的賭場。

You must go to see a show when visiting New York City.

當你去紐約市玩的時候，一定要去看一場表演。

The nightlife in Las Vegas is just amazing.

拉斯維加斯的夜生活是在太棒了。

 Words

campground [`kæmp͵graʊnd] *n.* 營地	amusement park 遊樂園
designate [`dɛzɪg͵net] *v.* 標出；表明；指定	casino [kə`sino] *n.* 賭場
exotic [ɛg`zɑtɪk] *adj.* 異國情調的	nightlife [`naɪtlaɪf] *n.* （都市）夜生活

 旅遊主題式對話

詢問一日行程 ......

C: Is there any one-day excursion package to places around Tokyo?

來電者: 有那種一天的旅遊套裝行程到東京附近的地方的嗎？

A: Yes. We have a lot of choices. If this is your first time to Tokyo, I would definitely suggest you the package to Mount Fuji.

旅行社人員：有的，我們有很多種選擇。如果這是你第一次來東京的話，我一定會建議你選擇到富士山的行程。

C: Sounds fun. Is the fare all-inclusive?

來電者: 聽起來挺有意思的。這個費用是全包的嗎？

A: Yes. The transportation cost, entrance fee, and one meal are all included in this fare. It is worth it.

旅行社人員：是的。交通費，入場費，還有一餐全部都包在這個費用了。這是很划算的。

(C: Caller；A: Travel Agent)

遊樂園 .....

G: We will go to Disneyland tomorrow.

導遊: 我們明天去迪士尼樂園。

T: Did we buy the two-day ticket?

旅客: 我們買的是兩天的套票嗎?

G: Yes! The ticket we bought is cheaper than the one sold in the ticket booth. Are you excited to go to the haunted house?

導遊: 對啊,我們買的票比在售票廳賣的還便宜。要去鬼屋了,你會感到興奮嗎?

T: Not at all. What I expect most about Disneyland is the parade and fireworks at night.

旅客: 一點也不。我去迪士尼樂園最期待的就是遊行跟晚上的煙火了。

(G: Tour Guide;T: Tourist)

夜生活 .....

G: We can all hang out together tonight. I know a few good bars in the city.

導遊: 我們今天晚上可以大夥一起玩,我知道這個城市一些不錯的酒吧。

T: That would be great. Shall we go to a lounge bar or a dancing club?

遊客: 太好了。我們要去喝酒聊天的酒吧還是舞廳呢?

G: We can go to a bar first and see if we want to go to a dancing club later.

導遊: 我們可以先去一個酒吧,然後到時候再看看我們要不要去舞廳。

(G: Tour Guide;T: Tourist)

🔍 Words

excursion [ɪkˋskɝˑʒən] n. 遠足;短途旅行

all-inclusive [ˋɔlɪnˋklusɪv] adj. 包括一切的

worth [wɝθ] adj. 有(…的)價值

booth [buθ] n. 亭;攤棚

parade [pəˋred] n. 遊行;行列

hang out (待在某處,或與某人待在一起)玩、閒晃、打發時間

表演活動

A: I want to go to see a musical.

A: 我想去看一齣音樂劇。

B: What is it?

B: 看什麼呢？

A: I haven't decided yet. I guess I will go to the ticket office around the hotel later and see what tickets are available.

A: 我還沒有決定。我想我等下會先去飯店附近的售票處看一下，然後看看還有什麼票。

B: You better hurry up before the tickets are sold out.

B: 你最好快一點，在票都賣完以前。

按摩SPA

T: Excuse me. What kind of spa treatment can I have in the villa?

旅客: 不好意思，請問我在度假別墅裡面可以做什麼樣的水療按摩的服務呢？

R: We have several packages that you can choose from depending on the massage time and the kind of essential oil you want to have.

接待人員：我們有幾個套裝可以讓你選擇的，根據你想要的按摩時間跟精油種類。

T: I prefer the scent of flowers, and I don't know how much time is suitable for me.

旅客: 我喜歡花香的味道，但我不知道我適合做多久的時間。

R: It's ok. I will have our therapist go to your villa to give you some advice.

接待人員：沒關係，我會讓我們的治療師到你的度假別墅裡面給你一些建議。

(T: Tourist ; R: Receptionist)

詢問景點

T: I happen to have this afternoon free. Could you give me some suggestion of what to do?

旅客: 我剛好這個下午有空。你可以給我點建議,關於可以做些什麼嗎?

V: What kind of activities do you like to do? We have outdoor, cultural, and recreational activities that you can participate in. Oh! Do you like to go to farmers'markets? There is one in the square today, and it's fun.

旅遊服務中心義工:你喜歡從事什麼樣的活動呢?我們有戶外的、文化的、還有休閒的活動你可以參加。哦!你喜歡去農夫市場嗎?今天在廣場有一個,很好玩的。

T: Sounds good. I will go to take a look. Thank you.

旅客: 好像不錯,我去看看好了。謝謝你。

(T: Tourist;V: Tourist information center volunteer)

Words

musical [`mjuzɪk!] *n.* 歌舞劇;音樂劇

sold out 售罄的;(門票等)全部預售完的

package [`pækɪdʒ] *n.* (有關聯的)一組事物,套裝

therapist [`θɛrəpɪst] *n.* 治療學家;特定療法技師(或專家)

happen to 碰巧;剛好

square [skwɛr] *n.* (方形)廣場

05 Unit 住宿會用到的英語

 輕鬆學旅遊短句　　念過一次請你打「√」

 訂房

Do you have any room available during the Chinese New Year?
你們在中國新年期間有任何的空房嗎？

I would like to book two non-smoking rooms with an ocean view.
我想要訂兩間有海景的禁煙房。

Is there any discount if we stay here for a week?
如果我們住在這裡一個禮拜的話，會有什麼折扣嗎？

We have several room types that you can choose from.
我們有幾種房型你可以選擇。

Our rooms are fully booked this weekend.
我們的房間在這個週末都被訂滿了。

登記入住

You can leave your luggage here and come back at 3 p.m. The room will be ready for you by then.
你可以把你的行李放在這裡，然後三點再回來。房間到那個時候就會為你準備好了。

I have made a reservation in your hotel. This is my confirmation letter.
我在你們的飯店做了預定，這是我的確認信。

Can we ask for an extra bed for our child?
我們可以加床給小孩嗎？

How would you like to pay for your room?

你想要怎麼付你的房費呢？

We have upgraded you to the deluxe room at no extra charge.

我們把你的房間免費升級為豪華客房了。

 Words

available [ə`veləb!] *adj.* 可用的；可得到的	leave [liv] *v.* 把……交給；委託
book [bʊk] *v.* 預訂；預約	confirmation [ˌkɑnfɚ`meʃən] *n.* 確定；確證
discount [`dɪskaʊnt] *n.* 折扣	deluxe [dɪ`lʌks] *adj.* 豪華的；高級的

詢問設施與服務

Could you tell me where the elevator is?

可以請你告訴我電梯在哪裡呢？

I will show you all the facilities we have, and they are all free of charge for our guests.

我會帶你看我們這裡的設施，它們都是免費讓我們的客戶使用的。

We have a vending machine on each floor, and you can buy water, soft drinks, beer, and snacks in the machine.

我們在每一層樓都有一個販賣機，你可以在機器裡買到水、汽水、啤酒、還有點心。

You may call room service and have them bring breakfast to your room.

你可以叫客房服務，讓他們把早餐送到你的房間。

I would like to ask for the laundry service.

我想要洗衣服務。

退房 .... 🛎

Our check out time is at 11 a.m.

我們的退房時間是早上的十一點。

Did you enjoy your stay in our hotel?

在我們酒店的住宿還可以嗎？

Please check your bill and put your signature here.

請確認你的賬單，並在這裡簽名。

If you check out later than the expected time, you may be asked for an extra charge.

如果你在預定的時間之後退房的話，你可以會被要求交額外的費用。

We will meet in the lobby at 9 a.m. tomorrow.

我們明天早上九點酒店在飯店大廳集合。

📝 Words

elevator [`ɛləˌvetə] n. 電梯	soft drink 汽水
facility [fə`sɪlətɪ] n. 設備，設施	laundry [`lɔndrɪ] n. 洗衣店，洗衣房
vending machine 自動販賣機	signature [`sɪgnətʃə] n. 簽名

 旅遊主題式對話

訂房 .... 🛎

G: I would like to reserve a room with a queen-size bed.

賓客：我想要預定一個大床的房間

R: I am sorry. We only have rooms with twin beds or a single king-sized bed.

飯店接待員：很抱歉，我們只有兩個單人床或者一個特大床的房間。

G: No problem. I will take the one with a king-size bed.

賓客：沒問題，我要那個特大床的房間。

R: Great. Please give me your name and contact information. I will book it for you.

飯店接待員：好的，請給我你的名字還有聯繫方式，我來幫你預定。

(G: Guest；R: Receptionist)

取消訂房 ......

T: I have a bad news. I will have to postpone my trip to Europe.

旅客：我有一個壞消息，我必須要延遲我的歐洲旅行了。

A: Whoops. We have arranged your travel accommodations!

旅行社人員：哎呀！我們已經幫你訂了住宿了啊！

T: This is what I am worrying about.

旅客：這正是我在擔心的。

A: I will check the cancellation policies and contact them as soon as possible.

旅行社人員：我看一下取消的規定，然後儘快跟他們聯絡。

(T: Tourist；A: Travel Agent)

詢問早餐 ......

C: The breakfast is included in your room rate. It will be served from 7 a.m. to 10 a.m. You can just go there and tell them your room number.

櫃台人員：早餐是包含在你的房費裡面的，供應時間從7點到10點，你可以直接過去那裡，然後告訴他們你的房號。

G: Awesome. Where is it served?

賓客：太棒了，在哪裡呢？

C: It is in the second floor. The waiter there will help you find a table.

櫃台人員：在二樓，那邊的服務生會幫你找到桌子。

(C: Front Desk Clerk；G: Guest)

Words

queen-size [`kwin͵saɪz] *adj.* （床、床單等）大號的	postpone [post`pon] *v.* 使延期；延遲
twin [twɪn] *adj.* 雙人的；成對的	accommodation [ə͵kɑmə`deʃən] *n.* 住宿
king-size [`kɪŋ͵saɪz] *adj.* （床、床單等）特大號的	rate [ret] *n.* 費用；價格

詢問房間用品

C: Hi, how may I help you?

櫃台人員：嗨，我可以幫你什麼嗎？

G: I am the guest in room 605, and I wonder if the shampoo is included in the room amenities. I don't see it in the room.

賓客: 我是605房間的客人，我在想洗髮精是不是附在房間裡面的呢？我在房間沒有看到。

C: I am so sorry. I will get some for you immediately.

櫃台人員：我真的很抱歉。我立刻幫你送過去。

G: Thank you. I will be waiting in the room.

賓客: 謝謝你。我會在房間裡面等的。

(C: Front Desk Clerk；G: Guest)

詢問設施與服務

A: I forgot to bring my laptop but I want to check in for my flight tomorrow on the Internet.

A: 我忘了帶我的筆電，但是我想要在網路上為我明天的飛機辦理登機。

B: Let me check the hotel facilities. Oh, they have business center on the ground floor. You should be able to access the computer and Internet there.

B: 讓我看看這個飯店的設施。哦，他們在一樓有商務中心，你應該能夠用一下那邊的電腦跟網路。

A: Is it free?

A: 那是免費的嗎？

B: I am not sure. Let's call the front desk and ask them.

B: 我不確定。我們打電話問問櫃台吧。

詢問飲用水

G: Excuse me. Is the tap water drinkable?

賓客：不好意思，自來水是可以喝的嗎？

C: No. It is not. There are two bottles of mineral water in the fridge. They are complimentary.

櫃台人員：不可以喝的。在冰箱裡面有兩瓶礦泉水，它們是贈送的。

G: Okay. Thanks!

賓客：好的，謝謝。

(G: Guest；C: Front Desk Clerk)

📝 Words

shampoo [ʃæm`pu] *n.* 洗髮精

amenity [ə`minətɪ] *n.* 便利設施；文化設施；福利設施

tap water 自來水（非蒸餾水）

mineral water 礦泉水

fridge [frɪdʒ] *n.* 冰箱

complimentary [ˌkɑmplə`mɛntərɪ] *adj.* 贈送的

餐廳會用到的英語

輕鬆學旅遊短句　　念過一次請你打「√」

找餐廳／訂位

Could you recommend some restaurants in this area?
你可以推薦一些在這個區域的餐廳嗎？

The restaurant is very popular, so you need to make a reservation.
這個餐廳非常受歡迎，所以你需要先做預約。

Can I reserve a table for two tonight?
我可以預定今晚一個兩人的桌子嗎？

What are the opening hours of the restaurant?
這個餐廳什麼時間開門呢？

Is there any dress code in this restaurant?
在這個餐廳有什麼服裝儀容的要求嗎？

餐廳帶位

We have made a reservation under the name of Frank.
我們用Frank的名字做了一個預訂。

How long do we have to wait?
我們要等多久呢？

Can we get a table by the window?
我們可以坐在窗戶旁邊嗎？

Do you mind sitting at the bar?

你介意坐在吧台嗎？

I would like to sit in the non-smoking area.

我想要坐在非吸煙區。

Words

Make a reservation 訂位，預訂	under the name of 用 ... 的名字；以 ... 的名義
A table for two 供兩人用的餐桌	mind [maɪnd] v. （用於否定句和疑問句中）介
opening hours 營業時間	意；反對
dress code 穿衣法則；著裝標準	

點菜

Do you have a Chinese menu?

你們有中文菜單嗎？

This is my first time here. Could you give me some suggestions?

這是我第一次來，你可以給我一些建議嗎？

Are you ready to order?

你準備好點餐了嗎？

What is the specialty in your restaurant?

你們餐廳的特色是什麼？

I am allergic to seafood.

我對海鮮過敏。

西式餐點點餐

What would you like to drink first?

你要先喝點什麼呢？

You can try our appetizers. They are very famous in this town.

你可以試試我們的開胃菜，它們在這個鎮是很有名的。

What kind of dressing would you like to have?

你想要什麼種類的沙拉醬呢？

 Do you want to order a side dish with your main course?

你要點個配菜搭配你的主食嗎？

Would you like to have some dessert?

你要來點甜點嗎？

 Words

specialty [`spɛʃəltɪ] n. 專業；專長	dressing [`drɛsɪŋ] n. （拌沙拉等用的）調料
allergic [ə`lɜdʒɪk] adj. 過敏的	side dish 小菜；配菜
appetizer [`æpə͵taɪzɚ] n. 開胃的食物；開胃 小吃	dessert [dɪ`zɜt] n. 甜點心；餐後甜點

旅遊主題式對話

找餐廳

A: Could you tell me where to find a vegetarian restaurant?

A: 你可以告訴我哪裡可以找到素食餐廳嗎？

B: There are a lot of great vegetarian restaurants in this neighborhood. Do you prefer western style or Chinese style?

B: 這個附近有很多很棒的素食餐廳。你喜歡西式的還是中式的？

A: I prefer Western style.

A: 我喜歡西式的。

B: OK. Give me your notebook, and I will draw the map and show you the one that I like a lot.

B: 好的，給我你的筆記本，我把我很喜歡的一家的地圖畫給你吧。

點酒

W: This is our drink menu. Can I bring you anything to drink?

服務生：這是我們的飲料單。我可以給你送點什麼喝的嗎？

C: Do you have wine?

顧客: 你們有葡萄酒嗎？

W: Sure! We have a variety of wine. If you are drinking alone, you may order our house wine. It is served by glass.

服務生：當然！我們有各種各樣的酒。如果你是一個人喝酒的話，你可以點我們的招牌酒，這是一杯一杯供應的。

C: Nice. I will start with a glass of red wine. Thank you.

顧客: 太好了。我先來一杯紅酒吧。謝謝。

(W: Waiter；C: Customer)

Waiter: What can I get for you?

服務生：你要點什麼呢？

C: Would you give me one more minute?

顧客: 可以給我再一點時間嗎？

Waiter: Absolutely. I will come back later.

服務生：當然沒問題！我等等再過來。

(W: Waiter；C: Customer)

Words

neighborhood [`nebɚ͵hʊd] n. 鄰近地區

draw [drɔ] v. 畫；繪製；描寫

wine [waɪn] n. 葡萄酒

a variety of 各種各樣的

house [haʊs] n. （用於餐飲場所的名稱）餐廳；餐館

absolutely [`æbsə͵lutlɪ] adv. 絕對地；完全地

牛排熟度 🛒

W: How would you like your steak? Rare, medium, medium-well, or well -done?

服務生：你想要牛排幾分熟呢？三分熟、五分熟、七分熟、還是全熟？

C: Medium, please.

顧客: 請給我五分熟。

W: No problem! What kind of sauce do you want to have? We have black pepper sauce and mushroom sauce.

服務生：沒問題！你想要哪一種醬汁呢？我們有黑胡椒醬跟蘑菇醬。

C: I will go with black pepper sauce. Thanks.

顧客: 我要配黑胡椒醬。謝謝。

(W: Waiter；C: Customer)

打包 🛒

C: The food in your restaurant is tasty, but the portion of the set meal is too large. I cannot finish it.

顧客: 你們餐廳的食物很好吃，但是套餐的份量太大了，我吃不完。

W: Do you want me to pack the leftovers for you? You can go back home and microwave them.

服務生: 你要我幫你打包嗎？你可以回家再微波加熱來吃。

C: That will be great. Please do it for me, except the salad. It is not very fresh.

顧客: 那就太棒了。請幫我打包，除了沙拉。沙拉不是很新鮮。

W: I am sorry. Let me tell my manager, and he will come to express our apology.

服務生：抱歉。讓我告訴我的經理，他會來跟你表示我們的歉意。

(C: Customer；W: Waiter)

結賬

C: The check, please.

顧客: 請給我賬單。

W: Yes, this is your bill.

服務生：好的，這是你的賬單。

C: I will pay by cash. Please give me the receipt. Thanks.

顧客: 我付現金，請給我收據，謝謝。

(C: Customer；W: Waiter)

Words

sauce [sɔs] n. 調味醬；醬汁	check [tʃɛk] n.（餐廳的）帳單
portion [`porʃən] n.（食物等的）一份；一客	bill [bɪl] n. 帳單
apology [ə`pɑlədʒɪ] n. 道歉；陪罪	receipt [rɪ`sit] n. 收據；收條

07
Unit

逛街購物會用到的英語

▶ 輕鬆學旅遊短句　念過一次請你打「√」

尋找商店

I am looking for a grocery store.
我在找雜貨店。

Is there any flea market in this city?
這個城市有跳蚤市場嗎？

Do they sell local crafts in this souvenir shop?
這個紀念品店有賣當地的手工藝品嗎？

The convenient store is located on the ground floor of the hotel.
便利商店就在飯店的一樓。

What is the town famous for?
這個城鎮有名的是什麼？

買食物

What is the expiration date of the milk?
牛奶的有效日期是哪一天？

Do you know how to use the self-checkout machine?
你知道怎麼用自助結賬機器嗎？

Where can I weigh the fruit?
我可以在哪裡秤水果呢？

Should we buy poultry or beef for our meal tonight?

我們今天的晚餐應該買家禽還是牛肉？

Can I get a plastic bag?

可以給我一個塑膠袋嗎？

Words

grocery store 雜貨店	self-checkout 自助收銀機；自助結帳系統
flea market 廉價市場；跳蚤市場	weigh [we] v. 秤……的重量
craft [kræft] n. 工藝，手藝	poultry [`poltrɪ] n. 家禽

買衣服

I want to buy men's suits.

我想要買男生的西裝。

The large size is out of stock. Do you want me to order it for you?

大號的缺貨了，你要我幫你訂貨嗎？

Do you have clothes that are made of cotton?

你們有棉質的衣服嗎？

I am looking for the fitting room.

我正在找試衣間。

Can I try it on?

我可以試穿嗎？

買女性珠寶／化妝品／用品

They sell fine jewelry in the boutique.

在這個精品店裡面有賣珠寶。

Can I try the perfume?

我可以試試這個香水嗎？

This is the tester. You can try it.

這是試用品，你可以試用看看。

Where can I buy sanitary napkins?

哪裏可以買到衛生棉呢？

I want to buy sunscreen and sunglasses.

我想要買防曬乳還有太陽眼鏡。

 Words

suit [sut] *n.* （一套）衣服	boutique [bu`tik] *n.* 精品店；流行女裝商店
out of stock 無庫存	sanitary napkin 衛生棉
fitting room 試衣間	sunscreen [`sʌn͵skrin] *n.* 防曬油；防曬乳

 旅遊主題式對話

殺價 🛒

C: How much is it?

顧客: 這個多少錢呢？

V: It is 80 US dollars.

小販：這個是80美金。

C: Isn't it too expensive? It is beyond my budget. Can I get some discount?

顧客: 這不會太貴嗎？超過我的預算了，可以給我打折嗎？

V: No. The price is fixed. You can go to see the items in that area. They are similar to this one, but the price is a lot cheaper.

小販：不行，這個價格是不二價的。你可以去那一區看看那些品項，它們都跟這個很像，但是價格要便宜很多。

(C: Customer；V: Vendor)

包裝 🛒

A: Where have you been?

A: 你去哪裡了呢？

B: I was in the shop. I bought a beautiful necklace for my mom as a souvenir.

B: 我在那個商店。我買了一條漂亮的項鍊給我媽媽，作為紀念品。

A: Sounds great. Did you ask them to wrap it as a gift?

A: 聽起來很棒，你有請他們包裝成禮物嗎？

B: Yes. I ask them to take the price tag off for me and wrap the necklace for me.

B: 有的，我請他們把價格標籤拿掉，並且把項鍊包好。

退稅

C: I would like to ask for the tax refund.

顧客: 我想要要求退稅。

S: No problem. This is the tax refund form. Please give me your passport and let me check if you are eligible for the refund.

銷售人員：沒問題。這是退稅的表格，請把你的護照給我，我來幫你看看你是不是符合退稅資格。

C: Here is my passport. Please show me how to fill out the form.

顧客: 這是我的護照，請教我怎麼填這個表格。

(C: Customer；S: Sales)

Words

budget [`bʌdʒɪt] n. 預算；預算費	refund [rɪ`fʌnd] n. 退還；歸還；償還
souvenir [`suvə͵nɪr] n. 紀念品；紀念物	eligible [`ɛlɪdʒəb!] adj. 有資格當選的；法律上
wrap [ræp] v. 包，裹	合格的
tag [tæg] n. 牌子；標籤；貨籤	

退貨 🛒

A: I want to return these shoes.

A: 我想要去退回這雙鞋子。

B: Why? What's wrong with them?

B: 為什麼呢？它們有什麼問題呢？

A: They are too small for me. I need to exchange for larger ones.

A: 它們對我來說太小了，我需要換成更大的。

B: Okay, I got it. Don't forget to bring the receipt with you!

B: 好的，我知道了。別忘了把收據帶在身上！

買皮件 🛒

A: I am looking for a shoulder bag.

A: 我正在找一個單肩背包包。

B: What kind of material would you like?

B: 你想要什麼材質的？

A: I like leather. However, it is always heavier than other materials.

A: 我喜歡皮革的，但是，它們總是比別的材質來的重。

B: Not necessarily. There are a lot of designer brands in the mall. Let's go there and take a look.

B: 不一定啦。在購物中心裡面有很多設計師品牌，我們去那裡看看吧。

買相機

S: What type of camera are you looking for? Any brand and any model number?

銷售人員：你在找什麼樣的相機呢？找什麼品牌跟型號嗎？

C: Not really. I am looking for a camera with larger pixels and lighter weight.

顧客: 也沒有。我在找一台畫素比較大、又比較輕的相機。

S: No problem. I will show you the ones that fit your need.

銷售人員：沒有問題，我把符合你的需求的那些拿給你看。

(S: Sales；C: Customer)

Words

exchange [ɪks`tʃendʒ] v. 交換；調換	necessarily [`nɛsəsɛrɪlɪ] adv. 必定；必然地
shoulder bag 有肩帶的女用手提包	pixel [`pɪksəl] 畫素；圖素
leather [`lɛðɚ] n. 皮革	fit [fɪt] v. 適合；符合

08 Unit

其他時候會用到的英語

輕鬆學旅遊短句　　念過一次請你打「√」

買藥

Where can I find a pharmacy?
我在哪裡可以找到藥局呢？

Can I buy drugs without a prescription?
我如果沒有處方箋的話可以買藥嗎？

The medicine has some side effects.
這種藥會有一些副作用。

I am looking for drugs to treat constipation.
我正在找可以治療便秘的藥。

How many pills can I take a day?
我一天可以吃多少顆呢？

看醫生

May I get a doctor who speaks Mandarin?
可以找一個說中文的醫生嗎？

I am having serious diarrhea.
我拉肚子很嚴重。

I have a fever. I might have got a cold.
我發燒了，可能感冒了。

I sprained my ankle.

我的腳踝扭傷了。

I am allergic to some drugs.

我對某些藥物過敏。

Words

pharmacy ['fɑrməsɪ] *n.* 藥局；藥房	diarrhea [ˌdaɪə'rɪə] *n.* 腹瀉
prescription [prɪ'skrɪpʃən] *n.* 處方；藥方	fever ['fivɚ] *n.* 發燒；發熱；熱度
side effect 副作用	sprain [spren] *v.* 扭傷

郵寄

Is there any post office nearby?

這附近有郵局嗎？

I want to send postcards back to my country.

我想要寄明信片回我的國家。

Where can I buy stamps?

我在哪裡可以買到郵票呢？

How much is the postage?

郵資是多少呢？

Can I send it by express mail?

我可以寄快捷郵件嗎？

交通／問路

Excuse me. Could you tell me how to go back to this hotel?

不好意思，你可以告訴我怎麼走回這個飯店嗎？

I am lost. Do you know how to get to the metro station?

我迷路了，你知道怎麼到這個地鐵站嗎？

Where can I get the bus route map?

我在哪裡可以買到公車路線圖呢？

If you will stay here for three more days, you should get the three-day pass.

如果你會在這裡多留三天的話，你應該要買三日通票。

I missed my station. Can I get off here?

我坐過站了，可以在這裡下車嗎？

Words

post office 郵局	postage [`postɪdʒ] n. 郵資；郵費
postcard [`post͵kɑrd] n. 郵政明信片	express [ɪk`sprɛs] adj. 快遞的；快運的
stamp [stæmp] n. 郵票	pass [pæs] n. 通行證；入場證

旅遊主題式對話

買網路卡

G: Do you know where can I buy a prepaid mobile phone card with Internet access?

賓客: 你知道我在哪裡可以買到能夠上網的手機電話預付卡嗎？

R: We sell it in our hotel. Do you want to buy an unlimited data plan?

飯店接待人員：我們飯店有賣。你要買無限制的數據方案嗎？

G: I don't know if I need it or not.

賓客： 我不知道我需不需要。

R: It depends on how long and how often you will need to use the Internet. If you use it a lot, it's definitely cheaper.

飯店接待人員：要看你需要用網路的時間有多長與多頻繁。如果你使用量很大，那當然會比較便宜。

(G: Guest；R: Hotel Receptionist)

東西遺失

A: My wallet was stolen.

A: 我的皮夾被偷了。

B: What? When did it happen?

B: 什麼？什麼時候發生的呢？

A: I don't know. I haven't realized it until we got back to the hotel.

A: 我不知道。我直到回到飯店才發現。

B: Let's go to the police station and report the theft.

B: 我們去警察局通報竊案吧。

買維他命

A: I am looking for a pharmacy.

A: 我在找藥局。

B: What do you want to buy?

B: 你想要買什麼呢？

A: My uncle asked me to buy some vitamins for him, but he did not tell me what kind of vitamins he needs. I will need advice from a pharmacist.

A: 我的叔叔叫我買一些維他命給他，但是他沒有告訴我他需要哪種維他命，我需要藥師來給我建議。

Words

prepaid [pri`ped] *adj.* 預先付的；已付的	vitamin [`vaɪtəmɪn] *n.* 維他命，維生素
steal [stil] *v.* 偷；竊取	advice [əd`vaɪs] *n.* 勸告；忠告
theft [θɛft] *n.* 偷竊；盜竊	pharmacist [`fɑrməsɪst] *n.* 藥劑師

掛號

T: I want to make an appointment.

旅客: 我想要預約。

N: Have you registered at our hospital before?

護士：你有在我們的醫院掛號過嗎？

T: No. I am a foreigner, and it is my first time to this country.

旅客: 沒有，我是外國人，這是我第一次來到這個國家。

N: OK. Please give me your information, and I will register it for you.

護士：好的，給我你的資料，我來幫你掛號。

(T: Tourist；N: Nurse)

發生意外

G: Where can I report an accident? My friend was hit by a car.

賓客: 我可以在哪裡通報意外呢？我的朋友被車撞了。

R: Please call 110 if there is any emergent accident. Do you need me to do it for you?

飯店接待人員：如果有緊急意外，請打110。你需要我幫你打嗎？

G: My friend is injured. Please send an ambulance here. It's an emergency.

賓客: 我的朋友受傷了，請叫救護車來這裡。這是緊急事件。

R: No problem. I will do it immediately.

飯店接待人員：沒有問題，我現在馬上處理。

(G: Guest；R: Hotel Receptionist)

A: I lost my passport. What should I do now?

A: 我的護照掉了，我現在應該怎麼做？

B: You should go to the embassy or the local representative office to report the loss.

B: 你應該去大使館或者當地代表處掛失。

A: Okay. I will do it as soon as possible.

A: 好的，我會儘快去做。

Words

accident [`æksədənt] n. 事故；災禍；意外

injure [`ɪndʒɚ] v. 傷害；損害；毀壞

ambulance [`æmbjələns] n. 救護車

emergency [ɪ`mɝdʒənsɪ] n. 緊急情況

embassy [`ɛmbəsɪ] n. 大使館

representative [rɛprɪ`zɛntətɪv] adj. 代表的；代理的

PART 3

近年試題練習

GO!

01 Unit 101 外語領隊英語考試—試題

101 專門職業及技術人員普通考試導遊人員、領隊人員考試試題
等別：普通考試
類科：外語領隊人員（英語）
科目：外國語（英語）
考試時間：1 小時 20 分
※注意：本試題為單一選擇題，請選出一個正確或最適當的答案，複選作答者，該題不予計分。

1. If the tapes do not meet your satisfaction, you can return them within thirty days for a full _____ .
   (A) fund   (B) refund   (C) funding   (D) fundraising

2. There was a slight departure delay at the airport due to _____ weather outside.
   (A) forbidden   (B) inclement   (C) declined   (D) mistaken

3. For safety reasons, radios, CD players, and mobile phones are banned on board, and they must remain _____ until the aircraft has landed.
   (A) switched on   (B) switch on   (C) switch off   (D) switched off

4. During take-off and landing, carry-on baggage must be placed in the overhead compartments or _____ the seat in front of you.
   (A) parallel   (B) down   (C) underneath   (D) lower

5. While many couples opt for a church wedding and wedding party, a Japanese groom and a Taiwanese bride _____ in a traditional Confucian wedding in Taipei.
   (A) tied the knot   (B) knocked off   (C) wore on   (D) stepped down

6. If the air conditioner should _____ , call this number immediately.
   (A) break up   (B) break down   (C) break into   (D) break through

7. _____ , the applicant was not considered for the job.

   (A) Due to his lack of experience   (B) Because his lack of experience

   (C) His lack of experience   (D) Due to his experience lack

8. The company _____ by a nationally-known research firm.

   (A) the surveyed market had   (B) had the surveyed market

   (C) had the market surveyed   (D) the market had surveyed

9. _____ the first computers, today's models are portable and multifunctional.

   (A) Alike   (B) Unlike   (C) Dislike   (D) Unlikely

10. The hotel _____ for the conference featured a nine-hole golf course.

    (A) that he selected   (B) that he selected it

    (C) that selected   (D) he selected it

11. Now you can purchase a seat and pick up your boarding pass at the airport on the day of departure _____ simply showing appropriate identification.

    (A) together   (B) for   (C) by   (D) with

12. The downtown bed-and-breakfast agency has _____ .

    (A) a two-night minimum reservation policy

    (B) a policy two-night minimum reservation

    (C) a reservation two-night policy minimum

    (D) a minimum policy two-night reservation

13. Finding an accountant _____ specialty and interests match your needs is critically important.

    (A) who   (B) which   (C) whose   (D) whom

14. Smokers who insist on lighting up in public places are damaging not only their own health but also that of _____ .

    (A) another   (B) each other   (C) one another   (D) others

15. The Internet is creating social isolation _____ people are spending more time on computers.

    (A) unless   (B) so that   (C) though   (D) as

16. _____ the offer is, the more pressure we will have to bear.

    (A) The greatest   (B) The greater   (C) More of   (D) Most of

17. Ecotourism is not only entertaining and exotic; it is also highly educational and

    _____ .

    (A) rewarded   (B) rewards   (C) reward   (D) rewarding

18. Readers _____ to the magazine pay less per issue than those buying it at a

    newsstand.

    (A) subscribe   (B) subscribing   (C) subscribed   (D) are subscribing

19. Passengers _____ to other airlines should report to the information desk

    on the second floor.

    (A) have transferred   (B) transfer   (C) are transferred   (D) transferring

20. _____ is first to arrive in the office is responsible for checking the voice

    mail.

    (A) The person   (B) Who   (C) Whoever   (D) Whom

21. Members of the design team were not surprised that Ms. Wang created the

    company logo _____ .

    (A) itself   (B) herself   (C) themselves   (D) himself

22. In the interests of safety, passengers should carry _____ dangerous items

    nor matches while on board.

    (A) either   (B) or   neither   (D) not

23. I am sure that if he _____ the flight to Paris, he would have arrived there

    by now.

    (A) makes   (B) made   (C) is making   (D) had made

24. "We are approaching some turbulence. For your safety, please keep your belts

    _____ until the 'seat belt'sign goes off.'"

    (A) fasten   (B) fastened   (C) fastening   (D) be fastened

25. Each country has its own regulations _____ fruit and vegetable imports.

    (A) pertaining   (B) edible   (C) allowable   (D) regarding

26. Those wishing to be considered for paid leave should put _____ requests

    in as soon as possible.

    (A) they   (B) them   (C) theirs   (D) their

27. The convenience store _____ owner just won the grand lottery will be

Super 英文領隊導遊

closed next month.

(A) which   (B) who   (C) whose   (D) that

28. The flight will make a _____ in Paris for two hours.

(A) stopover   (B) stepover   (C) flyover   (D) crossover

29. All of the students cried out excitedly _____ knowing that the midterm examination had been canceled.

(A) for example   (B) because   (C) as long as   (D) upon

30. If you carry keys, knives, aerosol cans, etc., in your pocket when you pass through the security at the airport, you may _____ the alarm, and then the airport personnel will come to search you.

(A) let on   (B) let off   (C) set on   (D) set off

31. My father always asks everyone in the car to _____ for safety, no matter how short the ride is.

(A) tight up   (B) fast up   (C) buckle up   (D) stay up

32. Client: What are this hotel's _____ ?

Agent: It includes a great restaurant, a fitness center, an outdoor pool, and much more, such as in-room Internet access, 24-hour room service, and trustworthy babysitting, etc.

(A) installations   (B) utilities   (C) amenities   (D) surroundings

33. Tourist: What is the baggage allowance?

Airline clerk: _____

(A) Please fill out this form.

(B) Sorry, cash is not suggested to be left in the baggage.

(C) It is very cheap.   (D) It is 20 kilograms per person.

34. The manager gave a copy of his _____ to his secretary and asked her to arrange some business meetings for him during his stay in Sydney.

(A) visa   (B) boarding pass   (C) itinerary   (D) journey

35. A tour guide is _____ informing tourists about the culture and the beautiful sites of a city or town.

(A) afraid of   (B) responsible for   (C) due to   (D) dependent on

36. A bus used for public transportation runs a set route; however, a _____ bus travels at the direction of the person or organization that hires it.

(A) catering   (B) chatter   (C) charter   (D) cutter

37. I was overjoyed to learn that I had accumulated enough _____ to upgrade myself from coach to business class.

(A) loyalty points   (B) credit cards   (C) grades   (D) degrees

38. Palm Beach is a coastline _____ where thousands of tourists from all over the world spend their summer vacation.

(A) airport   (B) resort   (C) pavement   (D) passage

39. Before you step out for a foreign trip, you should _____ about the accommodations, climate, and culture of the country you are visiting.

(A) insure   (B) require   (C) inquire   (D) adjust

40. Our flight _____ to Los Angeles due to the stormy weather in Long Beach.

(A) was landed   (B) had averted

(C) had been transformed   (D) was diverted

41. After disembarking the flight, I went directly to the _____ to pick up my bags and trunks.

(A) airport lounge   (B) cockpit   (C) runway   (D) baggage claim

42. Disobeying the airport security rules will _____ a civil penalty.

(A) result in   (B) make for   (C) take down   (D) bring on

43. I would like to express our gratitude to you _____ behalf of my company.

(A) at   (B) on   (C) by   (D) with

44. The security guards carefully patrol around the warehouse at _____ throughout the night.

(A) once   (B) odds   (C) intervals   (D) least

45. _____ the father came into the bedroom did the two little brothers stopped fighting.

(A) Only when   (B) Only if   (C) If only   (D) While

46. Working as a hotel _____ means that your focus is to ensure that the needs and requests of hotel guests are met, and that each guest has a memorable stay.

(A) commander　(B) celebrity　(C) concierge　(D) candidate

47. Mount Fuji is considered _____ ; therefore, many people pay special visits to it, wishing to bring good luck to themselves and their loved ones.

(A) horrifying　(B) scared　(C) sacred　(D) superficial

48. The non-smoking policy will apply to any person working for the company _____ of their status or position.

(A) regardless　(B) regarding　(C) in regard　(D) as regards

49. This puzzle is so _____ that no one can figure it out.

(A) furry　(B) fuzzy　(C) fury　(D) futile

50. If I had called to reserve a table at Royal House one week earlier, we _____ a gourmet reunion dinner last night.

(A) can have　(B) will have had　(C) would have had　(D) would have eating

51. _____ unemployed for almost one year, Henry has little chance of getting a job.

(A) Having been　(B) Be　(C) Maybe　(D) Since having

52. The school boys stopped _____ the stray dog when their teacher went up to them.

(A) bully　(B) bullied　(C) to be bullying　(D) bullying

53. The teacher had asked several students to clean up the classroom, but _____ of them did it.

(A) all　(B) both　(C) none　(D) either

54. Before the applicant left, the interviewer asked him for a current _____ number so that he could be reached if he was given the job.

(A) connection　(B) concert　(C) interview　(D) contact

55. If you have to extend your stay at the hotel room, you should inform the front desk at least one day _____ your original departure time.

(A) ahead to　(B) forward to　(C) prior to　(D) in front of

56. I will be very busy during this weekend, so please do not call me _____ it is urgent.

(A) except　(B) besides　(C) while　(D) unless

57. Prohibited items in carry-on bags will be confiscated at the checkpoints, and no _____ will be given for them.

(A) argument (B) recruitment (C) compensation (D) decision

58. All the employees have to use an electronic card to _____ in when they arrive for work.

(A) clock (B) access (C) enter (D) apply

59. I called to ask about the schedule of the buses _____ to Kaoshiung.

(A) leaving (B) heading (C) binding (D) taking

60. As for the delivery service of our hotel, FedEx and UPS can make _____ at the front desk Monday through Friday, excluding holidays.

(A) posts (B) pickups (C) picnics (D) practices

Many visitors to Italy avoid its famous cities, preferring instead the quiet countryside of Tuscany, located in the rural heart of the country. Like the rest of Italy, Tuscany has its share of art and architectures, 61 travelers are drawn more by its gentle hills, by its country estates, and by its hilltop villages. This is not an area to rush through but to enjoy slowly, like a glass of fine wine produced here. Many farmhouses offer simple yet comfortable 62. From such a base, the visitors can 63. the nearby towns and countryside, 64. up the sunshine, or just 65. in the company of a good book.

61. (A) if   (B) once   (C) but   (D) because
62. (A) accommodations   (B) replacements
    (C) customs   (D) privileges
63. (A) explain   (B) explore   (C) explode   (D) expose
64. (A) leap   (B) mount   (C) soak   (D) creep
65. (A) register   (B) relax   (C) reduce   (D) repeat

Vancouver Island is one of the most beautiful places in the world. It is situated off the west 66. of Canada, about one and a half hour by ferry from Vancouver on the mainland. Victoria, the capital city, 67. over one hundred and fifty years ago and is famous for its old colonial style buildings and beautiful harbor. It is the center of government for the province of British Columbia, so many of the people living there are __68.__ as public servants. The lifestyle is very relaxed, __69.__ to other cities in Canada, and this is __70.__ a lot of people to move there after they retire. The island is also popular with tourists because of the magnificent mountain scenery and the world-renowned Butchart Gardens.

66. (A) quarter   (B) position   (C) coast   (D) site

67. (A) was founded   (B) founded   (C) was founding   (D) found

68. (A) regarded   (B) employed   (C) included   (D) treated

69. (A) compared   (B) to compare   (C) comparing   (D) compare

70. (A) hindering   (B) demanding   (C) attracting   (D) prohibiting

      After 16 weeks of labor contract disputes, Wang Metals workers say they have had enough. At 10:30 this morning, hundreds of workers walked out of work and onto the picket line. Wang Metals has more than 800 workers, and the union says about 90 percent of them are participating in the strike. They plan to continue to picket factory office here in four-hour shifts. The union representative claims workers have taken these measures as a last resort. " We had met and decided to wait for the company to put a decent offer on the table, and when it finally did last night, it turned out to be unacceptable. So, we voted to strike." The representative said that union members will strike as long as necessary. Extra security has been ordered by the plant, and guards are blocking passage through the main entrance to the factory. Local business leaders are concerned because any kind of prolonged dispute could have a negative effect on other sectors of the community as well. "Wang Metals is the backbone of our local economy. Everything from food to entertainment, to houses…it all connects to the plant," says one business owner.

71. Which of the following is the best headline for this news report?

(A) Wang Plant Orders Extra Security

(B) 800 Workers Stage Walkout at Wang

(C) Wang Metals Loses Money During Strike

(D) Wang Workers Start Strike Today

72. What triggered the strike?

(A) The company being the backbone of the local economy.

(B) An offer by the company that the union found unacceptable.

(C) 90 percent of the workers picketing the factory offices.

(D) The company ordering extra security guards.

73. How long do the workers intend to strike?

(A) For four weeks.　　　　　　　(B) A number of weeks.

(C) Indefinitely.　　　　　　　　(D) Late into the night.

74. If some of the plant workers were to lose their jobs, what might be the effect on the community as a whole?

(A) Hardly any effect. Things would stay the same.

(B) There would be more houses available for other people to live in.

(C) The economy of the community would suffer.

(D) The economy of the community would prosper.

75. Who blocked the passage through the main entrance to the factory?

(A) Security guards.　　　　　　(B) Local business leaders.

(C) Union representatives.　　　　(D) Company officials.

　　Vacation rentals are fully private homes whose owners rent them out on a temporary basis to tourists as an alternative to hotels. They are available in all kinds of destinations, from a rustic cabin in the mountains to a downtown apartment in a major city. They can be townhouses, single-family-style homes, farms, beach houses, or even villas.

　　Vacation rentals are generally appealing for many reasons. They are, to name some on the top, cost-saving, spacious, great for large groups, separated from crowds, and no tips or service charges. Besides, they have kitchens for cooking, living rooms for gathering, outdoor spaces for parties or barbeques, and they offer the appeal of living like locals in a real community. They are usually equipped with facilities such as sports and beach accessories, games, books and DVD libraries, and in warmer locations, a swimming pool. Many vacation rentals are pet-friendly, so people can take their pets along with them when traveling.

　　Customers who choose hotels often enjoy the advantages of brand recognition, familiar reservation processes, and on-site service, while booking a vacation rental may mean stepping out of that comfort zone in order to get privacy, peace and quietness they offer -- things that are hard to obtain in a hotel room. For tourists, choosing a vacation rental over a hotel means more than short-term lodging -- vivid experiences and lifelong memories are what they value.

76. What is this reading mainly about?

(A) Planning leisure trips.

(B) The values of different vacation destinations.

(C) Alternative accommodations for tourists.

(D) Booking accommodations for fun trips.

77. What is the major concept of a vacation rental?

(A) Private houses rent out on weekdays only.

(B) Private homes rent out to tourists.

(C) Furnished homes for rent when owners are on vacations.

(D) Furnished rooms for short-term homestays.

78. Which of the following is NOT considered the reason that makes vacation rentals appealing?

(A) Familiar booking processes.

(B) Being economic.

(C) Being equipped with many useful facilities.

(D) Being pet-friendly.

79. What is the major advantage when tourists choose hotels rather than vacation rentals?

(A) Fame and wealth.   (B) Living like locals.

(C) Fair prices.   (D) On-site service.

80 Which of the following statements is a proper description of vacation rentals?

(A) They are shared by many owners.

(B) Tipping is not necessary at vacation rentals.

(C) They are built for business purpose.

(D) Daily cleaning is usually included in the rental contract.

1. **B**；中譯：假如你不滿意這卷錄音帶，你在三十天內退還可以享有完全的退費。

   解析：(A) fund 資金　(B) refund 退款　(C) funding 基金　(D) fundraising 基金籌措 meet one's satisfaction 滿足某人需求，購物時對物品不滿意返還店家，店家就會退費，退費為 refund，所以答案為 (B)。

2. **B**；中譯：由於外面惡劣天氣的緣故，在機場出發的時間有一些延誤。

   解析：(A) forbidden 禁止的　(B) inclement 惡劣的　(C) declined 被拒絕　(D) mistaken 錯誤的／空格中需用形容詞形容天氣。飛機會延誤常常是因為惡劣天氣的因素，所以選項中用 inclement（惡劣的）最恰當，故答案為 (B)。

3. **D**；中譯：基於安全的原因，在飛機上禁止使用 CD 播放器及行動電話，且它們需保持關機直到飛機落地。

   解析：(A) switched on 開機　(B) switch on 開機　(C) switch off 關機　(D) switched off 關機／on board（在飛機、船上），飛機上不可以使用 3C 產品，所以這些東西都要保持關機，也就是 remain switched off，需注意需用過去分詞 switched（當形容詞用），故答案為 (D)。

4. **C**；中譯：在飛機起飛及落地過程中，隨身行李必須放置在上方的置物櫃或你前面座位的下面。

   解析：(A) parallel 平行的　(B) down 下方　(C) underneath 在…下方　(D) lower 較低的 空格前是有一個介系詞片語 in the overhead compartments（在上方置物櫃），所以連接詞 or 後面也需用介系詞片語，選項中只 (C) underneath 是介系詞，且符合題意，表示在座位下方，故答案為 (C)。

5. **A**；中譯：當許多新人選擇教堂婚禮及辦婚禮派對時，一個日本新郎及台灣新娘在台北以傳統的儒家婚禮結婚。

   解析：(A) tied the knot 結婚　(B) knocked off 被擊倒　(C) wore on 穿上　(D) stepped down 步下／opt for sth（選擇某事）。空格內需用動詞或動詞片語，其中以 tied the knot 結婚最符合題意，故答案為 (A)。

6. **B**；中譯：假如空調故障，立即打這個電話。

   解析：(A) break up 拆開　(B) break down 故障　(C) break into 強行進入　(D) break through 突破／本題為假設語句，if +S+ should+V…表示說話者認為發生的可能性很低，空格中需用動詞原形，選項中以 break down（故障）最符合題意，故答

案為 (B)。

7. Ⓐ；中譯：由於缺乏經驗，這位應徵者沒有獲得這項工作。

解析：本題需用表原因的副詞子句或介系詞片語，來說明應徵者未獲錄取原因。(A) 正確，Due to+受詞，表由於…原因 (B) 錯誤，because 需接子句 (C) 錯誤，無介系詞引導 (D) 錯誤，介系詞片語後面有動詞 lack。故答案為 (A)。

8. Ⓒ；中譯：這家公司有經國際聞名的研究公司調查過市場。

解析：本題考關係詞的省略，原句可改寫為 The company had the market (which was) surveyed by a nationally-known research firm，故答案為 (C)。

9. Ⓑ；中譯：不同於最初的電腦，現代的機型都是可攜式且多功能的。

解析：(A) Alike 一樣 adv；adj　(B) Unlike 不像 prep.　(C) Dislike 不喜歡 v.　(D) Unlikely 未必的 adj.；adv. 空格中需用介系詞引導介系詞片語，當副詞修飾全句，選項中只有 Unlike（不像）為介系詞，且符合題意，故答案為 (B)。

10. Ⓐ；中譯：他選擇召開研討會的這家飯店以設有九個洞的高爾夫球場為其特色。

解析：關係詞代名詞 that 在句中即為動詞 select 的受詞，所以不需再有 it 出現，故答案為(A)。

11. Ⓒ；中譯：現在，你只要簡單出示適當的身分證明文件就可以在出發的那天到機場買個座位並且拿到你的登機證。

解析：空格中用表示用什麼方式的介系詞，其中以 by 最恰當，表示以出示身分證明文件方式，故答案為 (C)。

12. Ⓐ；中譯：市中心附贈早餐的住宿機構有最少二個晚上前先預約的要求。

解析：bed-and-breakfast 為一種住宿並提供早餐的機構，提前二晚預訂的講法選項中以 two-night minimum reservation policy 最恰當，故答案為 (A)。

13. Ⓒ；中譯：要找一個專長與利益符合你需求的會計是非常地重要的。

解析：本題考關係代名詞的運用，先行詞是 accountant ，在關係子句中需用所有格，表示他的專長及利益，所以要用 whose，故答案為 (C)。

14. Ⓓ；中譯：那些堅持在公共場所吸菸者不僅為害他們自己的健康，也同時為害別人的健康。

解析：lighting up 點燃、照明，在此作吸菸的意思，not only…but also（不僅…而且）。that 在句中代表 health，不定代名詞 others 表示是剩餘的全部（複數），所以空格中意思為別人的健康應用 that of others，答案為 (D)。

15. Ⓓ；中譯：網路正造成社會隔離，因為人們花愈來愈多時間在電腦上面。

解析：空格後面是一個表示原因的副詞子句，所以空格需填入表原因連接詞，選項中以 as（因為）最恰當，答案為 (D)。

16. Ⓑ；中譯：我們投資的愈多，我們所承受的壓力就愈大。

解析：本題是考比較級，the+ 形容詞比較級 +(be)，the+ 形容詞比較級 +…表示愈是…，就會愈…之意，故空格內用 greater，故答案為 (B)。

17. (D)；中譯：生態之旅不僅好玩且吸引人，它同時也是非常有教育及回饋意義的。

解析：空格前是對等連接詞 and，所以空格內需用形容詞作為主詞補語，選項中都是動詞 reward（報答）的變化型式，因該處 it 是指 Ecotourism（生態之旅，表示事務），形容事物的補語分詞要用現在分詞，故答案為 (D)。

18. (B)；中譯：訂閱雜誌的讀者每期付出的錢少於那些在書報攤買雜誌的人付的錢。

解析：subscribe（訂閱），本題考分詞用法，現在分詞可當形容詞用修飾名詞，表示主動之意，所以空格處用 subscribing，修飾前面 reader，表示雜誌訂閱者，故答案為 (B)。

19. (D)；中譯：轉機到其他航空公司的旅客應到二樓的服務台報到。

解析：本題考分詞用法，現在分詞可當形容詞用修飾名詞，表示主動之意，所以空格處用 transferring，故答案為 (D)。

20. (C)；中譯：最先抵達辦公室的人要負責查看電話語音留言。

解析：第二個動詞 is 前面的名詞子句為本句主詞，空格置於句首無先行詞，所以要用複合關係代名詞 Whoever，故答案為 (C)。

21. (B)；中譯：設計團隊的成員都不會驚訝王小姐自己設計公司的識別標誌。

解析：本題空格處要用反身代名詞，表示設計的人就是主詞（Ms. Wang）自己本身，所以用 herself，故答案為 (B)。

22. (C)；中譯：基於安全考量，乘客在機上既不能攜帶危險物品也不能帶火柴。

解析：neither…nor 既不能…也不能，故空格需填入 neither，答案為 (C)。

23. (D)；中譯：我相信假如這班機是飛往巴黎，他現在將已經抵達這裏了。

解析：本題考假設語句，由題意研判這架飛機當時並未飛往巴黎，所以為與過去事實相反的假設，句型為 if +S+ 過去完成式，S+would+ 現在完成式，所以空格需用過去完成式，故答案為 (D)。

24. (B)；中譯：「我們正要接近些許亂流，為了您的安全，請繫緊安全帶直到『繫緊安全帶』燈熄滅為止。」

解析：空格內需用形容詞，做為受詞補語 belt 的補語，因為安全帶是被繫緊的，故用過去分詞 fastened，答案為 (B)。

25. (D)；中譯：每個國家有關於各國的水果與蔬菜輸入的規定。

解析：(A) pertaining 附屬的 adj.　(B) edible 可食用的 adj.　(C) allowable 允許的 adj.　(D) regarding 關於 prep./空格前為名詞 regulations（規定），故空格內需用介系詞引導的片語修飾前面的名詞，選項中以 regarding（關於）最符合題意，答案為 (D)。

26. (D)；中譯：那些需要獲得帶薪休假的人應該儘快提出申請。

解析：paid leave（帶薪休假），空格應該填入代表複數的所有格，故應用 their，答案為 (D)。

27. (C)；中譯：這間老闆剛剛贏得大樂透的便利商店下個月將要關閉。

解析：本題考關係代名詞，先行詞是 store，關係子句的主詞 the owener，空格要用所有格，表示是這家店的老闆，故用 whose，答案為 (C)。

28. **A**；中譯：這班機將中途停留巴黎二個小時。

解析：(A) stopover 中途下車　(B) stepover 足球術語　(C) flyover 飛越 n.　(D) crossover 轉變／make a stopover 就是中途停留某站（地點）之意，故答案為 (A)。

29. **D**；中譯：在得知期中考已經取消後，所有的學生興奮地尖叫。

解析：空格後面是動名詞 knowing（後面接名詞子句為受詞），所以空格需用介系詞，選項中只有 upon 為介系詞，且符合題意，故答案為 (D)。

30. **D**；中譯：假如你隨身包中攜帶鑰匙、小刀、噴霧罐等，當經過機場的安全檢查門時可能會觸動警鈴，而這時機場人員會前來盤查你。

解析：(A) let on 洩漏　(B) let off 流失　(C) set on 決定　(D) set off 引起
set off the alarm 意思就是引起警報，故答案為 (D)。

31. **C**；中譯：我父親總是要求在車內的人都要繫上安全帶以策安全，不管路程有麼多短。

解析：buckle up 為繫上安全帶，故答案為 (C)。

32. **C**；中譯：顧客：飯店的便利設施有哪些？代辦處：這個飯店有一個很棒的餐廳、一座健身中心、一座室外游泳池，另外還有許多，例如室內可上網、24 小時房間服務、以及可靠的托育服務等。

解析：(A) installations 設置　(B) utilities 公共事業　(C) amenities 便利設施　(D) surroundings 周圍環境 n.／代理商所說的應是指飯店的各種便利設施，故應用 amenities，故答案為 (C)。

33. **D**；中譯：觀光客：行李限重是多少？

解析：航空公司櫃員：(A) 請填這張表格　(B) 抱歉，零錢不能放在行李裏面　(C) 它非常便宜　(D) 每人 20 公斤／ baggage allowance 就是指行李限重的重量，所以選項中以 (D) 最適合題意。

34. **C**；中譯：這位經理給了一份行程表給他的秘書，並要求他在停留雪梨期間幫他安排一些商務拜會。

解析：(A) visa 簽證　(B) boarding pass 登機證　(C) itinerary 行程表　(D) journey 旅程
秘書要安排行程是要依據行程表（itinerary），故答案為 (C)。

35. **B**；中譯：導遊要負責告知觀光客一個城市或小鎮的歷史及漂亮的景點。

解析：(A) afraid of 擔心　(B) responsible for 負責　(C) due to 由於　(D) dependent on 依靠／導遊的責任就是告知旅客相關訊息，所以用 be responsible for（對…負責），故答案為 (B)。

36. **C**；中譯：公共運輸用的巴士繞行固定的路線，然而租賃巴士行走的路線則是依僱用他的個人或機構指定的方向。

解析：(A) catering 迎合　(B) chatter 碎碎念　(C) charter 租賃　(D) cutter 裁衣人／a set route 固定的路線，charter bus 就是租賃的巴士，故答案為 (C)。

37. **A**；中譯：我得知我已經累積足夠的信用卡點數來讓我可以從經濟艙升等頭等艙後，我欣喜若狂。

    解析：依據題意，空格是要填入信用卡點數之意，要用 loyalty points，答案為 (A)。

38. **B**；中譯：棕梠灘是全球數以千計的觀光客前來渡暑假的一個海岸勝地。

    解析：(A) airport 機場　(B) resort 勝地　(C) pavement 鋪過的路面　(D) passage 通行
    由題意知，空格應為渡假勝地之意，故答案為 (B)。

39. **C**；中譯：在你動身前往國外旅行前，你必須先要打聽你所要造訪的國家的居住環境、氣候及文化等。

    解析：(A) insure 保險 (B) require 要求　(C) inquire 打聽　(D) adjust 調整／空格需填入
    動詞，依題意要先瞭解你要造訪國家的一些事物，所以選項中以 inquire（打聽）
    最為符合題意，故答案為 (C)。

40. **D**；中譯：因為長灘地區的惡劣天氣，我們的航班轉降到洛杉磯。

    解析：空格需用適當的動詞時態，因發生時間在過去且已完成，並考量班機是被迫轉降
    （divert），所以用過去被動式，故答案為 (D)。

41. **D**；中譯：在下機後，我直接到行李提領處提取我的袋子及行李箱。

    解析：(A) airport lounge 機場候機室　(B) cockpit 駕駛艙　(C) runway 跑道　(D)
    baggage claim 行李提領處／提取行李要到 baggage claim，故答案為 (D)。

42. **A**；中譯：不遵守機場的安全規定將會被處以民事罰款。

    解析：(A) result in 導致　(B) make for 向…走　(C) take down 取下　(D) bring on 引起
    Disobey（不遵守），依題意為不守規定就會導致被罰款，所以空格中動詞用
    result in（導致），故答案為 (A)。

43. **B**；中譯：我想要代表我們公司向您表達感謝之意。

    解析：express our gratitude（表達我們感謝），on behalf of 即為代表某人或某事物之
    意，故答案為 (B)。

44. **C**；中譯：安全警衛們整晚每隔一段時間小心地在倉庫周遭巡邏。

    解析：at intervals 指每隔一段時間，所以答案為 (C)。

45. **A**；中譯：只有當父親進入房間時兩兄弟才會停止爭吵。

    解析：本題考倒裝句型，當 only 出現於句首時需用倒裝句，所以空格內需用 Only
    when，表示只有當…時候，所以答案為 (A)。

46. **C**；中譯：作為一個飯店的接待人員，表示你必須專注於確保飯店客人的需求都能被滿
    足，且讓每個客人都有難忘的住宿經驗。

    解析：(A) commander 指揮官　(B) celebrity 知名人士　(C) concierge 接待員　(D)
    candidate 候選人／Working as 做為（某工作職位），題意是指飯店內的某個職
    務的工作就是要滿足客人需求等，選項中以 concierge（接待員）最恰當，故答案
    為 (C)。

47. C；中譯：富士山被認為是神聖的，因此許多人特地造訪它，希望帶給他們及他們所愛的人好運。

解析：(A) horrifying 毛骨悚然的　(B) scared 受驚嚇的　(C) sacred 神聖的　(D) superficial 膚淺的／由題意知富士山應該是指神聖的（後面提到希望帶來好運），故答案為 (C)。

48. A；中譯：禁煙政策將實施於公司的任何人，不論其身分及地位。

解析：regardless of sth 是指不管、不論何事，所以答案為 (A)。

49. B；中譯：這謎題是如此模稜兩可以致於沒有人能猜出來。

解析：(A) furry 毛皮的 adj.　(B) fuzzy 模糊的 adj.　(C) fury 憤怒 n.　(D) futile 無用的 adj.／figure it out（解決，猜出來），so+adj+that+子句（如此…以致於），依題意，謎題的性質應該是用模糊的 fuzzy，故答案為 (B)。

50. C；中譯：假如我有再早一個星期打電話到皇家酒樓訂桌，我們昨晚就會吃到團圓大餐了。

解析：本題考為假設句，由 if 子句用過去完成式，可推測是與過去事實相反的假設，主要子句要用 would+ 現在完成式，故答案為 (C)。

51. A；中譯：失業將近一年以後，亨利很難再找到工作。

解析：本題為分詞構句，空格內需填入完成式（表示已經一段時間）的現在分詞構句，當作表示原因的副詞結構來修飾主要子句，故用 Having been unemployed…，故答案為 (A)。

52. D；中譯：當他們的老師往他們走過去的時候，那些男學童停止霸凌這隻流浪狗。

解析：go up to（走過去），stop+Ving 表示停下某件正在做的事，stop+to+V 表示停下來去做某件事，依本題意思應該是停止霸凌狗，要用 stop bullying，故答案為 (D)。

53. C；中譯：這位老師已經要求幾個學生清掃教室了，但他們都沒有做。

解析：沒有一個人有做要用 none of them did it，故答案為 (C)。

54. D；中譯：在應徵者離開以前，面試者問了他目前的連絡電話，以便假如他可以獲得這份工作時可以連絡上他。

解析：asked him for sth（問他某件事），contact number 是指連絡電話，所以答案為 (D)。

55. C；中譯：假如你要延長你在飯店停留時間，你必須至少在你原預定離開前一天通知櫃台。

解析：(A) ahead to 到前面去　(B) forward to 向前　(C) prior to 在…之前　(D) in front of 在前面／在某時間之前要用 prior to+時間，故答案為 (C)。

56. D；中譯：在這週末期間我都會很忙，所以除非緊急的事否則不要打電話找我。

解析：urgent（緊急的，急迫的），空格內需填入連接詞引導副詞子句，依據題意用 unless（除非…）最符合，故答案為 (D)。

57. C；中譯：在隨身袋子中的違禁品在檢查處將會被沒收，並且這些將不會獲得賠償。

解析：(A) argument 爭論　(B) recruitment 募兵　(C) compensation 賠償　(D) decision 決定／Prohibited items（違禁品），confiscate（沒收），違禁品沒收就表示沒有賠償，故答案為 (C)。

58. A；中譯：所有員工當他們到班時必須使用電子卡片打卡。

解析：上班打卡為 clock in/on，故答案為 (A)。

59. B；中譯：我打電話去問開往高雄的巴士時刻表。

解析：schedule（時刻表），開往某地用 heading to，故答案為 (B)。注意：leaving for 是指動身前往。

60. B；中譯：至於我們飯店的遞送服務，FedEx 跟 UPS 從星期一到星期五，例假日除外，會在我們的櫃台收件。

解析：as for（說到、至於），收件為 make pickups，故答案為 (B)。

61-65；中譯：許多來到義大利的遊客會避免到一些有名的城市，而寧願到安靜的鄉下地方托斯卡尼，它位於義大利的鄉下核心。如同義大利其他地方一樣，托斯卡尼擁有它獨有的藝術與建築，但是遊客更被當地柔和的山丘、鄉村莊園以及山頂村落所吸引。這不是一個走馬看花的區域而是應該慢慢欣賞，就像一杯這裏釀造的葡萄酒一樣。許多農莊都有提供簡單但舒適的住所。以此為基地，觀光客們可以探索附近的城鎮以及鄉村，沉浸在陽光中，或只是以一本好書放鬆。

61. C；

解析：空格前提到這地方有與義大利其他地方相同處，後面提到更有不同之處吸引觀光客，表示語氣的轉折及加強，所以用對等連接詞 but，答案為 (C)。

62. A；(A) accommodations 住宿　(B) replacements 替代　(C) customs 風俗　(D) privileges 特權

解析：空格有形容詞 simple yet comfortable（簡單但舒適的）來形容空格內的名詞，再考量本句提到農莊可提供的，所以選項中以 accommodations（住宿）最符合，故答案為 (A)。

63. B；(A) explain 解釋　(B) explore 探索　(C) explode 爆破　(D) expose 使曝露

解析：空格中需填入動詞原形，由後面受詞是村莊及城鎮，所以動詞用 explore（探索）最適合，表示旅客可以探索附近的村莊及城鎮，故答案為 (B)。

64. C；(A) leap 跳躍　(B) mount 登上　(C) soak 浸泡　(D) creep 爬行

解析：空格中需填入動詞原形，配合後面介系詞 up，用 soak up（沉浸在）表示沉浸在陽光中，故答案為 (C)。

65. B；(A) register 登記　(B) relax 放鬆　(C) reduce 減少　(D) repeat 重複

解析：空格中需填入動詞原形，由空格後面提到用一本好書來陪伴，所以選項中以 relax（放鬆）最適合，表示用讀好書來放鬆自己，故答案為 (B)。

66-70 ；中譯：溫哥華島是世界最漂亮的地方之一，它位處加拿大西岸外海，大約距離大陸城市溫哥華市一個半小時的渡輪時間。維多利亞市，首都，建於 150 多年前，並以殖民時期的古建築物及美麗的海港著稱。它是不列巔哥倫比亞省政府的中心所在，所以許多生活在這裏的民眾都是受雇的公務員。比起其它加拿大的城市，這邊的生活步調是非常令人舒適的，且這一直吸引很多人在退休後搬到這邊來。這個島也因擁有壯麗的山景及世界聞名的布查花園而廣受觀光客喜愛。

66. **C**；(A) quarter 四分之一　(B) position 位置　(C) coast 海岸　(D) site 現場

解析：由後面提到需要由溫哥華搭船一個半小時航程，所以溫哥華島應該是位於海岸外，選項中應用表 coast（海岸），也就是表示加拿大的西部海岸外，故答案為 (C)。

67. **A**；

解析：空格需用動詞，且主詞是指城市，城市是需要被創立的，要用被動式，故用 was founded，故答案為 (A)。

68. **B**；(A) regarded 關心　(B) employed 雇用　(C) included 包括　(D) treated 對待

解析：空格前有 be 動詞，後面提到公務員，公務員是被雇用的，所以需用被動式 be employed，故答案為 (B)。

69. **A**；

解析：空格中需用分詞形成分詞構句，說明主要子句，且比較是要用被動的，所以用過去分詞 compared，故答案為 (A)。

70. **C**；(A) hindering 妨礙　(B) demanding 要求　(C) attracting 吸引　(D) prohibiting 禁止

解析：空格中需填入動詞現在分詞，形成現在進行式，表示一直持續發生的事。由後面提到許多人退休後搬到這地方，所以選項中以 attracting（吸引）最適合，故答案為 (C)。

71-75 ；中譯：在經過 16 週的勞動合約爭議後，王氏金屬的工人們說他們已經受夠了。今天上午 10:30，數以百計的工人放下工作上街示威。王氏金屬有超過 800 名工人，工會說大約百分之九十的員工參加這場罷工。他們計畫繼續以每四小時一輪的方式包圍工廠辦公室。工會代表聲稱工人們已將這些方法做為最後的手段了。「我們已經開過會並且等待公司能給個合理待遇拿到談判桌上，但當昨晚公司提出後，那結果我們不能接受，所以我們投票決定罷工」。工會代表說只要有必要，工會成員就會罷工。工廠已經增援安全人員，且警衛封鎖從正大門進入工廠的通道。當地的企業領導人們也表達關心，因為任何形式的長時間動亂也可能對社會的其他方面造成負面的影響。一位企業主說：「王氏金屬是我們這個區域經濟的骨幹，從餐飲到娛樂到住屋…等每件事都與工廠有關聯。」

71. **D**；中譯：下列何者是這篇新聞報導的最佳標題？　(A) 王氏金屬雇請更多警衛　(B) 800 個員工策劃在王氏金屬罷工　(C) 王氏金屬在罷工中蒙受損失　(D) 今天王氏金屬員工開始罷工

解析：本篇報導一開始就指出今天上午數以百計的工人放下工作走上示威罷工，再來說明罷工的原因是因為待遇的談判已經破裂，最後是當地企業對該公司罷工對當地經濟影響的憂慮，所以報導主要是說明從今天開始的罷工示威相關事情，故答案為 (D)。

72. **B**；中譯：甚麼原因引發這場罷工？(A) 這家公司是當地經濟的骨幹　(B) 公司提出工會認為無法接受的提議　(C) 90%的員工包圍工廠辦公室　(D) 工廠雇用額外的安全警衛

　　解析：由 We had met and decided to wait for the company to put a decent offer on the table, and when it finally did last night, it turned out to be unacceptable. So, we voted to strike…，知是因為公司沒有提出一個讓工會可以接受的合理待遇才會引發罷工，所以答案為 (B)。

73. **C**；中譯：員工打算罷工多久？(A) 四個禮拜　(B) 數個禮拜　(C) 無限期　(D) 入夜以後

　　解析：(A) 由 The representative said that union members will strike as long as necessary…，知罷工的期限沒有設定，只要有必要就持續下去，所以答案為 (C)。

74. **C**；中譯：假如有些這家工廠的員工失去工作，整體來說會對這社區造成什麼影響？
(A) 幾乎沒有影響，所有事情都會一如往常　(B) 那裏將會有更多的房子讓其他人可以住　(C) 社區的經濟將會受傷害　(D) 社區的經濟將會繁榮

　　解析：由 Local business leaders are concerned because any kind of prolonged dispute could have a negative effect on other sectors of the community as well.，可知動亂可能對社會的其他方面造成負面的影響，也就是使社區的經濟受到傷害，所以答案為 (C)。

75. **A**；中譯：誰封鎖從正大門進入工廠的通道？　(A) 警衛　(B) 當地企業負責人　(C) 工會代表　(D) 公司官員

　　解析：由…guards are blocking passage through the main entrance to the factory.知是警衛負責封鎖的，答案為(A)。

76-80；中譯：假日租賃屋是完全私有的房子，而屋主將房子以暫時的方式出租給觀光客做為旅館的替代品。在各種地點都可以看得到，從山中的樸素小屋到主要城市的市中心公寓都有。它們可能是透天厝、獨棟家庭房、農場、海邊小屋或甚至別墅都有。

假日租賃屋通常訴求有許多理由，最常見的理由是省錢、空間大、可以供大團體、可避開人群、且不需小費或服務費用。除此之外，它有廚房可以烹煮，有客廳可聚會，有戶外空間可烤肉或開派對，並且訴求生活就像當地人在真實的社區一樣。它們通常配備有一些設施，像是運動與海灘相關用品、遊戲、書籍與 DVD 收藏，並且在較為溫暖的地方會有游泳池。許多假日租賃屋都是可以帶寵物的，所以人們在旅行中就可以帶寵物同行。

會選擇飯店的顧客通常是喜歡品牌認知、熟悉的訂房程序及提供網上服務等等優點，然而預定一間假日租賃屋意味著要跳脫那個舒適的方式，來獲得日租賃屋所提供的隱私、安靜與安詳，而這是飯店房間所難以提供的。對遊客來說，選擇一間日租賃屋而不是飯店代表著不只是短期居住——鮮明的經驗及一生的回憶會是他們想要的。

76. **C**；中譯：這篇主要講的是甚麼？　(A) 規劃休閒行程　(B) 不同度假地點的價值觀　(C)

觀光客住宿的不同選擇　(D) 歡樂旅行的住宿預訂

解析：由一開始就提到假日租賃屋是出租給觀光客做為旅館的替代品，再提到假日租賃的優點及與一般飯店所能提供不一樣之處，所以重點主要是談觀光客住宿可以有不同選擇，答案為 (C)。

77. B；中譯：假日租賃屋的主要概念是甚麼？ (A) 私人的房子只在平日出租　(B) 私人的房子出租給觀光客　(C) 當屋主外出度假時將附有家具的房子出租　(D) 將附有家具的房間出租給短期居住的人。

解析：由…owners rent them out on a temporary basis to tourists as an alternative to hotels…，所以假日租賃屋是屋主將房子以暫時的方式出租給觀光客，答案為 (B)。

78. A；中譯：下列何者不被認為假日租賃屋訴求的理由？ (A) 熟悉的預訂方式　(B) 省錢　(C) 有很多實用的設施　(D) 可以帶寵物

解析：(A) 由 Customers who choose hotels …, familiar reservation processes，…，知熟悉的預訂方式為選擇訂傳統飯店的理由，非假日租賃屋的訴求　(B) 由 They are, to name some on the top, cost-saving,…，知省錢為訴求之一　(C) 由 Besides, they have kitchens for cooking, living rooms for gathering…，知很多實用的設施為訴求　(D) 由 Many vacation rentals are pet-friendly…，知可以帶寵物為訴求之一。故答案為 (A)。

79. D；中譯：何者是觀光客不選擇假日租賃屋而選擇飯店的主要優點？(A) 名聲與財富　(B) 生活像當地人　(C) 平實的價格　(D) 有網站服務

解析：由 Customers who choose hotels often enjoy the advantages of brand recognition, familiar reservation processes, and on-site service, while booking a vacation rental may mean stepping out of that comfort zone…，知觀光客選擇飯店有許多優點，但一想到要訂假日租賃屋就不是那麼容易，也就暗示它是無法上網預訂的，所以答案為 (D)。

80. B；中譯：下列何項有關假日租賃屋的敘述是適當的？　(A) 它們是由許多人所共有的　(B) 假日租賃屋是不需要給小費的　(C) 它們是為了商業目的而建的　(D) 日常清潔通常包含在租賃契約中。

解析：(A) 由 Vacation rentals are fully private homes whose owners…知它們是完全私人的，並沒提到是由許多人所共有，敘述不適當　(B) 由 They are, to name some on the top, cost-saving… and no tips or service charges,知假日租賃屋是不需要給小費的，敘述適當　(C) 文中僅提到假日租賃屋是私人擁有的，並未提到它們是為了商業目的而建的，敘述不適當　(D) 文中沒有提到日常清潔事宜，敘述不適當。所以答案為 (B)。

102 專門職業及技術人員普通考試導遊人員、領隊人員考試試題

等別：普通考試

類科：外語領隊人員（英語）

科目：外國語（英語）

考試時間：1 小時 20 分

※注意：本試題為單一選擇題，請選出一個正確或最適當的答案，複選作答者，該題不予計分。

1. The _____ of touring in this city is that it's very pricey.

   (A) convenience   (B) downside   (C) confusion   (D) opportunity

2. Seeing the rise of new media technology, many people predict newspapers will soon be _____ .

   (A) widespread   (B) prevalent   (C) obsolete   (D) accessed

3. Am I _____ to compensation if my ferry is canceled?

   (A) asked   (B) entitled   (C) qualified   (D) requested

4. It is the high season, and I'm not sure whether the hotel could provide enough _____ for the whole group.

   (A) vacation   (B) locations   (C) recommendation   (D) accommodations

5. Due to the delay, we are not able to catch up with our _____ flight.

   (A) connecting   (B) connected   (C) connect   (D) connectional

6. _____ of the death penalty say it is an important tool for preserving law and order in the society.

   (A) Components   (B) Respondents   (C) Opponents   (D) Proponents

7. Even though John has returned from Bali for two weeks, he is still _____ the memories of his holidays.

   (A) missing   (B) forgetting   (C) savoring   (D) remembering

8. The park does not allow pets; _____, we would have brought our puppy with us.

(A) unless　(B) therefore　(C) likewise　(D) otherwise

9. This traveler's check is not good because it should require two _____ by the user.

(A) insurances　(B) accounts　(C) signatures　(D) examinations

10. Shelly has adhered _____ a low-fat diet for over two months and succeeded in losing 12 pounds.

(A) on　(B) at　(C) in　(D) to

11. Violent video games have been _____ for school shootings, increases in bullying, and violence towards women.

(A) influenced　(B) acclaimed　(C) decided　(D) blamed

12. My car wouldn't start this morning, and then I realized the battery was _____.

(A) empty　(B) low　(C) weak　(D) dead

13. Recently, extreme weather and climate events in the form of heat waves, droughts and floods seem to have become the norm rather than the _____ .

(A) condition　(B) objection　(C) exception　(D) question

14. Many _____ users of mobile phones would get anxious and panic once the phone is missing.

(A) friendly　(B) familiar　(C) heavy　(D) careful

15. After looking at the map, Tom suggested that we _____ heading east.

(A) continue　(B) continued　(C) have continued　(D) are continuing

16. In 2060, people over 65 will account _____ more than 41 percent of the population in Taiwan.

(A) for　(B) no　(C) in　(D) at

17. Despite his effort to combat fear of height, the dip and turn of the roller coaster still _____ Jeff.

(A) excited　(B) terrified　(C) convinced　(D) stimulated

18. We have seen a marked increase in the number of visitors to the theme park, but cannot understand why the total income indicates _____ .

(A) a demand (B) a decline (C) a distinction (D) a disruption

19. The Union has filed a protest _____ behalf of the terminated workers.

(A) for (B) in (C) on (D) at

20. Paul didn't go to the baseball game yesterday; _____ , he went fishing.

(A) not to mention (B) instead (C) in that case (D) moreover

21. The manager lacked coordination and communication skills; likewise, his crew was altogether _____ .

(A) disciplined (B) disjointed (C) dismayed (D) discriminated

22. The chemicals in these cleaning products can be _____ to our health.

(A) hazardous (B) hapless (C) rueful (D) pitiful

23. It took us no time to clear _____ at the border.

(A) costume (B) costumes (C) custom (D) customs

24. Good luck for your interview today. I'll keep my fingers _____ and wish you the best.

(A) bent (B) crossed (C) pointed (D) knitted

25. Our new neighbors next door will have a _____ party this weekend.

(A) homecoming (B) homebasing (C) housewarming (D) housemoving

26. Aliens who overstay their visas would be _____ back to their country of birth.

(A) deported (B) discharged (C) departed (D) disclaimed

27. Computer chess games are getting cheaper all the time; _____ , their quality is improving.

(A) indeed (B) in short (C) therefore (D) meanwhile

28. Stay calm and clear-minded. I'm sure you'll have no problem _____ the exam.

(A) to pass (B) passing (C) pass (D) passed

29. Sorry, we don't have these shoes in size seven. They are out of _____ . Would you like to try a different style?

(A) order   (B) business   (C) stock   (D) sale

30. A: How often do you eat out?

B: _____.

(A) Five times a week.

(B) For thirty minutes.

(C) Every one hour.

(D) In a second.

31. A: Sir, you just triggered the security alarm. Are you carrying any metal item?

B: _____.

(A) No, I have emptied all my coins from my pockets.

(B) No, I didn't pull the trigger.

(C) Yes, it's a very sensitive detector.

(D) Yes, you can never be too careful.

Recently a cheating scandal has rocked the world: Lance Armstrong, an American professional road racing cyclist, finally admitted that he had used performance-enhancing drugs in his seven Tour de France wins. In the past, he persistently denied the _32._ of doping, even under oath, and persecuted former close associates who went public _33._ him.

Now, he confesses his years of denial as "one big lie" for keeping up a fairy tale image: a hero who overcame cancer, a winner of the Tour repeatedly, and a father with a happy marriage and children. Armstrong's cheat has rekindled the long-term debate on _34._ performance-enhancing drugs should be accepted in sports. On one side, it is argued that these drugs' harmful health effects have been overstated, and using drugs is part of the _35._ of sports much like improved training techniques and new technologies. On the other side, it is argued that these drugs are harmful and potentially fatal, and that athletes who use them are cheaters who gain an unfair _36._ and violate the spirit of competition.

32. (A) implementation   (B) exploitation

(C) persecution   (D) allegation

33. (A) for   (B) upon   (C) over   (D) against

34. (A) how   (B) lest   (C) whether   (D) which

35. (A) evolution   (B) satisfaction   (C) cooperation   (D) distribution

36. (A) viewpoint   (B) advantage   (C) share   (D) control

37. Jennifer is very good with specific details, but she doesn't always get the

   _____ .

   (A) big frame   (B) big image   (C) big picture   (D) big book

38. Do they have a _____ plan if it rains tomorrow and they can't go hiking?

   (A) convenience   (B) contingency   (C) continuous   (D) constituent

39. The past years have seen many _____ in the telecommunications industry,

   such as the development of phones that can receive e-mail and images.

   (A) innovations   (B) invitations   (C) instructions   (D) installations

40. Joe works around the clock. He's really _____ to make money and get

   ahead in the company.

   (A) deluded   (B) driven   (C) disappointed   (D) depressed

41. Most of my friends don't eat meat. _____ we always go to vegetarian

   restaurants when we go out for dinner.

   (A) Because   (B) As a result,   (C) If   (D) When

42. We decided to take our vacation during the winter this year _____ we

   realized that we could save a lot of money that way.

   (A) till   (B) then   (C) so   (D) because

43. When you stay in a hotel, what basic _____ do you think are necessary?

   (A) activities   (B) capabilities   (C) facilities   (D) abilities

44. Airport limousine service, valet parking service, and concierge service are some

   of the most poplar items among our _____.

   (A) car services   (B) guest services   (C) sales services   (D) retail services

45 The "Ambassador" is centrally located in Hsinchu, a few minutes by car from

   the station. It offers a _____ view of the metro Hsinchu area.

   (A) panoramic   (B) pacific   (C) pastoral   (D) premodern

46. I would like to _____ my American Express card, please.

(A) choose this to   (B) charge this to   (C) chain this to   (D) change this to

47. Guest: I have made a reservation for a suite overnight.

Clerk: Yes, we have your reservation right here. Would you please fill out this__

_____ form and show me your ID?

(A) reimbursement   (B) registration   (C) refund   (D) registrar

48. He's got a new job in Paris. He has been _____ there for three months.

(A) live   (B) lived   (C) living   (D) life

49. As Tim has no experience at all, I _____ he is qualified for this job.

(A) describe   (B) deliberate   (C) develop   (D) doubt

50. How _____ you feel if your best friends from high school mistook you for someone thirty years older at the reunion?

(A) would   (B) would have   (C) will   (D) will have

51. Taiwan Mountain Tea and Red Sprout Mountain Tea are _____ subspecies of the island. They were discovered in Taiwan in the 17th century.

(A) inscribed   (B) indigenous   (C) incredible   (D) industrial

52. A group of young students has taken the _____ through social media to organize a rally against the austerity plans.

(A) invitation   (B) initiative   (C) instruction   (D) inscription

53. Wild Formosa Sika deer became _____ due to extensive hunting of the animal during the Dutch colonization period.

(A) extinct   (B) excite   (C) exact   (D) explicit

54. Many emerging countries are facing economic uncertainty after the _____ with former union.

(A) making up   (B) breaking up   (C) setting up   (D) taking up

55. Would you please pick up the groceries from the store _____ your way home?

(A) on   (B) in   (C) through   (D) of

56. Releasing the prisoners for fear of overcrowding might _____ the current rule of law.

(A) understand   (B) undermine   (C) underdevelop   (D) underfund

57. Getting _____ the city in a foreign country can be tricky as many locals don't speak English or welcome foreigners.

(A) around   (B) up   (C) with   (D) along

58. Your detailed _____ is as follows: leaving Taipei on the 14th of June and arriving at Tokyo on the same day at noon.

(A) item   (B) identification   (C) itinerary   (D) inscription

59. _____ you listen to the conclusion, you should continue to take notes as completely as possible.

(A) But   (B) Whether   (C) How   (D) As

60. Many people engage in risky tasks only for personal satisfaction—they are _____ only with their self-esteem.

(A) concerned   (B) contained   (C) complained   (D) completed

61. The term *rites of passage* was introduced by the Flemish anthropologist Arnold van Gennep in 1090 to describe the _____ that make important transitions in people's lives.

(A) cemeteries   (B) certainties   (C) celebrities   (D) ceremonies

62. With the same consumption of fuel, this motorbike goes _____ that one.

(A) as twice fast as   (B) twice fast as

(C) as fast as twice of   (D) twice as fast as

63. One of the most important parts of these activities is for students to share the _____ of a group discussion with the rest of the class.

(A) lowlights   (B) brightlights   (C) highlights   (D) headlights

64. Still to come _____ BBC World News, our Paris correspondent will update us on the Euro crisis.

(A) by   (B) on   (C) through   (D) in

65. Many people have made "getting in shape" one of their new year _____.

(A) recreations   (B) revolutions   (C) revelations   (D) resolutions

66. Upon _____ to the plan, the organizers are to set out the procedures.

(A) agreeing   (B) agree   (C) agreed   (D) agreeable

67. Client: Are there any direct flights to Paris?

Clerk: No, you would have to _____ in Amsterdam.

(A) transfer   (B) transport   (C) translate   (D) transform

68. Client: Could you give us a table _____ ?

Waiter: Certainly. Follow me, please.

(A) with the window   (B) to the window

(C) through the window   (D) by the window

69. Pineapple cakes and local teas are some of the most popular _____ of Taiwan.

(A) sights   (B) souvenirs   (C) services   (D) surprises

70. A _____ breakfast of coffee and rolls is served in the lobby between 7 and 10 am.

(A) complete   (B) complimentary   (C) continuous   (D) complicate

71. The hotels in the resort areas are fully booked in the summer. It would be very difficult to find any _____ then.

(A) vacations   (B) visitors   (C) views   (D) vacancies

72. _____ on the board for more than two decades, the president knows all the details necessary to persuade the new members.

(A) Having served   (B) Serving   (C) Services   (D) Served

73. On occasions of loss and grief, we should use the most appropriate words to express our _____ .

(A) considerations   (B) contemplations   (C) condolences   (D) complacency

74. _____ the use of personal pronouns such as *he* or *she*, it can be used to refer to an entire idea or concept that is comprehensive and complex.

(A) In order to   (B) In reference to   (C) In contrast to   (D) In speaking to

75. Steve created quite _____ when he introduced that controversial idea at the advisory meeting.

(A) a stock   (B) a stare   (C) a stir   (D) a star

76. This sleek and sophisticated design might be _____ to some of you who don't believe in the aesthetics of products.

(A) an eye opener   (B) a can opener   (C) an ear opener   (D) a beer opener

Mount Rushmore is perhaps one of North America's most distinguished and famous landmarks, right after the Statue of Liberty. It features the busts of four U.S. Presidents, Washington, Jefferson, Lincoln and Roosevelt.

This place has an interesting story. First, a New York lawyer named Charles E. Rushmore visited the Black Hills in 1885. He asked a local the name of the granite mountain before them. Since the peak had no name, the man replied humorously, "Mount Rushmore." The name has never been changed since! In 1923 state historian Doane Robinson suggested carving some giant statues in South Dakota's Black Hills. However, the formations chosen, known as the Needles, were too fragile, and the sculptor, Mr. Gutzon Borglum, decided to use the granite mountain instead. Born in a family of Danish Mormons in Idaho in 1867, Borglum studied art in Paris and enjoyed moderate fame as a sculptor after remodeling the torch for the Statue of Liberty. Borglum chose the presidents "in commemoration of the foundation, preservation and continental expansion of the United States." President Calvin Coolidge dedicated the memorial in 1927.

At this very moment, near this mountain, there is another colossal monument **in progress**: the Crazy Horse Memorial, to honor this courageous Indian leader. In this way, history is preserved, as big as the heritage is, to be shared with everyone in an attractive way.

77. What is the second paragraph mainly about?

    (A) A brief history of Mount Rushmore.

    (B) The geographical features of Mount Rushmore.

    (C) Other attractions near Mount Rushmore.

    (D) A comparison between Mount Rushmore and the Statue of Liberty.

78. What does "**in progress**" imply about the Crazy Horse Memorial in the last paragraph?

    (A) It is better than the other monuments.

    (B) It will change to an Indian name.

    (C) It is still under construction.

    (D) It gives more fun to the tourists.

79. Mr. Gutzon Borglum _____.

    (A) was an unknown artist before he carved the giant statues

    (B) suggested carving some statues in South Dakota's Black Hills

    (C) chose the subjects for his sculptures

    (D) was a sculptor from France

80 The four U.S. presidents featured in Mount Rushmore do NOT include _____.

    (A) Jefferson   (B) Coolidge   (C) Roosevelt   (D) Washington

02 Unit
102外語領隊
英語考試—解析

1. **B**；中譯：這個城市觀光量減少是因為費用昂貴的緣故。
   解析：(A) convenience 便利性　(B) downside 下降趨勢　(C) confusion 困惑　(D) opportunity 機會／這此題中，因費用昂貴所帶來對該城市觀光的影響，唯一相關的是 (B) 下降趨勢。

2. **C**；中譯：看到新的媒體科技的興起，許多人預測報紙將很快會被淘汰。
   解析：(A) widespread 普及的　(B) prevalent 盛行的　(C) obsolete 已過時的　(D) accessed 進入／報紙本就已經是日常生活中相當普遍的媒體之一，所以新科技對報紙帶來的影響應該選 (C)。

3. **B**；中譯：如果我所要搭的渡輪班次取消了，我是否有權要求賠償呢？
   解析：(A) asked 要求　(B) entitled 給予…權力　(C) qualified 有資格　(D) requested 要求／be 動詞+動詞過去分詞-被動時態，故選 (B)，被給予權力求償。

4. **D**；中譯：正值旺季，我不確定飯店是否能提供整團所需的房間。
   解析：(A) vacation 假期　(B) locations 地點　(C) recommendation 意見　(D) accommodations 住宿／飯店所最主要提供的是住宿，故選 (D)。

5. **A**；中譯：因為航班誤點的緣故，所以我們趕不上我們的銜接航班。
   解析：(A) connecting 連接（動名詞）　(B) connected 連接的　(C) connect 連接　(D) connectional 無此字／connecting flight 銜接班機，轉接班機。故選 (A)。

6. **D**；中譯：死刑的支持者認為其為維護法律及社會秩序的重要工具。
   解析：(A) Compoments 成分　(B) Respondents 回答者　(C) Opponents 反對者　(D) Proponents 支持者／認為死刑為維護社會秩序的重要工具，必定為支持死刑的人，故選 (D)。

7. **C**；中譯：儘管 John 已經從峇里島度假回來兩個星期了，但他仍沈浸在假期的回憶當中。
   解析：(A) missing 想念　(B) forgetting 忘記　(C) savoring 反覆品味　(D) remembering savoring the memory 細細地、反覆地品嚐回憶，沈浸在回憶當中。

8. **D**；中譯：這一個公園不准寵物進入；要不然我們就會帶著小狗了。
   解析：(A) unless 除非　(B) therefore 因此　(C) likewise 照樣地　(D) otherwise 要不然 would have brought(p.p.) 是一個與過去事實相反的用法，所以是沒有帶小狗來，故選 (D)。

Super 英文領隊導遊

9. Ⓒ；中譯：這張旅行支票沒效，因為它應該要有使用者的兩個簽名。

解析：(A) insurances 保險　(B) accounts 帳戶　(C) signatures 簽名　(D) examinations 檢驗／一般旅行支票上，在購買時，使用者會被要求在上面簽名，使用時需再簽一次，故選 (C)。

10. Ⓓ；中譯：Shelly 已經連續兩個月以上都堅持低脂飲食，並且成功的減掉 12 磅。

解析：adhere to 堅持；遵循。故選 (D)。

11. Ⓓ；中譯：暴力的電動遊戲被歸咎為造成校園槍擊事件、霸凌增加及對女性暴力行為的原因。

解析：(A) influenced 影響　(B) acclaimed 歡呼　(C) decided 決定　(D) blamed 譴責 blame for 因…而責備，譴責；歸咎於。故選 (D)。

12. Ⓓ；中譯：我的車子今天早上無法發動，然後我發現是電池沒電了。

解析：(A) empty 空　(B) low 低　(C) weak 弱　(D) dead 死／英文中形容電池、電瓶沒電會用 dead 來形容，一般說 the battery was dead，所以選 (D)。

13. Ⓒ；中譯：最近，極端的天氣及熱浪、乾旱及水災的氣候問題看起來已經變成是常態而不是異常。

解析：(A) condition 情況　(B) objection 反對　(C) exception 異常、例外　(D) question 問題／四個選項皆為名詞，選擇切合整句意思的 (C)。

14. Ⓒ；中譯：許多手機的重度使用者在手機遺失時會感到焦慮及慌張。

解析：(A) friendly 友善的　(B) familiar 熟悉的　(C) heavy 重　(D) careful 仔細的／在英文中用 heavy 除了形容重量重之外，也可形容使用程度，依句意選擇 (C)。

15. Ⓐ；中譯：在看過地圖後，Tom 建議我們繼續向東走。

解析：此題考 suggest 的特殊句型：人＋ suggest ＋ that 某人＋(should)＋原形動詞。因為 that 子句省略助動詞 should，所以子句的動詞不論人稱皆用原形動詞。

16. Ⓐ；中譯：在 2060 年時，在台灣 65 歲以上的人口將超過 41%。

解析：(A) for 為了　(B) no 不　(C) in 在…內　(D) at 在 account for 在（數量、比例上）占，答案選 (A)。

17. Ⓑ；中譯：儘管他努力地要克服對高度的恐懼，雲霄飛車的傾斜小轉彎還是把 Jeff 給嚇壞了。

解析：(A) excited 使興奮　(B) terrified 使驚嚇　(C) convinced 使信服　(D) stimulated 使興奮／despite 儘管 prep.；fear of height 懼高。選擇 (B) 才切合題意。

18. Ⓑ；中譯：我們在主題樂園的來客數量上有看到明顯的增加，但卻無法理解為什麼總收入卻呈現下滑。

解析：(A) a demand 需求　(B) a decline 下滑　(C) a distinction 區別　(D) a disruption 分裂／來客量增加，一般來說，總收入應該也會增加。但在後半段以 but（但是）來作為連接詞，並提及總收入，可以推測是下滑，所以選 (B)。

19. Ⓒ；中譯：工會為了被開除的工人們提出抗議。

解析：(A) for　(B) in　(C) on　(D) at

on behalf of 為了…的利益；代表。選 (C)。

20. **B**；中譯：Paul 昨天沒有去參加棒球賽；他反倒是去釣魚了。

解析：(A) not to mention 更不用說　(B) instead 反而　(C) in that case 那樣的話　(D) moreover 並且／依題意，可先刪去 (C)、(D) 選項。not to mention 後面一般會加 that 或是子句，不能直接加逗號，所以選 (B)。

21. **B**；中譯：經理缺乏協調以及溝通的技巧；同樣地，他的部屬也完全不協調。

解析：(A) disciplined 有紀律的　(B) disjointed 不協調　(C) dismayed 驚慌的 (D) discriminated 區別／likewise 同樣地，所以空格需選擇與經理所缺乏協調及溝通技巧相關的選項，選 (B)。

22. **A**；中譯：在清潔用品中所含的化學物質可能有害於我們的健康。

解析：(A) hazardous 有害的　(B) hapless 不幸的　(C) rueful 後悔的　(D) pitiful 可憐的 依題意選擇(A)。

23. **D**；中譯：在邊界上，我們一下子就通過海關檢查了。

解析：(A) costume 戲服 (B) costumes 戲服（複數）(C) custom 習俗 (D) customs 海關 clear customs 通過海關檢查，選 (D)。

24. **B**；中譯：祝你今天面試好運。我會交叉我的手指並祝你好運。

解析：(A) bent 彎曲　(B) crossed 交叉　(C) pointed 指　(D) knitted 編織 keep my fingers crossed = cross my fingers 交叉手指以祈求好運，選 (B)。

25. **C**；中譯：我們隔壁新搬來的鄰居在這個週末將舉辦一個喬遷派對。

解析：(A) homecoming 返家、歸國　(B) homebasing 無此字　(C) housewarming 喬遷　(D) housemoving 無此字／housewarming party 喬遷派對。句中為新搬來的鄰居要舉辦派對，依題意選擇 (C)。

26. **A**；中譯：逾期滯留的外國人將會被強制解送至他們出生的國家。

解析：(A) deported 驅逐出境　(B) discharged 免除　(C) departed 出發　(D) disclaimed 否決／overstay 停留超過（時間）；visa 簽證。對於停留超過簽證允許時間的外國人，依法需強制遣返，所以選 (A)。

27. **D**；中譯：電腦的西洋棋遊戲愈來愈便宜了；同時，它們的品質也不斷的提高。

解析：(A) indeed 確實 adv.　(B) in short 總之（介係詞片語）　(C) therefore 因此 adv.　(D) meanwhile 同時 adv.／依題意可先刪去 (A)、(B) 選項，一般而言，當某樣物品價錢變低時，無法構成品質提高的理由，所以選擇 (D)。

28. **B**；中譯：保持鎮定及冷靜。我確定你將能毫無問題地通過考試。

解析：have no problem V-ing 表示對某事沒有問題，have no problem with+名詞。故本題選(B) passing 動名詞。

29. **C**；中譯：對不起，我們這一款的鞋子沒有 7 號的尺寸了。都沒有庫存了。你要不要試試其他的款式呢？

解析：(A) order 次序　(B) business 生意　(C) stock 庫存　(D) sale 銷售／out of stock 缺貨，沒有庫存片語用法。選 (C)。

30. (A)；中譯：你多久會外出吃飯一次？

解析：(A) Five times a week. 一週 5 次　(B) For thirty minutes. 30 分鐘　(C) Every one hour. 每一小時。　(D) In a second 等一下／依照問題回答，所以要選 (A)。

31. (A)；中譯：先生，您剛剛觸動了警報系統。您是否有攜帶任何的金屬物品呢？

解析：(A) No, I have emptied all my coins from my pockets. 沒有，我已經將我口袋中的零錢都掏出來了。　(B) No, I didn't pull the trigger. 沒有，我沒有扣扳機。　(C) Yes, it's a very sensitive detector. 是的，這是一個非常靈敏的偵測器。　(D) Yes, you can never be too careful. 是的，你越小心越好／依照問題回答，需選擇 (A)。

32-36；中譯：最近一樁醜聞事件震驚全球：蘭斯‧阿姆斯壯，美國職業公路競速選手，終於承認他在環法自行車賽七連霸中有服用興奮劑。在過去，他始終否認有服用興奮劑的指控甚至宣示，以及迫害公開出面反對他的前任密友。

現在，他承認他過去幾年的否認是「一個大謊言」，為的是要保持童話故事般的形象：一個抗癌成功的英雄，比賽的常勝軍，以及擁有快樂婚姻及孩子的父親。阿姆斯壯的欺騙行為重新引發了對於在運動比賽當中是否能使用興奮劑的長期辯論。有一方認為興奮劑對於人體健康的傷害效用有被誇大，使用藥物是體育當中一部分的進化過程就像是改良的訓練技巧及新的科技。另一方則認為，這些藥物會造成傷害，以及致命的潛在可能性，使用這些藥物的運動員是獲得不公平利益及違反競賽精神的作弊者。

32. (D)；(A) implementation 成就　(B) exploitation 剝削　(C) persecution 迫害　(D) allegation 指控

解析：doping 用興奮劑，選 (D) 以切合句意。

33. (D)；(A) for 為了　(B) upon 在…上面　(C) over 在…上面　(D) against 反對

解析：go public against 公開反對；went 為 go 的過去式，故選 (D)。

34. (C)；(A) how 如何　(B) least 最少的　(C) whether 是否　(D) which 哪一個

解析：文章中有提到 debate（辯論），及針對興奮劑的使用兩個立場不同的意見，所以這裡選 whether，(C) 選項。

35. (A)；(A) evolution 進化　(B) satisfaction 滿意度　(C) cooperation 合作　(D) distribution 貢獻

解析：35 題的這一個句子當中後半段有提到改良的訓練技巧及新的科技，所以選擇 (A)。

36. (B)；(A) viewpoint 觀點　(B) advantage 優點　(C) share 股份　(D) control 控制

解析：36 題的句子是闡述贊成使用興奮劑這一方的意見，其認為使用興奮劑是進步，選 (B) 優點，以切合題意。

37. (C)；中譯：Jennifer 非常擅長具體細節的部分，但她並不是總能把握住重點。

解析：(A) big frame 大框框　(B) big image 大影像　(C) big picture 大局，重點　(D) big book 大書／big picture 整體局勢；重點、大局。選 (C) 符合題意。

38. B；中譯：如果明天下雨，而不能去健行的話，他們是不是有預備的方案呢？

解析：(A) convenience 方便的　(B) contingency 預防的　(C) continuous 連續的　(D) constituent 組成的／contingency plan 應急計畫、預備方案。題中詢問如果沒有辦法去健行的話，是否有其他的計畫，所以選 (B)。

39. A；中譯：在過去幾年，電訊業中有許多的創新，例如是可以接收 email 及影像電話的發展。

解析：(A) innovations 創新　(B) invitations 邀請　(C) instruction 指令　(D) installations 設備／句子的後半段有提到電話的發展，所以依題意，應選擇 (A)。

40. B；中譯：Joe 日夜不停的工作。他非常急切的賺錢及在公司中出人頭地。

解析：(A) deluded 受騙的　(B) driven 急切的　(C) disappointed 失望的　(D) depressed 沮喪的／work around the clock 夜以繼日地不斷工作；選 (B) 急切的。

41. B；中譯：我大部分的朋友不吃肉。因此，當我們出去吃晚餐時總是會選擇素食餐廳。

解析：(A) Because 因為　(B) As a result 因此　(C) If 如果　(D) When 當／第一句可被視為是解釋第二句中所說選擇素食餐廳的原因，所以此題選擇 (B) 因此才恰當。

42. D；中譯：我們決定要在今年冬天時去度假，因為我們意識到這樣的話我們能省下更多的錢。

解析：(A) till 直到　(B) then 然後　(C) so 所以　(D) because 因為／realize 了解，意識到。句子的前半段說明所決定的事情，後半段在空格後接 we realized…，表示在說明原因，故選 (D)。

43. C；中譯：當你住在一家飯店時，什麼樣的基本設備是你覺得必須的？

解析：(A) activities 活動　(B) capabilities 性能　(C) facilities 設備　(D) abilities 能力 stay（在某城市、飯店、別人家）暫住，逗留。住在飯店大多為短時間暫住，所以在英文中多半說 stay in a hotel。依句意，空格處應填 (C) 最為恰當。

44. B；中譯：機場巴士接送服務、代客泊車服務、以及禮賓服務是我們的客戶服務中最受歡迎的幾種。

解析：(A) car services 汽車服務　(B) guest service 客戶服務　(C) sales services 銷售服務　(D) retail services 零售服務／句中提到的三種服務，其服務對象是以人為主，所以選擇 (B) 客戶服務。

45. A；中譯：國賓飯店位在新竹的中心位置，數分鐘車程即可到達火車站。在這可以看到新竹市區的全景。

解析：(A) panoramic 全景的　(B) pacific 太平洋的　(C) pastoral 鄉村的　(D) premodern 現代化之前的／metro 大都市的。句中提到的景象是屬於新竹市區的，所以刪去 (C)、(D)；選 (A) 以切合題意。

46. (B)；中譯：我想以我的美國運通卡來支付這一筆款項。

   解析：(A) choose this to 將這選擇到　(B) charge this to 將這記帳到　(C) chain this to 將這束縛到　(D) change this to 將這改變到／American Express card 美國運通卡。美國運通卡是信用卡的一種，其功能為在購物時用以支付款項，所以根據題意，需選擇與付款相關的選項，故選 (B)。

47. (B)；中譯：客人：我有預訂一個晚上的套房。職員：是的，我們這有您的預約紀錄。可不可以麻煩您填寫一下這一張登記表格以及出示您的證件？

   解析：(A) reimbursement 補償　(B) registration 登記　(C) refund 退款　(D) registrar 登記人員／這一題是在入住飯店時，客人與櫃臺人員間的對話，可以從 reservation ，suite 等字看出來。所以選擇 (B) 登記表格。

48. (C)；中譯：他在巴黎找到新工作。他已經在那住三個月了。

   解析：(A) live 住 v.　(B) lived 住 p.p.　(C) living 住 V-ing　(D) life 生活 n.／He has been… 完成式。句中提到他住在巴黎的原因是因為找到新工作，而工作可被視為是一個持續性的狀態，可推定他還住在巴黎，所以在這裡應該用現在完成進行式 have been + Ving 來表示已經進行一陣子，且持續進行的狀態，故選 (C)。

49. (D)；中譯：因為 Tim 完全沒有經驗，我不敢肯定他有資格做這份工作。

   解析：(A) describe 描述　(B) deliberate 故意的　(C) develop 發展　(D) doubt 懷疑 句中說明 Tim 完全沒有經驗，而後半段提到有資格做這個工作，選(D) 與句意相符，對 Tim 的資格抱持懷疑的態度。

50. (A)；中譯：如果你中學時最好的朋友在同學會上將你誤認成比你老 30 歲的人時，你有什麼感覺？

   解析：(A) would　(B) would have　(C) will　(D) will have
   (B) 和 (D) 文法不通順，所以先刪去。would 和 will 的差別在於 would 所敘述的事發生機率較小，而 will 比較肯定。依題意，would 比較符合。

51. (B)；中譯：台灣高山茶和紅心高山茶是這個島上的原生亞種。它們是在 17 世紀時在台灣被發現。

   解析：(A) inscribed 刻、雕　(B) indigenous 原生的　(C) incredible 不可思議的　(D) industrial 工業的／subspecies （動植物的）亞種。第一句中的 island 指的是台灣，在第二句中說明這兩種茶是在 17 世紀在台灣被發現的，所以選擇 (B) 原生的。

52. (B)；中譯：一群年輕的學生在社群網站上發起抗議財政緊縮的活動。

   解析：(A) invitation 邀請 n.　(B) initiative 主動自發 n.　(C) instruction 教學　(D) inscription 銘文／take the initiative 主動，自發去做，常用片語。

53. (A)；中譯：野生的台灣梅花鹿絕種的原因是因為在荷蘭殖民時期大量的狩獵動物。

   解析：(A) extinct 絕種的　(B) excite 使興奮　(C) exact 準確的　(D) explicit 明確的 空格前為 became，所以先將動詞選項 (B) excite 刪去。句子後半段說明因為在荷蘭殖民期間的大量狩獵，所以我們可以猜測此舉會造成動物的數量減少甚至是絕種，所以選擇 (A)。

54. **B**；中譯：在脫離前聯盟國之後，許多新興的國家都正面臨著經濟上的不確定性。

解析：(A) making up 和好　(B) breaking up 與…斷絕關係　(C) setting up 組織，計畫　(D) taking up 重新開始／依照題意，選擇 (B)。

55. **A**；中譯：你在回家的路上可不可以順道去雜貨店買些東西？

解析：on someone's way home 在某人回家的路上。故選 (A)。

56. **B**；中譯：因為擔心牢裡人滿為患而釋放囚犯可能會危害現今的法制。

解析：(A) understand 理解　(B) undermine 危害　(C) underdevelop 使發展不充分　(D) underfund 對…提供資金不足／prisoner 囚犯、犯人。本題中敘述釋放囚犯的原因是因為獄中的犯人太多，以常理推論對於法制的影響應該是 (B) 危害。

57. **A**；中譯：在國外的城市四處隨意走走有可能會有點棘手，因為許多當地人不會說英文或是不歡迎外國人。

解析：(A) around　(B) up　(C) with　(D) along／get around 隨意走走，四處走動。本題考的是片語，所以依題意選擇 (A)。

58. **C**；中譯：你的詳細行程安排如下：6 月 14 日從台北出發，當天中午抵達日本東京。

解析：(A) item 品項　(B) identification 身份證明　(C) itinerary 行程安排　(D) inscription 銘文／本句中，在冒號後說明了出發及抵達的日期及地點，可被視為是行程的安排，所以選 (C)。

59. **D**；中譯：當你在聽到結論時，你應該要繼續做筆記，要盡可能的完整。

解析：(A) But　(B) Whether　(C) How　(D) As
(D) 當連接詞有「當……時」的意思。

60. **A**；中譯：許多參與危險任務的人只是為了個人的滿足感－他們只關心他們的自尊。

解析：(A) concerned 關心　(B) contained 包含　(C) complained 抱怨　(D) completed 完成／engage in 從事、參加；concern with 關心。依題意空格處應應選擇 (A)。

61. **D**；中譯：通過儀式這一個詞是在西元 1090 年時由法蘭德斯的人類學家 Arnold van Gennep 所提出的，描述人生進入重要轉換時所舉行的儀式。

解析：(A) cemeteries 墓園　(B) certainties 必然之事　(C) celebrities 名人　(D) ceremonies 儀式／rites of passage 通過儀式，人類學中的用語，指的是人生中經歷重要轉換時所有的儀式，如出生、結婚、死亡等都會有相關的儀式，有宣告身份轉換及祈福之意。依句子最後部分「在人生中造成重大轉變」來選擇，應以 (D) 儀式最為恰當。

62. **D**；中譯：同樣的耗油量，這一輛摩托車跑得是那一輛的兩倍快。

解析：倍數詞 + as + 原級 Adj. + as，故選 (D)。

63. **C**；中譯：這些活動當中最重要的一部分是要讓學生分享與其他人在團體討論中的重點。

解析：(A) 無此字　(B) 無此字　(C) highlights 重要部分　(D) headlights 頭燈

highlights 最重要的部分，精彩部分。此題選 (C)。

64. **B**；中譯：接下來在 BBC 的世界新聞中，我們駐派在巴黎的記者將為我們報導最新的有
關歐元危機的消息。

解析：(A) by　(B) on　(C) through　(D) in
on news 在…新聞（節目）中，和 on TV 的用法相同。come by 是從旁邊穿過，
而 come through 為穿過，與 news 連用均不符合題意。而 in news 則是指所指的
人事物在這一則新聞故事中，所以應選擇 (B)。

65. **D**；中譯：許多人將塑身列為新年新希望之一。

解析：(A) recreation 消遣娛樂　(B) revolutions 革命　(C) revelations 啟示錄　(D)
resolutions 決心／new year resolution 在新的一年所下的決心，意即新年新希望。

66. **A**；中譯：一旦計畫通過，組織者們就將開始流程。

解析：(A) agreeing　(B) agree　(C) agreed　(D) agreeable 四個選項皆為同意，但
詞性不同，(A) 為 V-ing，(B) 為原形動詞，(C) 為過去式或過去分詞，(D) 為形容
詞。upon 置於句首加動名詞為「一…就」的句型，故選擇 (A)，以切合題意。

67. **A**；中譯：客人：有沒有直飛巴黎的航班？員工：沒有，你必須在阿姆斯特丹轉機。

解析：(A) transfer 轉乘　(B) transport 運輸　(C) translate 翻譯　(D) transform 變形
客人詢問是否有直達巴黎的班機，但員工回答沒有，所以可推論需以轉機的方式
到達，故選 (A)。

68. **D**；中譯：客人：可不可以給我們窗邊的位子？服務生：當然可以，請跟我來。

解析：(A) with the window 有窗戶的　(B) to the window 到窗戶的　(C) through the
window 進入窗內　(D) by the window 窗戶旁

69. **B**；中譯：鳳梨酥和本地的茶葉是台灣最受歡迎的土產。

解析：(A) sights 名勝　(B) souvenirs 紀念品、土產　(C) services 服務　(D) surprises
驚喜／(B) 最適合題意。

70. **B**；中譯：附贈的早餐有咖啡和麵包捲，早上 7 點到 10 點之間在大廳供應。

解析：(A) complete 完整的　(B) complimentary 贈送的　(C) continuous 連續的　(D)
complicate 複雜的／依題意，最恰當的為 (B) 選項。

71. **D**；中譯：位在旅遊勝地的飯店夏天時都訂滿了。要找到空的房間非常的困難。

解析：(A) vacations 假期　(B) visitors 旅客　(C) views 風景　(D) vacancies 空房
vacancy 空房間／第一句已經説了飯店都被預訂光了，所以意為沒有空房故選
(D)。

72. **A**；中譯：在董事會任職超過 20 年以上，總裁熟知所有説服新成員所需的細節。

解析：此題考分詞構句的用法。第一句話 The president has served on the board for
more than two decades. 第二句話 The president knows all the details necessary
to persuade the new members. 將兩句結合，第一句的 The president 去掉，並
將動詞改為現在分詞表主動，形成一個分詞片語。故選 (A) Having served。

73. **C**；中譯：在失去與悲傷的場合當中，我們應該用最恰當的話來表達我們的哀悼之意。

解析：(A) considerations 考慮　(B) contemplations 沈思　(C) condolences 哀悼之意　(D) complacency 自滿／loss 失去；grief 悲傷、悲痛。本句中的 loss 失去指的是失去所愛的人，occasions of loss and grief 可被視為是弔唁的場合中，所以選擇 (C) 哀悼之意。

74. **C**；中譯：與人稱代名詞裡的 he 或是 she 不同的是，it 可以被用在表示一個廣泛及複雜的想法或是概念。

解析：(A) In order to 為了　(B) In reference to 關於　(C) In contrast to 與…相反的　(D) In speaking to 無此片語／根據題意，選 (C) 較適當。

75. **C**；中譯：Steve 製造了一陣的騷動，當他在諮詢顧問會議中提出了一個頗具爭議的觀點。

解析：(A) a stock 一隻股票　(B) a stare 一瞪　(C) a stir 一片混亂　(D) a star 一個星星　create a stir 引起騷動；controversial idea 頗具爭議的論點。當在會議中提出了具爭議的觀點時，通常會引起的是騷動或是混亂，所以本題選 (C)。

76. **A**；中譯：這一個時尚且精緻微妙的設計會讓你們這一些不相信產品美感的人大開眼界。

解析：(A) an eye opener 大開眼界　(B) a can opener 一個開罐器　(C) an ear opener 大開耳界　(D) a beer opener 一個啤酒開瓶器　an eye opener 大開眼界，令人瞠目吃驚的事物。依題意，選擇 (A)。

77-80；中譯：羅斯摩爾山或許是北美最顯著及著名的地標之一，排名僅次於自由女神像。它有四位美國總統的半身雕像，分別是華盛頓、傑佛遜、林肯和羅斯福。

這個地方有個有趣的故事。首先，一位名為查爾斯 E. 羅斯摩爾的紐約律師在 1885 年時到布拉克山來。他在這一片山脈前詢問一位當地人這一座花崗岩山的名字。因為這一個山峰並沒有被命名，所以這個人幽默的回答是羅斯摩爾山。從此之後，這個名字就未曾被更動！在 1923 年時，歷史學家多恩羅賓遜建議在南達科他州的布拉克山雕刻巨大的雕像。然而，結構決定一切，被稱做尼德爾斯的山太過脆弱，雕刻家格曾博格勒姆就決定要用這一座花崗岩山代替。出生於 1867 年愛達荷州的丹麥裔摩門家庭，博格勒姆曾在巴黎學習藝術，並在成為改造自由女神像火把的雕刻家之後，小有名氣。博格勒姆選擇幾位總統以「紀念美國的奠基，維持及國土的擴張」。卡爾文柯立芝總統在 1927 年時推動這一項紀念計畫。

在這個非常的時刻，這座山的附近，還有一項巨大的紀念碑工程在進行：瘋馬酋長雕像，用以紀念這一位英勇的印地安領袖。用這樣子的方法，歷史被保存，和古蹟一樣的巨大，能以引人注目的方式來與每一個人分享。

77. **A**；中譯：第二段的主旨是？

解析：(A) 羅斯摩爾山的簡短歷史。(B) 羅斯摩爾山的地理特徵。(C) 其他鄰近羅斯摩爾山的景點。(D) 羅斯摩爾山與自由女神像的比較。第二段的第一句話說 "This place has an interesting story." 這個地方有個有趣的故事。之後便是敘述名稱由來，雕像的起源，雕刻家等的介紹，所以是在簡短的介紹此地的歷史，故選 (A)。

78. **C**；中譯：在最後一段中，指瘋馬酋長雕像還在 "in progress" 是什麼意思？

解析：(A) 比其他的紀念碑好。(B) 它將被改成印地安名字。(C) 它仍在建造中。(D) 它帶給遊客更多的樂趣／in progress 正在進行中的。選 (C)。

79. **C**；中譯：格曾博格勒姆_____。

解析：(A) 在他雕刻巨像前是一個沒沒無名的藝術家。　(B) 建議在南達科他州的布拉克山雕刻一些雕像　(C) 選擇他的雕像的主題　(D) 是位法國的雕刻家

在第二段中有一句 "Borglum chose the presidents in commemoration of ….." 這一句話是指博格勒姆對於要在羅斯摩爾山雕刻的總統雕像的選擇標準，所以可以被認為博格勒姆選擇他的雕像主題，所以選 (C)。其他的選項則為非，因為博格勒姆在接下羅斯摩爾山的雕刻前就已經因為改造了自由女神的火把雕刻而享有名氣；而建議在南達科他州的布拉克山雕刻巨大的雕像是歷史學家多恩羅賓遜；博格勒姆出生於愛達荷州的丹麥裔摩門家庭。

80. **B**；中譯：在羅斯摩爾山所呈現的四位總統雕像中不包括。

解析：(A) 傑佛遜　(B) 柯林芝　(C) 羅斯福　(D) 華盛頓

本文中的第二句話便有指出四位總統分別是華盛頓、傑佛遜、林肯和羅斯福。故選 (B)，柯林芝總統是當年推動此計畫的人，並不在這四個總統雕像之中。

03 Unit

103 外語領隊 英語考試—試題

103 專門職業及技術人員普通考試導遊人員、領隊人員考試試題
等別：普通考試
類科：外語領隊人員（英語）
科目：外國語（英語）
考試時間：1 小時 20 分
※注意：本試題為單一選擇題，請選出一個正確或最適當的答案，複選作答者，該題不予計分。

1. Tourists often remark that Taiwan is a beautiful island worthy of visiting; that is a nice _____ .

   (A) complaint　(B) compliment　(C) compromise　(D) complement

2. Jane enjoys traveling, and she always travels with great _____.

   (A) entertainment　(B) enormousness　(C) enthusiasm　(D) enthronement

3. From a traveler's _____ , I have to admit that the city has superfluous amount of new statues and monuments.

   (A) assumptive　(B) anticipative　(C) prescriptive　(D) perspective

4. If you arrive in Skopje before 2014, expect to see quite a bit of construction as the city is currently undergoing a massive _____ .

   (A) transformation　(B) transaction　(C) confirmation　(D) confrontation

5. The passage read by the tour guide is an _____ from a longer work.

   (A) excess　(B) excerpt　(C) exception　(D) exemption

6. During the trip, whenever Sarah does not understand what the tour guide says, she always _____ her hand and asks questions.

   (A) arises　(B) rises　(C) arouses　(D) raises

7. Shall we _____ it will not rain tonight, and plan the outdoor party?

   (A) resume　(B) assume　(C) consume　(D) subsume

8. _____ and you will overcome these difficulties.

(A) Persecute　(B) Predominate　(C) Persevere　(D) Preserve

9. My friend did not _____ his dream to be a tour leader.

　　(A) relinquish　(B) distinguish　(C) furnish　(D) astonish

10. The manager made it clear that he intended to _____ down some new rules to enforce workplace discipline.

　　(A) lied　(B) laid　(C) lay　(D) lie

11. Internet technology has nowadays _____ time and space.

　　(A) coincided　(B) collapsed　(C) collaborated　(D) consisted

12. We must not allow our creative protest to _____ into physical violence.

　　(A) defect　(B) betray　(C) resist　(D) degenerate

13. The young man _____ to dazzle everyone by scoring 25 points and handing out 7 assists, leading the team to victory.

　　(A) proceeded　(B) provided　(C) devolved　(D) precancelled

14. Human knowledge is now in the process of being _____ into always-available digital formats.

　　(A) convicted　(B) condescended　(C) converted　(D) confronted

15. If you require an _____ response to a current incident, please telephone our switchboard on 101.

　　(A) immature　(B) inconvenient　(C) immigrant　(D) immediate

16. Taipei, Taiwan's _____ capital city, is one of CNN's top ten New Year Eve destinations.

　　(A) vicious　(B) vibrant　(C) vigilant　(D) vicarious

17. Being a tour guide, one needs to be more concerned about the major important matters instead of spending too much time on _____ issues.

　　(A) sensible　(B) voluble　(C) effusive　(D) frivolous

18. Father always takes his _____ vacation in July so the family can go abroad together.

　　(A) ambient　(B) ambivalent　(C) annual　(D) ancillary

19. The document was finally proved _____ and accepted by the court.

　　(A) authentic　(B) confident　(C) dubious　(D) fragile

20. Applicants who do not have strong computer skills will not be as _____ as those who do.

(A) compensative (B) comprehensible (C) comprehensive (D) competitive

21. Let's continue to work with the faith that unearned suffering is _____ .

(A) preemptive (B) redemptive (C) emotive (D) promotive

22. When traveling in Switzerland, you may see some high mountains _____ covered by ice and snow.

(A) desperately (B) imminently (C) perpetually (D) radically

23. Our tour guide was _____ that we felt hesitant to complain to her about the hotel service.

(A) so a sweet lady (B) such a sweet lady

(C) so such sweet (D) such sweet

24. What _____ our tour guide has provided!

(A) useful information (B) an useful information

(C) useful information (D) useful informations

25 I believe the trip I took last summer was _____ interesting than yours.

(A) very much (B) so much (C) much (D) much more

26. By the time he receives this letter I am writing, I _____ around the country.

(A) may be traveling (B) travel (C) had traveled (D) am traveling

27. The dispute over who should be the leader _____ before we got there.

(A) has been settled (B) had been settled (C) settled (D) will settle

28. Our tour leader speaks English and French well, and _____ .

(A) so does our tour guide (B) so our tour guide can

(C) neither does our tour guide (D) nor can our tour guide

29. Tourism usually brings much-needed money to developing countries. _____ , it provides employment for the local people.

(A) However (B) Therefore (C) Furthermore (D) For instance

30. If Jane had won the race, she would have been given a free trip to England; in other words, _____ .

(A) Jane won the race (B) Jane got a free trip

(C) Jane gave a free trip (D) Jane lost the race

31. Tourist: Excuse me. Where's the check-in _____ for American Airlines?

Worker: It's in Terminal 2. This is Terminal 1.

(A) carrel (B) barrier (C) counter (D) concord

32. Worker: If you're on an international flight, I believe you have to check in three hours before your flight.

Tourist: And for _____ flights?

Worker: On those flights you have to check in one and a half hours before.

(A) domestic (B) country (C) neighboring (D) foreign

33. Worker: Can I see your ticket and your passport, please?

Tourist: Sure. Here's my passport, and here's my _____.

(A) paper (B) e-ticket (C) boarding pass (D) online purchase

34. Worker: Excuse me, sir. One of your bags is overweight. I'm going to have to charge you for the excess weight.

Tourist: I see. How much _____ do I have to pay? And can I pay by credit card?

Worker: 30 dollars, sir, and yes, we do accept credit cards.

(A) cash (B) over (C) extra (D) additional

35. Dihua Street is a great place to purchase traditional Chinese foods which _____ _____ great gifts, and many shops will seal purchases for plane travel.

(A) making (B) make (C) makes (D) made

36. National Taiwan Museum _____ way back in 1908 during the Japanese occupation of Taiwan.

(A) builds (B) built (C) is built (D) was built

37. The second floor explores aboriginal culture, _____ visitors about the aboriginal tribes so important to Taiwanese history.

(A) teaches (B) taught (C) teaching (D) is taught

38. You can carry a cell phone with you _____ you go but you can't do this with your PC.

(A) however   (B) whichever   (C) wherever   (D) whatever

39. With special rates and _____ breakfasts for two, our Bed & Breakfast packages are the perfect way for you to relax and recharge.

(A) complimentary   (B) compulsory   (C) condescending   (D) commodious

40. Anything that gives travelers a taste of the local culture or a personal greeting upon arrival _____ the favorable experience of an airport and the city or country where it's located.

(A) is available for   (B) adjusts to   (C) adds to   (D) gets over

41. During our journey through the desert, our food, clothes, and other possessions _____ a team of pack animals.

(A) were mailed to   (B) were enforced to

(C) were transported by   (D) were kept by

42. Last year, I wanted to go trekking in the Gobi Desert, but my doctor did not allow me to because I was not in very good _____.

(A) enjoyable figure   (B) physical shape

(C) social mind   (D) careful attention

43. Several new government policies are scheduled to _____ today.

(A) take effect   (B) avoid contact   (C) go over   (D) work off

44. Most people will tell you that using a phone at the table is not polite while simultaneously _____ to being guilty of having used their phone at the table.

(A) conducted   (B) admitting   (C) disappoint   (D) explanatory

45. Online classes _____ enabling teachers and students to communicate, even when they are across the world from each other.

(A) take care of   (B) make up

(C) make an appointment to   (D) hold the promise of

46. Dutch artist Florentijn Hofman was upset about the arrangement for his *Rubber Duck* installation _____ in Keelung.

(A) in show   (B) on display   (C) in sail   (D) for touring

47. Hand soaps _____ in restrooms in public venues have been found to

contain exceedingly high numbers of viable bacteria.

(A) provide (B) providing (C) are provided (D) provided

48. He got up _____ to watch the first ray of the rising sun.

(A) as earliest (B) enough early (C) very earlier (D) early enough

49. The Flight 506 to Amsterdam, scheduled to depart at 11:30 a.m., has been delayed _____ a big fog.

(A) on account of (B) in case of (C) by way of (D) aware of

50. _____ allowing people to buy single shoes, once a season the single shoes bank gives unwanted single shoes to members for free.

(A) Before (B) On the contrary (C) By taking chance (D) In addition to

51. Many people, when traveling in Southeast Asia, try to avoid the monsoon season as it is _____ to travel around.

(A) very harder (B) much harder (C) too harder (D) so harder

52. This tour group got a special promotion fare, which requires one stop-over in Japan for about two hours with _____ .

(A) a connecting flight (B) a non-stop flight

(C) a direct flight (D) a daily flight

53. There are many small and practical ways you can _____ energy and help protect the environment.

(A) conserve (B) observe (C) deserve (D) serve

54. Only on Sundays _____ without paying.

(A) they could visit the museum (B) you will visit the museum

(C) can you visit the museum (D) we will visit the museum

55. Twins aren't always twice as nice; they have much higher risks of being born _____ and having serious health problems.

(A) preliterate (B) premature (C) prejudiced (D) prescribed

56. A: Excuse me, sir. We are going to leave early tomorrow morning for our flight schedule. Shall we have an early breakfast arrangement for my group?

B: _____ .

(A) Sure. The breakfast is not available in the morning.

(B) What time do you want to have breakfast?

(C) How long does it take from the hotel to the airport?

(D) Sure. May we serve your people now?

57. It is always a good idea to buy _____ . If you get sick or lose one of your possessions while traveling, the insurance company will pay your medical expenses or give you money.

(A) medicines   (B) travel guide   (C) duty free goods   (D) travel insurance

58. A national bird survey is to be conducted around the New Year's Day holiday to both celebrate the new year and _____ public awareness about wildlife protection.

(A) raise   (B) switch   (C) divide   (D) arise

59. Soon all our natural resources will be used up if we do not _____ our levels of consumption.

(A) calcify   (B) multiply   (C) generate   (D) reduce

60. A: I see your company has invested in some new machinery.

B: _____ .

(A) Yes, they are cutting down on new machines.

(B) Yes, and it's already up and running.

(C) Yes, they are interfering with other machines.

(D) Yes, it is taking advantages in a short time.

61. The group leader carefully reminds the group that no agricultural products _____ into the USA territory.

(A) are required   (B) are claiming   (C) are allowed   (D) are bringing

62. A: How many countries are you going to visit when you go on vacation to Asia?

B: _____ .

(A) Korea is the country I love best.

(B) Unfortunately I don't have much time left.

(C) Sure, many countries in Asia have wonderful cultures.

(D) Not very many. I don't have a lot of money.

63. A: My husband and I are leaving for Paris. We are taking a second honey moon.

B: _____ .

(A) Oh, nice! Business or pleasure?

(B) How romantic. Paris is a beautiful city.

(C) Well, that's the great thing about Paris.

(D) Sounds like you are a little busy.

64. At the end of the train there is an open _____ car where you can stand and smell the jungle, listen to the birds, and breathe in the sweet Asian air.

(A) primary   (B) installation   (C) observation   (D) moderation

65. If you are not delighted with your purchase, you can take the goods back to your retailer who will _____ you the purchase price.

(A) deliver   (B) refund   (C) exchange   (D) inform

66. Many tourists arriving in Japan naturally _____ their sightseeing in large cities such as Tokyo, Osaka, and Kyoto, not far from the international airports where they arrive.

(A) commence   (B) embrace   (C) navigate   (D) resemble

67. When it comes to catching the bad guys, a _____ camera is a police officer's best friend.

(A) medium   (B) protection   (C) surveillance   (D) treasure

68. A census analysis published in 2011 showed that almost all of the city's population increase since 2000 can _____ by an increase in residents between the ages of 20 and 35.

(A) be responsible for   (B) be accounted for

(C) be popular with   (D) be important for

69. China Airlines said yesterday it will work with U.S. based GE Aviation to improve the carrier's fuel efficiency _____ the volatile nature of fuel prices.

(A) in light of   (B) in spite of   (C) in proportion of   (D) in need of

70. Some retailers, desperate for sales and customer loyalty, have begun training their employees in the art of _____ with customers.

(A) playing   (B) cheating   (C) bargaining   (D) persuading

It is my first visit to the land where I was born, where most people have hair and eyes like mine, where I'm about as tall (or as short) as everyone else. Still, I am a foreigner, *laowai*. I left Taiwan in 1974, when I was an eight-month-old infant, to __71.__ by an American family in Detroit. Taipei, __72.__ about one hundred miles from the southeast coast of China, is a crowded landscape of skyscrapers, Buddhist temples, and weaving traffic.

I'd never wanted to visit Taiwan or my __73.__ family before, but here I am, feeling as if I never want to leave, magically __74.__ to a place and people I'd never known. Later, I'll look back and wonder if this intense sense of __75.__ was a dream, an illusion of desire.

71. (A) bringing up   (B) taken to live   (C) be raised   (D) being taken care

72. (A) located   (B) mapped   (C) carried   (D) placed

73. (A) economical   (B) biological   (C) premiere   (D) revolutionary

74. (A) similarly   (B) assimilating   (C) interesting   (D) uninterested

75. (A) losing   (B) missing   (C) longing   (D) belonging

You might think that a good tour guide needs to have a PhD in Art History or a family that dates back for seven generations in the area. **Neither could be further from the truth.** If you are reading this, you already have the best quality in a tour guide: curiosity. A good tour guide always wants to know about his/her surroundings and to learn about new things. Besides, a good tour guide also possesses the following qualities.

A good tour guide is sensitive to the needs of others. Although he/she can be as **gregarious** and funny as Robin Williams, or as knowledgeable as a professor, **neither talent will make for a great experience** unless the tour guide is sensitive enough to realize when someone's feet hurt. In other words, a good tour guide needs to be aware of the needs and limitations of his/her guests and to realize when they are tired, hungry, bored or simply unable to do the things they have signed up for.

A good tour guide is well organized. He/She always has plans, back up plans and contingency back up plans to help deal with unforeseen problems and complications. Being organized also means that a guide does not forget to meet someone or show up in the wrong place. He/She also knows when the museums, parks, restaurants and other attractions are open, and stays current on all local events so that he/she can suggest lots of things to do and see.

A good tour guide is knowledgeable about the local area. This includes places to go, places to eat, things to do, museums, and local attractions. A good tour guide always puts together a collection of local attraction brochures and keeps them with him/her. He/She also sends such materials to his/her guests before they arrive so that they can tell him/her what they are interested in seeing and doing.

76. The best title for this passage is _____ .

(A) Things to Be in Your City　　(B) Job as a Tour Guide

(C) Qualities of a Good Tour Guide　(D) Practice and Perfect Your Tours

77. The sentence "**Neither could be further from the truth**" in the first paragraph implies that _____ .

(A) a good tour guide needs to have a PhD in Art History

(B) a good tour guide needs to have his/her family living in an area for several generations

(C) a good tour guide needs to have both a PhD in Art History and residence in an area for generations

(D) a good tour guide needs to have neither a PhD in Art History nor residence in an area for generations

78 The word "**gregarious**" in the second paragraph means _____ .

(A) obsequious　　(B) convivial　　C) concerned　　(D) ludicrous

79. The phrase "**make for**" in the clause "**neither talent will make for a great experience**" means "_____ ."

(A) contribute to　　(B) take into consideration

(C) move toward　　(D) bear down on

80. As indicated in this passage, the best quality of a good tour guide is _____ .

(A) being sensitive　　　　　(B) being organized

(C) being knowledgeable　　　(D) being curious

03 Unit 103外語領隊英語考試——解析

1. Ⓑ；中譯：觀光客常常評論台灣是一個值得造訪的美麗寶島，那是一個美好的讚美語。

   解析：(A) complaint 抱怨 (B) compliment 恭維語 (C) compromise 協調 (D) complement 補充／由句子前面的說明知對台灣是表達肯定的，所以空格內應該是表達讚美的名詞，選項中以 compliment（恭維語）最適合，故答案為 (B)。

2. Ⓒ；中譯：珍喜歡旅行，且她抱著很大的熱情去旅行。

   解析：(A) entertainment 娛樂 (B) enormousness 巨大的 (C) enthusiasm 熱情 (D) enthronement 崇拜／因為她很喜歡旅行，推論她應該是對旅行有 enthusiasm（熱情），故答案為 (C)。

3. Ⓓ；中譯：從一位旅客的觀點來說，我必須承認這個城市有過多的新雕像及紀念碑。

   解析：(A) assumptive 假設的 (B) anticipative 預期的 (C) prescriptive 規定的 (D) perspective 看法／superfluous（多餘的、過多的），空格內需用名詞作為所有格 traveler's 的受詞，選項中只有 perspective（看法）為名詞且符合題意，故答案為 (D)。

4. Ⓐ；中譯：你如果在 2014 年前到達思科普里，你會看到有不少的建設，因為這個城市正進行一個大規模的變化。

   解析：(A) transformation 變化 (B) transaction 處理 (C) confirmation 確認 (D) confrontation 遭遇／quite a bit of（有不少的），因為有許多新的建設，城市應該是進行大規模的轉變，選項中以 transformation（變化）最適合，故答案為 (A)。

5. Ⓑ；中譯：導遊唸的這一段文章是摘錄自一篇長篇作品中。

   解析：(A) excess 超過 (B) excerpt 摘錄 (C) exception 例外 (D) exemption 豁免 passage 是指文章中的一小段，故由題意知該段文章為長篇文章中的一段，所以空格內用 excerpt（摘要）最符合題意，故答案為 (B)。

6. Ⓓ；中譯：在旅途期間，每當莎菈不瞭解導遊所說的事情時，她總是舉手發問。

   解析：(A) arises 興起 (B) rises 上升 (C) arouses 喚醒 (D) raises 舉起 由題意知空格內的動詞應為舉起手來的意思，需用 raises（舉起），故答案為 (D)。

7. Ⓑ；中譯：我們是否可以假設今晚不會下雨，並且籌劃戶外派對？

   解析：(A) resume 收回 (B) assume 假設 (C) consume 消費 (D) subsume 包含／先認為今晚不會下雨為前題再來籌畫派對，故空格內動詞以 assume（假設）最符合題意，答案為 (B)。

8. (C)；中譯：堅持下去你將會克服那些困難的。

   解析：(A) Persecute 迫害　(B) Predominate 統治　(C) Persevere 堅持　(D) Preserve 保存／本題為祈使句，句首空格內用原形動詞，由題意表示你最後將會克服困難，用原形動詞 Persevere（堅持）最恰當，故答案為 (C)。

9. (A)；中譯：我的朋友沒有放棄成為一位旅行領隊的夢想。

   解析：(A) relinquish 放棄　(B) distinguish 區別　(C) furnish 供應　(D) astonish 使驚訝 空格中需用動詞，依題意為沒有放棄成為領隊的夢想，動詞以 relinquish（放棄）最適合，故答案為 (A)。

10. (C)；中譯：這位經理強調他想要立下一些新的工作規則來加強工作場所的紀律。

    解析：make it clear（強調），由題意知空格內動詞應為設立、立訂之意，要用 lay down（制定），故答案為 (C)。

11. (B)；中譯：今日網路科技已經打破了時間及空間的藩籬。

    解析：(A) coincided 相符合　(B) collapsed 使崩潰　(C) collaborated 合作　(D) consisted 存在於／網路無遠弗屆，可以突破時間及空間的限制，所以空格中動詞用 collapsed（使崩潰）最適合且符合題意，答案為 (B)。

12. (D)；中譯：我們不允許我們思想的抗議變成實質的暴力。

    解析：(A) defect 叛變　(B) betray 出賣　(C) resist 反抗　(D) degenerate 變質／題意表達為無形思想的抗議變成為實質的暴力衝突，表示一種轉變，所以動詞用選項中的 degenerate（變質）最符合題意，故答案為 (D)。

13. (A)；中譯：這個年輕男子以得到 25 分以及送出 7 次助攻讓人眼睛為之一亮，並幫他的球隊獲勝。

    解析：(A) proceeded 進行　(B) provided 以⋯為條件　(C) devolved 轉交　(D) precancelled 已付郵資後取消／dazzle（耀眼），依題意表達這個人用好的表現讓人注目，故空格內動詞以選項中 proceeded（進行）最適合且符合題意，故答案為 (A)。

14. (C)；中譯：人類的知識現在是在轉換成永遠可用的數位型式的過程中。

    解析：(A) convicted 宣告有罪　(B) condescended 屈就　(C) converted 轉換　(D) confronted 面對／always-available（永遠可用的），空格內需用動詞過去分詞形成被動語態，題意是指知識轉變成數位型式，故用 be converted into（轉換成為），故答案為 (C)。

15. (D)；中譯：如果你在當時的情況要有立即的回應，請撥打我們的電話 101。

    解析：(A) immature 不成熟的　(B) inconvenient 不方便的　(C) immigrant 移民的　(D) immediate 立即的／由題意表示緊急狀況需要打緊急電話，故選項中以 immediate（立即的），表示立即的回應最符合題意，故答案為 (D)。

16. (B)；中譯：台北，台灣活力的首都城市，是 CNN 的全球最佳十個跨年地點之一。

    解析：(A) vicious 罪惡的　(B) vibrant 生氣勃勃的　(C) vigilant 不睡的　(D) vicarious

替代的／空格中的形容詞來形容這個城市，選項中以 vibrant（生氣勃勃的）最適合，表示是個有活力的城市，故答案為 (B)。

17. **D**；中譯：作為一個導遊，你需要更為關心一些重要的事情，而不是花費太多時間在瑣碎的事務上。

解析：(A) sensible 有知覺的　(B) voluble 流利的　(C) effusive 熱情洋溢的　(D) frivolous 瑣碎的／instead of（而不是），由題意知導遊要注意重要的事，而不要浪費時間在其他一些事情上，選項中以 frivolous（瑣碎的）最符合題意，故答案為 (D)。

18. **C**；中譯：父親總是在七月使用他的年度休假，讓我們能在海外團聚。

解析：(A) ambient 包圍的　(B) ambivalent 有矛盾感情的　(C) annual 年度的　(D) ancillary 輔助的／take vacation（渡假），空格中形容詞來形容這種假期，選項中以 annual（年度的）最適合，表示年度休假之意，故答案為 (C)。

19. **A**；中譯：這文件最後被證實為真且為法庭採信。

解析：(A) authentic 真實的　(B) confident 有信心的　(C) dubious 存疑的　(D) fragile 脆弱的／空格中需用形容詞作為主詞補語，説明文件的狀態。由題意知文件已被接受，空格內以 authentic（真實的）最符合題意，故答案為 (A)。

20. **D**；中譯：沒有堅強的電腦技能的求職者將不會像有這方面能力的人一樣具有相同的競爭力。

解析：(A) compensative 賠償的　(B) comprehensible 能理解的　(C) comprehensive 全面的　(D) competitive 競爭的／as +形容詞+ as 表示與…相同，依題意是説沒電腦能力的人其競爭力會不如有這方面能力的人，故空格內形容詞用 competitive（競爭的），答案為 (D)。

21. **B**；中譯：我們用自己不該受的苦難可以為自身贖罪的這種信念來繼續工作。

解析：(A) preemptive 先買的　(B) redemptive 贖罪的　(C) emotive 感情的　(D) promotive 提升的／unearned suffering 意思是不屬於（我們）的苦難，空格中用形容詞當主詞（unearned suffering）的補語，本句的意思是指受苦可以贖罪，所以選項中以 redemptive（贖罪的）最適當，故答案為 (B)。

22. **C**；中譯：當在瑞士旅行時，你可以看到一些永久被冰雪覆蓋的高山。

解析：(A) desperately 絕望地　(B) imminently 立即地　(C) perpetually 永久地　(D) radically 激進地／瑞士有許多終年被白雪覆蓋的高山，所以空格中的副詞以 perpetually（永久地）最為適當，用來修飾 covered（動詞過去分詞當形容詞用），故答案為 (C)。

23. **B**；中譯：我們的導遊是一位如此的甜美的女士，以致於我們不想去向她抱怨關於飯店服務的事。

解析：本題考「如此…以致於」的句型，可用 such a sweet lady that…或 so sweet a lady that…，故答案為 (B)。

24. (C)；中譯：我們的導遊提供的資訊是多麼有價值啊！

　　解析：有用的資訊要用 useful information，所以答案為 (C)。注意 information 為不可數名詞，不可使用複數型及不加不定冠詞 a 或 an。

25. (D)；中譯：我相信我去年夏天參加的旅行比你參加的要有趣的多了。

　　解析：本題考比較級，多音節的形容詞比較級為 more+ 形容詞，本題前面可以再用副詞修飾，故為 much more interesting，故答案為 (D)。

26. (A)；中譯：當他收到這封我正在寫的信時，我也許正在這個國家四處旅行。

　　解析：本題考時態，副詞子句用簡單現在式表未來時間，主要子句用 may+現在式或進行式，表示未來可能的狀態，所以答案為 (A)。

27. (B)；中譯：關於誰才是領導者的爭議，在我們到那邊之前已經解決了。

　　解析：牽涉到二個過去時間先後發生的動作時，先發生者用過去完成式，後發生者用過去式，本題中，爭議的解決（動詞要用被動）是在我們到之前就發生，空格內應用過去完成被動式，故答案為 (B)。

28. (A)；中譯：我們領隊英語和法語講得很好，並且導遊也是一樣。

　　解析：表示導遊英語和法語講得也很好，要用 so does our tour guide，其中 does 替代 speaks English and French well，且 so 置於句首，該句要用倒裝，故答案為 (A)。

29. (C)；中譯：旅遊通常會帶給開發中國家他們急需的錢，此外，旅遊會給當地居民帶來就業。

　　解析：(A) However 不論如何　(B) Therefore 因此　(C) Furthermore 除此之外　(D) For instance 例如／前面提到旅遊會帶來收入，後一句表示更會給當地帶來就業，所以空格用副詞 Furthermore（除此之外）最恰當，表示更加強調這些旅遊帶來的好處，故答案為 (C)。

30. (D)；中譯：假如珍有贏得那場比賽，她將已經獲得一趟免費的英國旅遊了，換句話說，珍輸了那場比賽。

　　解析：本題考假設語氣，題目中 if 子句中用過去完成式，主要子句用 would+現在完成式，所以該句為與過去事實相反的假設，也就是珍沒能贏得那場比賽，她輸掉那場比賽，故答案為 (D)。

31. (C)；中譯：旅客：抱歉！哪裡是美國航空的報到櫃台？

　　　　　工作人員：它在第二航站，這裡是第一航站。

　　解析：由題意知旅客應該是問報到櫃台 check-in counter，故答案為 (C)。

32. (A)；中譯：工作人員：假如你搭乘國際航班，我認為你必須要在你起飛前三小時報到。

　　　　　旅客：如果是國內線呢？

　　　　　工作人員：在那些航線，你必須在一個半小時前報到。

　　解析：班機分為國際線（international flight）及國內線（domestic flight），由題意知旅客是問國內線，故答案為 (A)。

33. (B)；中譯：工作人員：抱歉！我可以看一下你的護照及機票嗎？

　　　　　旅客：當然，這是我的護照，而這是我的電子機票。

解析：工作人員表示要看護照及機票，旅客除了給護照外，空格的選項中有電子機票（e-ticket），故答案為 (B)。

34. (C)；中譯：工作人員：先生，抱歉，你的其中一個袋子超重了，我將向您加收超重的費用。

　　　　　旅客：我想想看，我該付多少額外費用？還有我能刷卡付帳嗎？

　　　　　工作人員：30 元，先生，還有是的，我們可以接受信用卡。

解析：行李超重需另外付費，額外費用為 extra，故答案為 (C)。

35. (B)；中譯：迪化街是購買傳統中式食材的好地方，這些食材被視為貴重的禮物，許多商店都會為航空旅行需要來密封採購項目。

解析：空格處需填入關係形容詞子句的動詞，先行詞是 foods（複數），故動詞需用簡單現在式 make（意思當被認為），故答案為 (B)。

36. (D)；中譯：國立台灣博物館早在 1908 年當日本佔據台灣時候就建造了。

解析：way back（很早以前），空格中動詞需用被動過去式，所以用 was built，答案為 (D)。

37. (C)；中譯：二樓可以探索原住民文化，讓訪客瞭解關於原住民部落對台灣歷史的重要性。

解析：空格處需用表示目的分詞構句，且因表示主動所以用 teaching，故答案為 (C)。

38. (C)；中譯：你不論你去哪裏皆可以隨身攜帶一隻手機，但你不能將你的電腦也一併帶去。

解析：空格中需用連接詞引導副詞子句，依題意應表示無論你去哪裏，所以用表地方的 wherever，故答案為 (C)。

39. (A)；中譯：享有特價優待及兩客免費早餐，我們的住宿加早餐的組合是你放鬆及充電的最佳方式。

解析：(A) complimentary 免費的　(B) compulsory 強制的　(C) condescending 屈尊的　(D) commodious 方便的／由題意知該類行程是指住房優惠及附贈二客免費早餐，空格處用 complimentary（免費的）最符合題意，故答案為 (A)。

40. (C)；中譯：任何讓旅客可以有當地文化氛圍的事，或是一個在抵達時候私人的問候，都可增加這個機場以及它所在的城市及國家給人討喜的經驗。

解析：(A) is available for 可用於　(B) adjusts to 適應　(C) adds to 增加　(D) gets over 克服／空格內為該句的動詞，由題意知讓旅客體驗文化及親切的問候等會使這個機場或國家給人的印象有正面的影響，選項中以 adds to（增加）最合題意，也就是增加旅客對這地區的好感，故答案為 (C)。

41. (C)；中譯：在我們穿越沙漠的旅程中，我們的食物、衣物及其他物品是被一支駝獸隊伍所運送。

解析：possessions（所有物），空格為本句動詞，依題意可知這些物品是被一些動物所運送，所以需用被動式，且為過去時間，故空格內需用 were transported by，故答案為 (C)。

42. **B**；中譯：去年我想要到戈壁沙漠長途跋涉，但我的醫生不允許我去，因為我的身體狀況不佳。

解析： trekking（長途跋涉），到沙漠長途跋涉需要良好的身體狀況，身體的狀況為 physical shape，故答案為 (B)。

43. **A**；中譯：有幾項政府的新政策預定今天要生效。

解析：(A) take effect 生效　(B) avoid contact 逃避接觸　(C) go over 查看　(D) work off 償清／be scheduled to（預定），新的政策會有開始實施的時間，故空格內以選項 take effect（生效）最符合題意，答案為 (A)。

44. **B**；中譯：大部分的人會告訴你在吃飯時講手機是不禮貌的，然而同時自己也犯了在吃飯中講手機的錯。

解析：at the table（吃飯時），be guilty of（犯…的錯誤），題意應指告訴別人吃飯時不可講手機，卻容許自己犯同樣的錯，所以空格中用動名詞 admitting（容許）當介係詞 while 受詞，故答案為 (B)。

45. **D**；中譯：線上課程能讓教師及學生互相交流，甚至是當他們是在相隔兩地的情況下。

解析：(A) take care of 照顧　(B) make up 補足　(C) make an appointment to 預約去　(D) hold the promise of 保證／空格為本句動詞，由題意表示線上課程可以讓學生與老師互動交流，依選項中各動詞片語代入，其中以 hold the promise of（保證）最合理，，故答案為 (D)。

46. **B**；中譯：荷蘭藝術家霍夫曼對他的黃色小鴨裝置在基隆展出的安排感到失望。

解析：be upset about（對…感到失望），由題意可知霍夫曼對展出的安排感到失望，展出應用 on display，故答案為 (B)。

47. **D**；中譯：在公共廁所提供的洗手肥皂已經被發現含有超過很高數量的生菌數。

解析：空格內需用動詞的過去分詞當形容詞，修飾前面的 soaps，所以用 provided（被提供，表示被動）最適合，故答案為 (D)。

48. **D**；中譯：他起得夠早所以看得到日出的第一道曙光。

解析：要注意 enough 修飾形容詞時要置於形容詞後面，故答案為 (D)。

49. **A**；中譯：往阿姆斯特丹的 506 航班，原訂上午 11:30 起飛，因為濃霧緣故已經延誤了。

解析：(A) on account of 由於…原因　(B) in case of 如果　(C) by way of 經由　(D) aware of 知道／由題意知延誤的原因是由於濃霧的緣故，選項中應用 on account of（由於…原因），答案為 (A)。

50. **D**；中譯：除了允許人們買單鞋，每季一次這些沒人要的庫存單鞋會免費送給會員。

解析：(A) Before 在之前　(B) On the contrary 相反地　(C) By taking chance 碰運氣　(D) In addition to 除了…之外／once a season（每季一次），空格需用介係詞（片語）來引導後面名詞片語，依題意是指除了可以用買的以外，每季還能有機會獲得免費贈送，故空格中用 In addition to（除了…之外）最適合且符合題意，答案為 (D)。

51. (B)；中譯：許多人要到東南亞旅行時，都會設法避開雨季，因為那會使得到處遊玩變得更加困難。

解析：monsoon season（雨季），空格內需用形容詞當主詞補語，依題意為使旅遊更加困難，故用選項中的 much harder，答案為 (B)。注意副詞要用 much，不用 very。

52. (A)；中譯：這個旅行團拿到優惠的促銷價格，而這需要有一次中途停留在日本大約二個小時轉機。

解析：(A) a connecting flight 轉機航班　(B) a non-stop flight 直飛航班　(C) a direct flight 直飛航班　(D) a daily flight 延誤航班 stop-over（中途停留），由題意知這團的行程需在日本停留並轉機，故空格用 a connecting flight（轉機航班），答案為 (A)。

53. (A)；中譯：有許多微小但實用的方法讓你可以節約能源，並且幫助保護環境。

解析：(A) conserve 節約　(B) observe 觀察　(C) deserve 應得　(D) serve 服務
由題目中提到幫助環保，所以空格處應該指節約能源之意，故選項中以 conserve（節約）最符合題意，答案為 (A)。

54. (C)；中譯：只有在星期天你才可以免費參訪這座博物館。

解析：本題考倒裝語句，only 放在句首時，後面主詞及動詞位置要對調（也就是倒裝），如有助動詞需移至主詞前面，所以空格內需用 can you visit the museum，答案為 (C)。

55. (B)；中譯：雙胞胎不必然都是好的，他們有較高的早產及嚴重健康問題的風險。

解析：(A) preliterate 沒有文字前的　(B) premature 不成熟的　(C) prejudiced 有偏見的　(D) prescribed 指示／twice as nice 是指雙倍的好，也就是雙重的保險之意。由題意知他們可能會有嚴重的健康風險及其他出生時的風險，選項中以 premature（不成熟的）最適合，表示初生時尚未成熟，也就是早產之意，故答案為 (B)。

56. (B)；中譯：A：抱歉，先生。我們明天需一大早離開去搭我們的航班，我們團可以比較早安排用早餐嗎？

B：(A) 沒問題，早上是沒有早餐的　(B) 你需要幾點鐘用早餐？　(C) 從飯店到機場需要多久？　(D) 沒問題，需要我們現在幫你們服務嗎？

解析：A 問 B 是否能安排較早時段用餐，B 的回答以 (B) 你需要幾點鐘用早餐？最適當，故答案為 (B)。

57. (D)；中譯：購買旅遊保險總是個好主意，假如你在旅途中生病或是遺失你的物品，保險公司將會付你的醫藥費或付你錢。

解析：(A) medicines 藥品　(B) travel guide 導遊　(C) duty free goods 免稅商品　(D) travel insurance 旅遊保險／句中提到生病或物品遺失都可以獲得理賠，所以推定

空格中建議要購買的東西是 travel insurance（旅遊保險），答案為 (D)。

58. (A)；中譯：一項全國性的鳥類調查將大約在新年假期開始實施，以慶祝新年並且喚醒大眾對野生動物保護的意識。

解析：(A) raise 叫醒　(B) switch 擺動　(C) divide 分開　(D) arise 上升／空格後面表示大眾對野生動物保護的意識等，故空格中動詞應用 raise（叫醒、喚醒）最適合，故答案為 (A)。

59. (D)；中譯：如果我們不減少消耗的程度，不久我們的天然資源將消耗殆盡。

解析：(A) calcify 使硬化　(B) multiply 成倍增加　(C) generate 產生　(D) reduce 減少　used up（用完了），由題意知是要我們減少消耗地球資源，所以空格內的動詞用 reduce（減少）最符合題意，故答案為 (D)。

60. (B)；中譯：A：我看到你們公司已經投資了一些新的機器。

B：(A) 是的，他們正削減新機器　(B) 是的，新機器已經備好並運轉中　(C) 是的，它們正與其他機器產生干擾　(D) 是的，它在短間內獲得優勢。

解析：A 問 B 它們公司投資新機器的事，B 回答以 (B) 新機器已經備好並運轉中最為恰當，來說明現在機器的狀況，故答案為 (B)。

61. (C)；中譯：這團領隊仔細地提醒團員們農產製品不可以攜入美國境內。

解析：空格處為 that 子句的動詞，依題意應為農產品不被允許進入美國，應用被動式，所以空格用 are allowed（被允許），故答案為 (C)。

62. (D)；中譯：A：在你去亞洲度假時，你將到多少國家去？

B：(A) 韓國是我最喜歡的國家　(B) 很遺憾的我沒有剩下很多時間　(C) 當然，亞洲的許多國家都有令人驚奇的文化　(D) 沒有多少國家，我沒有太多錢。

解析：A 問 B 去亞洲會去幾個國家，重點是問多少國家，所以回答時以(D) 沒有多少國家，我沒有太多錢最恰當，故答案為 (D)。

63. (B)；中譯：A：我及我先生將要到巴黎去，我們要二度蜜月。

B：(A) 啊，太好了！公務或者去旅遊？　(B) 好羅曼蒂克啊！巴黎是個漂亮的城市　(C) 嗯，這正是巴黎很棒的一點。　(D) 聽起來你有一點忙。

解析：A 向 B 說要去巴黎二度蜜月，已經清楚說明去的目的，回答時以 (B) 好羅蒂克阿，巴黎是個漂亮的城市，表示贊同這個地點最為適當，故答案為 (B)。

64. (C)；中譯：在火車的末端有一個開放的景觀車廂，在那裏你可以站立著，聞到叢林的味道、聽到鳥叫聲以及呼吸到亞洲芬芳的空氣。

解析：(A) primary 主要的　(B) installation 裝置　(C) observation 觀察　(D) moderation 緩和／題意指出在這個車廂中你可以用聽覺、嗅覺及呼吸到自然的事物，所以空格中應是指 observation car（景觀車廂），故答案為 (C)。

65. (B)；中譯：如果你不滿意你買的物品，你可以將物品帶回到零售商，他將會退你購買價格的錢。

解析：(A) deliver 遞送　(B) refund 退款　(C) exchange 交換　(D) inform 通知

be delighted with（對…感到高興），由題意知空格內應是指買到不滿意的東西要退款之意，應用 refund（退款），答案為 (B)。

66. (A)；中譯：許多抵達日本的旅客自然地會從一些大城市像是東京、大阪及京都開始觀光行程，不會離他們抵達的國際機場太遠。

解析：(A) commence 著手開始　(B) embrace 擁抱　(C) navigate 導航　(D) resemble 相似／空格中要填入本句的動詞，由題意表示觀光客一般會從機場附近的城市去觀光，所以動詞用選項中 commence（著手開始）最恰當，表示從這些地方開始觀光行程，故答案為 (A)。

67. (C)；中譯：當說到要逮捕不良份子時，監視攝影機是警察最好的朋友。

解析：(A) medium 媒介　(B) protection 保護　(C) surveillance 監視　(D) treasure 財富 When it comes to+Ving（當提到要…），由題意知空格處是指監視器的意思，所以用 surveillance camera，答案為 (C)。

68. (B)；中譯：2011 年出版的一份戶口普查分析指出，從 2000 年起幾乎所有這個城市的增加的人口是由於年紀介於 20 到 35 歲的居民增加所致。

解析：(A) be responsible for 為…負責　(B) be accounted for 歸因於　(C) be popular with 因…受歡迎　(D) be important for 因…重要 census（人口統計） 由題意可知該年齡群人口增加是這個城市人口增加的主因，故選項中以 be accounted for（歸因於）最適當，答案為 (B)。

69. (A)；中譯：中華航空公司昨天說有鑑於油價的波動特性，它將與美國的 GE 航太公司合作來改善客機的燃油效率。

解析：(A) in light of 有鑑於　(B) in spite of 雖然　(C) in proportion of 與成正比　(D) in need of 需要／volatile（反覆無常的），題意是說因為油價波動的特性，華航要與 GE 公司合作提高燃油效率，而選項中以 in light of（有鑑於）符合題意，表示是基於這種因素，故答案為 (A)。

70. (C)；中譯：有些零售商極度渴望銷售業績及顧客忠誠，已經開始訓練他們的員工用與顧客討價還價的詭計。

解析：(A) playing 玩　(B) cheating 欺騙　(C) bargaining 討價還價　(D) persuading 說服／desperate for（渴望），in the art of 表示用…的詭計，依題意是指零售商為業績不擇手段，所以用一些詭計訓練他們的銷售員，選項中以 bargaining（討價還價）最適當，故答案為 (C)。

71-75；中譯：那是我第一次造訪我出生的地方，在那裏大部份的人和我一樣有著相同的頭髮及眼睛，在那裏我與其他的人一般高（或一樣矮）。但是，我依然是個外國人，老外。我在 1974 年離開台灣，當我還是一個八個月大的嬰兒時，被一個在底特律的家庭撫養長大。台北，位於中國東南沿海約一百英哩外，是一個聚集了摩天大樓、佛教寺院及交通川流不息的地方。

我以前從沒想到過去造訪台灣，或者我出生的家庭，但現在我來了，感覺如同我從來不想要離開，很奇妙地，對一個我從未認識的地方及人似曾相識。以後，我將會回顧並懷疑是否這深刻歸屬的感覺是一場夢、一場渴望的幻想。

71. C ；

解析：空格處需用動詞形成不定詞片語，且依前後句意表示被撫養長大，需要用被動式，所以空格內用 be raised，故答案為 (C)。

72. A ；

解析：空格處說明台北的位置，以過去分詞使用當形容詞用，修飾前面的名詞，所以用 located，答案為 (A)。

73. B ；中譯：(A) economical 經濟的 (B) biological 生物學上的 (C) premiere 最早的 (D) revolutionary 革命的

解析：由前後文知，空格處的家庭應該是指作者原來出生的地方，選項中以 biological（生物學上）來形容最適合，也就是指出生地的意思，故答案為 (B)。

74. B ；中譯：(A) similarly 相似地 (B) assimilating 使相似（分詞） (C) interesting 有趣的 (D) uninterested 公平地

解析：該句意為對從未認識的地方及人好像似曾相識，空格處需用動詞的現在分詞形成分詞構句，表示這一種結果，選項中以 assimilating（使相似）最適合，故答案為 (B)。

75. D ；

解析：空格為介係詞 of 的受詞，故用動名詞，句子的意思是指歸屬的感覺（因為前面提到未到過這地方卻感覺來過），所以空格應用 belonging，答案為 (D)。

76-80 ；中譯：你也許會認為一個好導遊需要具有藝術史博士學位，或是在居住這個地區已經住了 7 個世代的家族。二者皆錯得離譜，如果你正讀到這裏，你已經具備了一個導遊的最大特質：好奇心。一個好的導遊總是想要去瞭解他/她周遭環境以及學習新的事物，除此之外，一個好的導遊也具有以下特質。

一個好導遊對其他人的需求是敏感的，雖然他或她可能是像羅賓威廉斯一樣的喜歡與人相處且風趣，或者是像教授一樣學問淵博，這兩種本事都不足以成為一個好的經驗，除非導遊具有足夠的敏感度來瞭解當一個人腳受傷時的感受。換句話說，一個好的導遊必須知道他或她的客人的需求及限制因素，並且能瞭解當他們累了、餓了、厭煩或單純不能夠做一些他們已經報名要做的事。

一個好的導遊是條理清楚的，他或她總是有計畫、備份計畫以及偶發事件的備份計畫來處理無法預見的問題及抱怨。條理清楚也意味著一個導遊不會忘記與某人見面或出現在錯誤的地方，他或她也知道何時博物館、公園、餐廳或其它景點開放的時間，並且對所有當地活動瞭若指掌，使他或她可以建議許多可以去做以及去看的東西。

一個好的導遊對當地必須是有見識的，這包含可以去的地方、可以吃的地方、可以做的事情、博物館、以及當地的景點。一個好的導遊總是收集當地的景點簡介手冊並隨身攜帶。他或她也會將這些資料在客人抵達前送給他或她的客人，讓他們可以先指出他們有興趣去看或是去做的事。

76. ⓒ；中譯：這篇文章最佳的題目是：(A) 在你的城市要做的事　(B) 關於導遊的工作　(C) 一個好導遊的特質　(D) 熟練讓你的旅遊達到完美

解析：文章一開始談到好導遊需具備的人格特質，再談到好導遊要有敏感度，並要有同理心去感受團員的需求等，都是圍繞在一位好導遊的各種特質，所以最佳題目應為一個好導遊的特質，答案為 (C)。

77. ⓓ；中譯：在文章中第一段的 "二者皆不是事實" 這句話意謂著　(A) 一個好導遊需要有藝術史的博士學位　(B) 一個好導遊他/她的家族在這個區域已經數個世代　(C) 一個好導遊需要有藝術史的博士學位且在這個區域已經居住數個世代　(D) 一個好導遊既不需要有藝術史的博士學位且不需在這個區域已經居住數個世代

解析：文章中提到二者分別是具有博士學位及家族已經住在當地好幾代，文中的意思是一個好導遊既不需要有藝術史的博士學位且不需在這個區域已經居住數個世代，答案為 (D)。

78. ⓑ；中譯：在文章第二段中 "gregarious" 這個字表示(A) obsequious 奉承的　(B) convivial 歡樂的，友好的　(C) concerned 擔心的　(D) ludicrous 可笑的

解析： "gregarious" 是合群的意思，這個在句中表示喜歡與人相處之意，與選項中的 convivial（歡樂的，友好的）意思相近，故答案為 (B)。

79. ⓐ；中譯： "neither talent will make for a great experience" 句中的 "make for" 這片語意思是 (A) contribute to 幫助　(B) take into consideration 考慮到　(C) move toward 朝某方向　(D) bear down on 逼近

解析：這句話是指這兩種才能也無法造就出一個好的經驗，"make for"故在此意思為對…有幫助之意，也就是選項中 contribute to（幫助）之意，故答案為 (A)。

80. ⓓ；中譯：就本文所提到，一個好導遊最重要的特質是(A) 要感覺靈敏的　(B) 要有系統的　(C) 要有知識的　(D) 要有好奇心

解析：由第一段…you already have the best quality in a tour guide: curiosity…，知一個好導遊最重要的特質是要有好奇心，答案為 (D)。

NOTE

04 Unit
101 外語導遊
英語考試—試題

101 專門職業及技術人員普通考試導遊人員、領隊人員考試試題
等別：普通考試
類科：外語導遊人員（英語）
科目：外國語（英語）
考試時間：1 小時 20 分
※注意：本試題為單一選擇題，請選出一個正確或最適當的答案，複選作答者，該題不予計分。

1. At the annual food festival, you can _____ a wide variety of delicacies.

   (A) sample   (B) deliver   (C) cater   (D) reduce

2. On my flight to Tokyo, I asked a flight _____ to bring me an extra pillow.

   (A) clerk   (B) employer   (C) chauffeur   (D) attendant

3. Cloud Gate, an internationally _____ dance group from Taiwan, demonstrated that the quality of modern dance in Asia could be comparable to that of modern dance in Europe and North America.

   (A) refunded   (B) reflected   (C) retained   (D) renowned

4. The complex is _____ of the main building, a tennis court, and a wonderful garden.

   (A) organized   (B) collected   (C) occupied   (D) comprised

5. The zoo features more than 1,000 animals in their natural _____ .

   (A) habitats   (B) playgrounds   (C) landmarks   (D) facilities

6. A good tour guide has to be _____ to the people in his group.

   (A) considered   (B) conditioned   (C) confided   (D) committed

7. I just spent a relaxing afternoon taking a _____ along the river-walk.

   (A) trot   (B) dip   (C) stroll   (D) look

8. In the entrance hall of the natural history museum, you can find a full-sized _____ of a dinosaur.

(A) replica   (B) revival   (C) remodel   (D) revision

9. The _____ of our trip to Southern Taiwan was A Taste of Tainan where we had a lot of delicious food.

(A) gourmet   (B) highlight   (C) monument   (D) recognition

10. Sara bought a beautiful dress in a _____ in a fashionable district in Milan.

(A) boutique   (B) brochure   (C) bouquet   (D) balcony

11. Bopiliao, _____ in Wanhua District, Taipei, and serving as the setting for the film, *Monga*, is a popular tourist spot.

(A) selected   (B) featured   (C) located   (D) directed

12. Before we left the hotel, our tour guide gave us a thirty-minute _____ on the local culture.

(A) exhibition   (B) presentation   (C) construction   (D) invitation

13. Chichi is a town in Central Taiwan that is _____ by rail.

(A) accessible   (B) approached   (C) available   (D) advanced

14. The man at the passport _____ did not seem to like the photo in my passport, but in the end he let me through.

(A) station   (B) custom   (C) security   (D) control

15. Success does not happen by chance. It's achieved through hard work and _____.

(A) expiration   (B) reception   (C) preparation   (D) irritation

16. If you want, I can _____ it easier for you.

(A) weigh   (B) act   (C) be   (D) make

17. All resources are _____ in the sense that there are not enough to fill everyone's wants to the point of satisfaction.

(A) scarce   (B) absent   (C) plentiful   (D) fertile

18. Thanks to India's economic _____ and the booming growth of its airline industry, more Indians are flying today than ever before.

(A) prosperity   (B) souvenir   (C) decline   (D) evidence

19. The tour guide is a _____ man; he is very polite and always speaks in a kind manner.

(A) careless　(B) persistent　(C) courteous　(D) environmental

20. This restaurant features _____ Northern Italian dishes that reflect the true flavors of Italy.

(A) disposable　(B) confident　(C) authentic　(D) dimensional

21. On my first trip to Taipei, my _____ about the city is close to zero.

(A) consensus　(B) knowledge　(C) restoration　(D) honor

22. _____ excellence in running a hotel restaurant is considered by many hotel managers the most difficult challenge of all.

(A) Achieving　(B) Resembling　(C) Dictating　(D) Exhausting

23. Take your time. I don't need an answer _____ .

(A) consistently　(B) regularly　(C) immediately　(D) frequently

24. Don't over pack when you travel because you can always _____ new goods along the way.

(A) watch　(B) acquire　(C) promote　(D) throw

25. Whales are _____ , like we are, and must swim to the surface to breathe air.

(A) teenagers　(B) performers　(C) giants　(D) mammals

26. The landscape of this natural park is best seen on bike or foot, and there are _____ trails in the area. All paths offer breath-taking sceneries.

(A) sole　(B) simultaneous　(C) numerous　(D) indifferent

27. If you need a ride to the airport, please don't _____ to call me. I'll be available all this afternoon.

(A) pursue　(B) hesitate　(C) stop　(D) think

28. With crystal clear water, emerald green mountains and various outdoor activities to offer, it's not _____ that Sun Moon Lake is one of the most visited spots in Taiwan.

(A) identified　(B) apparent　(C) grateful　(D) surprising

29. Taiwan is well known for its mountain _____ spots and urban landmarks such as the National Palace Museum and the Taipei 101 skyscraper.

(A) scenic　(B) neutral　(C) vacant　(D) feasible

30. Trash can be _____ for creatures that live in the water. Every year, plastic trash kills millions of sea birds, marine mammals and sea turtles.

(A) invaluable   (B) dangerous   (C) spoiling   (D) tedious

31. Many concerns were _____ about South Africa hosting the World Cup in 2010, but in the end South Africa pulled it off and did an excellent job.

(A) surpassed   (B) licensed   (C) implemented   (D) raised

32. The notion that fashionable shopping takes place only in cities is_____ , thanks to the Internet.

(A) outdated   (B) approximated   (C) rehearsed   (D) motivated

33. Night markets in Taiwan have become _____ tourist destinations. They are great places to shop for bargains and eat typical Taiwanese food.

(A) tropical   (B) popular   (C) edible   (D) responsible

34. It has been my honor and pleasure to work with him for more than 10 years. His insight and analysis are always_____.

(A) distant   (B) superficial   (C) impressive   (D) premature

35. The tragedy could have been avoided but for the _____ of the driver.

(A) carefulness   (B) prediction   (C) negligence   (D) alertness

36. According to the meeting _____, three more topics are to be discussed this afternoon.

(A) agenda   (B) invoice   (C) recipe   (D) catalog

37. Taroko National Park _____ high mountains and steep canyons. Many of its peaks tower above 3,000 meters in elevation.

(A) lacks   (B) features   (C) excludes   (D) disregards

38. The local tour guide has a _____ personality. Everybody likes him.

(A) windy   (B) stormy   (C) sunny   (D) cloudy

39. Tomorrow I will be able to let you know _____ how many people will join the trip.

(A) tremendously   (B) highly   (C) rationally   (D) precisely

40. _____ fireworks shows lit up the sky of cities around the world as people celebrated the start of 2012.

(A) Invisible　(B) Spectacular　(C) Dull　(D) Endangered

41. A: "Excuse me. Can I take this seat?" B: "Sorry, it is _____."

(A) empty　(B) closed　(C) occupied　(D) complete

42. Many teenagers _____ late to play online games.

(A) grow up　(B) break up　(C) take place　(D) stay up

43. To _____ health and fitness, we need proper diet and exercise.

(A) maintain　(B) apply　(C) retire　(D) contain

44. From the evidence, it seems quite _____ that someone broke into my office last night.

(A) humble　(B) inspiring　(C) obvious　(D) promising

45. I hate to go through the _____ process of application again. I need an assistant to do it for me.

(A) interesting　(B) energetic　(C) fascinating　(D) tedious

46. I was very scared when our flight was passing through _____ from the nearby storm.

(A) turbulence　(B) breeze　(C) currency　(D) brilliance

47. Most critics _____ the failure of the movie to its lack of humanity.

(A) caused　(B) imputed　(C) rewarded　(D) dedicated

48 It is _____ impossible to train cats to do what you want them to do, but this one called Sasha can not only shake hands with people but also use the toilet.

(A) unlikely　(B) casually　(C) virtually　(D) secondly

49. My most memorable trip is climbing Mount Fuji. Getting to the _____ and seeing the sunrise from the top of the clouds was amazing.

(A) depth　(B) remark　(C) twig　(D) peak

50. Jennifer is _____ in several languages other than her mother tongue English.

(A) fluent　(B) quiet　(C) universal　(D) tall

51. The heavy rain in the valley often affects my _____ , so I sometimes have to pull my car over to the side of the road and wait until the rain stops.

(A) landscape (B) sight (C) image (D) taste

52. Costa Brava is a popular tourist destination in northeastern Spain, thanks to its
_____ climate, beautiful beaches, and charming towns.

(A) dreadful (B) contemporary (C) moderate (D) bitter

53. I really like your scarf. Can I _____ my hat for that?

(A) expand (B) exist (C) exchange (D) expel

54. At the Welcome Center, you will find plenty of _____ , including maps,
brochures, and wireless internet access.

(A) resources (B) reformation (C) documents (D) assistance

55. With its palaces, sculptured parks, concert halls, and museums, Vienna is a city
_____ in cultures.

(A) chronic (B) elite (C) provincial (D) steeped

56. The oldest of all the main Hawaiian islands, Kauai is _____ for its
secluded beaches, scenic waterfalls, and jungle hikes.

(A) due (B) known (C) neutral (D) ripe

57. _____ in 1730, Lancaster's Central Market is the oldest continuously
operating farmers market in the United States.

(A) Demolished (B) Established (C) Imported (D) Located

58. High in the mountains of Chiapas, San Cristóbal del la Casas is one of the most
_____ spots in Mexico: colorful, historic, and remarkably complex.

(A) antarctic (B) cosmetic (C) photogenic (D) synthetic

59. A single visit to Rome is not enough. The city's layered complexity _____
time.

(A) assists (B) demands (C) evolves (D) lingers

60. Right now, there are more tigers in _____ than there are left in the wild.
We need to take action to save the big cats.

(A) captivity (B) debt (C) haste (D) quality

61. After a shipwreck, cruise companies try to _____ back hesitant passengers
with discounts.

(A) bounce (B) coil (C) lure (D) ransom

62. A canal _____ along a leafy bike pass, through green parks, and pass the city's four remaining windmills.

(A) injects   (B) meanders   (C) pollutes   (D) rumbles

63. Tourists have a wide range of budget and tastes, and a wide variety of resorts and hotels have developed to _____ for them.

(A) cater   (B) desire   (C) mourn   (D) pray

64. The developments of technology and transport infrastructure have made many types of tourism more _____ .

(A) affordable   (B) considerable   (C) exclusive   (D) illusive

65. For many, vacations and travel are increasingly being viewed as a _____ rather than a luxury and this is reflected in tourist numbers.

(A) community   (B) dynasty   (C) necessity   (D) sincerity

66. The view of _____ waterfalls in the rainforest is spectacular.

(A) ascending   (B) cascading   (C) flourishing   (D) overflowing

67. If you plan and time it right, some home _____ can let you stay somewhere for free.

(A) abiding   (B) boosting   (C) meditating   (D) swapping

68. Preservation Hall is one of the many jazz _____ in New Orleans, but some of the best music can still be found on street corners, in backyards and at funerals.

(A) ceremonies   (B) distractions   (C) habitats   (D) venues

69. As a general rule, it's best to avoid wearing white clothing and accessories when traveling. Go with darker colors that _____ dirt well.

(A) delete   (B) hide   (C) parade   (D) imply

70. People love to socialize, and Facebook makes it easier. The shy become more _____ online.

(A) modest   (B) outgoing   (C) pious   (D) timid

Let's picture a huge public gathering – like the hajj to Mecca. Think of the World Cup, the Olympics, or a rock concert. When thousands or even millions of people get together, what will be the biggest health concern? Traditionally, doctors and public health officials were most concerned about the spread of infectious diseases. Robert Steffen, a professor of travel medicine at the University of Zurich, says that infectious diseases are still a concern, but injuries are a bigger threat at so-called mass gatherings.

According to Professor Steffen, children and older people have the highest risk of injury or other health problems at mass gathering events. Children are at more risk of getting crushed in stampedes, while older people are at higher risk of heat stroke and dying from extreme heat.

Stampedes at mass gatherings have caused an estimated seven thousand deaths over the past thirty years. The design of an area for mass gathering can play a part. There may be narrow passages or other choke points that too many people try to use at once. The mood of a crowd can also play a part. Organizers of large gatherings need to avoid creating conditions that might lead to stampedes and heat stroke.

So what advice does Professor Steffen have for people attending a large gathering? First, get needed vaccinations before traveling. Then, stay away from any large mass of people as much as possible. Also, be careful with alcohol and drugs, which can increase the risk of injuries.

71. Which of the following would be the most appropriate title for this passage?
   (A) How to avoid mass gatherings
   (B) Mass gathering: New escape skills
   (C) Infectious diseases: New cures found
   (D) Health risks in a crowd: Not what you may think

72. Which of the following is closest in meaning to **stampede** in the passage?
   (A) A plane crash
   (B) A steamy factory
   (C) A sudden rush of a crowd
   (D) Heat stroke due to mass gathering events

73. According to Professor Steffen, which of the following is more threatening to

the health of people attending a huge public gathering?

(A) Injuries

(B) Infectious diseases

(C) The mood of event organizers

(D) Insufficient budget for an event

74. Which of the following is clear from the passage?

(A) Infectious disease is no longer a concern of the public.

(B) Event organizers should be more careful to avoid stampedes.

(C) A proper place for mass gathering should have one narrow passage.

(D) Children and older people are prohibited to attend mass gatherings.

75. Which of the following statements is LEAST supported in the passage?

(A) Extreme heat can cause death at mass gatherings.

(B) Infectious diseases will not spread at mass gatherings.

(C) Alcohol can increase the risk of injuries at mass gatherings.

(D) Older people are likely to suffer from heat stroke at a large gathering.

The historic center of Hoi An looks just how Vietnam is supposed to look: narrow lanes, wooden shop houses, a charming covered bridge. Hoi An's well preserved architecture –from the 16th century onward, the harbor town attracted traders from China, India, Japan and as far as Holland and Portugal – led United Nations Educational, Scientific and Cultural Organization (UNESCO) to deem it a World Heritage site, praising it as an outstanding demonstration of cultural blending over time in an international commercial port.

When Hoi An was first recognized as a World Heritage site in 1999, the city welcomed 160,300 tourists. In 2011, 1.5 million tourists arrived. Today, tour buses crowd the edge of Hoi An's old town. Tourists flood the historic center. Hundreds of nearly identical storefronts – providing food and selling the same tailored clothes, shoes and lanterns – colonize the heritage structures. To squeeze tourism revenue, a hospital has been forced to move out. Its building, built in the 19th century, now houses a tailoring business.

While local government officials and business owners view changes in the old town positively, tourists are beginning to notice the loss of authenticity in Hoi An. A 2008 UNESCO report sounded the alarm that "unless tourism management can be improved, the economic success generated by tourism will not be sustainable in the long term."

76. What is the main idea of the passage?

(A) Sustainable tourism revenue in the long run should not be a concern of the government.

(B) Hoi An should sell its old town to a modern tailoring business to increase economic revenue.

(C) UNESCO should urge Hoi An to build more narrow lanes, wooden houses, and covered bridges.

(D) Tourism management of historic sites should put a focus on protecting their authenticity and integrity.

77. What country is Hoi An located in?

(A) China   (B) Vietnam   (C) Japan   (D) Thailand

78. According to the passage, the old town of Hoi An is now _____.

(A) an empty place   (B) a famous theme park

(C) a popular tourist spot   (D) a center of modern arts

79. According to the passage, UNESCO believes World Heritage sites should be

_____.

(A) abandoned   (B) modernized   (C) preserved   (D) exploited

80. According to the passage, which of the following is true?

(A) Hoi An has never been influenced by foreign cultures and has never traded with other countries.

(B) Hoi An has become a UNESCO World Heritage site since the 16th century.

(C) Tourists are attracted to Hoi An to admire its modern architecture and related arts.

(D) The number of tourists to Hoi An has increased substantially after it was recognized as a World Heritage site.

1. **A**；中譯：在這年度的美食節，你可以品嚐各式各樣的佳餚。

   解析：(A) sample 取樣　(B) deliver 投遞　(C) cater 供應　(D) reduce 減少／本題考動詞。a wide variety of（各式各樣的），美食節有很多各式各樣的美食可以品嚐，空格內動詞用 sample 最恰當，所以答案為 (A)。

2. **D**；中譯：在飛往東京的途中，我要求空服員多給我一個枕頭。

   解析：(A) clerk 事務員　(B) employer 員工　(C) chauffeur 機師　(D) attendant 服務員

3. **D**；中譯：雲門舞集，一個來自於台灣的國際性知名舞蹈團體，展現出亞洲的現代舞蹈已足以比擬在歐洲或是北美洲的水準。

   解析：(A) refunded 償還 v.　(B) reflected 反映 v.　(C) retained 保留 v.　(D) renowned 有名的 adj.／空格前有副詞，後面接名詞，故需用形容詞，選項中以 renowned（有名的）最恰當，故答案為 (D)。

4. **D**；中譯：這個綜合建築包含一座主建築、網球場、以及漂亮的庭園。

   解析：(A) organized 組織　(B) collected 收集　(C) occupied 佔據　(D) comprised 包含片語 be comprised of（包含有…），故答案為 (D)。

5. **A**；中譯：這座動物園的特色是有超過 一千隻動物在他們的自然棲息地中。

   解析：(A) habitats 棲息地　(B) playgrounds 遊樂園　(C) landmarks 地標　(D) facilities 設備／feature（以…為特色），動物園中的動物應該是在棲息地的環境，所以答案為 (A)。

6. **D**；中譯：一位好的導遊必須對他的團員效力。

   解析：(A) considered 考慮過的　(B) conditioned 有條件的　(C) confided 信賴　(D) committed 忠誠／片語 be committed to（致力於…），故答案為 (D)。

7. **C**；中譯：我剛才沿著河岸漫步度過一個輕鬆的午後時光。

   解析：(A) trot 慢跑　(B) dip 浸泡　(C) stroll 漫步　(D) look／看題意為沿河岸漫步，漫步用 take a stroll，故答案為 (C)

8. **A**；中譯：在這座自然歷史博物館的入口處，你將會發現一座全尺寸的恐龍複製品。

   解析：(A) replica 複製品　(B) revival 再生　(C) remodel 重新塑造　(D) revision 修訂依題意應是指全尺寸的模型或複製品，故答案為 (A)。

9. **B**；中譯：我們到台灣南部旅遊最重要的事就是台南美食，在那裏我們享用了很多美味的食物。

解析：(A) gourmet 美食家　(B) highlight 重點　(C) monument 紀念　(D) recognition 確認／美食之旅是一種旅遊中的重點，所以選項中以 highlight（重點）最符合題意，故答案為 (B)。

10. A；中譯：莎拉在一間位於米蘭的流行時尚區的時裝店買了件漂亮的連身裙。

解析：(A) boutique 流行女裝店　(B) brochure 小冊子　(C) bouquet 花束　(D) balcony 陽台／買衣服合理判斷應該在服裝店，故選項中以 boutique（流行女裝店）最符合，故答案為 (A)。

11. C；中譯：剝皮寮，位於台北市萬華區，做為電影《艋舺》的場景，是一個很受觀光客喜愛的景點。

解析：(A) selected 選擇　(B) featured 以…為特色　(C) located 位於　(D) directed 導演／表示位於某地方的用法可用 located in（at），所以答案為 (C)。

12. B；中譯：在我們離開飯店前，我們導遊為我們講解三十分鐘有關當地的文化。

解析：(A) exhibition 展示　(B) presentation 介紹；報告　(C) construction 建築　(D) invitation 邀請／依據題意，應該是指導遊解說有關當地文化，空格中的名詞以選項中 presentation（介紹；報告）最符合，故答案為 (B)。

13. A；中譯：集集是台灣中部一個火車可到達的小鎮。

解析：(A) accessible 可進入的　(B) approached 接近的　(C) available 可用的　(D) advanced 先進的／空格需為主詞補語，說明這個小鎮，依題意是指火車可以到達之意，選項中以 accessible（可進入的）最適合，故答案為(A)。

14. D；中譯：那個在護照查驗的人看起來不喜歡我在護照中的照片，但最後還是讓我過去了。　(A) station 車站　(B) custom 習俗　(C) security 安全　(D) control 控制

解析：do not seem to like（不喜歡），護照查驗應用 passport control，故答案為 (D)。

15. C；中譯：成功不會偶然發生，它必須努力工作並做好準備才能得到。

解析：(A) expiration 截止日期　(B) reception 接待　(C) preparation 準備　(D) irritation 憤怒／by chance（偶然），選項中以 preparation（準備）最合理，表示成功必須要努力並有準備，故答案為 (C)。

16. D；中譯：如果你要的話，我可以幫你讓它變得更容易些。

解析：變得更容易些為 make it easier，故答案為 (D)。

17. A；中譯：所有的資源都是不夠的，也就是說沒有足夠的東西去讓每個人都能滿意。

解析：(A) scarce 不足的　(B) absent 缺席的　(C) plentiful 豐富的　(D) fertile 肥沃的

18. A；中譯：由於印度經濟的繁榮以及航空產業的快速發展之賜，今天印度人比以往更常搭飛機。

解析：(A) prosperity 繁榮　(B) souvenir 紀念品　(C) decline 下降　(D) evidence 跡象

19. C；中譯：這位導遊是一個謙恭有禮的人，他非常有禮貌並且講話很親切。

解析：(A) careless 粗心的　(B) persistent 頑固的　(C) courteous 謙恭的　(D) environmental 環境的／由句子後面的描述可知這位導遊是個有禮貌並態度和藹的

人，所以選項中以 courteous（謙恭的）最恰當，故答案為 (C)。

20. **C**；中譯：這家餐廳以真正的義大利北方菜為特色，真實呈現出義大利的風味。

解析：(A) disposable 可拋棄的　(B) confident 自信的　(C) authentic 真實的　(D) dimensional 尺寸的／features（以…為特點），表示真正的義大利菜，選項中以 authentic（真實的）最恰當，故答案為 (C)。

21. **B**；中譯：在我第一次到台北旅遊的時候，我對這個城市毫無所知。

解析：(A) consensus 共識　(B) knowledge 知識　(C) restoration 恢復　(D) honor 光榮

22. **A**；中譯：要把一間在飯店中的餐廳經營的有聲有色，對許多飯店經理人來說是最困難的挑戰。

解析：(A) Achieving 獲得　(B) Resembling 類似　(C) Dictating 命令　(D) Exhausting 耗盡／空格內需用動名詞來當作句子主詞，依題意是指要成功經營一家飯店中的餐廳，選項中以 Achieving（獲得）最恰當，表示獲致良好的經營之意，故答案為 (A)。

23. **C**；中譯：慢慢來就好，我不需要馬上要有答案。

解析：(A) consistently 一致地　(B) regularly 規律地　(C) immediately 立即地　(D) frequently 時常地／Take your time 為不急、慢慢來之意，所以不需要立即有答案，故答案為 (C)。

24. **B**；中譯：當旅遊時行李不要帶太多，因為你沿途總是會買到新的東西。

解析：along the way（沿途中），不要裝過多的東西是因為沿途中可以買的到，所以空格內的動詞以選項中 acquire（獲得）最符合題意，故答案為 (B)。

25. **D**；中譯：鯨魚就像我們一樣是哺乳動物，必須游到水面上呼吸。

解析：(A) teenagers 青少年　(B) performers 表演者　(C) giants 巨人　(D) mammals 哺乳動物／本句意思是要表達鯨魚是哺乳動物，空格內要用 mammals（哺乳動物），故答案為 (D)。

26. **C**；中譯：欣賞這座自然公園的景觀最好是騎單車或步行，在這個區域裏有許多的步道，所有的小徑都能看到令人屏息的美景。

解析：(A) sole 單獨的　(B) simultaneous 同時的　(C) numerous 許多的　(D) indifferent 無關的／landscape（景觀），breath-taking（令人屏息的），空格內需用形容詞來形容 trail，依句意知應該是指很多的步道，選項中以 numerous（許多的）最恰當，故答案為 (C)。

27. **B**；中譯：如果你需要搭車去機場，不要客氣儘管打電話跟我說，我今天下午有空。

解析：a ride 就是搭車的意思，要表示不要客氣的慣用語是 don't hesitate to…，所以答案為 (B)。

28. **D**；中譯：日月潭有著水晶般清澈的湖水，祖母綠般的山巒及各式各樣的戶外活動，難怪在台灣日月潭是最多觀光客造訪的景點之一。

解析：要表達一件事是令人（或不令人）驚訝用法為 it is (not) surprising that…，故答

案為 (D)。注意：如果主詞是人的話，那就需用過去分詞，例：I was surprised…

29. (A)；中譯：台灣以它的高山景點及城市地標著名，如故宮博物院及台北 101 大樓。

解析：(A) scenic 風景的　(B) neutral 中立的　(C) vacant 空的　(D) feasible 可行的
be known for（以…著稱），空格需用形容詞修飾後面名詞 spot，題目中提到高山景點，景點用 scenic spot，故答案為 (A)。

30. (B)；中譯：垃圾對水中生物造成危害，每年有數以百萬的海鳥、海洋哺乳類及海龜死於塑膠垃圾。

解析：(A) invaluable 無價的　(B) dangerous 危險的　(C) spoiling 掠奪　(D) tedious 沉悶的／空格處為主詞補語，說明垃圾與海洋生物的關係，由題目後面說明知道垃圾是對海洋生物有危害的，所以選項中以 dangerous（危險的）最恰當。

31. (D)；中譯：南非在 2010 年舉辦世界杯足球賽曾引起很多疑慮，但最終南非還是順利完成且做得很好。

解析：(A) surpassed 超過　(B) licensed 准許　(C) implemented 執行　(D) raised 升高
pulled off（完成），空格處要填入動詞過去分詞形成被動式，表示憂慮是被升高，選項中以 raised 最適合，故答案為 (D)。

32. (A)；中譯：由於網路的關係，購買流行商品只能在市區來進行這種想法已經過時了。

解析：(A) outdated 過時的　(B) approximated 使接近　(C) rehearsed 排練　(D) motivated 激發／空格處需用主詞補語，說明這種想法，網路造成購物型態改變，所以從前的想法已經不合時宜，選項中以 outdated（過時的）最符合。

33. (B)；中譯：台灣的夜市已經成為受歡迎的觀光地點，那裡是可以買到便宜的東西且吃到傳統台灣小吃的地方。

解析：(A) tropical 熱帶的　(B) popular 受歡迎的　(C) edible 可吃的　(D) responsible 負責的／所以選項中以 popular（受歡迎的）來形容夜市觀光最恰當，故答案為 (B)。

34. (C)；中譯：能與他一起工作超過十年一直是我的榮幸，他的眼光與解析能力都令人印象深刻。

解析：(A) distant 遠方的　(B) superficial 表面的　(C) impressive 印象深刻的　(D) premature 不成熟的／空格處為主詞補語，說明他給人的感覺，由題意知道他的能力是非常優秀的，所以選項中以 impressive（印象深刻的）最恰當。

35. (C)；中譯：如果不是司機的疏忽，這場悲劇原本是可以避免的。

解析：(A) carefulness 謹慎　(B) prediction 預言　(C) negligence 疏忽　(D) alertness 警告／but for（若非、要不是），由題意知要不是司機如何，悲劇就不會發生，選項中以 negligence（疏忽）最合理，故答案為 (C)。

36. (A)；中譯：根據會議議程，今天下午有超過三個主題要討論。

解析：(A) agenda 會議程序　(B) invoice 帳單　(C) recipe 食譜　(D) catalog 目錄。

37. (B)；中譯：太魯閣國家公園的特色是高山及深邃的峽谷，裏面許多山峰都超過海拔 3000

公尺。

解析：(A) lacks 缺乏　(B) features 以…為特色　(C) excludes 把…排除　(D) disregards 輕視／空格中需用動詞，表示太魯閣國家公園的狀況，選項中以 features（以…為特色）最符合題意，表示公園是以具有高山及峽谷為特色。

38. C；中譯：這位當地的導遊有開朗的個性，每個人都喜歡他。

解析：導遊要讓人喜歡，他的性格以應以選項中 sunny（陽光的）最合理。

39. D；中譯：明天我會精確地告訴你要參加這趟旅遊的人數。

解析：(A) tremendously 大量地　(B) highly 高度地　(C) rationally 理性地　(D) precisely 精確地／空格需用副詞修飾前面動詞 know，因為提到有關旅遊人數，故選項中應用 precisely（精確地），表示精確地確認人數，答案為 (D)。

40. B；中譯：當人們慶祝 2012 的新年到來時，絢爛的煙火秀照亮了全世界各地的天空。

解析：(A) Invisible 看不見的　(B) Spectacular 壯麗的　(C) Dull 呆滯的　(D) Endangered 快絕種的／lit up（照亮，lit 為 light 的過去式），空格內要用形容詞形容煙火，選項中以 Spectacular（壯麗的）最恰當，故答案為 (B)。

41. C；中譯：A：請問我可以坐這個座位嗎？

B：抱歉！它有人坐了。

解析：表示座位已經有人佔（或坐）用 it's occupied，故答案為 (C)。

42. D；中譯：許多青少年熬夜玩線上遊戲。

解析：(A) grow up 長大　(B) break up 打碎；分手　(C) take place 發生　(D) stay up 熬夜／晚上不睡覺熬夜打電動遊戲，熬夜為 stay up，故答案為 (D)。

43. A；中譯：為了保持健康與身材，我們需要適度飲食與運動。

解析：(A) maintain 維持　(B) apply 運用　(C) retire 後退　(D) contain 包含。

44. C；中譯：從跡象看來，很明顯的昨天晚上有人闖進我的辦公室。

解析：(A) humble 恭敬的　(B) inspiring 激勵的　(C) obvious 明顯的　(D) promising 有希望的／broke into（強行進入）（broke 是 break 的過去式動詞），空格需用形容詞當主詞補語，說明這件事情的狀態，選項中以 obvious（明顯的）最符合，表示跡象很明顯的顯示出有人闖入，故答案為 (C)。

45. D；中譯：我討厭再經歷一次進行冗長的申請程序，我需要一個助理來幫我做。

解析：(A) interesting 有趣的　(B) energetic 精力旺盛的　(C) fascinating 迷人的　(D) tedious 冗長乏味的／go through（進行、經歷），句中提到討厭這件事，故空格中的形容詞以選項中的 tedious（冗長乏味的）最恰當，故答案為 (D)。

46. A；中譯：當我們的航班穿越附近風暴的亂流區時，我非常害怕。

解析：(A) turbulence 亂流　(B) breeze 微風　(C) currency 流通　(D) brilliance 光輝

47. B；中譯：大部分評論家歸咎這部電影的失敗在於缺乏人性。

解析：(A) caused 起因　(B) imputed 歸咎原因　(C) rewarded 報酬　(D) dedicated 奉獻／表示失敗的原因的歸屬，動詞用選項中 imputed（歸咎原因）最適當。

48. **C**；中譯：要訓練貓去做你想要牠們去做的事實際上是不可能的，但是這隻叫做莎哈的貓不但能與人握手，還會上廁所。

解析：(A) unlikely 不可能 (B) casually 偶然 (C) virtually 實際上 (D) secondly 其次 not only…but also（不僅…而且），空格中需用副詞修飾形容詞 impossible，選項中以 virtually（實際上）最符合題意，表示正常情況下是不可能訓練的。

49. **D**；中譯：我最難忘的旅行是去爬富士山，爬到山頂並看著太陽從雲端升起是非常令人驚奇的。

解析：(A) depth 深度 (B) remark 評論 (C) twig 細樹枝 (D) peak 山頂
空格需填入山頂的名詞，所以用 peak（山頂），答案為 (D)。

50. **A**；中譯：珍妮佛除了她的母語英語外，還會流利的講其他幾種語言。

解析：other than（除…之外），mother tongue（母語），講流利的語言可以用 be fluent in…，故答案為 (A)。

51. **B**；中譯：山谷中的大雨時常會影響我的視線，所以有時候我必須把車停在路邊等雨停。

解析：(A) landscape 風景 (B) sight 視線 (C) image 影像 (D) taste 味覺／依題意大雨會影響開車視線，所以空格以選項中 sight（視野、視線）最符合，答案為 (B)。

52. **C**；中譯：由於其溫和的氣候、美麗的海岸及迷人的小鎮，布拉瓦海岸是位於西班牙東北部一個很受歡迎的度假區。

解析：(A) dreadful 可怕的 (B) contemporary 現代的 (C) moderate 溫和的 (D) bitter 嚴寒的／空格內需用表示氣候的形容詞，觀光勝地應該是溫和的氣候，故選項中以 moderate（溫和的）最符合，所以答案為 (C)。

53. **C**；中譯：我真的很喜歡你的圍巾，我能用我的帽子與你交換嗎？

解析：用 A 來交換 B 的說法可用 exchange A for B，故答案為 (C)。

54. **A**；中譯：在服務中心，你將會發現有很多資源可用，包括地圖、簡介以及無線上網。

解析：(A) resources 資源 (B) reformation 改革 (C) documents 文件 (D) assistance 協助／句中所列的地圖、簡介以及無線上網等項目都屬於一些有用的資源，故答案為 (A)。

55. **D**；中譯：維也納擁有許多城堡、雕塑公園、音樂廳及博物館，是一個沉浸在文化中的城市。

解析：(A) chronic 慢性的 adj. (B) elite 精華 n. (C) provincial 鄉下的 adj. (D) steeped 沉浸 v.／維也納是個文化之都，空格中需用 steeped（沉浸，過去分詞）當形容詞，修飾前面的名詞 city，故答案為 (D)。

56. **B**；中譯：夏威夷所有主要島嶼中最古老的是可愛島，它以幽靜的海濱、風光明媚的瀑布及叢林步道而聞名。

解析：be known for…表示以…而聞名，故答案為 (B)。

57. **B**；中譯：設立於 1730 年，蘭卡斯特的中央市場是美國現在還繼續營運中最悠久的農夫市場。

　　解析：(A) Demolished 毀壞　(B) Established 設立　(C) Imported 輸入　(D) Located 位於／句首空格應填入過去分詞（表被動），且因為空格後為時間，故應用選項中的 Established（設立），表示創立的時間點，故答案為 (B)。

58. Ｃ；中譯：位處契亞帕斯山的高處，San Cristóbal del la Casas 是墨西哥最佳拍照景點之一：色彩繽紛的、歷史的、醒目地交錯著。

　　解析：(A) antarctic 南極的　(B) cosmetic 化妝的　(C) photogenic 適宜拍照的　(D) synthetic 合成的／空格中需用形容詞形容這個景點，依題意指這地方有各種色彩及歷史等交織而成，選項中以 photogenic（適宜拍照的）最恰當，故答案為 (C)。

59. Ｂ；中譯：只到訪羅馬一次是不夠的，要了解這城市層層交錯的複雜性是需要時間的。

　　解析：(A) assists 幫助　(B) demands 需要　(C) evolves 發展　(D) lingers 徘徊
　　依題意知，羅馬這個城市是很複雜的，需要多一點的時間來瞭解，所以空格內動詞用 demands，故答案為 (B)。

60. Ａ；中譯：現在，圈養的老虎比野生的老虎還多，我們需要採取行動來保護這些大貓。

　　解析：本題句型為比較級，in capacity 就是指人類圈養的，in the wild 就是指野生的，故答案為 (A)。

61. Ｃ；中譯：在一場船難後，遊輪公司們設法用折扣來挽回猶豫的旅客。

　　解析：(A) bounce 彈起來　(B) coil 盤繞　(C) lure 引誘　(D) ransom 贖回／船難後很多遊客會猶豫不決，所以要用折扣來吸引遊客，選項中 lure（引誘）最恰當，lure back 表示吸引回來，故答案為 (C)。

62. Ｂ；中譯：一條運河蜿蜒地沿著枝葉茂盛的單車道、穿過翠綠的公園且經過這城市四座續存的風車。

　　解析：(A) injects 注入　(B) meanders 曲折流過　(C) pollutes 汙染　(D) rumbles 轟隆作響／canal（運河），bike pass（腳踏車道），空格內要用描述運河的動詞，選項中以 meanders（曲折流過）最恰當，的故答案為 (B)。

63. Ａ；中譯：觀光客們的預算及喜好的範圍很大，且有很多不同種類的度假村及飯店已經為迎合他們而設立了。

　　解析：(A) cater 迎合　(B) desire 渴望　(C) mourn 悲傷　(D) pray 祈求／句意為業者已經發展不同等級的飯店來滿足觀光客的不同需求，所以空格內動詞用 cater（迎合）最恰當，表示迎合需求不同的觀光客，故答案為 (A)。

64. Ａ；中譯：科技的發展及交通運輸的建設已經使得許多樣態的旅遊讓人更加負擔得起。

　　解析：(A) affordable 可負擔的　(B) considerable 相當的　(C) exclusive 排外的　(D) illusive 幻覺的／空格需填入形容詞說明這些旅遊，選項中以 affordable（可負擔的）最恰當，表示讓人負擔得起，故答案為 (A)。

65. Ｃ；中譯：對許多人來說，度假與旅遊逐漸被視為一種必需品而不是一種享受，而這也反映在旅遊人數上面。

解析：(A) community 社會　(B) dynasty 朝代　(C) necessity 必需品　(D) sincerity 真實／由題意知旅遊不被認為只是一種享受，而有其他的意涵，選項中以 necessity（必需品）最適宜，故答案為 (C)。

66. **B**；中譯：這座雨林中的層級式瀑布景象是很壯觀的。

解析：(A) ascending 上升的　(B) cascading 層級式的　(C) flourishing 茂盛的　(D) overflowing 過剩的／空格中需用描述瀑布的形容詞，選項中以 cascading（層級式的）最適當，也就是像一層一層階梯狀的瀑布，故答案為 (B)。

67. **D**；中譯：如果你有計畫並時間安排妥當，有些地方的一些住宅交換是可以讓你免費住的。

解析：Home swapping 是指旅遊時和別的國家的屋主交換地方住宿，答案為 (D)

68. **D**；中譯：Preservation Hall 是在紐奧良的許多爵士樂表演地之一，但一些最好的音樂仍然可在街頭角落、後院及喪禮中被發現。

解析：(A) ceremonies 儀式　(B) distractions 分心　(C) habitats 居住地　(D) venues 舉辦地點／Preservation Hall 為爵士樂的聖地之一，選項中以 venues（舉辦地點）最適合，故答案為 (D)。

69. **B**；中譯：原則上，旅途中避免穿白色的衣服及配件，穿深色一點的可以隱藏髒污。

解析：(A) delete 刪掉　(B) hide 隱藏　(C) parade 遊行　(D) imply 暗示／As a general rule（原則來說），空格處需用適當的動詞，表示讓髒汙看不出來，選項中以 hide（隱藏）最適當，故答案為 (B)。

70. **B**；中譯：人都是喜歡社交的，而臉書讓這變得更容易，害羞的人在網路上變得更開朗。

解析：(A) modest 謹慎的　(B) outgoing 開朗的　(C) pious 虔誠的　(D) timid 膽小的 The shy 是指生性害羞的人，而害羞的人在網路環境中無須拘謹，會變的外向開朗，所以選項中用 outgoing（開朗的）最恰當，故答案為 (B)。

71-75 ；中譯：讓我們想像一場眾多人群聚集場面——像是麥加朝聖。想想看世界盃、奧運、或是搖滾音樂會。當數以千計或甚至百萬的群眾聚集在一起時，什麼是健康最大的考慮因素呢？傳統上，醫生以及公共衛生官員最擔心的是傳染性疾病的散播。羅伯特‧史蒂芬，一位蘇黎士大學的旅遊醫學教授，認為傳染病確實是個考慮因素，但在所謂眾多人群聚集時，意外傷害是個更大的威脅。

依據史蒂芬教授的說法，在眾多人群聚集時，孩童及老年人遭受意外傷害或其他健康問題的風險最高。孩童的風險在於可能因推擠而受到擠壓，而老年人則有較高熱中暑以及死於酷熱的風險。

因眾多人群聚集而造成的群眾推擠在過去的三十年間據估計已經造成七千人死亡，場地的設計會影響群眾聚集，狹窄的通道或其他阻塞的地點會使得太多群眾同時使用，群眾的情緒也可能扮演一定的角色，群眾聚集的規畫者必須避免可能導致推擠與熱中暑的情況發生。所以什麼是史蒂芬教授對人們參與群聚活動的建議呢？首先，在出發前先注射必要的疫苗，再者，儘可能遠離過多的人群。還有，要小心酒類以及藥物使用，那會增加意外傷害的風險。

71. (D)；中譯：下列何者是這篇文章最適合的標題？(A) 如何避免眾多人群聚集　(B) 眾多人群聚集：新的逃離技巧　(C) 傳染性疾病：發現新療法　(D) 在人群中的健康風險：跟你想的不一樣

解析：本文一開始提到眾多人群聚集場合的健康風險，一般認為最大的風險應該是傳染病，然而一位學者認為事實上意外傷害才是最大的風險，後面分別提到孩童及老人可能遭受的傷害及如何避免造成傷害，都與一般人想像的不一樣，所以最適合的標題為選項 (D)。

72. (C)；中譯：下列何者最接近文章中出現的 stampede 這個字的意思？(A) 一架飛機墜毀　(B) 一間蒸氣工廠　(C) 洶湧的人潮　(D) 人群聚集造成熱中暑

解析：stampede 意思是群眾蜂擁，推擠之意，所以選項中最接近的為 (C) 洶湧的人潮

73. (A)；中譯：根據史蒂芬教授看法，下列何者對參與人群聚集的人是更加具有威脅？(A) 意外傷害　(B) 傳染疾病　(C) 活動規畫者的情緒　(D) 活動缺乏預算

解析：由 Robert Steffen,…says that infectious diseases are still a concern, but injuries are a bigger threat…，知意外傷害是更大的威脅，所以答案為 (A)。

74. (B)；中譯：下列何者由文章中可清楚得知？　(A) 傳染病不再是大眾關注的事　(B) 籌畫者應更小心避免發生群眾推擠　(C) 一個適當的眾多人群聚集場合應該要有個狹小的通道　(D) 小孩及老年人被禁止參與眾多人群聚集場合。

解析：(A) 由… says that infectious diseases are still a concern…，故傳染病仍是大眾應關心的事　(B) 由 Organizers of large gatherings need to avoid creating conditions that might lead to stampedes …，故知籌畫者應更小心避免發生群眾推擠　(C) 文中表示狹小的通道使眾多人群聚集場合容易發生群眾推擠，應該要避免　(D) 文中沒有提到小孩及老年人要被禁止參與眾多人群聚集場合。故本題答案為 (B)。

75. (B)；中譯：下列何項敘述在文章中最不被認同？(A) 極端的熱在眾多人群聚集場合可能造成致死　(B) 傳染病不會在眾多人群聚集場合傳播　(C) 在眾多人群聚集場合酒精可能增加意外傷害的風險　(D) 老年人在眾多人群聚集場合可能會有熱中暑的風險。

解析：(A) 文中有提到熱中暑是眾多人群聚集場合的風險　(B) 文中仍然認為傳染在眾多人群聚集場合仍是健康問題考量因素之一，表示仍然可能發生傳染病，敘述非文章本意　(C) 文中有提到在眾多人群聚集場合酒精可能增加意外傷害的風險　(D) 文中有提到老年人在眾多人群聚集場合可能會有熱中暑的風險。故本題答案 (B)。

76-80；中譯：歷史古都會安看起來就如同越南給人的印象：狹窄的街道，木造的商店，迷人的遮蓬橋。會安具有保存良好的建築——自從十六世紀以來，這個港口小鎮吸引著從中國、印度、日本、甚至遠至荷蘭與葡萄牙的貿易商——而這讓聯合國教科文組織(UNESCO)認證它為世界遺產，讚揚它是一個融合各種文化的古代國際商業港之具體展現。

當會安在 1999 年剛獲得世界遺產認證時，這個城市吸引了 160,300 名觀光客。到 2011

年時，150 萬觀光客來到這裏。今天，觀光巴士擠滿了會安老街的外緣，觀光客湧進了這個歷史古都，數百間幾近相同的店面——提供飲食、販賣著相同的合身衣物、鞋子以及燈籠——充斥著各個古建築物。為了賺取觀光財，一間醫院已經被迫遷離，而一座建於 19 世紀的建築物，現在成為一家成衣公司。

就在當地政府官員及企業老闆視古都的這些改變表示肯定之同時，觀光客也開始注意到會安真實性的流失。一個 2008 年聯合國教科文組織報告發出警告指出：「除非旅遊管理能改進，否則因觀光而帶來的經濟成果長期來看將不會持續。」

76. Ⓓ；中譯：這篇文章的大意是什麼？(A) 持續的觀光收益最終不應該成為政府關心的事　(B) 會安應該將他的老街賣給現代的成衣企業以增加觀光收益　(C) UNESCO 應該要求會安建更多狹窄的街道，木造的商店及遮蓬橋　(D) 歷史古蹟的旅遊管理應該注意保護其真實性及完整性。

　解析：本文先描述會安為何成為世界遺產，再提到成名後因觀光客湧進造成的亂象，最後提到觀光客也發現會安的真實性越來愈受質疑，聯合國也提出警告要管理當局注意其管理，所以本文大意為選項 (D) 歷史古蹟的旅遊管理應該注意保護其真實性及完整性。

77. Ⓑ；中譯：會安位於哪裏？　(A) 中國　(B) 越南　(C) 日本　(D) 泰國

　解析：由 The historic center of Hoi An looks just how Vietnam is supposed to look…，知應該是位於越南，答案為 (B)。

78. Ⓒ；中譯：根據本文，會安舊城現在是(A) 一個空蕩的地方　(B) 一個有名的主題樂園　(C) 一個觀光勝地　(D) 一個現代藝術中心

　解析：由 Today, tour buses crowd the edge of Hoi An's old town. Tourists flood the historic center…，知會安現在湧入很多觀光客，是一個觀光勝地，答案為 (C)。

79. Ⓒ；中譯：根據本文，UNESCO 認為世界遺產應被　(A) 遺棄　(B) 現代化　(C) 保存　(D) 開發

80. Ⓓ；中譯：根據本文，下何者為真？(A) 會安從未被其他外國文化影響也未曾與其他國家貿易　(B) 會安自從 16 世紀就已經是 UNESCO 世界遺產地　(C) 觀光客被吸引到會安讚歎它的現代建築及相關藝術　(D) 到會安的觀光客人數在它被認證為世界文化遺址後已經大大地增加。

　解析：(A) 由 Hoi An's well preserved architecture– from the 16th century onward, the harbor town attracted traders from China, India…，可知會安自古以即與其他國家貿易且來被其他外國文化影響，敘述為非　(B) 由 Hoi An was first recognized as a World Heritage site in 1999…，知會安於 1999 年才成為 UNESCO 世界遺產地，敘述為非　(C) 會安是個歷史舊城，所以觀光客是因歷史古建築而來，敘述為非　(D) 文中提到，剛獲認證時觀光客是 16 萬多，到 2011 年是 150 多萬，所以到惠安的觀光客人數在被認證為世界文化遺址後已經持續地增加，敘述為真。所以答案為 (D)。

05 Unit

102 外語導遊
英語考試—試題

102 專門職業及技術人員普通考試導遊人員、領隊人員考試試題
等別：普通考試
類科：外語導遊人員（英語）
科目：外國語（英語）
考試時間：1 小時 20 分
※注意：本試題為單一選擇題，請選出一個正確或最適當的答案，複選作答者，該題不予計分。

1. Macau, a small city west of Hong Kong, has turned itself into a casino head-quarters in the East. Its economy now depends very much on tourists and visitors whose number is more than double that of the local _____ .

    (A) man　(B) shop　(C) worker　(D) population

2. Three meals a day means that _____ one will have breakfast, lunch and dinner each day.

    (A) contrarily　(B) nevertheless　(C) normally　(D) regardless

3. A _____ is simply another name for a small specialty shop.

    (A) boutique　(B) body shop　(C) bonus　(D) beauty parlor

4. When the table filled with some _____ refreshments was removed, the host announced that dinner would be served.

    (A) strong　(B) heavy　(C) light　(D) bright

5. It is important to note that the brochure represents only a small _____ of a much larger bulk of rules and regulations that we have to observe.

    (A) article　(B) selection　(C) election　(D) writing

6. Looking back over his 50 years of living in the village, Peter does not _____ that he did not move to a large city earlier.

    (A) regret　(B) remember　(C) claim　(D) announce

7. The easiest way to look for the shop that you want to visit in a shopping center

is to go to the _____ or information desk when you fail to find out the answer from passers-by.

(A) direct   (B) directory   (C) dictionary   (D) director

8. Taiwan is short of _____ resources but full of educational opportunities.

   (A) physical   (B) chemical   (C) geometric   (D) natural

9. Taiwan has plentiful annual _____ but unfortunately its rivers are too short and too close to the sea.

   (A) cloud   (B) water   (C) rainfall   (D) temples

10. Strictly speaking, Venice is now more of a _____ city than a maritime business city.

    (A) waterfront   (B) Italian   (C) tourism   (D) modern

11. I like Rome very much because it has many historic _____ and it is friendly to visitors.

    (A) stories   (B) glory   (C) sites   (D) giants

12. Kyoto is my _____ city because I prefer traditional Japanese culture to electronic culture.

    (A) favorite   (B) hobby   (C) disliked   (D) wonderful

13. Either the _____ or the cashier's desk of the hotel can help us figure out the exact amount of money and other details we need to join a local tour.

    (A) receiving   (B) reception   (C) resignation   (D) recognition

14. When traveling in a foreign country, we need to carry with us several important documents at all times. One of them is our passport together with the _____ permit if that has been so required.

    (A) entering   (B) entry   (C) exit   (D) ego

15. The 79 year-old Kaohsiung woman has repeatedly _____ NT$120,000 every year for some 10 years to the Home for the Aged in her hometown in Pingtung.

    (A) donated   (B) spent   (C) borrowed   (D) aided

16. I have collected so many art objects in my house that there is no more _____ for new ones.

(A) pace   (B) speed   (C) time   (D) space

17. Though most airlines ask their passengers to check in at the airport counter two hours before the flight, some international flights _____ their passengers to be at the airport three hours before departure.

(A) revise   (B) require   (C) record   (D) reveal

18. Most cities that can date back to ancient _____ tend to either create their own myth or fabricate an unspeakable tradition that combines facts and fiction.

(A) knee   (B) history   (C) pass   (D) tool

19. Before taking a bus, it is advisable to check out its route on a computer or read carefully the route _____ at the bus stop.

(A) way   (B) chart   (C) label   (D) hostel

20. No Chinese musical instrument is like the pi-pa that has been in use for almost two thousand years either in solo performance or in _____ . Critics describe the string instrument to have a unique timbre that can somewhat be matched by western lute.

(A) choir   (B) orchestra   (C) athletics   (D) chamber music

21. The question of what kind of _____ law this city upholds cannot be answered by your fallacious argument.

(A) civilized   (B) civil   (C) citizen   (D) civic

22. The Philippines is a country with more than 7000 islands and it has dozens of native languages. What is even more amazing is the _____ between the north and the south, particularly their people's religious belief and political conviction.

(A) contrast   (B) competition   (C) construction   (D) condition

23. I love to go wandering; often I take my bicycle to _____ around the countryside on weekends.

(A) tour   (B) speed   (C) stroll   (D) drive

24. The cellphone is very _____ because it connects us with the world at large and even provides us with the necessary information on crucial moments.

(A) expensive   (B) rare   (C) fashionable   (D) handy

25. When answering questions of the immigration officer, it is advisable to be straight forward and not _____ .

(A) historic   (B) hesitating (C) hospitable   (D) heroic

26. When a train arrives, the first thing you need to do is to check if its _____ matches with where you want to go before you step in.

(A) design   (B) destination   (C) destiny   (D) dedication

27. Customs officers usually have a _____ face and they have the right to ask us to open our baggage for searching.

(A) good-looking   (B) funny-looking   (C) stern-looking   (D) silly-looking

28. Some cities do not have passenger loading zones. It is advisable to follow the instruction of the tourist guide to get off or get on the tour bus to _____ safety and comfort.

(A) prevent   (B) guarantee   (C) keep away   (D) attend to

29. In some airports, there is the final call announcement, but in others, they only have _____ signals on the sign board. Passengers are responsible for their own arriving at the boarding gate in time.

(A) image   (B) blinking   (C) faulty   (D) traffic

30. Paris' Cultural Calendar may be bursting with fairs, salons and auctions, but nothing can quite _____ the Biennale des Antiquaires.

(A) compete with   (B) comment on   (C) complain about   (D) compose of

31. Someone _____ her house last night and stole almost all her valuable things.

(A) broke through   (B) broke up   (C) broke in   (D) broke down

32. _____ all the recent criticism of free trade and free markets, it's important to remember that in the last 25 years more people worldwide moved from poverty to the middle class than at any other time in history.

(A) In spite of   (B) For the sake of   (C) By all accounts,   (D) Were it not for

33. Mingling with tourists from different backgrounds helps tour guides _____ and learn new things in answering curious visitors' various questions.

(A) blow their own horn   (B) take their breath away

(C) fall from grace (D) broaden their horizons

34. Pingxi District in New Taipei City of Taiwan holds an annual Lantern Festival in which releasing sky lanterns has become a tradition. _____ that sky lanterns were the invention of an ancient Chinese politician and military leader "Kong Ming."

(A) As a consequence   (B) Legend has it

(C) It isn't worth the trouble (D) It is high time

35. I have _____ on my research project and couldn't make any progress forward, so I need to rethink my design and get some help.

(A) come to a standstill (B) come out ahead

(C) come to light   (D) come through

36. We need to _____ how we can walk out of this maze and get home safe.

(A) figure out (B) count on (C) back up (D) give up

37. Money changing can be complicated. When in doubt, always ask someone who is _____.

(A) ignorant (B) shaky (C) prejudiced (D) knowledgeable

38. If we remember our social _____, particularly in a big crowd, we shall win people's admiration though we may not feel it.

(A) ages (B) manners (C) news (D) recruits

39. Dress codes are basically some _____ about what people wear in an organization or on a particular occasion.

(A) pros and cons   (B) ups and downs

(C) dos and don'ts   (D) ways and means

40. A: I'm going on a five-day trip to Thailand next week.

B: That's great! Wish _____ a wonderful trip.

(A) you (B) you have (C) you having (D) you to have

41. This time next year I _____ in France.

(A) am traveling   (B) have been traveling

(C) will be traveling (D) have traveled

42. The airlines _____ to us about the long flight delay, but they just kept us

waiting and did not say anything.

(A) could explain   (B) had explained

(C) should be explaining   (D) could have explained

43. When something wrong happens, _____ let me know immediately.

(A) do not manage to   (B) do not hesitate to

(C) do not think to   (D) do not hide to

44. A prominent survey has ranked Taipei as the second greenest metropolis among 22 major Asian cities, _____ only Singapore.

(A) surpassing   (B) trailing   (C) traversing   (D) conflicting

45. Taiwan is the home of hot springs. Located along Wenshui River, the Taian Hot Springs were developed during the Japanese _____.

(A) oration   (B) operation   (C) orientation   (D) occupation

46. This is the final _____ call for China Airline Flight 009 to Hong Kong at Gate C2.

(A) landing   (B) taking off   (C) riding   (D) boarding

47. Taiwan government said yesterday it will not give up restrictions it imposes on imported beef, after a warning by U.S. lawmakers that the issue could _____ free trade talks.

(A) facilitate   (B) advance   (C) delight   (D) cripple

48. According to a new study, the continuing _____ of immigrants to American shores is encouraging business activity and producing more jobs with the supply of abundant labors.

(A) threat   (B) arrival   (C) removal   (D) selection

49. The financial _____ that started in the U.S. and swept the globe was further proof that—for better and for worse—we can't escape one another.

(A) data   (B) tadpole   (C) advent   (D) crisis

50. In order to make traveling easier, especially for those who rely on public transportation, the Tourism Bureau worked with local governments to _____ the Taiwan Tourist Shuttle Service in 2010.

(A) terminate   (B) initiate   (C) annotate   (D) depreciate

51. Technology, such as cellphones, often _____ equality and helps lift people out of poverty.

(A) fosters　(B) discourages　(C) likens　(D) diminishes

52. In the story about belling the cat, the mice know that life would be much safer if the cat were stuck with a bell around its neck. The problem is, who will _____ his life to bell the cat?

(A) achieve　(B) resolve　(C) gamble　(D) persist

53. Master Sheng Yen _____ his entire life to spreading the Dharma, using simple and practical language to help bring people from all walks of life closer to Buddhism.

(A) saved　(B) donated　(C) devoted　(D) savored

54. Simply put, no society can truly _____ if it smothers the dreams and productivity of half its population, women.

(A) deteriorate　(B) flourish　(C) ravage　(D) smuggle

55. Increasing tourism infrastructure to meet domestic and international demands has raised concerns about the _____ on Taiwan's natural environment.

(A) impact　(B) input　(C) itinerary　(D) identity

56. Sweets aren't an intrinsic part of a meal, but their presence on the dining table is often a great _____ of happiness.

(A) link　(B) source　(C) pardon　(D) ordeal

57. Wushantou Reservoir began its _____ in 1920 and was completed in 1930. It became the Wushantou Scenery Park in 1969.

(A) construction　(B) congestion　(C) contamination　(D) confrontation

58. I'll pay a visit to the Wolfsonian, an _____ museum in Miami. I love its collection of decorative artifacts and propaganda materials from 1885 to 1945.

(A) edible　(B) outrageous　(C) awful　(D) extraordinary

59. The support for suspending death penalty has gained _____ , and it is very likely that someday the congress of the country will pass its suspension.

(A) monument　(B) motivation　(C) module　(D) momentum

60. Thailand is a pleasure for the senses. Tourists come from around the world to

visit the nation's gold-adorned temples and sample its delicious _____ .

(A) sky diving   (B) cuisine   (C) bungee jumping   (D) horseracing

61. The world is full of beautiful places, many with _____ stories to tell.

(A) vast   (B) urgent   (C) occasional   (D) enchanting

62. If you've ever seen a jazz band _____ or tried your hand at playing a saxophone, there is a good chance that the instrument you've seen in action or handled yourself came straight from the township of Houli, Taiwan.

(A) perform   (B) vanish   (C) perish   (D) vomit

63. Music was one of the first industries that have been disrupted by the Internet because _____ files are so easy to share, but it is found that when paying for songs is made easier than stealing them, people will pay.

(A) audio   (B) visual   (C) physical   (D) psychological

64. In a world that is ever more complex, turbulent and dangerous, Secretary Clinton has made a great _____ to strengthening the United States' relationships with allies, partners and friends.

(A) confirmation   (B) ambition   (C) contribution   (D) satisfaction

65. A bill to legalize gay marriage in Washington State has won final legislative __ _____ and taken effect starting 2012.

(A) approval   (B) rejection   (C) veto   (D) admission

66. One of the most painful things you may experience in life is that a friend you trust most _____ you.

(A) protects   (B) bores   (C) betrays   (D) persuades

67. Out of ignorance and selfishness, many people _____ against others based on their races, sexual orientation, age, or other reasons.

(A) falter   (B) discriminate   (C) respect   (D) beam

68. Dogs are said to be our most _____ friends because they enrich our life with their loyal company and never complain.

(A) faithful   (B) stink   (C) passive   (D) vulnerable

69. Be _____ to the people who make us happy because they are the charming gardeners who make our souls blossom.

(A) grateful   (B) resentful   (C) shameful   (D) mournful

70. Only love is powerful enough to overcome _____ , an often underestimated emotion that deprives us of our happiness.

(A) passion   (B) admiration   (C) worship   (D) hatred

71. Men often give excuses to _____ their wrongdoings.

(A) justify   (B) reject   (C) knit   (D) irritate

72. Recovering from the depression of losing one's beloved, you need all the help you can get, so I very much _____ a meditation program.

(A) recruit   (B) shrug   (C) recommend   (D) shudder

73. When visiting Alishan, one of the most popular tourist destinations in Taiwan, it's worth spending a few days to learn about the indigenous people living in mountain villages and _____ the marvelous scenery.

(A) prick on   (B) take in   (C) put off   (D) pick up

74. At 3,952 meters, Yushan is not only Taiwan's tallest _____ ; it is also the tallest mountain in Northeast Asia.

(A) peak   (B) dip   (C) vale   (D) creek

75. Having secured political and economic stability and overcome severe flooding, Thailand's ability to bounce back is _____ to investors.

(A) annoying   (B) enduring   (C) appealing   (D) scaffolding

76. _____ that much of the world is still mired in an economic slowdown, but some of the brightest examples of significant and lasting opportunity are right under our nose.

(A) All around the world   (B) There is no denying

(C) In the meantime,   (D) It is a turning point

Businesses often want to find out the level of service that is being provided by the employees in a particular store or place of business. In order to do this, they hire people who are known as mystery shoppers. These are people who shop at a store and secretly gather information about the store and the employees. They often also give their opinions about the overall experience they have while shopping.

Any type of business that deals with the public may be visited by a mystery shopper. These businesses include but are not limited to hotels, restaurants, retail stores, gas stations, and banks. Practically any business whose management needs to learn what the end consumer sees and experiences can benefit from mystery shopping.

Mystery shopping has become a big industry in the U.S., with estimated value of this industry at over $600 million in 2004. However, most people who work as mystery shoppers are unable to make a living doing it. Rather, they simply do it for fun and get free meals, merchandise, and sometimes money. The industry has also been hit in recent years by criminals who try to get people to pay in order to become **certified** as mystery shoppers.

77. According to the passage, what does a mystery shopper do?

(A) Observe how customers behave.

(B) Gather specific information about services.

(C) Visit some stores and talk with managers.

(D) Exchange information in a mysterious way.

78. According to the passage, which of the following is true?

(A) Mystery shoppers wear special costumes at work.

(B) Gas stations are among the potential places mystery shoppers will visit.

(C) There are over 600 million mystery shoppers in the U.S.

(D) Mystery shoppers are in danger because they may be beaten by criminals.

79. Which of the following is implied in the passage?

(A) Mystery shopping began in 2004.

(B) One has to look great in order to be a mystery shopper.

(C) One earns a lot of money by working as a mystery shopper.

(D) In reality, mystery shopping is just another market research tool.

80. Which of the following is closest in meaning to "**certified**" in the last line of this passage?

(A) qualified　　(B) talented　　(C) instructed　　(D) identified

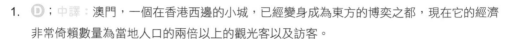

1. **(D)**；中譯：澳門，一個在香港西邊的小城，已經變身成為東方的博奕之都，現在它的經濟非常倚賴數量為當地人口的兩倍以上的觀光客以及訪客。

   解析：turned into（變成），表示當地人口用 local population，所以答案為 (D)。

2. **(C)**；中譯：一天三餐意謂正常情況下，一個人每天需要有早餐、中餐及晚餐。

   解析：(A) contrarily 相反地　(B) nevertheless 不過　(C) normally 正常情況下　(D) regardless 不論如何／本題考副詞。一天吃三餐應是指正常的情況，所以選項中用 normally（正常情況下）最適合，故答案為 (C)。

3. **(A)**；中譯：流行女裝店不過是小型專用品店的另一種稱呼。

   解析：(A) boutique 流行女裝店　(B) body shop 汽車修理廠　(C) bonus 紅利　(D) beauty parlor 美容院／specialty shop 指賣專門用品的店，選項中以 boutique（流行女裝店）最符合題意，其實就是賣專門的用品，故答案為 (A)。

4. **(C)**；中譯：當擺滿輕食點心的桌子被移開後，主人宣佈晚餐即將開始。

   解析：句中 filled with…為過去分詞片語修飾桌子，表示滿桌子的點心，點心為一種輕食，所以空格內形容詞用 light，故答案為 (C)。

5. **(B)**；中譯：要注意的是，手冊中所列的只是我們必須遵守的眾多規定及法令中所節錄的一小部分而已。

   解析：(A) article 物品　(B) selection 挑選　(C) election 選舉　(D) writing 書寫
   a bulk of sth（一大堆的東西），題意是指小冊子中的規定只是從一大堆規定中選出一部分而已，所以空格內名詞用 selection（挑選），故答案為 (B)。

6. **(A)**；中譯：回顧他過去生活在這個村莊的五十年的歲月，彼得不後悔他沒有早一點搬到大城市。

   解析：(A) regret 後悔　(B) remember 記得　(C) claim 主張　(D) announce 宣布

7. **(B)**；中譯：在一間購物中心，你要找尋一間你想要去的店，當問旁人也得不到答案時，最容易的方法是看指南或是問服務台。

   解析：(A) direct 直線的　(B) directory（工商）指南　(C) dictionary 字典　(D) director 指導員／要找尋一家店除問人外，還可以問服務台及用其它方式，選項中以 directory（指南）最合理，也就是查看指南，故答案為 (B)。

8. **(D)**；中譯：台灣缺乏天然資源，但是到處都教育的機會。

   解析：(A) physical 物質的　(B) chemical 化學的　(C) geometric 幾何的　(D) natural

天然的／short of（缺乏），台灣缺乏的資源，選項中以 natural（天然的）最恰當，也就是缺乏天然資源，故答案為 (D)。

9. C；中譯：台灣有充沛的年降雨量，但遺憾的是河流太短且太靠近海。

解析：annual（每年的），年降雨量用 annual rainfall，故答案為 (C)。

10. C；中譯：嚴格來說，威尼斯目前與其說是個沿海的商業城，倒不如說是個觀光城市。

解析：more of + 名詞…than + 名詞（與其說…倒不如說是…），威尼斯目前應該比較像是一座觀光的城市，故答案為 (C)。

11. C；中譯：我很喜歡羅馬，因為它有許多歷史遺跡且對遊客很友善。

解析：be friendly to（對某人或事情是友善的），歷史遺蹟（historic sites），故答案為 (C)。

12. A；中譯：京都是我最喜歡的城市，因為我對傳統日本文化的喜愛勝過電子文化。

解析：prefer…to（寧願…而不），由題意知道他喜歡京都這個城市，所以選項中用形容詞 favorite（喜愛的）最恰當，故答案為 (A)。

13. B；中譯：這間飯店不管是在接待或是結帳櫃台，都可以讓我們知道參加當地旅遊行程切確的費用及其他細節。

解析：(A) receiving 接收　(B) reception 接待　(C) resignation 辭職　(D) recognition 辨認／figure out（計算出；明白指出），飯店有結帳櫃檯（cashier's desk）及接待櫃台（reception desk），故答案為 (B)。

14. B；中譯：當在國外旅遊時，我們必須要全程隨身攜帶一些重要文件，其中之一就是我們的護照連同入境許可放在一起，假如要求是要這麼做的話。

解析：together with（連同），護照需與其他東西放在一起，空格後面是 permit（許可），所以選項中以 enter（進入）最恰當，也就是 enter permit（入境許可），故答案為 (B)。

15. A；中譯：這位 79 歲家住高雄的老婦人，大約有 10 年之久每年捐獻新台幣十二萬元給在她老家屏東的老人之家。

解析：捐贈的動詞為 donate，故答案為 (A)。

16. D；中譯：我在家裡已經蒐集了如此多的藝術品，以致於我沒有多餘的空間可以再容納一些新的東西。

解析：so…that（如此…以致於…），東西蒐藏多了就會沒有空間擺放，所以選項中用 space（空間）最符合題意，故答案為 (D)。

17. B；中譯：雖然大部分的航空公司要求旅客們在飛行前二小時到機場櫃檯報到，但是一些國際航線要求乘客必須在飛機起飛前三小時到機場。

解析：(A) revise 修訂　(B) require 要求　(C) record 記錄　(D) reveal 顯露

18. B；中譯：大部分可追溯到古代歷史的城市，通常會創造它們的神話，或者編造出一個很難解釋且混雜著事實與虛構的傳統歷史。

解析：(A) knee 膝蓋　(B) history 歷史　(C) pass 經過　(D) tool 工具

19. B；中譯：在搭乘巴士之前，最好先在電腦上查看一下它的路線，或仔細看一下在巴士停靠站的路線表。

解析：it is advisable to（最好是去…），check out（檢查），依題意是要看停靠站的路線圖（rout chart），故答案為 (B)。

20. B/D；中譯：沒有其他傳統中國的樂器像琵琶一樣已經被使用將近二千年了，不論是在獨奏或是在樂隊合奏方面。評論家描述這種弦樂器具有一種獨特的音質，而這有一點與西方魯特琴相匹配。

解析：(A) choir 唱詩班　(B) orchestra 管絃樂隊　(C) athletics 田徑運動　(D) chamber music 管樂／空格前有對等連接詞 or，所以空格需填入與 solo performance（獨奏）對應的名詞，選項中以 orchestra 管絃樂隊最符合題意，所以答案為 (B)。此題選 (D) 亦可。

21. B；中譯：有關這個城市支持哪一類民法的這個問題不應由你荒謬的論點來決定。

解析：(A) civilized 文化的　(B) civil 公民的　(C) citizen 市民　(D) civic 城市的 uphold（支持，維護），fallacious（荒謬的），民法用 civil law，故答案為 (B)。

22. A；中譯：菲律賓是個擁有 7000 多個島嶼的國家且有數十種原住民語言，更令人驚訝的是，南方與北方的不同點，特別是他們人民的宗教信仰以及政治的傾向。

解析：(A) contrast 差異　(B) competition 競爭　(C) construction 建築　(D) condition 狀況／空格中需填入一個表示南方與北方狀態的名詞，由題意研判應該南北大不同，所應用選項中的 contrast（差異），故答案為(A)。

23. A；中譯：我喜歡去漫遊，我時常在周末騎著我的腳踏車繞著村莊遊蕩。

解析：(A) tour 周遊　(B) speed 加速　(C) stroll 散步　(D) drive 開車

24. D；中譯：手機非常方便，因為它讓我們可充分地與全世界連結，且甚至提供我們在關鍵時刻必要的資訊。

解析：(A) expensive 昂貴的　(B) rare 稀有的　(C) fashionable 時尚的　(D) handy 方便的／at large（充分地），空格內需用形容詞說明手機的特性，由句意提到手機可以連接全世界並提供協助，所以用選項中的 handy（方便的）最適合，故答案為 (D)。

25. B；中譯：當回答移民官的問題時，最好是能率直的回答而不要遲疑。

解析：(A) historic 歷史上的　(B) hesitating 猶豫的　(C) hospitable 好客的　(D) heroic 英雄的 it is advisable to（最好是要…），straight forward（直率的），回答移民官的問題要直接，不要有所疑慮，否則會讓人起疑，所以選項中以 hesitating（猶豫的）最符合題意，故答案為 (B)。

26. B；中譯：當火車到達時，你需要做的第一件事就是在你上車之前，查看它的目的地是否符合你要去的地方。

解析：(A) design 設計　(B) destination 目的地　(C) destiny 命運　(D) dedication 奉獻

27. C；中譯：海關人員通常會有一張嚴肅的臉，並且他們有權力要求我們打開行李受檢。

解析：(A) good-looking 看起來好看　(B) funny-looking 看起來好笑　(C) stern-looking 看起來嚴肅　(D) silly-looking 看起來愚蠢

28. **B**；中譯：有些地點沒有乘客上下車處，最好是跟著導遊的指示來上下旅遊巴士以確保安全與舒適。

解析：(A) prevent 阻止　(B) guarantee 保證　(C) keep away 遠離　(D) attend to 處理旅程中聽從導遊的指示以確保安全，空格內動詞用選項中 guarantee（保證）最符合題意，故答案為 (B)。

29. **B**；中譯：在一些機場有最終呼叫廣播通知，但在其他機場，它們只有訊息顯示看板上閃動的訊息，乘客們有義務自行及時抵達登機門。

解析：(A) image 影像　(B) blinking 閃動的　(C) faulty 有缺點的　(D) traffic 交通 final call announcement（機場的最終呼叫廣播），依題意是指訊息顯示看板上會有閃動的訊息提醒旅客該登機，所以空格內用選項中的 blinking（閃動的）最適當，故答案為 (B)。

30. **A**；中譯：巴黎的文化行事曆充滿各種市集、沙龍及拍賣等活動，但是沒有什麼比的上巴黎古董雙年展。

解析：(A) compete with 與…競爭　(B) comment on 對…評論　(C) complain about 對…抱怨　(D) compose of 包含／be bursting with（裝滿），由題意知巴黎的文化行程雖多，但巴黎古董雙年展是最重要的，其它的活動都比不上它，所以空格內動詞用選項中的 compete with（與…競爭）最符合題意，故答案為 (A)。

31. **C**；中譯：有人昨晚闖入她家中並且偷走所有值錢的東西。

解析：(A) broke through 突破　(B) broke up 結束　(C) broke in 闖入　(D) broke down 失敗／由題意知有人進入她家偷東西，選項中以動詞用 broke in（闖入）最符合，故答案為 (C)。

32. **A**；中譯：儘管近來所有自由貿易與自由市場的批判，但要記住在最近的 25 年中，比起歷史上任何其他時期中，全世界有更多人由貧窮走向中產階級。

解析：(A) In spite of 儘管　(B) For the sake of 由於　(C) By all accounts 據說　(D) Were it not for 要不是／空格置於句首，後面接名詞片語，故需用介系詞引導介系詞片語當副詞修飾全句，依題意為雖然對自由貿易有所批判…，所以用選項中 In spite of（儘管）最符合題意，故答案為 (A)。

33. **D**；中譯：與不同背景的觀光客一起相處可以使導遊開闊眼界，且在回答好奇的觀光客問題時能學習到新的事物。

解析：(A) blow their own horn 自吹自擂　(B) take their breath away 令人屏息　(C) fall from grace 墮落　(D) broaden their horizons 開闊眼界／Mingle with（與…混雜一起），與不同的背景人相處可以使導遊增廣見聞，所以選項中以 broaden their horizons（開闊眼界）最符題意，故答案為 (D)。

34. **B**；中譯：在台灣新北市平溪區，會在每年一度的元宵節那天放天燈已成為一個傳統，據説天燈是由一位名為孔明的中國古代政治軍事家發明的。

解析：(A) As a consequence 因此　(B) Legend has it 傳説中　(C) It isn't worth the trouble 這不值得你煩惱　(D) It is high time 早就該如此／空格後面是 that 引導的名詞子句，説明天燈的由來，所以空格以中 Legend has it（傳説中）最符合題意，故答案為 (B)。

35. (A)；中譯：我的研究專題已經遭遇瓶頸且無法再往前推進，所以我需要重新思考我的設計並找人幫忙。

解析：(A) come to a standstill 停滯不前　(B) come out ahead 最後得到利益　(C) come to light 顯露出來　(D) come through 克服困難／由題意知研究已經遭遇困難無法前進，所以空格中應以 come to a standstill（停滯不前）最符合，故答案為 (A)。

36. (A)；中譯：我們必須找出如何走出這個迷宮的方法並且安全回家。

解析：(A) figure out 解決　(B) count on 依賴　(C) back up 支持　(D) give up 放棄

37. (D)；中譯：貨幣兌換是很複雜的，當有疑慮時，就要問懂這方面知識的人。

解析：(A) ignorant 無知的　(B) shaky 站不穩無法走的　(C) prejudiced 偏見的　(D) knowledgeable 有知識的／When in doubt 是指當有疑慮時，有不懂時應該要問懂的人，所以空格用 knowledgeable（有知識的）來形容這樣一個人最適當，故答案為 (D)。

38. (B)；中譯：假如我們能牢記社交禮儀，特別是在一個大群體中，我們將贏得人們的讚佩，雖然我們可能感覺不到。

解析：題意是要知道社交的方法才好在群體中得到敬重，所以空格內用 manners（方式），也就是 social manners（社交禮儀），故答案為 (B)。

39. (C)；中譯：衣著規定是一些基本有關人們在一個組織或特定場合中應有穿著的行為準則。

解析：(A) pros and cons 正反方　(B) ups and downs 盛衰　(C) dos and don'ts 行為準則　(D) ways and means 方式／Dress codes（服裝規定）是一種規定在何時該穿何種衣服的準則，所以空格應用 dos and don'ts（行為準則），答案為 (C)。

40. (A)；中譯：A：我下禮拜將要到泰國去五天。

B：那太棒了！祝你有個愉快的旅程。

解析：祝你旅途愉快需用祈使句 Wish you a wonderful trip，答案為 (A)。另也可以用 Have you a wonderful trip.

41. (C)；中譯：明年的這個時候我將在法國旅行。

解析：題意是指未來時間（明年的這個時間），空格內動詞需用未來式或未來進行式，依選項可用未來進行式，故答案為 (C)。

42. (D)；中譯：航空公司理應向我們解釋班機長時間延誤的原因，但他讓我們等待而沒説什麼。

解析：「could+have+p.p.」表示過去可以做而沒有做。所以答案為 (D)。

43. (B)；中譯：當錯誤發生時，請馬上讓我知道。

解析：do not hesitate to+V 為慣用語，表示馬上、立即之意，故答案為 (B)。

44. B；中譯：一項著名的調查將台北市列為二十二個亞洲都會中最佳綠色城市的第二名，僅次於新加坡。

　　解析：prominent（著名的），因為新加坡是第一名，台北緊跟其後，所以空格中用分詞 trailing（在…後面），故答案為 (B)。

45. D；中譯：台灣是溫泉之鄉，泰安溫泉位於文水河，在日據時代就已經開發了。

　　解析：(A) oration 演說　(B) operation 活動　(C) orientation 適應　(D) occupation 佔據
　　由題意知空格處應是指日據時代（Japanese occupation），故答案為 (D)。

46. D；中譯：這是中華航空 009 班機飛往香港班機在 2 號登機門登機最後一次登機廣播。

　　解析：登機前的廣播用 boarding call，故答案為 (D)。

47. D；中譯：在美國議員警告這個爭議可能會傷害自由貿易談判後，台灣政府昨天表示仍不會放棄對進口牛肉所設定的嚴格規定。

　　解析：(A) facilitate 促進　(B) advance 前進　(C) delight 使喜歡　(D) cripple 削弱
　　由題意知，空格內的動詞應該是指對雙方自由貿易談判有負面影響之意，所以選項中以 cripple（削弱）最適當，故答案為 (D)。

48. B；中譯：依據一項新的研究顯示，持續來到美國沿岸的移民人口正促進商業活動，且因更多的勞力供給而產生更多的工作機會。

　　解析：(A) threat 威脅　(B) arrival 抵達　(C) removal 移動　(D) selection 選擇
　　句中提到移民人口增加助長美國的商業及就業等狀況，所以選項中 arrival（抵達）最符合題意，表示持續出現的移民人口，故答案為 (B)。

49. D；中譯：開始於美國且橫掃全球的金融危機被更進一步證實了——不論如何——我們彼此都逃不掉。

　　解析：for better and for worse（不論好壞，不論如何），句中提到金融危機用 financial crisis，故答案為 (D)。

50. B；中譯：為了讓旅行更容易些，特別是對那些倚賴公共運輸的人們，觀光局與地方政府合作在 2010 年推動台灣旅遊巡迴巴士服務。

　　解析：(A) terminate 使停止　(B) initiate 發動　(C) annotate 註解　(D) depreciate 貶低
　　由題意知活動是由政府與民間開始推動，故空格中的動詞以選項中 initiate（發動）最恰當，故答案為 (B)。

51. A；中譯：科技，例如行動電話，常常可以促進平等並幫助人們脫離貧困。

　　解析：(A) fosters 促進　(B) discourages 阻止　(C) likens 比做　(D) diminishes 減少
　　equality（平等），科技讓人可以在平等的基礎上有發展的機會，所以空格內動詞用 fosters（促進）最符合題意，故答案為 (A)。

52. C；中譯：在貓掛鈴鐺的故事中，老鼠知道假如貓在脖子被掛上一個鈴鐺，牠們的生命就會安全多了，但問題是，誰要賭上牠的命去把鈴鐺掛在貓身上。

　　解析：(A) achieve 完成　(B) resolve 決定　(C) gamble 賭博　(D) persist 堅持／空格內

需用動詞，依題意為誰要冒這個危險去掛鈴鐺，選項中以 gamble（賭博）最符合題意，故答案為 (C)。

53. (C)；中譯：聖嚴法師畢其一生弘揚佛法，他用簡單且實用的語言使來自各行各業的人們都能更親近佛教。

解析：all walks of life(各行各業)，devote one's entire life to…為投入一生心力做某事，故答案為 (C)。

54. (B)；中譯：簡而言之，如果一個社會讓占一半人口的女性沒有夢想及生產力的話，這個社會就不會真正地繁榮。

解析：(A) deteriorate 惡化　(B) flourish 繁茂　(C) ravage 劫掠　(D) smuggle 走私 Simply put（簡單來說），smother（使…窒息），題意表示讓婦女能有夢想及生產力才可促進社會發展，空格內動詞用選項中的 flourish（使繁茂）最符合題意，故答案為 (B)。

55. (A)；中譯：增加觀光設施來迎合本地及國際的觀光需求已經讓人關注到台灣的自然環境受到衝擊。

解析：(A) impact 衝擊　(B) input 輸入　(C) itinerary 行程表　(D) identity 一致性 raised concerns about（引起…關注），建設可能會引起環境的破壞，所以空格中以 impact（衝擊）最符合題意，故答案為 (A)。

56. (B)；中譯：甜點不是餐點的要角，但它們出現在餐桌時常是一個快樂重要的來源。

解析：(A) link 連結　(B) source 來源　(C) pardon 原諒　(D) ordeal 折磨 intrinsic（真正的），看到餐桌上出現甜點就會覺得很快樂，由其是小孩子，所以甜點應該是快樂的 source（來源），答案為 (B)。

57. (A)；中譯：烏山頭水庫開始建造於 1920 年而於 1930 年落成，它在 1969 年成為烏山頭風景區。

解析：(A) construction 建築　(B) congestion 擁擠　(C) contamination 汙染　(D) confrontation 對抗／由題意知空格內應為表示建築的名詞，故答案為 (A)。

58. (D)；中譯：我將造訪沃爾夫索妮婭，一間在邁阿密非常特別的博物館，我喜歡這裡手工的裝飾品以及從 1885 到 1945 年的宣傳物等收藏品。

解析：(A) edible 可吃的　(B) outrageous 粗暴的　(C) awful 可怕的　(D) extraordinary 特別的／pay a visit to（拜訪），空格內需用適當的形容詞來形容該博物館，由後面所列的物品，研判應用 extraordinary（特別的）最適合，故答案為 (D)。

59. (D)；中譯：支持廢止死刑已經有了契機，而且非常可能有一天這國家的國會將通過廢止死刑。

解析：(A) monument 紀念碑　(B) motivation 動機　(C) module 模型　(D) momentum 契機／suspending（停止），由本句後面提到國會有機會通過廢止死刑的法律，故空格內用選項中 momentum（契機）最符合題意，故答案為 (D)。

60. (B)；中譯：泰國是一個充滿感官享受的地方，世界各地而來的觀光客造訪這個國家金碧輝煌的寺院並且品嚐它的美食。

解析：(A) sky diving 跳傘　(B) cuisine 菜餚　(C) bungee jumping 高空彈跳　(D) horseracing 賽馬／for the senses（感官的饗宴），sample 在此解釋為品嚐，所以空格中以 cuisine（菜餚）最符合題意，故答案為 (B)。

61. (D)；中譯：世界上有很多漂亮的地方，而許多都有迷人的故事可以述說。

解析：(A) vast 廣大的　(B) urgent 急促的　(C) occasional 偶爾的　(D) enchanting 迷人的／be full of（充滿著），漂亮的地方常有一些故事，選項中以 enchanting（迷人的）最恰當，表示這地方迷人的故事，故答案為 (D)。

62. (A)；中譯：假如你曾經看過一個爵士樂團表演，或自己親自吹奏薩克士風，很有可能你看到正在演奏的樂器或你自己手上拿的是來自於台灣小鎮后里。

解析：(A) perform 表演　(B) vanish 消失　(C) perish 滅亡　(D) vomit 嘔吐／there is a good chance（很有可能），依題意，爵士樂團應該是要演奏或表演，故選項中以 perform（表演）最符合題意，故答案為 (A)。

63. (A)；中譯：音樂是最早遭受網路殘害的產業之一，因為音樂檔是如此容易分享，但後來發現當買音樂變得比偷音樂來得容易時，人們將願意付錢。

解析：(A) audio 聲音的　(B) visual 視覺的　(C) physical 物質的　(D) psychological 心理學的／be made easier（被變得更容易），空格處是指音樂檔案，音樂檔案為 audio file，故答案為 (A)。

64. (C)；中譯：在一個比以前更為複雜、紛亂以及險惡的世界裏，國務卿柯林頓已經在於強化美國與盟邦、夥伴及朋友的關係上作出巨大的貢獻。

解析：(A) confirmation 確定　(B) ambition 野心　(C) contribution 貢獻　(D) satisfaction 滿意／強化美國與盟邦等關係對是柯林頓對美國做出的貢獻，也就是 make a great contribution to…故答案為 (C)。

65. (A)；中譯：在華盛頓州，一個使同性戀結婚合法的法案已經贏得最後立法通過，且從 2012 年開始生效。

解析：(A) approval 同意　(B) rejection 否決　(C) veto 禁止　(D) admission 承認 take effect（生效），法案立法通過用 legislative approval，故答案為 (A)。

66. (C)；中譯：你人生中有可能所經歷過最為痛苦的事之一是被你最信任的朋友出賣。

解析：(A) protects 保護　(B) bores 鑽入　(C) betrays 出賣　(D) persuades 說服 被最信任的好朋友出賣是一件很痛苦的事，空格內動詞用 betrays（出賣），表示一個你最信任的朋友出賣，故答案為 (C)。

67. (B)；中譯：由於無知與自私，許多人基於種族、性別傾向、年紀及其他原因而歧視他人。

解析：(A) falter 搖晃　(B) discriminate 歧視　(C) respect 尊敬　(D) beam 照耀 Out of（因為），歧視別人動詞用 discriminate against，故答案為 (B)。

68. (A)；中譯：狗被認為是我們最忠實的朋友，因為牠們用不離不棄的態度來充實我們的生活。

解析：(A) faithful 忠心的　(B) stink 惡臭的　(C) passive 被動的　(D) vulnerable 有價值的／be said to be（被認為是），狗是人類最忠實的朋友，所以空格內用 faithful（忠心的）來形容狗，故答案為 (A)。

69. (A)；中譯：要對那些讓我們快樂的人心存感恩，因為他們是讓我們心靈得以綻放的迷人園丁。

解析：(A) grateful 感恩的　(B) resentful 憤怒的　(C) shameful 可恥的　(D) mournful 悲哀的／be+ 形容詞 +to 某人，表示要對某人…，為祈使句用法，依題意空格應用 grateful（感恩的），表示對人要感恩，故答案為 (A)。

70. (D)；中譯：只有愛有足夠的力量來戰勝仇恨，一種通常被低估且剝奪我們快樂的情緒。

解析：(A) passion 熱情　(B) admiration 讚美　(C) worship 崇拜　(D) hatred 仇恨後面句子來說明空格中的名詞，所以選項中以 hatred（仇恨）最符合題意，也呼應前面提到用愛來化解仇恨之意，故答案為 (D)。

71. (A)；中譯：男人通常會找藉口來為他們做錯的事辯護。

解析：(A) justify 為…辯護　(B) reject 否認　(C) knit 編織　(D) irritate 激怒／excuse（藉口），為做錯的事找理由來解釋，選項中用 justify（為…辯護）最適當，故答案為 (A)。

72. (C)；中譯：為了從失去你所最愛的人的沮喪中恢復過來，你需要所有你能得到的幫助，所以我非常推薦一個冥想課程。

解析：(A) recruit 徵募　(B) shrug 聳肩　(C) recommend 推薦　(D) shudder 發抖 beloved（心愛的人），題意是指介紹給人一個課程，動詞用選項中 recommend（推薦）最恰當，故答案為 (C)。

73. (B)；中譯：當造訪阿里山時，台灣最受歡迎的觀光區之一，那值得多花幾天來瞭解有關生活在山間部落的原住民以及奇異的景觀。

解析：(A) prick on 驅使　(B) take in 觀賞　(C) put off 延遲　(D) pick up 搭載／奇異的景觀是要用欣賞的，所以動詞用選項中 take in（觀賞）最符合，故答案為 (B)。

74. (A)；中譯：高達 3952 公尺，玉山不僅是台灣最高山，她也是東北亞最高的山。

解析：(A) peak 山峰　(B) dip 浸泡　(C) vale 溝槽　(D) creek 小溪／玉山為台灣最高山，選項中用 peak（山峰）最符合題意，故答案為 (A)。

75. (C)；中譯：由於已經具有可靠的政治與經濟穩定度，且克服了嚴重的水患，泰國復原的能力對投資者是有吸引力的。

解析：(A) annoying 惱人　(B) enduring 持久　(C) appealing 有吸引力　(D) scaffolding 搭鷹架／該句主詞為 Thailand's ability 屬事物，空格係中需用現在分詞當形容詞用作為主詞補語，選項中以 appealing（有吸引力）最適當，表示對投資者是有吸引力的，故答案為 (C)。

76. (B)；中譯：不可否認的是世界上許多地方仍在經濟衰退的泥淖中，但是有些最亮眼的例子都有顯著且持久的機會，而這已都在我們眼前。

解析：空格置於句首，後面是接 that 名詞子句，選項中只 There is no denying（不可否認的是）符合句意及用法，故答案為 (B)。

77-80；中譯：商場上時常需要了解員工在一家特定的店或企業場所提供服務的水準，為此，他們僱用被稱為神秘客的人。這些人會在一家店消費並暗中蒐集關於這家店及員工的資訊，他們通常也會提供關於在他們消費時所得到的整體經驗及意見。

任何與公眾往來有關的各種行業都有可能被神秘客所造訪，這些行業不限於飯店、餐廳、零售店、加油站以及銀行。特別是那些管理者需要去了解終端顧客所看到以及體驗的行業，都可以經由神祕的消費而受益。

神秘消費在美國已經變成一大產業，據估計這個產業產值在 2004 年已超過六億美元。然而大部分擔任神秘客的人不會靠此維生，反而是，他們純粹因為興趣或可以獲得免費餐點、商品或有時候有錢領而從事。這產業近年也被一些要人付錢就可以成為認證的神秘客的罪犯行為而備受抨擊。

77. (B)；中譯：根據本文，神秘客做甚麼？(A) 觀察消費者行為是如何　(B) 蒐集有關服務的特定資訊　(C) 造訪一些店家並與經理交談　(D) 用神秘的方式交換資訊

解析：由 These are people who shop at a store and secretly gather information about the store and the employees…，知神秘客會暗中蒐集店家及員工服務的資訊，答案為 (B)。

78. (B)；中譯：根據本文，下列敘述何者為真？(A) 神秘客工作時穿著特殊服裝　(B) 加油站名列神秘客會造訪的潛在地點　(C) 在美國有六億個神秘客　(D) 神秘客們有危險因為他們可能會被罪犯們毆打。

解析：(A) 文中沒提到這點，敘述為非　(B) 由…business…may be visited by a mystery shopper. These businesses include but are not limited to hotels, restaurants, retail stores, gas stations,…，故知加油站名列神秘客會造訪的潛在地點，敘述為真　(C) 文中沒提到這點，敘述為非　(D) 文中沒提到這點，敘述為非。

79. (D)；中譯：下列何項在文章中有暗示到？(A) 神秘消費開始於 2004 年　(B) 人必須長得好看才能成為神秘客　(C) 有人因為擔任神秘客而賺很多錢　(D) 事實上，神祕消費只是另一種市場調查工具。

解析：文中提到神秘客暗中蒐集消費時店家的服務等各種資訊，提供企業作為改進服務的參考，與市場調查意義相類似，故可視為另一種市場調查工具，其他敘述文中均無提到，答案為 (D)。

80. (A)；中譯：下列哪一個字的意思與 certified 最相近？(A) qualified 有資格的　(B) talented 有才能的　(C) instructed 受委任的　(D) identified 被辨認出的。

解析：certified 在文中的意思是被認證過的，也就是具有某些資格之意，所以與選項中的 qualified（有資格的）意思最相近，故答案為 (A)。

103 年專門職業及技術人員普通考試導遊人員、領隊人員考試試題
等別：普通考試
類科：外語導遊人員（英語）
科目：外國語（英語）
考試時間：1 小時 20 分
※注意：本試題為單一選擇題，請選出一個正確或最適當的答案，複選作答者，該題不予計分。

1. One advantage of staying in apartment-style hotels is that you can either eat out or keep costs down by self-_____ .

   (A) branding   (B) catering   (C) flavoring   (D) navigating

2. The world-class Kruger National Park, known for its _____ of wildlife, has an astonishing variety and number of animals.

   (A) breakdown   (B) diversity   (C) hospitality   (D) prescription

3. As one source of human-induced global warming, airplanes _____ large volumes of greenhouse gases.

   (A) permit   (B) shovel   (C) emit   (D) vanish

4. Bus trips in the city cost $2.50 for adults. Children under 12 years old are _____ a half-fare.

   (A) abided by   (B) entitled to   (C) indifferent from   (D) oriented toward

5. We arrived at the airport two hours before _____ in order to check in, but we were told that we could not do so as the flight was overbooked.

   (A) demand   (B) departure   (C) dismissal   (D) dispute

6. _____ to the theme park and a ten minutes' stroll from it, the hotel offers you the best location for your holiday accommodation.

   (A) Adjacent   (B) Aggressive   (C) Applicable   (D) Approximate

7. An airline _____ travelling in secret should act normally first and then test

the flight attendant with abnormal behaviors such as being drunk, noisy, or difficult to please.

(A) individual　(B) inspector　(C) intern　(D) inventor

8. Provision for people with disabilities on public transport is only average in this city, although some new buses are now wheelchair- _____ .

(A) accessible　(B) correlative　(C) inclusive　(D) skeptical

9. Although the city is relatively untroubled by crime in comparison with other cities, there is now more street crime than _____ .

(A) it used to　(B) there used to be　(C) was there　(D) it has been

10. Many bus companies offer day passes at the cost of a short-distance ticket. They are good for unlimited _____ within the company's network on the same day.

(A) bites　(B) feet　(C) prices　(D) rides

11. Travelling by long-distance bus is generally the cheapest way to reach the destination, but spending 12 hours on the road is very time- _____ .

(A) consuming　(B) misleading　(C) relieving　(D) violating

12. Ask for _____ before you take close-up photographs of people, and if payment is requested, either pay up or put the camera away.

(A) capital　(B) justice　(C) permission　(D) substance

13. Under this travel insurance plan, you are _____ to make a claim when your journey has to be cancelled for reasons beyond your control.

(A) dispensable　(B) eligible　(C) hospitable　(D) invaluable

14. We believe travelers can make a positive contribution to the countries they visit if they respect their _____ communities and spend their money wisely.

(A) guest　(B) host　(C) port　(D) source

15. There is no reason to stay in the city center; after the shops close, the center becomes a _____ ghost town.

(A) customary　(B) feasible　(C) spectacular　(D) virtual

16. Stroll west from the Maritime Museum along the waterfront and you will soon _____ the Amsterdam Center for Architecture.

(A) chase   (B) hold   (C) reach   (D) stop

17. Located in one of the city's poorer neighborhoods, many old houses in this area have been torn down to _____ for new and better public housing.

(A) date back   (B) fall short   (C) get around   (D) make way

18. To order room service, you call the reception and ask for food items listed on the hotel's menu. The food _____ your room for you to enjoy.

(A) is then brought to   (B) may then bring in

(C) to bring is then at   (D) has then brought to

19 In the United States, about 1.8 million people in the _____ industry work in establishments such as hotels, restaurants, casinos, and amusement parks.

(A) hospitality   (B) missionary   (C) renaissance   (D) sanctuary

20. Budget airlines boosted their _____ of passenger traffic to nearly 40% last year; at the same time major traditional airlines saw lower volumes.

(A) flow   (B) model   (C) net   (D) share

21 The climate in the city is tropical, with monthly _____ temperatures in the range of 19 to 29 degrees and relative humidity between 70 and 80%.

(A) mean   (B) plain   (C) rare   (D) surface

22. Once we were seated at the restaurant, it took almost no time before big bamboo steamers full of dumplings arrived, along with _____ on how to eat those *xiao long bao*.

(A) brunches   (B) chopsticks   (C) directions   (D) functions

23. Youbike is a bicycle rental service that _____ with the MRT Easycard, and is widely thought of as the "last mile" in public transportation after you have ridden the bus, train, or MRT.

(A) books   (B) calls   (C) uses   (D) works

24. Taipei Zoo will accept reservations for up to 300 visitors per day to meet the panda family. Visitors without reservation can _____ up for the ticket, though numbers will be limited.

(A) catch   (B) follow   (C) keep   (D) queue

25. _____ you purchase good tea, keep it in a dry cool place, avoiding direct

sunshine. An airtight container is a good choice.

(A) After   (B) Though   (C) Before   (D) Whereas

26. When the 6.3 magnitude earthquake struck Taiwan, the railway administration immediately suspended train service _____ it checked for any possible damage to tracks.

(A) where   (B) that   (C) whether   (D) while

27. This _____ features Spain's major cities including stops at several famous cathedrals.

(A) forecast   (B) itinerary   (C) restriction   (D) allowance

28. When arriving in Thimphu, the capital of Bhutan, some visitors find it difficult to adjust to the city's high _____ and need to seek medical help.

(A) altitude   (B) superstition   (C) significance   (D) economy

29. A _____ flight is a form of commercial flight where the departure and the arrival take place in the same country.

(A) foreign   (B) domestic   (C) rural   (D) connecting

30. When the show was cancelled, the people who had bought tickets had their money _____.

(A) purchased   (B) prescribed   (C) replaced   (D) refunded

31. There are many baggage claim _____ at most international airports. Once you have collected your baggage there, move toward the customs clearance area.

(A) escalators   (B) cylinders   (C) tunnels   (D) carousels

32. Taj Mahal, regarded by many as the finest example of Mughal architecture, is one of the most popular tourist _____ in India.

(A) attractions   (B) departments   (C) surroundings   (D) promises

33. Some hotels require their guests to leave a _____ to cover incidental charges to the room.

(A) custom   (B) discount   (C) deposit   (D) currency

34. The chef uses only the finest _____ to make his special salsa.

(A) ingredients   (B) properties   (C) vouchers   (D) characteristics

35. When you are in public places, be sure not to leave your personal _____ unattended.

    (A) boarding (B) amusement (C) themes (D) belongings

36. Don't miss out on the best London art _____ including sculptures, paintings, and photography.

    (A) civilizations (B) exhibitions (C) preparations (D) distributions

37. You can buy washing machines, dishwashers, or other household _____ on the fifth floor of this department store.

    (A) pamphlets (B) oysters (C) appliances (D) chores

38. This restaurant is famous for its exotic flavors of Indian _____.

    (A) cuisine (B) ornament (C) necessities (D) costumes

39. Most countries have passed laws to protect their national _____ such as valuable historical buildings or things that are important to cultural preservation.

    (A) habitat (B) continent (C) anthem (D) heritage

40. After many years of travelling, the couples decided to stay in London forever and have a _____ home there.

    (A) swollen (B) permanent (C) lethal (D) temporary

41. After cleaning the hallway, the janitor left a sign saying that the floor was wet and _____.

    (A) slightly (B) enormous (C) slippery (D) enchanted

42. John asked the waitress for a _____ to drink his iced tea.

    (A) straw (B) grinder (C) fiber (D) sausage

43. A _____ park is a large area of land reserved for wild animals, in which they can move freely and be seen by the public who usually drive through the park in cars.

    (A) shrine (B) botanical (C) descendent (D) safari

44. Petronas Twin Towers in Kuala Kumpur are the world's tallest twin towers. Visitors can see the views of the city from the Skybridge as well as from the _____ at Level 86.

    (A) environment (B) observatory (C) glacier (D) latitude

45. It is said that even today men and women still struggle to achieve a balance in their co-existence. In many parts of the world, women are still _____ to occupy positions previously closed to them.

(A) striving   (B) abolishing   (C) discerning   (D) inspecting

46. I missed the meeting this morning. Can someone _____ me in on what happened?

(A) send   (B) deal   (C) fill   (D) read

47. Oil price _____ is always regarded as the barometer of worldwide economy.

(A) confrontation   (B) fluctuation   (C) prevention   (D) substitution

48. Chloe McCardel, an Australian endurance athlete, had to abandon her attempt to swim from Cuba to Florida after she was _____ by a jellyfish.

(A) stung   (B) drowned   (C) stabbed   (D) dunk

49. To take advantage of some good bargains, many consumers choose to become members of warehouse clubs and start to buy things _____.

(A) at large   (B) in terms   (C) off base   (D) in bulk

50. Many parents send their children to some after-school music programs in order to explore their musical interests and _____ their talents.

(A) cultivate   (B) disguise   (C) subside   (D) moderate

51. Cold symptoms usually last for about a week. If the symptoms _____ or worsen, you will want to see a doctor immediately.

(A) postpone   (B) persist   (C) converse   (D) comply

52 The jazz concert will be held at the high school _____ in town and is going to be one event you do not want to miss out on.

(A) circumstance   (B) embassy   (C) monument   (D) auditorium

53. Please make sure to keep your receipts so we can _____ you for your travel expenses.

(A) supervise   (B) reimburse   (C) relocate   (D) scatter

54. In general, drivers must be careful about walkers. Under current law, motorists must _____ to pedestrians in a crosswalk.

(A) yield   (B) confess   (C) proceed   (D) resist

55. To save money, Susan always clips _____ from the newspaper to use at the grocery store.

(A) certificates   (B) warranties   (C) coupons   (D) pouches

56. Bollywood movies have recently _____ to a global market and drawn hundreds of millions of viewers all over the world.

(A) increased   (B) appealed   (C) speculated   (D) enriched

57. Visitors to San Francisco this morning might be quite disappointed because the Golden Gate Bridge was barely _____ through the dense fog.

(A) durable   (B) visible   (C) amiable   (D) audible

58. Hawaii is a great location for all kinds of water sports. Some like to go windsurfing _____ others like to go water-skiing.

(A) despite of   (B) therefore   (C) whenever   (D) whereas

59. More and more public _____ stations can be found in places like restaurants, department stores, and airports. Smartphone owners can make use of them when the battery is low.

(A) charging   (B) hacking   (C) fueling   (D) boosting

60. Prices of hotel rooms are very _____ to demand, so special deals and discounts during weekdays could always attract more people.

(A) commercial   (B) frequent   (C) gradual   (D) sensitive

61. A U.S. flight bound for New York last month experienced _____ shortly after take-off from Houston, causing minor injuries to five crew and passengers.

(A) jet lag   (B) boundaries   (C) turbulence   (D) atmosphere

62. This 2.5km-long tree-lined _____ featuring flower shops and boutiques is one of the most beautiful places in Paris.

(A) colleague   (B) delicacy   (C) ambulance   (D) boulevard

63. Although guests are not allowed to eat durians inside the hotel because of their offensive odor, some people manage to _____ them in.

(A) calculate   (B) exclude   (C) achieve   (D) smuggle

64. More money is needed to improve the _____ of the nation's rural areas

including building roads and establishing clinics.

(A) infrastructure (B) obstacle (C) commodities (D) diagnosis

65. Taking a photograph in a court is often _____ and sometimes can even be seen as a serious offense.

(A) prohibited (B) accumulated (C) celebrated (D) disordered

66. Each room of this hotel has large windows that provide _____ views of the sparkling Atlantic Ocean.

(A) cautious (B) spectacular (C) experimental (D) ambitious

67. Gift _____ refers to the act of enclosing a present in some sort of material. In many cases, it also adds much value to the gift.

(A) editing (B) spelling (C) containing (D) wrapping

68. Sunday is the best day to visit the market. There are many fantastic _____ selling fresh local fruits and vegetables.

(A) stalls (B) recipes (C) pitchers (D) buns

69. Every year the school prepares a celebratory dinner _____ for the graduating class. The event will be held at San Francisco's Ritz-Carlton Hotel this year.

(A) engagement (B) complex (C) disposal (D) banquet

70. Many skin diseases are _____ and can be passed from one person to another.

(A) energetic (B) fictional (C) contagious (D) abundant

Culinary tourism is when people travel to a different country to enjoy local cuisine. Travelers often look specifically for places with a rich cuisine, food and drink festivals, and cooking classes. Many different destinations are popular for culinary tourism, such as France, Thailand, India, and Japan.

The most basic form of culinary tourism is when travelers go to a country with the aim of trying local dishes. Culinary tourists are interested in dishes that cannot be found in other places. Food and drink festivals increase culinary tourism because they give travelers a chance to sample many different dishes. Cooking classes also

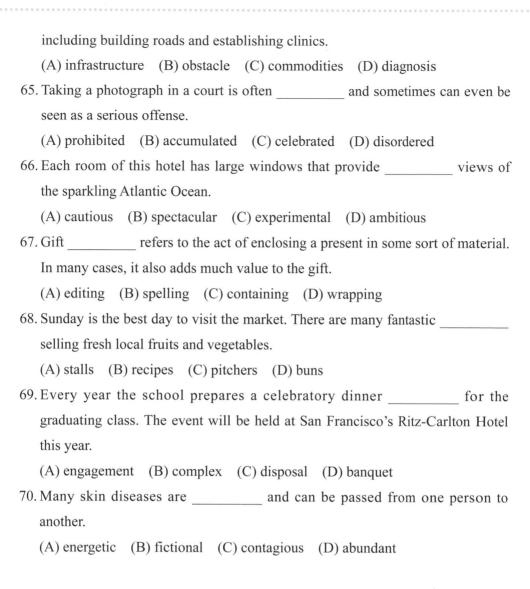

give tourists the chance to learn how to cook local dishes and teach them new techniques in the process. A culinary tour may include a mixture of these activities.

Particularly in Thailand, there are cooking schools with a huge range of prices, locations, and cuisines to choose from. A typical half-day course includes an introduction to fundamental ingredients, cooking techniques, and a hands-on chance to prepare and cook at least four dishes. Most schools offer a **revolving** cast of dishes, making it possible to study for a week without repeating a lesson. Courses often start with a visit to a market and end with a communal lunch where you get to taste your hard work.

The courses at smaller Thai cooking schools in Bangkok offer an ideal home-style learning environment that is different from most of the hotels and restaurants in Thailand. You can experience Thai culture through the arts and secrets of fragrant and delicious Thai cooking with the local people. Experienced chefs will show you the secret recipe of authentic Thai cuisine step-by-step. But keep in mind that Thai cooking is extremely flexible. Although you will be given recipes, the emphasis is on understanding the ingredients and flavors and using your senses to make adjustments when you cook. Classes are intended to be relaxed and fun, reflecting the Thai approach to life. There is no need to have any previous cooking experience, just a love of food and a willingness to experiment.

71. What does the passage suggest about culinary tourism?

(A) Thailand is by far the best destination for culinary tourists.

(B) Most culinary tourists do not express concern about weight watching.

(C) International fast food chain stores are usually not on the itinerary of culinary tourists.

(D) To boost culinary tourism, free samples are provided to tourists in food and drink festivals.

72. Which of the following is true about cooking courses in Thailand?

(A) Most cooking classes do not start until the afternoon.

(B) Ingredients are usually purchased by the chef for tourists.

(C) There is a wide selection of cooking courses in Thailand for tourists.

(D) Smaller cooking schools are preferred over famous hotels and restaurants.

73. Which of the following is closest in meaning to **"revolving"** in the third paragraph?

(A) reviving   (B) reversing   (C) regulating   (D) rotating

74. According to the passage, which of the following statement could be inferred?

(A) Thai people are generally very laid-back.

(B) A culinary tour is not complete without food festivals.

(C) Destinations for culinary tourism are limited to four specific countries.

(D) There is a lot of confidential information involved in cooking Thai food.

75 Where is this passage most likely from?

(A) Yellow pages.   (B) A travel website.

(C) A restaurant yearbook.   (D) An annual report of a travel agent.

The use of emoticons, punctuation to depict a facial expression, is an essential part of the **lexicon** of the Internet. Even if you don't use emoticons, you probably know what they are-little strings of characters, when looked at sideways, are like faces showing some emotion. For example, :-D means *laughing*, with eyes, a nose, and a capital D for a wide, happy mouth.

All this is the result of a half-joking computer post put up by a faculty member at Carnegie Mellon University on September 19, 1982. Scott Fahlman noticed that some of the jokes being sent around Carnegie Mellon's computer network were being taken seriously by a few people on campus. Someone who didn't get the joke might be upset by an all-in-fun comment and send out an angry response. This wasted a lot of people's time. Fahlman suggested the *smiley* as a solution. If you write something not to be taken seriously, he suggested, type :-) after it. **Some people took up his suggestion and it became part of the Internet shorthand at Carnegie Mellon.** The popularity of smiley turned out to be much more than Fahlman expected. Within a few months, it soon spread via messages to other universities and companies.

No one really knows how many emoticons there are, but lists of 100 or so are common. The most popular ones are actually turned into little pictures by word-processing or instant-messaging software. For instance, :-(meaning sadness or disappointment becomes ☹ on your computer screen.

76. What is the main purpose of the passage?

   (A) To convince the reader to use emoticons in electronic communication.

   (B) To introduce the reader to the origin of the smiley.

   (C) To provide a historical overview of the Internet development.

   (D) To explain the various meanings of the smiley.

77. What does the word **lexicon** in the first paragraph mean?

   (A) technology   (B) communication

   (C) vocabulary   (D) application

78 Which of the following best expresses the essential information in **the highlighted sentence** in the second paragraph?

   (A) Many people at his university liked his suggestion.

   (B) He was promoted to a better job because of his suggestion.

   (C) His suggestion helped create the Internet at the university.

   (D) His suggestion was shortened by the university faculty.

79. Which of the following can be inferred from the passage about Fahlman's colleagues at Carnegie Mellon?

   (A) They often posted jokes.

   (B) They tried to offend each other.

   (C) They didn't know how to write good messages.

   (D) They didn't like jokes at all.

80 According to the passage, which of the following is true about *emoticons*?

   (A) They can all be turned into little pictures by common word-processing software.

   (B) Nobody actually noticed the use of emoticons in text messages.

   (C) They are symbols used on a network to indicate emotion.

   (D) No more than 100 emoticons are found nowadays.

06 Unit 103外語導遊英語考試—解析

1. **B**；中譯：住在公寓型態的飯店的優點之一是你可以外食或者自己開伙來省錢。

   解析：(A) branding 標記　(B) catering 辦伙　(C) flavoring 提味　(D) navigating 導航　eat out（外食），either …or（不是…就是），依題意應是指可以外食或是自行開伙，空格用選項中的 catering（辦伙）最適合，故答案為 (B)。

2. **B**；中譯：世界級的克魯格國家公園以它多樣的野生動物聞名於世，它有令人嘆為觀止的種類及數量的動物。

   解析：(A) breakdown 崩潰　(B) diversity 多樣性　(C) hospitality 款待　(D) prescription 命令／（be）known for（以…聞名），句中後半部已經點出是以豐富的動物多樣性聞名，故空格中以 diversity（多樣性）最適合，答案為 (B)。

3. **C**；中譯：作為人類引起的全球暖化來源之一，就是飛機排放大量的溫室氣體。

   解析：(A) permit 允許　(B) shovel 鏟起　(C) emit 排放　(D) vanish 消失／human-induced（人類引起的），greenhouse gases（溫室氣體），飛機排出的氣體會造成溫室效應，空格內動詞應用 emit（排出），故答案為 (C)。

4. **B**；中譯：在這個城市內成人搭巴士票價是 2.5 元，未滿 12 歲的兒童享有半價。

   解析：(A) abided by 遵守　(B) entitled to 有資格　(C) indifferent from 與…不同　(D) oriented toward 導向／half-fare（半價），題意應為兒童享有半價搭乘的資格，選項中以 be entitled to（有…資格）最適合，故答案為 (B)。

5. **B**；中譯：我們在飛機起飛前二小時抵達機場想要報到，但我們被告知因機位超賣無法報到。

   解析：(A) demand 要求　(B) departure 出發　(C) dismissal 解雇　(D) dispute 駁斥 overbooked 是指機位超賣，搭飛機要在飛機起飛前數小時先至機場報到，所以空格中名詞用 departure（出發）最適當，故答案為 (B)。

6. **A**；中譯：緊鄰著主題公園只有十分鐘的步程，這家飯店是你渡假住宿的最佳地點。

   解析：(A) Adjacent 緊鄰的　(B) Aggressive 侵略的　(C) Applicable 適切的　(D) Approximate 大約的／stroll（漫步），由題意知距離公園只有十分鐘路程，表示是靠近公園之意，空格中用 Adjacent，也就是 be adjacent to（緊鄰著）最適合且符合題意，故答案為 (A)。

7. **B**；中譯：一個暗中跟隨一起飛行的航空檢查員一開始行為正常，之後會以不正常的行為，例如酒醉、吵鬧或難以安撫等來測試空服員。

解析：(A) individual 個人　(B) inspector 檢查員　(C) intern 實習生　(D) inventor 發明者／abnormal（反常的），空格後面現在分詞為修飾空格內的名詞，表示跟隨班機一起旅行的，由題意知他會以各種情況來測試空服員，空格內以 inspector（檢查員）最符合，故答案為 (B)。

8. **A**；中譯：這個城市中，在公共運輸提供殘障人士的各種設施只算是平均水準，但有些新型的巴士現在可以上下輪椅。

　　解析：(A) accessible 可進入的　(B) correlative 相關的　(C) inclusive 包括的　(D) skeptical 懷疑的／Provision（提供，供應），disabilities（殘障人士），巴士內有可供輪椅上下車的設備，選項中以 accessible（可進入的）最適合。

9. **B**；中譯：雖然這個城市相較於其他城市來說比較沒有治安問題，但現在比以前有較多的街頭犯罪。

　　解析：本題考比較句，used to +V 表示過去經常的事，句中意思為這個地方過去的狀況，比較的標地是"有街頭犯罪的狀況"，故用 there used to be 來呼應前面的比較 there is now…，故答案為 (B)。

10. **D**；中譯：許多客運業者以短程的票價提供一日票，它們可以在同一天內在這家公司的路網內無限制地使用。

　　解析：day passes（一日票），at the cost of（以…價格），good for（有效），由題意知空格處應是指無限制搭乘（unlimited rides）之意，故答案為 (D)。

11. **A**；中譯：搭長程巴士旅遊通常是到達目的地最便宜的方式，但是花費 12 個小時在路上是很耗時。

　　解析：(A) consuming 消耗　(B) misleading 誤導　(C) relieving 解脫　(D) violating 違反／依題意知搭長途巴士便宜但花費比較多時間，耗時為 time-consuming，故答案為 (A)。

12. **C**；中譯：在你拍攝人物特寫時，要先取得同意，且如果是要付費的，要拍就要付錢不然就放下相機。

　　解析：(A) capital 資金　(B) justice 公平　(C) permission 許可　(D) substance 內容
　　ask for（要求某事），close-up（特寫），pay up（付錢），題意是指拍攝人像前要先取得被拍照者的同意，並弄清楚是否需付費，空格處為取得同意之意，故用 permission（許可），答案為 (C)。

13. **B**；中譯：依據這個旅遊保險計畫，當你因不可抗拒因素而必須取消行程時，你可以申請理賠。

　　解析：(A) dispensable 不重要的　(B) eligible 有資格的　(C) hospitable 好客的　(D) invaluable 無價的／make a claim（請求理賠），題意為當行程取消你有權利請求理賠，be eligible to +V 為有資格去做某事的意思，故答案為 (B)。

14 **B**；中譯：我們相信遊客將可對他們造訪的國家做出正面貢獻，假如他們尊重當地居民並明智地消費。

解析：(A) guest 客人　(B) host 主人　(C) port 港口　(D) source 源頭／到一個國家觀光需尊重當地居民或社會，故空格處用 host（主人），host communities 意思是當地居民，故答案為 (B)。

15. (D)；中譯：沒有理由停留在市中心，在商店關門後，市中心變成一座真正的鬼城。

解析：(A) customary 風俗的　(B) feasible 可行的　(C) spectacular 壯觀的　(D) virtual 實際上的／歐美許多大城市中心的商店晚上關門就後人煙稀少，就像鬼城，故選項中用形容詞 virtual（實際上的）最符合題意，故答案為 (D)。

16. (C)；中譯：由海洋博物館向西沿著海濱步行，你不久就會到達阿姆斯特丹建築藝術中心。

解析：stroll（散步、漫步），題意是指由海洋博物館向西走就可到達藝術中心，動詞用 reach（到達），故答案為 (C)。

17. (D)；中譯：因為位於這個城市較為貧窮的鄰近區域之一，在這區域的許多舊房子已經被拆除以騰出空間給新的且較好的公共住宅使用。

解析：(A) date back 追溯　(B) fall short 缺乏　(C) get around 逃避　(D) make way 讓位／neighborhoods（鄰近地區），tear down（拆掉），由題意知要將舊房子處理掉以新建築取代，空格中用 make way（讓位）最符題意，故答案為 (D)。

18. (A)；中譯：如要叫客房服務，你可打電話到服務台並訂購列在飯店目錄中的餐點，餐點將會被送到你房間內供你享用。

解析：空格中需用適當的動詞型態，因餐點是被動送過來，所以需用被動式，且可用簡單現在式代替未來式，故答案為 (A)。

19. (A)；中譯：在美國，大約 180 萬人從事服務業的人在像是飯店、餐廳、賭場以及遊樂場等場所工作。

解析：(A) hospitality 招待　(B) missionary 傳教士　(C) renaissance 復興　(D) sanctuary 聖堂／establishment（場所），題目中所提到的這些場所工作的人都算是從事服務業，服務業稱為 hospitality industry，故答案為 (A)。

20. (D)；中譯：廉價航空在去年提升他們的市場佔有率幾乎達 40%，同時期主要的傳統航空公司僅小幅成長。

解析：(A) flow 流動　(B) model 模型　(C) net 網絡　(D) share 佔有率／budget airline（廉價航空），see lower volume 為只有較小的量，也就是小幅成長，題意是指廉價航空明顯提升乘客的搭乘數量，故空格用 share（佔有率）最適當，表示乘客的載客率，故答案為 (D)。

21. (A)；中譯：這個城市屬熱帶性氣候，月平均溫度介於 19 到 29 度之間，且相對濕度介於 70%到 80%。

解析：空格處應指月平均溫度之意，所以空格用 mean（平均），故答案為 (A)。

22. (C)；中譯：我們一在餐廳就座，沒多久時間一大籠裝滿湯包的竹製蒸籠端上來，伴隨著的是如何品嚐這些小籠包的說明。

解析：(A) brunches 早午餐　(B) chopsticks 筷子　(C) directions 指示說明；方向　(D) functions 功能／空格後面介系詞片語說明該如何品嚐這道美食，故空格內的名詞應用 directions（指示說明）最符合題意，答案為 (C)。

23. **D**；中譯：Youbike 是一種搭配捷運悠遊卡的腳踏車出租服務，且廣泛地在公共交通運輸中被視為在搭乘巴士、火車或捷運之後的最後一哩路。

解析：空格前面 that 引導形容詞子句修飾 service，空格中需用說明這項服務與悠遊卡間關係的動詞，由選項中以 works（with）最恰當，表示搭配使用之意，故答案為 (D)。

24. **D**；中譯：台北市立動物園將接受每天最高上限 300 位訪客來與貓熊家族見面，沒有預約的遊客可以排隊取票，然而數量有限。

解析：(A) catch 捕捉　(B) follow 跟隨　(C) keep 保持　(D) queue 排隊
依題意應為沒有預約的遊客到現場排隊等候取票，故選項中以 queue（排隊）最符合題意，故答案為 (D)。

25. **A**；中譯：在你買到好茶後，把它放到乾燥陰冷之處，避免直接曝曬陽光，使用密封罐是個好方法。

解析：句首空格需用連接詞引導副詞子句，依題意應為買到好茶以後…，所以空格內應用 After，故答案為 (A)。

26. **D**；中譯：當震度 6.3 級的地震襲擊台灣時，鐵路當局在檢查鐵軌是否有任何可能危害的同時，立刻暫停火車行駛。

解析：suspend（暫停），空格處需用表時間的連接詞來引導副詞子句，依題意為當檢查鐵軌的時候暫停火車行駛，故用 while（當…的同時）最恰當，故答案為 (D)。

27. **B**；中譯：這個行程的特色為到西班牙的主要城市，以及停留許多有名的天主教堂。

解析：(A) forecast 預測　(B) itinerary 行程　(C) restriction 限制　(D) allowance 零用錢
feature（以…為特色），stop 在此解釋作停留點，句中提到包含許多觀光景點為特色的事物，這些應該列在 itinerary（行程表）中的項目，故答案為 (B)。

28. **A**；中譯：當抵達廷布，不丹的首都，一些觀光客發現無法適應這座城市的高海拔並需要立刻尋求醫療協助。

解析：(A) altitude 高度　(B) superstition 迷信　(C) significance 意義　(D) economy 經濟／adjust to（適應），不丹位於高山上，旅客容易有高山症，也就是無法適應高海拔的環境，高海拔用 high altitude，故答案為 (A)。

29. **B**；中譯：國內航線是指起飛及降落都在同一國的商業飛航型式。

解析：(A) foreign 外國的　(B) domestic 國內的　(C) rural 鄉下的　(D) connecting 連接的／題目中所指的航線就是指國內航線，也就是 domestic flight，故答案為 (B)。

30. **D**；中譯：當表演被取消，那些已經買票的人退回他們的錢。

解析：(A) purchased 購買　(B) prescribed 指示　(C) replaced 取代　(D) refunded 退款／表演取消，已買票的人應該要退票，退票動詞為 refund，have(had) something + p.p 表示讓…某事發生，故答案為 (D)。

31. **D**；中譯：在大部份的國際機場都有許多行李轉盤，一旦你在那裏拿到你的行李，就往通關區域移動。

    解析：(A) escalators 電扶梯　(B) cylinders 圓筒　(C) tunnels 通道　(D) carousels 旋轉式輸送帶／customs clearance（通關、海關放行），由題意知空格處指的應是行李轉盤，所以空格內應用 carousels（旋轉式輸送帶），故答案為 (D)。

32. **A**；中譯：泰姬瑪哈陵，許多人認為是蒙兀兒建築最精緻的表現，是印度最受歡迎的觀光景點之一。

    解析：(A) attractions 吸引　(B) departments 部門　(C) surroundings 環境
    (D) promises 允許／泰姬瑪哈陵是一個非常吸引觀光的地方，所以空格內選項中以 attractions（吸引力）最適當，表示吸引觀光客的地方，故答案為 (A)。

33. **C**；中譯：一些飯店會要求他們的客人必須付押金來支付住房內非經常性費用。

    解析：(A) custom 習慣　(B) discount 折扣　(C) deposit 押金　(D) currency 通貨
    incidental charges（非經常性費用、雜費），由題意知該空格內應是指飯店住房的押金之意，所以答案為 (C)。

34. **A**；中譯：這位大廚只使用最好的原料來做他的特製莎莎醬。

    解析：(A) ingredients 成份　(B) properties 財產　(C) vouchers 證明人
    (D) characteristics 特性／要做出最好的成品應該是要用最好的原料來做，選項中以 ingredients（成份）最符合題意，故答案為 (A)。

35. **D**；中譯：當你在公共場所時，記住不要讓你個人物品沒人看管。

    解析：(A) boarding 上船　(B) amusement 娛樂　(C) themes 主題　(D) belongings 行李、物品／leave something unattended 表示丟下某事物沒人注意，在公共場所應將隨身的東西看管好，所以空格內應是指隨身的東西或行李，選項中用 belongings（行李、物品）最符合題意，故答案為 (D)。

36. **B**；中譯：不要錯過最棒的倫敦藝術展的作品，包括雕塑、畫作以及攝影。

    解析：(A) civilizations 文明　(B) exhibitions 展覽　(C) preparations 準備　(D) distributions 分配／miss out（錯過），依句中提到雕塑、畫作以及照片等項目，研判空格中應以 exhibitions（展覽）最符合題意，故答案為 (B)。

37. **C**；中譯：在這家百貨公司的五樓你可以買到洗衣機、洗碗機或其他家電用品。

    解析：(A) pamphlets 小冊子　(B) oysters 牡蠣　(C) appliances 用具　(D) chores 雜務
    洗衣機、洗碗機等均屬家電品，家電用品為 household appliances，故答案為 (C)。

38. **A**；中譯：這家餐廳以它異國風味的印度料理聞名。

    解析：(A) cuisine 菜餚　(B) ornament 裝飾　(C) necessities 必需品　(D) costumes 服裝／exotic（異國的），句中提到餐廳有充滿異國風味的東西，選項中以 cuisine（菜餚）最適宜，表示異國口味的料理，故答案為 (A)。

39. **D**；中譯：大部份的國家已經透過立法來保護他們國家的遺產，例如有價值的歷史建築，或對文化的保存有重要意義的事務。

解析：(A) habitat 居住地　(B) continent 大陸　(C) anthem 國歌　(D) heritage 遺產
句中提到的歷史建築或文化等均與國家傳承有關，故選項中以 heritage（遺產）
最符合題意，故答案為 (D)。

40. **B**；中譯：經過幾年的旅行，這對夫婦決定要永遠留在倫敦，並在那裏建立一個永久的家庭。

解析：(A) swollen 腫起的　(B) permanent 永久的　(C) lethal 致死的　(D) temporary
暫時的／句中提到要永遠停留在那裏，表示應該是要建立永久的而非暫時的家，
故選項中用 permanent（永久的）最適當，答案為 (B)。

41. **C**；中譯：在清潔過走道後，清潔工留了一塊表示地板濕滑的告示。

解析：(A) slightly 輕微地　(B) enormous 巨大的　(C) slippery 滑溜的　(D) enchanted
著迷的／依題意研判告示應是指地板是濕的且可能會滑倒，故空格用選項中的
slippery（滑溜的）最符合題意，答案為 (C)。

42. **A**；中譯：約翰向服務生要一根吸管來喝他的冰茶。

解析：(A) straw 麥稈、吸管　(B) grinder 研磨機　(C) fiber 纖維　(D) sausage 香腸
由題意可知約翰要這東西是為了要喝冰茶，所以選項中以 straw（麥稈、吸管）
最適合，也就是用吸管喝水，故答案為(A)。

43. **D**；中譯：野生公園就是一大片的野生動物的保留地，在裏面牠們可以自由活動，並讓坐
在車內開車遊歷公園的人們來觀看。

解析：由題意可知這種公園就是指野生公園（safari park= animal park），故答案為
(D)。

44. **B**；中譯：吉隆坡的雙子星大樓是世界上最高的雙塔建築，遊客可以從天橋以及位於 86
樓的景觀台來觀賞這個城市的景色。

解析：(A) environment 環境　(B) observatory 觀景台　(C) glacier 冰河　(D) latitude 緯
度／由高處觀賞城市風光應該是由 observatory（景觀台），故答案為 (B)。

45. **A**；中譯：據說直到今天，男人與女人們仍然設法在他們共處上取得平衡，在世界上許多
地方，女人仍然努力的佔有原來就屬於她們的位置。

解析：(A) striving 努力　(B) abolishing 取消　(C) discerning 分辨　(D) inspecting 檢
查／空格內需用動詞現在分詞，與前面 be 動詞形成現在進行式，表示動作仍持
續進行中，由題意知女人仍想要維持原有的位置，故動詞用選項中的 striving（努
力）最符合題意，故答案為 (A)。

46. **C**；中譯：我錯過了今天早上的會議，有人能告訴我有什麼事嗎？

解析：本題考片語用法，依題意為錯過會議要事後了解會議內容 fill sb. in on sth.對某人
提供（有關…的）情況，動詞要用 fill，故答案為 (C)。

47. **B**；中譯：石油價格波動通常被認為是全世界經濟的指標。

解析：(A) confrontation 對抗　(B) fluctuation 波動　(C) prevention 阻止　(D) substitution 替代／barometer 為氣壓計，在句中為指標之意，石油價格上下起伏就代表世界經濟的變化，所以選項中以 fluctuation（波動）最符合題意，故答案為 (C)。

48. **A**；中譯：Chloe McCardel，一位澳洲的極限運動家，在她遭到水母螫傷後放棄了她要從古巴游泳到佛羅里達的企圖。

解析：(A) stung 叮咬；螫　(B) drowned 溺死　(C) stabbed 刺傷　(D) dunk 喝 endurance athlete（極限運動員），空格中需用動詞過去分詞與 be 動詞形成被動式，由題意知她應該是被水母叮咬，故動詞要用 sting（過去式與過去分詞 stung-stung）最適合，故答案為 (A)。

49. **D**；中譯：為了要買到便宜商品，許多消費者選擇成為量販店的會員並開始買大包裝的商品。

解析：(A) at large 一般地　(B) in terms 明確地　(C) off base 錯誤的　(D) in bulk 大量 take advantage of（利用），good bargains（便宜商品），由句中提到量販店，所以空格處應是指採購大量的東西，故選項中用 in bulk（大量）最適合，故答案為 (D)。

50. **A**；中譯：許多父母會送他們的孩子去參加一些課後的音樂課程，為了是要發掘他們對音樂的興趣並培養他們的才能。

解析：(A) cultivate 培養　(B) disguise 假裝　(C) subside 下沉　(D) moderate 有節制的／talent（天份、才能），空格內需用原形動詞（前面 to 省略），由受詞是 talents（才能），故動詞用選項中的 cultivate（培養）最適合，故答案為 (A)。

51 **B**；中譯：感冒症狀可能持續一個星期之久，如果症狀持續或惡化，你將必須立刻去看醫生。

解析：(A) postpone 延期　(B) persist 持續　(C) converse 交談　(D) comply 允許 cold symptoms 是指感冒症狀，空格內需用動詞，題意是指如果感冒症狀一直沒有改善就必須看醫生，所以空格內用 persist（持續）最恰當，與後面的動詞 worsen（更惡化）相呼應，故答案為 (B)。

52. **D**；中譯：這場爵士演奏會將於鎮上的這所中學演奏廳舉行，並且將會是一場你不能錯過的盛會。

解析：(A) circumstance 環境　(B) embassy 大使　(C) monument 紀念碑　(D) auditorium 禮堂／miss out on（遺漏掉），由題意知這是一場演奏會，應該是要在禮堂（auditorium）舉行，故答案為 (D)。

53. **B**；中譯：請確實保存好你的收據，我們才能退還你的旅行花費。

解析：(A) supervise 監督　(B) reimburse 償還　(C) relocate 重新安置　(D) scatter 散播／make sure（確定），題意指依據收據來退還行程中花費的錢，故動詞應以選項中的 reimburse（償還）最適合，故答案為 (B)。

54. **A**；中譯：一般來說，駕駛者應該注意行人。依據現行法律，機車騎士在十字路口必須禮讓行人。

解析：(A) yield 禮讓　(B) confess 承認　(C) proceed 進行　(D) resist 反抗

be careful about（小心某事），pedestrians（行人），句子先前已提到駕駛者應

注意行人，空格後有提到騎士在路口遇到行人的狀況，故空格內的動詞以 yield

（禮讓）最符合題意，答案為 (A)。

55. C ；中譯：為了要省錢，蘇珊總是從報紙剪下折價卷在賣場使用。

解析：(A) certificates 執照　(B) warranties 保證書　(C) coupons 折價券　(D) pouches

錢包／clip（剪下來）。從報紙把折價券（coupons）剪下來，故選 (C)。

56. B ；中譯：寶萊塢的電影最近已吸引了全球市場，並且吸引全球數以百萬計的觀賞者。

解析：(A) increased 增加　(B) appealed 對…有吸引力　(C) speculated 推測　(D)

enriched 使豐富／空格需用動詞來描述電影對全球市場的情形，由題目後面提到

已經吸引了數以百萬的觀眾欣賞，故表示印度電影吸引全球市場，故動詞用選項

中的 appealed（對…有吸引力）最適合，故答案為 (B)。

57. B ；中譯：今天上午到舊金山的觀光客可能會相當失望，因為金門大橋在濃霧中幾乎看不

見。

解析：(A) durable 持久的　(B) visible 看見的　(C) amiable 和藹的　(D) audible 聽得見

的／barely 表示幾乎不，是一個表否定的副詞，用以形容空格中的形容詞，由題

意知金門大橋在濃霧中，應該是很難被看清楚的，所以形容詞要用 visible（看見

的），barely visible 表示很難被看見的，故答案為 (B)。

58. D ；中譯：夏威夷是個很適合各種水上運動的地點，一些人喜歡去玩風帆衝浪，而其他人

喜歡去滑水。

解析：(A) despite of 不管　(B) therefore 因此　(C) whenever 無論何時　(D) whereas

然而／空格內應用連接詞引導副詞子句，表示一些人如何，然而其他人如何，連

接詞應用表達轉折語氣的 whereas（然而），故答案為 (D)。

59. A ；中譯：愈來愈多的公共充電站可以在一些像是餐廳、百貨公司及機場中發現到，當手

機電池快沒電時，智慧型手機的使用者可以加以利用。

解析：(A) charging 充填　(B) hacking 砍劈　(C) fueling 加油　(D) boosting 提升

make use of（加以利用），由句中提到手機沒電時可以利用到，故空格處應該是

指充電站，充電用 charging，故答案為 (A)。

60. D ；中譯：飯店房間的價格對需求是很敏感的，所以在周末其間的一些特價及折扣總是能

吸引到更多人。

解析：(A) commercial 商業的　(B) frequent 頻繁的　(C) gradual 逐漸的　(D) sensitive

敏感的／由句子後半段中提到打折或優惠就能吸引到更多人，所以知房間價格是

對需求應該是 sensitive（敏感的），故答案為 (D)。

61. C ；中譯：一架美國飛往紐約的班機上個月由波士頓起飛不久後經歷了一場空中亂流，造

成五位機組員及乘客受輕傷。

解析：(A) jet lag 時差　(B) boundaries 邊界　(C) turbulence 亂流　(D) atmosphere 大氣／bound for（前往），由題意知該飛機遭遇的應該是空中的亂流（turbulence），故答案為 (C)。

62. (D)；中譯：這條 2.5 公里長具有花店及精品店特色的林蔭大道是巴黎最漂亮的其中一個地方。

解析：(A) colleague 同事　(B) delicacy 精巧　(C) ambulance 救護車　(D) boulevard 大道／tree-lined 為兩旁種有樹木的道路，所以空格中的選項以 boulevard（大道）最符合題意，表示這是一條充滿花店與精品店的林蔭大道，故答案為 (D)。

63. (D)；中譯：雖然因為榴槤味道重的原因使客人在飯店內不可以吃榴槤，有些人還是設法把它們夾帶進來。

解析：(A) calculate 計算　(B) exclude 排除　(C) achieve 達到　(D) smuggle 走私夾帶由題意知榴槤是不允許在飯店內吃，而一些人是用偷帶的方式帶入飯店，所以選項中用 smuggle（走私，夾帶）最適合，故答案為 (D)。

64. (A)；中譯：需要投入來更多的錢來改善這個國家鄉下地區的基礎設施，如修築道路及建立診所等。

解析：(A) infrastructure 基礎設施　(B) obstacle 障礙　(C) commodities 商品　(D) diagnosis 診斷／rural（鄉下的），由句子中提到的道路及醫院等設施都屬基礎建設，選項中用 infrastructure（基礎設施），答案為 (A)。

65. (A)；中譯：在法庭中攝影通常是被禁止的，且有時甚至被認為是一種嚴重的犯罪。

解析：(A) prohibited 禁止　(B) accumulated 累積　(C) celebrated 出名的　(D) disordered 使混亂／空格中需用動詞過去分詞，與前面 be 動詞形成被動式，由題意知應用選項中 prohibited（禁止）最恰當，表示在法庭中攝影是絕對被禁止的，故答案為 (A)。

66. (B)；中譯：這個飯店的每一個房間都有的大窗戶，可以看得到壯闊閃耀的大西洋景色。

解析：(A) cautious 謹慎的　(B) spectacular 壯觀的　(C) experimental 實驗的　(D) ambitious 野心勃勃的／空格中為形容大西洋的景色的形容詞，選項中以 spectacular（壯觀的）最適當，故答案為 (B)。

67. (D)；中譯：禮品包裝是指將禮物用一些材料包裹起來，在大多數情況下，它可以為禮物增加價值。

解析：(A) editing 編輯　(B) spelling 拼字　(C) containing 包含　(D) wrapping 包裹In many cases（在大多數情況下），由題意可知空格處是指禮品的包裝，要用 gift wrapping，答案為 (D)。

68. (A)；中譯：星期天是逛市集最好的日子，有許多很棒的小攤子賣著新鮮的當地蔬果。

解析：(A) stalls 售貨攤　(B) recipes 食譜　(C) pitchers 投手　(D) buns 小圓麵包空格後面的現在分詞當形容詞，說明前面的空格中的名詞，因其提到販賣新鮮的蔬果等東西，所以選項中以 stalls（售貨攤）最適合，故答案為 (A)。

69. **D**；中譯：每一年學校會為畢業班級準備一場慶祝晚宴，今年這場盛會將於舊金山的麗池卡爾頓飯店舉辦。

　　解析：(A) engagement 約定　(B) complex 合成物　(C) disposal 配置　(D) banquet 宴會／celebratory（興高采烈的），由題意知空格處應為晚宴之意，所以選項中用 banquet（宴會），故答案為 (D)。

70. **C**；中譯：許多疾病都具有傳染性且可由人傳染給其他人。

　　解析：(A) energetic 積極的　(B) fictional 虛構的　(C) contagious 傳染性的　(D) abundant 豐富的／句中提到有些疾病會人傳人，所以空格內形容詞以 contagious（傳染性的）最符合題意，故答案為 (C)。

71-75；中譯：烹飪旅遊就是指人們到不同的國家旅遊的同時享用當地美食，旅客們時常特地找尋些具有豐富美食、飲食節慶與烹飪課程的地方，有許多不同的地點是烹飪旅遊的大熱門，例如法國、泰國、印度及日本。

烹飪旅遊最基本的型式就是遊客到一個國家的目標為嘗試當地的菜，美食遊客會對在其他地方無法見到的菜色感到興趣，各種飲食節慶更豐富了美食之旅，因為這給了觀光客品嚐許多不同菜色的機會，烹飪課程同時也給觀光客學習如何料理當地菜色的機會，並教他們新技巧，一個烹飪旅遊也可能是這些活動的綜合。

特別是在泰國，那裏從價格、地點到菜色種類，有非常多的烹飪學校可供選擇，一種典型的半天課程包含簡介到基本原料、烹飪技術以及動手實做的機會來烹煮至少四道菜。大部分學校提供一個循環性的菜色內容，使得一個禮拜中的學習不會有重複，課程通常開始於造訪市場而以大家一起品嚐努力成果的午餐結束。

在曼谷的一些比較小的泰國菜學校的課程提供一種理想的家庭式學習環境，那是一個不同於其他大部分在泰國的飯店或餐廳的學習環境，你可以經由與當地居民一起研究泰國菜香料中所含的藝術及奧祕並體驗泰國的文化。有經驗的大廚會一步一步教你真正的泰式料理的秘方，但要知道泰式烹飪是很有彈性的，雖然你有食譜，重要的是要能了解內涵及香料，並在烹飪時要用你的感覺去做調整。課程都是輕鬆有趣的，這反映出泰國人對生活的觀點，不需要先前有任何烹飪方面的經驗，只要有對食物的喜愛及願意去做就可以了。

71. **C/D**；中譯：文中有關烹飪旅遊暗示為何？(A) 泰國到目前為止是最佳的烹飪旅遊地點　(B) 大部分烹飪旅客不會在意控制體重　(C) 國際性的速食連鎖店不會出現在烹飪旅遊的行程　(D) 為了促進烹飪旅遊，在美食節中會有免費食物樣品提供給觀光客

　　解析：由 Culinary tourists are interested in dishes that cannot be found in other places…，可知美食遊客只會對在其他地方無法見到的菜色感到興趣，所以國際性快餐店的東西四處可見，不會引起他們的興趣，故答案為 (C)。(D) 選項從寬。

72. **C**；中譯：下列何項關於在泰國的烹飪課程序數是正確的？(A) 大部分課程直到下午才開始　(B) 原料通常是由大廚買給觀光客　(C) 在泰國有許多樣的烹飪課程可提供觀光客選擇　(D) 比較小型的烹飪學校較有名的飯店或餐廳更令人喜愛。

　　解析：(A) 文中沒提到，敘述錯誤　(B) 由文意推論，應旅客去市場選購　(C) 由

Particularly in Thailand, there are cooking schools with a huge range of prices, locations, and cuisines tochoose from…，敘述正確。 (D) 由 The courses at smaller…offer an ideal home-style learning … different from most of the hotels and restaurants…，知較小的烹飪學校是提供不一樣的環境，沒有說比較受歡迎，敘述錯誤。故答案為 (C)。

73. **D**；中譯：下列哪一個字與第三段中 "revolving" 的意義最相近(A) reviving 甦醒　(B) reversing 迴轉　(C) regulating 規定　(D) rotating 輪流交替

　　解析："revolving" 這字在句中是指循環性的，所以選項中以 rotating(輪流交替)與其意義最相近，答案為 (D)

74. **A**；中譯：依據本文，下列哪項敘述有被提到？(A) 泰國人通常都很悠閒的　(B) 烹飪旅遊要是沒有美食節就不完整了　(C) 烹飪旅遊的地點限制在四個特定國家　(D) 烹調泰式食物有許多秘密的知識牽涉其中。

　　解析：(A) 由 Classes are intended to be relaxed and fun, reflecting the Thai approach to life.知泰國人生活是悠閒的　(B) 文中沒提到　(C) 文中舉例烹飪旅遊的熱門地有法國、泰國、印度及日本等地方，但不限於此四處　(D) 文中指提到烹調泰式料理要靠感覺調整，沒說到有許多秘密知識。故答案為(A)。

75. **B**；中譯：這篇文章最可能從何而來？(A) 黃頁　(B) 旅遊網站　(C) 餐廳年鑑　(D) 旅遊機構的年度報告。

　　解析：文章內容主要介紹烹飪旅遊的意義、好玩之處，並舉泰國為例介紹當地的烹飪學校狀況，主要還是介紹一種旅遊型態，最有可能是出自於旅遊網站，故答案為(B)。

76-80；中譯：表情符號的使用，用標點符號來描述一個臉部的表情，是網路特殊詞彙的一個主要部分。就算你不用表情符號，你可能也知道那是甚麼——一小串的字母，當你從側邊看時像是表現出情緒的各種臉型，例如,:-D 表示好笑，他有眼睛，一個鼻子，以及一個大寫的 D 當成一個寬闊、快樂的大嘴。

這一切都源自於 1982 年 9 月 19 日卡內基梅隆大學由一個學校職員半開玩笑的電腦郵件。斯科特·法爾曼注意到有些在卡內基梅隆的電腦網路中傳送的笑話被一些校園內的人士嚴肅看待。有些看不懂笑話的人可能被一個非常好笑的評語而感到煩擾，並傳送一個憤怒的回應，這樣就浪費了很多人的時間。法爾曼建議把笑容符號當做個解決方式，當你寫一些不是很嚴肅的事情的時候，他建議在後面打上 :-)，一些人採用他的建議並且變成卡內基梅隆網路速記文字的一部分。笑容符號受歡迎的程度最後遠超出法爾曼的想像，幾個月以後，它很快經由信件傳播到其他大學及公司中。

沒有人確知現在到底有多少表情符號，但隨便列都有超過 100 以上。最普通的一些已被文書處理或即時通訊軟體轉換成為小的貼圖，例如 :-(表示悲傷或失望，在你的電腦螢幕上會變成☹。

76. **B**；中譯：這篇文章主要目的為何？ (A) 來說服讀者在電子通訊中使用表情符號　(B) 向

讀者介紹微笑符號的起源　(C) 提供一個網路發展的歷史概觀　(D) 解釋微笑符號的不同含意。

　解析：本文一開始先解釋何為表情符號，再說明表情符號的源起故事及後來的發展，所以文章主要介紹表情符號或微笑符號的源起，故答案為 (B)。

77. C；中譯：在第文章一段中 lexicon 這個字的意思為何? (A) technology 科技　(B) communication 溝通　(C) vocabulary 字彙　(D) application 運用

　解析：lexicon 這個字的意思是專門詞彙，故與選項中 vocabulary（字彙）類似，故答案為 (C)。

78. A；中譯：下列何者最能表達出第二段中粗體標示的句子的實質的意思？(A) 在他大學內許多人喜歡他的建議　(B) 因為他的建議，他晉升到較好的工作　(C) 他的建議幫助創造了一個在大學的網際網路　(D) 他的建議被大學教職員給縮短。

　解析：該句翻譯為：一些人採用他的建議並且變成卡內基梅隆網路速記文字的一部分，意思就是大學中的同事都很贊同他的想法並且實際去做，故答案為(A)。

79. A；中譯：從本文中，下列何項有關法爾曼在卡內基梅隆大學的同事有被提到？(A) 他們時常寄送笑話　(B) 他們設法冒犯他人　(C) 他們不知如何寫好的訊息　(D) 他們一點也不喜歡笑話。

　解析：(A) 由…some of the jokes being sent around…were being taken seriously by a few people on campus…，知職員們時常寄送笑話　(B) 由 Someone who didn't get the joke might be upset by…可知是看不懂笑話才會生氣，不是要設法冒犯人　(C) 文中沒提到相關說法　(D) 文中沒提到相關說法。故答案為(A)。

80. C；中譯：依據本文，下列何項關於表情符號是對的？(A) 它們都能以一般的文書處理軟體變成小圖　(B) 沒有人會真正注意在文字訊息中表情符號的使用　(C) 它們是使用在一個網路上來表達情緒的符號　(D) 現今沒有超過 100 個表情符號被發明。

　解析：(A) 由 The most popular ones are actually turned into little pictures by word-processing or instant-messaging software. 知非所有表情符號都已變成圖型，敘述為非　(B) 文中沒提到相關內容，敘述為非　(C) 由 The use of emoticons…is an essential part of the lexicon of the Internet. 知它是使用在網路上來表達情緒的符號，敘述為真　(D) 由 No one really knows how many emoticons there are, but lists of 100 or so are common. 知現在至少有超過 100 種表情符號，敘述為非。故答案為 (C)。

附錄

必備單字一把抓，星星記號代表是超高頻率字。
背過請打 ☑

1. absent 缺席的
★ 2. accommodation 住宿
3. adventure 冒險
4. affordable 買得起的
5. agreement 協議
6. ahead 事先
7. aircraft 飛機
8. airplane 飛機、航空公司
9. airport 機場
10. aisle seat 靠走道的座位
★ 11. amenities 設施
12. appropriate 合宜的
13. approval 同意
14. arrival desk 入境櫃台
15. arrival time 到達時間
★ 16. arrive （人、飛機）到達
17. ban 禁止
18. baggage 行李
19. bargain 特價品
20. bill 法案
21. boarding gate 登機門
22. boarding pass 登機證
★ 23. boutique 精品店
★ 24. brochure 小冊子
25. budget airline 廉價航空
26. budget 預算
27. business class 商務艙
28. cabin crew 機組人員
29. capital 首都

30. captain 機長
31. carry 攜帶
32. challenge 挑戰
33. charge 費用、收費
34. charter bus 遊覽車
35. checked baggage 託運行李
36. check-in desk 辦理登機的櫃台
37. check-in 登記住房
38. check-in 辦理登機手續
39. check-out 結帳、退房
40. registration form 登記表
41. committed 致力於
42. compensate 補償
43. compete 競爭
44. competitive 競爭的
45. complimentary 贈送的
46. concierge 飯店禮賓人員
★ 47. connecting flight 轉機班機
48. conscious 有意識的
49. contagious 接觸傳染的
50. credit card 信用卡
51. crew 工作人員
52. cruise 飛行、航行
★ 53. cuisine 美食
54. currency exchange 換匯
55. custom 風俗
★ 56. customs officers 海關官員
★ 57. customs 海關
58. decline 下降

59. delay 延誤
60. delicacy 佳餚
61. delivery service 寄件服務
62. demand 需要、要求
63. demonstrate 論證、證明
64. departure lounge 候機室
65. departure time 起飛時間
66. deport 驅逐出境
67. deposit 訂金
68. destination 目的地
★ 69. direct flight 直飛班機
70. disaster 災害
71. disciplined 有紀律的
72. disembark 下飛機
★ 73. divert 轉向
★ 74. domestic flight 國內航班
★ 75. domestic 國內的
76. duty 職責
77. economy class 經濟艙
78. economical 節約的
79. edible 可食用的
80. employee 員工
81. entry permit 入境許可證
82. examine 檢查
83. exchange rate 匯率
84. expiration 期滿
85. export 出口
86. express 快車
87. facility 設施
88. fare （交通工具）車費
★ 89. fasten 繫緊
90. feature 特色
91. fee 費用
★ 92. final boarding call 最後登機廣播
93. first class 頭等艙
94. flight 班機
95. foreign currency 外幣

96. foreigner 外國人
97. front desk 櫃台
98. get off an airplane 下飛機
99. get on an airplane 上飛機
100. grateful 感謝的
101. greet 問候
102. guest service 客戶服務
103. hazard 危險
104. headquarters 總部
★ 105. high season 旺季
106. highlight 重點
107. history 歷史
108. historic 有歷史性的
109. historical 歷史的
110. identification 證件
★ 111. immigrant 移民者
★ 112. immigration officer 移民官
★ 113. immigration 移民
114. impact 影響、衝擊
115. import 進口
116. impose 徵（稅）
117. in advance 事先
118. income 收入
★ 119. indigenous 本地的
120. inflation 通貨膨脹
121. infrastructure 公共建設
122. initiate 開始、發起
123. initiative 主動的行動
124. inquire 詢問
★ 125. international flight 國際航班
★ 126. itinerary 旅程、路線、行程
127. jet lag 時差
128. journey 旅程
129. journal 期刊
130. landing 降落
131. landscape 風景、景色
132. lawmaker 立法者

133. legalize 合法化
134. light season 淡季
135. lobby 飯店大廳
136. luggage 行李
137. mature 成熟的
138. machinery 機器
139. metropolitan 大都市的
140. minority 少數人
141. modernize 現代化
142. mute 靜音
143. nature 自然
144. necessary 需要的
145. necessity 必需品
146. notion 概念、想法
147. noisy 吵鬧的
148. occasion 場合
149. operate 運作、運轉
150. orchestra 管弦樂
151. originate 創始
152. orerlook 俯視；監督
153. outgoing 外向的
154. overweight 超重的
155. ozone 臭氧
156. package holiday 套裝行程
★ 157. panoramic 全景的
158. participate in 參加
159. passenger 乘客
160. passport 護照
161. perform 表演
162. personal belongings 隨身物品

163. phenomenon 現象
★ 164. photogenic 上相的
165. pilot 飛行員
166. pollute 汙染
167. popular 受歡迎的
168. popularity 歡迎

169. population 人口
170. poverty 貧窮、貧困
171. present 出席的
172. promote 行銷
173. prosperity 繁榮
174. qualified 資格
175. quit 停止
176. quite 相當地
177. reasonable 價格合理的
178. reception 接待處
179. reconfirm 再次確認
180. refrain 抑制
★ 181. refund 退款
182. remarkably 明顯地、非常地
183. remind 提醒
184. replace 取代
185. require 需要、要求
186. requirement 需求
★ 187. reservation 預訂
188. reserve 預訂
189. reserved （被）保留的
190. resort 名勝
191. responsibility 責任
192. retreat 僻靜之處
193. revenue 稅收
194. reward 獎賞
195. rewarding 有價值的
196. round-trip ticket 來回票
197. route 路線、路程
198. rustic 鄉下的
199. safari 遠征旅行
200. sacred 神聖的
201. scene 風景；景
202. scenery 風景
203. security check 安全檢查
204. set route 固定的路線
205. shuttle service 接駁巴士服務

206. **sightseeing bus** 觀光巴士
207. **sign up** 報名登記
208. **significant** 有意義的、重要的
209. **single ticket** 單程票
★ 210. **souvenir** 紀念品
211. **spectacle** 奇觀
212. **spectacular** 壯觀的
213. **staple** 主食
214. **step out** 踏出
215. **stopover** 中途停留
216. **stuff** 物品、東西
217. **suite** 套房
218. **talent** 天份
219. **thrive** 興旺
220. **ticket** 票
221. **tour guide** 導遊
222. **tour manager** 領隊
223. **tour** 旅遊
224. **tourism** 觀光業
225. **tourist spots** 觀光景點
226. **tourist** 觀光客
227. **transfer** 轉機
228. **transit** 過境
229. **travel agent** 旅行社
230. **turbulence** 亂流
231. **unemployed** 失業的
232. **undergo** 經歷
233. **undertake** 從事
234. **urban** 都市的
235. **urge** 催促、力勸
★ 236. **vacancy** 空房、空位
★ 237. **vacant** 空的
238. **visa** 簽證
239. **violate** 違反
240. **violence** 暴力
241. **wander** 閒逛
242. **welfare** 福利

243. **window seat** 靠窗的座位
244. **withdraw** 提領
245. **within the law** 合法
246. **work independently** 獨立工作
247. **worthy** 值得的
248. **yield** 讓（座）
249. **zeal** 熱心
250. **zone** 地帶、地區

附錄

附錄

Learn Smart! 036

Super 英文領隊導遊 PAPAGO

考證照PASS，帶團GO！

作　　者	滴兒馬、方定國
發 行 人	周瑞德
企劃編輯	徐瑞璞
校　　對	劉俞青、陳欣慧
封面設計	高鍾琪
內文排版	菩薩蠻數位文化有限公司

印　　製	大亞彩色印刷製版股份有限公司
初　　版	2014 年 7 月
出　　版	倍斯特出版事業有限公司
電　　話	（02）2351-2007
傳　　真	（02）2351-0887
地　　址	100 台北市中正區福州街 1 號 10 樓之 2
E m a i l	best.books.service@gmail.com
定　　價	新台幣 329 元

港澳地區總經銷	泛華發行代理有限公司
地　　　　址	香港筲箕灣東旺道3號星島新聞集團大廈3樓
電　　　　話	（852）2798-2323
傳　　　　真	（852）2796-5471

國家圖書館出版品預行編目(CIP)資料

Super領隊導遊PAPAGO：考證照PASS,帶團GO!
滴兒馬, 方定國著. -- 初版. -- 臺北市：倍斯特,
2014.07
　　面；　公分.
　ISBN 978-986-90331-9-0(平裝)

　1. 英語 2.領隊 3.讀本

805.18　　　　　　　　　　　　　103011938